KIERAN MCLOUGHLIN

The Hateful 2: Forgiveness

First edition

ISBN (print): 9781739429645
ISBN (digital): 9781739429638

This book was professionally typeset on Reedsy.
Find out more at reedsy.com

Contents

Foreword

I didn't intend to write this, but I feel compelled to do so. Chapter 1 of this novel contains aspects readers may find upsetting. You may wish to avoid this chapter; this won't affect the rest of the story. *That being said, if you are sensitive to matters concerning suicide, please use your discretion.*

You might wonder 'Why include it, then?'

Simply, *The Hateful* is a very personal series. It deals with the deepest aspects and questions of myself and autism. I wanted to include aspects not mentioned often, especially the thoughts and feelings associated with them. I believe Chapter 1 offers a unique insight into a character that will play a central role in this novel.

Finally, this chapter is non-negotiable for me.

Again, please use discretion. Otherwise, I hope you enjoy this book. As with most things, the healing cycle includes multiple stages. This usually begins with a downfall.

Then comes forgiveness.

Acknowledgments

Its taken longer than I thought it would… But we're here. As always, thank you to the likes of Nick and Jonathan for the editing. Your work helps me to actually appear like a writer hahaha. Alejandro too, your cover, much like the first, blew me away. Your work is also appreciated. Then, I would also like to thank my amazing beta readers, Jack, Juliette and Winterlady. Your feedback helped shaped this book, and in turn made me a better writer.

I also want to thank my family. Mum, for always fighting and believing in what your autistic son could achieve, even when it was just the two of us. Mark, for becoming part of our family, and being the dad who stepped up. Tom, for being one of my greatest supporters throughout my life, and through my dream as an author. Hopefully this will be another step in getting you that yacht!

Finally, of course, I thank you too, my beloved reader. To know that you could've chosen another book to read, watched a TV show, or played a game, yet chose to read this instead. You have no idea how much that means to me. I can only hope that you find this book and my writing worth your time.

Thank you.

1

Shame

Gabriel wanders the streets of Kyrios as twinkles of snow fall from the sky, not sure if these moments will be his last.

Tonight, he wants to die.

It never makes sense how it happens. His black cloak feels like a noose tightening around his neck. Strands of his Hateful golden and silver hair land on his face, no matter how many times he brushes them back. Gabriel glances towards a desolate street, knowing that no one follows him.

Except darkness.

Gabriel can sense it: the imminence of death. Nihilism hangs on every thought. Hopelessness. Despite his effort. Despite his dreams. It had been for nothing. He was never meant to understand this world, nor it him.

And why would it? So much hate. Delusion. Apathy. What is the point of living? Why am I still breathing?

Gabriel notices the coldness in the air. He sees the little details his mind once decided were irrelevant. The closeness of death brings everything to his attention. Even the simple act of inhaling. It is all so precious, so fragile. Gabriel shivers, knowing that each breath takes him one step closer to the end, towards destroying the only thing responsible for his suffering.

Himself.

The days, sunless for thousands of years, now seem blacker. Gabriel can't remember the last time he slept. He's not been able to stop the same image from tainting his mind.

'Gabriel? Why?' He can hear Krista saying in his mind, seeing her on her knees with tears running down her face. She would wonder why he didn't speak. Why he said nothing. Gabriel knows you don't want to drag others to the depths in which you've allowed yourself to drown.

And so shame emerges.

You remember the person you once were, happy and innocent. Now, all you can see are your flaws, your failings. Despite everything you've done, people never change. Humans are fools lying to themselves. You realise your addictions were masquerades, the things you ran to, trying to escape the darkness you've always known exists within you.

Why did I even bother?

Gabriel staggers. His breathing is laboured. His head is heavy. He holds out an arm, letting his fingers brush against the cold metal wall that surrounds the city of Kyrios. He looks at the contorted rooftops, seeing only physical manifestations of pain and death, appearing to turn away as though ashamed of him. That makes him smile, as he casts his gaze up to the snowing sky, feeling tiny flakes land on his face.

'Oh, Divinity, why did you curse us like this? What did we do to deserve this?' he questions aloud, knowing that no one will answer him. His kind had been long forsaken by the god that created them. Besides, they weren't his precious humans. Not truly, anyway. They were monsters, disabled. They could tap into all four of his Blessings, but that changed nothing. Humans could only touch one, yet in return his infamous race was born with the curse, fractured of mind, broken before they took their first steps. Gabriel knew the truth. They had been abandoned. No angel was coming to guide them to heaven. Instead, Gabriel knew what was coming for them.

The realm of demons, the hell most humans feared.

But we're already in hell, aren't we? That's what they don't see. The demons... They walk among us, within...

There's a faint stirring within, the smirking presence that watches his every step.

You're just running, aren't you? it says, taking pleasure from his pain, from the thoughts spinning in his mind. Dizziness engulfs Gabriel as he forces his eyes closed, trying to calm himself. He is shaking, longing.

Krista. I need her. I need to—

Gabriel freezes. The answer is clear. It is obvious what he needs to do. There is only one way this can end.

'Die,' he says, his breath steaming out of him. Without hesitation, Hateful compulsion filling every part of his body, he staggers forward, making his way to a door not far from here. Just a few streets away.

'Krista… Krista…' Gabriel stammers, the presence within growing more prominent. He tries to ignore it, moving as fast as he can. In response, the presence within laughs, taking joy from every second.

What difference can she make? You will not confess your feelings for her. You don't know what love is. You've tried, haven't you?

3

You've searched for it. Longed for it. Yet deep down, you're not sure if you want it. After all, you don't want to drag her down with you, do you? Tell me, Gabriel, what can you offer her?

'Nothing,' Gabriel answers, forcing away tears. *I don't even know why I'm still breathing.*

Gabriel approaches the tiny staircase that leads to their home, struggling with each step. He just reaches the top, fumbling with his keys before stepping inside. A gust of snowy wind follows him as he drops to his hands and knees. The presence within laughs again while Gabriel cries. Still, he crawls forward, moving through a bare living room containing only a single chair. Books sit in a small pile alongside it. Krista's books.

I need this to end. I cannot take this anymore.

He ignores Krista's room, his heart aching. Gabriel staggers to his feet, heading towards the bathroom, switching on a light and closing the door behind him. He finds his greatest shame staring back at him in the mirror. He stands there, half disbelieving what he sees.

'Is this what I've allowed myself to become?' Gabriel asks, holding out his hand towards the sink beneath the mirror. His face is gaunt, his cheeks and chin narrow. The bags under his eyes betray his exhaustion. Gabriel shakes his head, despising the creature looking back at him.

He taps into his Transformative Blessing, summoning a tiny blade in his right hand, which he brings towards his throat.

Do it. Just end this.

A knock comes at the door, freezing Gabriel. Without waiting for an answer, Krista steps inside the bathroom, appearing as though she's just awoken. She rubs her eyes, before brushing her Hateful hair back. It's then she sees Gabriel, regarding the same reflection he's looking at, her eyes widening. They flicker between his face and the blade held to his neck.

'Gabriel?' Krista asks, her voice trembling, disbelieving.

Gabriel allows the blade to fall, relinquishing the Blessing.

'Krista… I…' he says, knowing there's nothing to say except the one thing that accompanies these moments.

'I'm so sorry,' he says, as Krista's arms wrap around him. Gabriel feels her shake, accompanying the sounds of her crying into his chest.

I caused this, Gabriel knows. *I caused her to suffer more. Why? Why am I like this?*

Inside, the presence emerges, encapsulating him.

Why? Because you are Hateful, fool, it says, causing Gabriel to squeeze his fists. He rests his head on Krista's, knowing that it was right. That was where it all began: his condition, his curse.

His hatred.

2

Change

A faint glow roused Lucifer from his sleep. His eyes fluttered open. Such radiance should be impossible here. He's deep within the Darklands now.

Then again, the snow was supposed to be impossible too.

Yet it lies around him, covering the trees and the ground. Lucifer didn't find it a coincidence that it had descended upon Ethero after what transpired in Exia. It was a premonition, a reminder of where he was going.

Kyrios.

Towards my past, Lucifer recalled, groaning, as he moved from his position lying against a tree, shivering from the cold. He looked to the forest surrounding him, reaching towards the snow and grabbing a fistful before taking a bite of it. It solved his thirst but didn't ease his hunger. His stomach grumbled. Lucifer hadn't eaten in days, not since leaving Exia. Often, his inclinations had told him to go back to Exia, but Lucifer rejected such notions. He had promised Ven that he'd return home. He had vowed he would change.

'I miss you so much,' Lucifer muttered, moving to sit back

against the tree. Faint white sparkles accompanied the falling snow, providing the glow that had woken him. Lucifer grimaced, unsure what to make of them. They reminded him of something.

Him. The sparkles fused, forming an outline of a figure Lucifer knew he'd seen before, a being much like Korai. However, unlike the Fallen, who he had not felt since leaving Exia, this being did not have tattoo-like markings across his skin, nor was he encased in an aura of violet and crimson. His skin was clear and white, his hair floating towards the sky, a perfect silver, and he studied Lucifer with eyes of a similar colour.

'What are you?' Lucifer asked. The being gave him a sense of peace and serenity. Then he remembered when he last saw this being: in a vision he had at the Institute before his first battle with Megidra.

Why are you here? Why now?

The being smiled. Unlike Korai, Lucifer perceived no mocking or condescension in that smile, but a genuine warmth he hadn't felt since...

'Who are you?'

'Hello, Lucifer,' the being answered. He did not appear cold despite being shirtless, his muscles defined but not bulky. There was a majesty about him. Lucifer was sure this was another entity, but not like Korai.

'Are you inside me too?' Lucifer asked. The being remained silent. Resentment filled Lucifer, but he forced himself to remain calm, remembering how easily he had allowed his emotions to control him in the past.

I almost did it again. After I promised Ven. I cannot repeat the same mistakes. I have to be better. I have to be—

7

'Be what, Lucifer?' the being asked. 'You're too harsh on yourself. You made a mistake, and you've learnt from it. Now, you pursue something else, something you weren't ready to pursue until you made your decision.'

'What decision is that?' Lucifer asked. 'Have you been waiting for this moment?'

'Yes,' the being answered, dropping to one knee in front of Lucifer. 'The second path begins, Lucifer.'

'But what makes you any different from him?' Lucifer asked, recalling what happened between him and Korai in Exia. 'What if I'm pursuing another poisonous dream? Another delusion?'

'Tell me, Lucifer Armedeus. What do you feel when I'm here?' the being asked.

Lucifer contemplated the feelings swirling within him. He recalled his last memories of Vennifer, lying in his arms as she said her last words.

Move forward. Forgive yourself...'

'Forgiveness,' Lucifer finally answered, lowering his head. 'With you, I feel forgiveness.'

Bitterness arose in his heart then, and he scowled.

'I do not deserve forgiveness. I deluded myself into thinking that I wished to save my race, that I could become a god. It was all a lie, so I could run from the truth, about how much I despise myself. Tell me, do you believe that merits forgiveness?'

He looked up. The being's expression hadn't changed at all. He was still smiling, compassionate.

'That's for you to discover, isn't it? That's why you're returning to where it all began,' the being said. He placed a gentle hand on Lucifer's shoulder, staring into his eyes. 'Do not fear repeating the same mistake, Lucifer. You've already changed. Now you must continue in your journey. You must find and understand forgiveness.'

The being rose to his feet, half turning away as Lucifer watched him move.

'Who are you? How do you know this?'

'I am the one who follows the downfall, Lucifer. The result of both order and chaos. This world is hurting so much. The price of my failure. Though you do not trust him, you will need Korai. A choice will have to be made.'

'A choice between what?' Lucifer asked.

'A choice between repeating the same cycle Ethero has followed since the beginning, or forgiveness. In time, you will understand. Go to Kyrios. Find the forgiveness that this world needs.'

The being faded then, dissipating into glistening silver sparkles. As his light diminished, Lucifer found himself alone within the almost black Darklands, barely lit by the grey sky above and the surrounding snow. Kyrios awaited him.

I've got to get up. I need to move forward.

Rustling caught Lucifer's attention. A pair of glowing green eyes stared right at him. Lucifer scrambled to his feet, tapping into his Transformative Blessing and shifting his hands into bladed claws as he lowered his posture, ready.

A deep growl came from the overgrowth. This was the reason most never ventured beyond the four cities.

A Machgar.

He could imagine it now, a bio-mechanical predator with an organic body and robotic legs. No one knew what colour their shaggy fur was supposed to be, but their teeth were made of metal, capable of tearing apart their prey. Lucifer had no intention of suffering such a fate. He placed his bladed fingertips together, before ripping them apart with a grinding sound that chimed into a metallic hiss.

The growling stopped and the green eyes froze.

Go. Do not force me to act.

The rustling resumed and the eyes turned away. Lucifer held his own breath, waiting to see if the danger had passed. It might be a ruse to trap him. He switched to his Elemental blessing, and fire ignited his hands.

'There,' Lucifer said, his expression darkening as he looked to his right. The Machgar emerged, its scruffy silver fur marred with patches of blood. Its green eyes flashed again, and it growled as it bared its teeth at Lucifer. He thought he heard a slight hiss from its mechanical legs, which gleamed as they reflected his flames. Two of its metal teeth were much longer than the others, extending from its mouth like silver daggers.

What now? Lucifer wondered, making no sudden movements. Instead, he tapped further into his Blessing, intensifying the flames and illuminating the surrounding forest.

The Machgar remained still, as though calling Lucifer's bluff.

'You do not want this fight,' Lucifer said.

The Machgar hesitated, then turned away, heading back into the overgrowth.

Lucifer released his Elemental Blessing, allowing the Darklands to return to their natural state. He sighed with relief, and turned in the direction he was sure led to Kyrios.

'He was right, whoever he was,' he said. 'I promised you, Ven. I will change. I will be better. I will find forgiveness.'

3

Leader of the Hateful

P auli's expression changed when he entered the office, looking concerned as she raised her head from what used to be Hela's desk.

No, now it's my desk. Diana half-smiled at Pauli as he closed the door behind him, his face hardening.

'You need to sleep in your room, Diana,' he said in his blunt tone; his way of being stern with her. It came from a place of caring, which made her smile.

He's so sweet, she thought, warmth radiating from within, and not from her Elemental Blessing.

Pauli still looked concerned. 'You'll burn out if you maintain this,' he said, sounding like the teacher he was. 'Are you intending to break yourself? Just days into the position?'

'No,' Diana said, tiredly, as she brushed her hair back and rubbed her eyes. 'The desk just looked so comfortable, and...'

Diana peeked over her knuckles, almost chuckling at her childishness. When Pauli returned this gesture with no hint of amusement, Diana sighed before allowing her hands to fall on the desk. She then turned her gaze to the various piles of papers that no longer possessed meaning or purpose.

What had I been doing? she wondered, shaking her head as no recollection came to her. She wasn't sure how long she'd been asleep, which agitated her.

'What is it?' Pauli asked.

Diana looked at him, observing his large physique, short hair, and well-groomed beard. She planted her elbow on the desk before resting her chin against the flat of her palm.

I wonder what beard product you're using today? Diana thought, realising she was losing herself again. She smiled in faint amusement: she needed to show organisation and leadership. After all, she was their leader now. It was time to act like one.

But I doubt I can hide anything from you, can I?

Diana appreciated that. She wanted Pauli to see the real her, not the leader of his race. Diana wondered if this was how Hela had felt during her tenure as leader of the Hateful. Isolated. Unsure. Afraid. Especially having taken over after her exiled brother. The issue, Diana had realised, was that no one explained what being a leader of their kind meant. She was sure Hela had gone through a similar induction.

Diana had taken over during a crisis herself. Again, one caused by Megidra's actions. Now, in the aftermath of his recent massacre, many humans were camping outside the Institute, launching regular attacks to hurt the Hateful. Thankfully, some brave few among them had positioned themselves across the wall between them and Exia, repelling anyone who attempted to scale the wall. They had resorted to non-harmful methods to defend themselves, like beating them back with bursts of water and non-toxic gas. Enough blood had been shed. The Institute felt the weight of that.

Still, that hasn't stopped my kind from trying, and it's snowing.

Something was changing. Diana could sense it, not just in Exia, but Ethero too. Few among humans or the Hateful were handling it well. There was no trace of the Titaniuses. It was like they had all disappeared. Though rumours suggested they had retreated within Exia Mountain, no one had confirmed it. Diana forced herself to stay firm. She straightened her posture, trying to show Pauli more confidence.

'Why did you just change your posture?' he asked, in his blunt Hateful way.

Diana sighed, still smiling. 'I was trying to make you feel confidence in me, despite having caught me sleeping in the office,' she said, stopping herself from chuckling.

Pauli's face relaxed. 'You don't need to do that,' he said. 'I'm always confident in you. We all are. It's just that I'm concerned you're pushing too hard, trying to do everything like Hela did.'

You're so genuine, Diana thought, the warmth rising again. She allowed herself to enjoy the sensation, before realising that Pauli had probably come for a reason.

'What's up?' she asked, before shaking her head in annoyance; the way she phrased her question wouldn't make sense to him. The Hateful needed more context. Diana considered a better way to phrase her question. 'Sorry. What I meant was, how can I help you, Pauli?'

He didn't respond, which informed Diana that she had already botched this interaction. Pauli seemed to consider what to say next before taking a deep breath.

'Diana, some of my kind wish to discuss with you the current state of affairs,' he said, before his demeanour became awkward. 'Your kind are becoming more ambitious in their attempts to scale the wall. Their anger doesn't seem to abate.'

'Anger fades, but pettiness can last a lifetime, Pauli,' Diana said, not surprised to hear this. She couldn't blame them: she often recalled the sounds of humans screaming among seething flames. The image of Exia burning was one she would never forget.

I don't have time to think about that. I'm the leader of the Hateful now. They need me.

Diana walked around her desk, moving towards the door as Pauli's gaze followed her.

'Come. Let's see if my kind has dented the wall.'

As Diana exited Tower 1 of the Institute, she gazed upon the now snow-covered ruins of the grounds, the aftermath of Megidra's assault. The sight made her recall the sounds of gunfire and blades clashing.

And the sound of the Descendants' horrifying cackling and gargled roars.

Diana stopped, shivering, remembering the last time she saw Hela, witnessing the hell her brother had created.

'Thank you so much for everything, Diana. The Hateful never forget.'

No, and I doubt I will either, Hela, Diana thought. She missed the former leader of the Hateful.

'Diana?' Pauli asked, his concern obvious as he spoke.

Diana forced herself to smile again. 'I'm alright, Pauli,' she said, not doubting that he would know she was lying. Knowing that he wouldn't say anything – not here, anyway – Diana looked ahead and continued towards the wall.

They had come during a rare moment of peace. Diana was

appreciative, hugging the black leather Hateful jacket she wore close to her neck, her breath suspended in clouds of steam.

'Do you want me to help you up?' Pauli asked.

Diana shook her head. 'No, I should be fine,' she said, opening her arms and allowing the cold to encapsulate her whole body, her jacket fluttering behind her. 'If I'm leader then I need to handle myself.'

Pauli made no further comment but tapped into his Physical Blessing, his musculature increasing within his Hateful attire. He jumped into the air, leaving a cloud of snow in his wake, before landing on top of the wall. Diana tapped into her own Blessing then, summoning the Elemental power of air. She wrapped herself in it, creating a sense of lightness that evolved into levitation. Then she summoned more of her Blessing, rising along the face of the wall until she reached the top. Unlike her first attempt at this, she landed as nobly as Pauli had. Diana smiled. She wondered what Hela would think if she could see that, comparing it to the first time they met.

So much has changed since then. I barely knew anything about myself. Your wonderful kind have changed my life. I must do the same for them.

Diana turned towards the city of Exia. Smoke was still rising towards the sky, another ugly trace of Megidra's massacre. Much had changed following the atrocities of the now infamous Devil of Anubi. Exia had become a battlefield of chaos and anarchy. Human factions arose from every district, competing for resources. The DFA had retreated to their base in Greyr after losing control of the streets. According to the brave scouts Diana had sent out, violence and death now lurked in every crevice of the city. This was apparent below them, in the no-man's-land between the Institute and the rest of Exia. There were makeshift campsites everywhere, made from whatever scrap metal the humans of Exia could get their hands on.

It was like the aftermath of an apocalypse. Campfires burned among the barbed-wired fences and ramshackle metal huts her kind had created. They all sheltered those who wanted to harm the Hateful. Humanity blamed the Hateful for Megidra's actions. Diana was thankful the war for the streets had taken most of their focus. For now.

But there's still a lot here, Diana noted, hearing footsteps pattering either side as a few volunteer guards approached. She noted their exhaustion. She made sure she appeared confident as they reached her.

'Seems quiet,' Diana said, knowing that she was stating the obvious. The Hateful guards nodded.

'Yes. We think the snow is having an effect,' one said, a male in his early twenties. 'As the covering gets thicker, the hum—sorry, I mean your kind – seem to struggle against it. Because of that, they aren't launching as many attacks. The only problem is that their strategies are becoming more sophisticated when they do attack.'

'What do you mean?' Pauli asked.

'They're launching multiple attacks at different points of the wall. I think they know there's few of us, so they're relying on us growing tired.'

Which you are, Diana thought.

'Is it a problem?' Pauli asked.

The guard shook his head. 'It's nothing we can't handle. Still, having a few more guards wouldn't hurt.'

'We'll get some more volunteers to help,' Diana said, folding her arms. 'We need to figure out something for the long term, assuming that my kind intends to try waiting us out. Could we build something on top of the walls? Even if it's just shelter to stay warm?'

'But wouldn't that serve as a massive target for your kind?' Pauli asked.

Diana acknowledged that with a nod. 'Probably, but it might make my kind's attacks more predictable. Easier to handle.'

'She has a fair point,' the young guard said, scratching his chin.

'We'll need resources,' another guard said, a young female.

Diana looked questioningly at Pauli. 'Where would we get supplies?' she asked. Then her eyes widened. 'Wait. Where do we get our supplies from? Food. Water. Power. Where does all of that come from?'

The group frowned at her, surprised she didn't know.

'My kind may decide to target vital supply routes rather than continue direct attacks. I need to know what they are. I should've been told this!'

Diana stopped herself then, taking in a breath. 'Sorry. I shouldn't blame any of you for that. I'm still trying to get a hold of this role.'

The group nodded, before Pauli gestured to prompt the guards to leave. As they did, he turned to Diana. 'I'm sorry, Diana. I should've told you.'

'No, we're both adjusting to this,' Diana said, softening. 'We'll get there.'

'That's the Diana I know,' Pauli said, smiling in a way that made Diana's heart skip a beat. She decided not to allow things to become awkward as they stared at each other. She turned her attention back towards the three towers of the Institute.

'I need to make sure I don't repeat her mistakes, Pauli,' Diana said, hating how her words sounded, but knowing them to be true. 'I can't lie to the others and act like I've got everything under control. Hela hid them from the truth. She isolated herself because of that. I have to be myself. That's why you all chose me. Now, take me to where your kind gets its supplies.'

The Hateful had many systems that allowed them to live independently. For food, a select group of them would organise supply drops by dragon riders at times when humans would most likely be asleep. It was a simple system, but Diana wondered how the recent changes in Exia's landscape would affect it.

As for the electricity source, Pauli was leading her there now, headed to the basement of Tower 2. There, Diana could see three massive turbines, cylindrical and connected by thick cables that ran from them before disappearing into the surface. Before them stood a console with two protruding handles.

'Those are where we charge the turbines,' Pauli explained, gesturing towards the console. 'Every week, one of us comes down to charge them with the Elemental Blessing. They then transfer the electricity through the rest of the Institute.'

'So why does most of the Institute use candlelight?' Diana asked.

Pauli smiled mischievously in a way Diana liked. 'They aren't candles, Diana. Could you imagine how often we'd need to replace them?'

It was a good point, but Diana didn't respond. She regarded Pauli expectantly; he almost seemed to hold himself from laughing.

'They're just normal lights, shaped to replicate candles,' he continued. 'They provide a soothing effect. Many of our kind have hypersensitivities, so we chose dim lighting to make things comfortable for them. As for heating and water, Tower 3's basement possesses a similar room to this one. Again, we use our Elemental Blessing to fill the tanks with water and to provide heating throughout the Institute.'

'So the Elemental is the best Blessing,' Diana said, nodding.

Pauli grinned, before letting out a slight chuckle as Diana fought herself from joining him. It felt wonderful to see Pauli act this way around her. More comfortable. More himself.

Should I be concerned with how much I like that? Diana wondered, before deciding to distract herself with matters she knew were important.

Every day she discovered something else that she needed to look after. It all strengthened the conclusion that had become apparent ever since she became the leader of the Hateful, that she couldn't repeat Hela's mistake.

That she needed help.

She moved towards the console, sad to hear Pauli's laughter dying behind her. His usual demeanour had returned, sensing the change in her mood.

I'm sorry, Pauli, but if we're going to do this, then I can't keep relying on you. Beyond everything I'm realising Hela went through, I haven't even begun working on the very reason you all chose me. It makes so much sense now why Hela ended up the way she did. So stressed, with no help. Is it any wonder why she retreated into her office more and more, placing her faith in the

19

children?

Diana sighed, folding her arms.

I can't do that. They deserve to choose how they live their lives. I need help from someone else.

Then she realised. 'I know what to do,' Diana began. 'Hela chose the wrong people to stack her hopes on. She shouldn't have relied on the children while ignoring the adults among you. I cannot do everything, never mind focus on the very mission you chose me for. Rather than repeat that mistake, I'll go the opposite way. It's time for those who feel abandoned to step up. It doesn't even have to be a job or a role we devise. If anyone here has a talent or skill, we will encourage them to pursue it. We're going to give them purpose, and hope…'

Diana paused then, gears clicking in her mind. She returned her gaze to Pauli. 'Call an emergency meeting, Pauli, right now. Make sure Reni is there. This new plan begins now.'

4

The Devil of Anubi

'C'mon son! Move!' a woman called to her child, scanning the snowy mist-filled streets of the Rai District.

'You're hurting my hand!' her little boy retorted, half moving with her, half fighting against her.

'It's just a little further, son. We're almost there!'

'Why are we rushing?' the boy asked.

His mother stopped and turned to him. 'You know why. He could be here any moment. The DFA never caught him. You know how Mommy said we gotta watch out for the bad people? Well, he's the one we've gotta watch out for most.'

'But… But he could be anywhere,' the boy said, gulping to contain his fear.

'Which is why we gotta move! We need to get home as soon as possible!' his mother said, pulling at his arm.

The boy resisted, tugging against her, looking up into her terrified eyes. 'What if he ran away?' he asked.

His mother leaned closer to him, her face mere inches from his. 'Devils don't run away, son. They—'

She stopped herself then, shaking her head before rising to her full height. When she pulled at her boy's arm, he no longer resisted. It's then they bumped into a man, causing him to stagger a few steps. Horror washed across their faces. The mother knew she should be afraid as she regarded the enormous figure.

He was the one humanity named the Devil of Anubi.

According to legend, the Divinity had unleashed the Devil as punishment for human sins, setting Exia aflame before unleashing a horde of demons upon the world. The legend said the Devil took on the guise of a dashingly beautiful man, armed with a charming smile and an eloquent voice, and donning a crimson cloak. While this was untrue, it hadn't stopped the legend from spreading, putting fear into every human heart. That was the greatest shame he felt as he regarded the mother and child now, watching as they cowered away from him.

If only you knew the reality, the Devil thought, knowing that what they saw was not a dashing gentleman of evil. The true Devil was a broken thing. He wore a tattered black cloak that covered almost all of his body, except for large black leather boots. His cloaked face was a blank void, like the tales of Ethero Fiends.

You think I'm about to kill you, the Devil thought, raising his hands beyond his cloak and studying them as though he hardly recognised they were his own. The mother and child were looking at his hands too, terrified of what he intended to do with them.

Nothing. Absolutely nothing. That is what I am now. Nothing...

The Devil allowed his hands to drop, returning to the

warmth of his cloak. It wasn't much, considering the weather. The snow fell in a light blizzard, while the fog allowed vision only a few meters ahead. An agitated whistle accompanied the snow, filling the silence between what the Devil knew were three very different lives.

Had this been another time, I wonder what I might've done. Would I have sought your approval and admiration, or would I have destroyed you both instead?

The latter thought caused him to wince and shake his head. He regarded the mother and child again.

'And to think I wanted to become you,' he said, before stepping around them. From there, he made his way towards one of the many streets he had spent the last few days roaming, each one reminding him of his shame and guilt. Exia and humanity had collapsed in the wake of his actions. All that remained were questions of how he had become a monster. Every time he asked himself that, his mind returned to one particular image.

Lucifer Armedeus weeping on his knees, holding the corpse of his love killed by Ryun's hand.

No, your hand, fool, the Fallen said within, causing the Devil to pause as he closed his eyes. Of course, Ryun was right. It had been his hands that killed her. The Devil understood that now. The sounds of screaming and gargled shrieks filled his mind, along with seething flames that had once given him so much pleasure. It had been his ultimate Hateful dream. Pain mixed with hatred, fuelling a sick desire that had manifested into the fantasy.

A fantasy that I somehow made into reality. Yet I regret everything now. I have nothing left, except—

'End your dream. Don't allow this to happen again.' The voice of Lucifer cut into his mind. The Devil opened his eyes and looked up at the sky, as tiny flakes of snow landed on his face.

'That's what I'm doing, Lucifer,' he murmured, before grimacing. 'But what happens now? Do I try to redeem myself? Is such a thing possible? I'm the Devil, so what's left for someone like me? Where do I go? What do I do?'

It surprised the Devil that Ryun didn't respond. The Fallen was all he had now. Hela had died by his hands, while their mother and father had cast them both aside long ago. Greene was gone as well. He had pushed the Titanius away.

'Everything that was good in my life, I ruined. All to pursue a poisonous dream, a delusion.'

To the end of all corrupted dreams, his mind recalled. The Devil shivered and lowered his gaze. Even that man seemed so distant now. He understood the truth now. He'd been running from so many truths, as Ryun would put it.

'Hey!'

He heard a voice in the distance that sounded like a small boy. The Devil looked around, seeing nothing. Guided by instinct, the Devil headed toward alleyways from which buildings rose like mangled metal spikes. He saw movement, accompanying the sounds of struggle: grunting interlaced with agitated murmurs. Familiar thoughts arose within the Devil, ones that belonged to the man he had wanted to be, the great delusion he had given a name.

Newman.

'Let go of me!' the young boy cried. He tried to sound tough, but the Devil could hear the betrayal of his fear and anxiety. The Devil quickened his steps, walking briskly through one back alley. He came upon an opening that led to a cross-section of streets, where figures moved under the heavily fogged streetlight. A group of humans appeared to be fighting with a small black boy, who was holding something in his hands. The Devil emerged from the alleyway, the air changing around him. The struggling stopped and everyone turned to face him.

'What d'ya want?!' a bulky figure demanded, his details obscured by the fog. The Devil did not answer, so the figure took a threatening step closer. The Devil regarded him then, unfazed, which seemed to spook the man.

'Hey!' the boy shouted, gaining the Devil's attention. 'Help me!'

'Shut up, boy!' a woman spoke from among the group. 'You stole our food! You deserve to be punished!'

Punished? the Devil thought, bitterness rising within, accompanying a stirring from Ryun. *No, it's me who deserves to be punished.*

'I didn't!' the boy protested, angry and defiant. The Devil guessed he was around twelve, his clothes too big for him. He struggled.

'I found it first!' the boy continued. 'These bastards ambushed me!'

Another of the adults stepped forward and slapped the boy hard in the face, making him yelp in surprise. Without thinking, the Devil moved, tapping into his Transformative Blessing. He summoned a large curving blade in his right arm, which extended from his cloak. The humans froze in horror. Old feelings and desires filled him, reminding the Devil of the monster he was. He wanted to kill them; all of them. He pictured the tree of blades in Anubi once more, hung around with human corpses. A haunting sense of dread followed.

No, what am I doing? the Devil thought, his lips parting before his knees dropped to the ground. Wetness soaked into them and his body shook. The group released the boy then, backing away.

'No, it's happening again,' the Devil murmured, imagining the humans running from him as his abominations gave chase, shrieking and roaring, tearing them apart. The snowy landscape of the present shifted and changed, turning into the burning hell he had created. Worst of all, he felt immense pleasure, remembering the relief that had come from finally ending his lies.

'I hate everyone and everything.'

'No,' the Devil whimpered, tears running down his cheeks. He looked up, seeing the last thing he wanted to.

Hela staggered towards him, a bleeding corpse trying to use multiple Blessings, dying as she bestowed him with a look he knew he had never deserved. The look he had longed for since he was a child.

A loving smile.

Inside, Ryun laughed, mocking his descent, knowing that the Devil was heading for another meltdown. Still, all the Devil could see was his own sister, staggering towards him before falling by his knees. Hela's smile never faded.

'I love you, brother. I just wish... you'd love yourself.'

'How, Hela? Tell me how!' the Devil screamed, his breathing growing ragged as dismay and hatred filled him. He staggered to his feet, power surging within him. Wisps of violet and crimson emitted from his body, reminding him of the being that still lived in him, now laughing at his misery.

And of his curse, of the simple fact that he was Hateful.

'No!' he bellowed, as the image of his sister faded, returning him to the snowy world that Exia had become. The adults had released the boy, who was regarding the Devil in amazement. The adults seemed horrified.

'I won't give in! I won't! You no longer have power over me!' the Devil screamed as the adults scrambled away, the boy seemingly unable to move. The wisps of violet and crimson intensified as his muscles grew and his hair floated upward, changing colour. The transformation was almost complete. Painful memories emerged. He recalled the moment he realised his mother and father had abandoned him and Hela. The way humans had treated him upon his first visit to Anubi.

'I refuse, Ryun! I am no longer your slave! Get out of my head!'

Is that so? Ryun responded, as he snickered within. *Then tell me, Devil of Anubi, what lie do you tell yourself now? Without your dream, what are you now?*

Sparks of electricity flickered around his body, and the Devil reared his head back and screamed. Everything around him shook, as though his will could break the world. His aura erupted like a wave of power before fading. Exia returned to its previous state, and the Devil fell to his knees again, panting with exhaustion, slick with sweat and relief. He turned his gaze towards the sky once more.

Without my dream, what am I? he asked himself. He heard the faint crunching of snow to his right. He looked in that direction, surprised to see the young boy approaching him, no doubt seeing that the Devil was...

Hateful.

'Go,' the Hateful man said, exhausted. His vision faded, and he fell onto his side.

5

Unknown Truths

The snow flickered through the leafless trees. Greene contemplated whether they ever had leaves to begin with. He had asked many questions like that over the past few days, making him realise how little he understood about Ethero.

Just like how my kind didn't choose to stay in Exia. They had no choice, Greene thought, trying to stave off ruefulness. At least, that's what he believed the emotion to be. It had risen with many others since his transformation. Anger. Scorn. Confusion. Greene was aware of these emotions because of his DFA training, having learned them to deal with the very humans who enslaved his race. That was what he had always thought, anyway. Now, he wasn't so sure. How did one understand emotions when they weren't supposed to feel them?

But you know the truth, don't you, Barbatos? Greene thought, regarding the blue-skinned sorcerer striding ahead of them. He was the reason they were on this journey. Greene glanced towards one of their new travelling companions, the Cybernetic known as Shallai.

And then there's you. Why is it every time I look at you, more feelings arise, but ones that feel wrong and forbidden?

Greene shook his head, not understanding those feelings. He gazed at his hands, studying how they had changed. His synthetic skin, once navy, was now jet black, and thin violet lines ran over his entire body like visible veins. He was taller too, around the size of an average human man, while possessing what seemed an endless pool of Life Essence within.

Is this what I'm supposed to be? Is this the true form of my race?

He already knew the answer to that. The transformation had only come from the potion created by Barbatos. No, the true form of the Titaniuses were the Great Machines they now sought to free.

The Titans.

Greene recalled the colossal being from his dreams. It had stood as tall as Exia Mountain, possessing a capacity for destruction matched only by the Demons that lived within the Hateful.

Like Newman, Greene thought, bitterness and melancholy filling his heart. Greene understood he couldn't have stopped his old friend, but he still felt ashamed about what had happened in Exia; for running. The memory of the cackling shrieks of Newman's monsters made him shiver, along with the human screams, the humans he had once sworn to protect.

The same humans who subjugated my kind...

Greene squeezed his fists then, torn between justification and responsibility. A hand falling on his shoulder jolted him back to the present. It was the last member of their party. Greene looked at the colossal being, almost entirely concealed in a black cloak. Only the hand of the giant Ethero Fiend showed, a ghostly white skin tone with long black fingernails like claws.

'*Guastva bvu myaskala,*' he said. Greene studied the black void that existed where its face should have been. Breaths of steam flowed gently from the void, but that made the creature no less terrifying, and snowflakes floated onto his cloak. The snow was another reminder of Greene's failure to stop Newman.

'I'm sorry?' Greene asked. The Ethero Fiend allowed his hand to fall, looking down on Greene like some great phantom of death. He offered no further words.

'He says to focus your anger, my dear Titanius,' Barbatos said. Greene was positive he could hear the smirk on the sorcerer's face. The sorcerer was just behind him, wielding his black sceptre with its glowing emerald tip. Like Shallai and Greene, Barbatos had put on no additional clothing despite the cold and the snow. He still wore his tight leather outfit with its multitude of protruding buckles and straps.

'Are you stewing, Greene?' the sorcerer asked, his eyes glinting with the suggestion that he already knew the answer. Greene scowled, turning his gaze on the Darklands they now roamed. They were no longer so dark, the snow and the grey sky illuminating them dimly. According to Barbatos, such a phenomenon hadn't been seen since the days when there had been a sun in the sky.

A herald for what is coming? Greene wondered, reflecting on the Fiend and Barbatos' suggestion that war was coming, and that they would face resistance soon. As far as his kind and humanity were aware, within the Darklands were the cities of Ethero, Dynames, Kyrios and Virtue, but Greene doubted that. There would be more, among other things. After all, everything he had once known had been a lie. Greene understood that now.

He also knew that they were barely scratching the surface.

Beginning with the open plains south of Exia, they had emerged in a swamp-like section of marshlands, before they entered the forests of lifeless trees they now traversed. What lay beyond, Greene couldn't guess, and Barbatos was not in the mood to share such information. Greene found himself tempted to question the sorcerer. In response, Barbatos grinned.

'Yes?' he asked.

'Where are we going?' Greene asked.

'To uncover your ancestors, of course,' Barbatos answered, before moving to walk ahead. He wanted to reach out and grab the sorcerer, but Greene held himself still. Shallai glanced at him, before folding her arms and moving toward Barbatos.

'If you don't tell him, I will,' she said.

Barbatos' eyes almost seemed to flash with anger, but he quickly recovered. He brushed back strands of long black hair before smiling at Shallai.

'And I thought you trusted me,' he said.

Shallai matched his smile then. 'You are self-aware enough to know that none of us here trust you, and that none of this would happen if you didn't benefit.'

'You question my benevolence now? My dear–'

'If you call me "my dear Cybernetic", like you do the Titanius, I will slap you,' Shallai warned.

Impressed, Barbatos gave her a nod, his smile never fading

as he half turned. He stopped himself then, looking back at Shallai. 'His name is Greene, not Titanius.'

'Perhaps you should remember that,' Shallai suggested, before Barbatos offered her a knowing wink. He spread his hands in an over-the-top sweep Greene was sure annoyed her, then opened his arms in a welcoming embrace.

'Go ahead, illuminate our friend,' he said. 'I'm not keeping anything from him. No one had asked.'

'Easy to say when three of us know where we're going, and what we're searching for,' Shallai said, unimpressed.

'True. But you forget that Greene has undergone many changes. He's processing them as we speak,' Barbatos said.

Green himself stepped forward, trying to contain his annoyance. 'I can speak for myself,' he said, addressing both of them. 'Please, Shallai, I appreciate you defending me. However, we all know what Barbatos says can fall into either truth or lie, while sounding much like the former. I don't doubt that what we're doing suits his own ends, but it suits mine too. Please, I mean no disrespect, but we're yet to understand what you and–' Greene hesitated, half considering whether to gesture or even turn towards the Fiend behind them. He decided to preserve his life a little longer and straightened himself, taking in a breath.

'Anyway, despite the myriad questions I have, I'm not sure whether I want to understand any of them. I will ask when I'm ready.'

'See,' Barbatos chimed in, gesturing with his sceptre towards Greene while regarding Shallai.

She glanced between the two of them before shaking her head. 'Nice try, Greene, but I know what you're doing. So does he,' she said, pointing at Barbatos. 'Don't feed into his bullshit. You need to understand what awaits us. Barbatos might make it seem like you two would be alright on your own, but you'll need us. Especially him.'

Shallai gestured towards the Fiend, before looking back at Barbatos. 'We should stop and get some rest. Then we'll talk. Anyone object?'

No one did, so Shallai raised her only mechanical arm, switching it into a long-barrelled firearm without a scope, reaching towards a handle that she cocked back.

'I'll get us some food first,' she said, before heading to the west.

Meanwhile, the Fiend turned and headed south. Greene followed him, knowing Barbatos would not move from his current location. The routine had been established, and soon they would have firewood and food. It fell to him and the wordless Ethero Fiend to scavenge for wood, which, despite the freezing cold and wet snow, they always found. Barbatos would then use magic to start the fire.

Within thirty minutes they had a fire going, with Barbatos conjuring strange black flames. Still, they generated a heat that melted some of the surrounding snow. Shallai returned with some unfortunate animal and then they ate. That didn't include Greene, who didn't need to eat or drink. He watched Shallai's gaze flicker towards Barbatos.

'Well?' she asked.

'Oh, I'm sorry, you wanted to discuss something, didn't you?' Barbatos smiled.

Shallai shot him an icy look before shaking her head. Her gaze found Greene. 'We're going to the cities of our races,' she said. 'Long ago, as you already know, our races swore an oath to hide ourselves from humanity, your kind and the

Hateful. Well, that's not the only oath we swore, and that's the reason you and Barbatos need us. To awaken the Great Machines, I'm guessing you will need each piece of the Titan core, which was split between our races and humanity. Am I right?'

Barbatos offered only a shrug, before his smile grew. 'I jest. Yes, that is what we seek. To awaken the Great Machines, we must assemble all four pieces of the Titan core,' he said. 'Of course, our Cybernetic friend here exaggerates her importance. Shallai is nervous, because news of our search will have already spread to the hidden races. They know we're coming. With that, division will arise, as our arrival brings tidings of war.'

Barbatos paused, and Shallai kept her icy look. That told Greene that his comments were not far off the mark.

'You say that,' he said, 'But you've hardly explained anything about this war. Who is fighting who?'

At first, Barbatos didn't answer. There was a glint in his eye, something like repressed anger. But then he quickly smirked, sealing the moment away.

'Between the Divinity and the Ether, of course,' he said. 'Our actions will renew the war that wasn't settled, and this time the line between ally and foe will be murkier, less obvious. Greene, the reason Shallai is making us have this conversation is because she knows, alongside our other friend, that there is no return from this. It has begun.'

Barbatos' confident smirk grew, as though this were all inevitable. A part of Greene wasn't sure. There was so much he didn't understand. Facets of the past he knew he hadn't been told.

'In due time, all shall be revealed,' Barbatos continued.

'Although none of you trust me, trust in my oath. I stand by the Eternal Mother, and in my belief the Divinity shall perish for what he's done, for this unjust world he created. For wanting something that could never be achieved.'

Greene frowned at that last sentence. The sorcerer closed his eyes and shook his head. 'A slip of the tongue, nothing more.'

'What did you mean by that?' Shallai said, as though sensing the same thing Greene had.

Before Barbatos could answer, the sound of movement caused the entire group to turn.

The Ethero Fiend rose to his feet and extended his sleeves towards his head, revealing his ghostly white skin and black claw-like hands. They gripped his hood, pulling it back to unveil a horrifying face. It was ghostly white like his hands, with large eternal black eyes. The Fiend's head was bald, emphasising the giant scar that curved from the top of his temple all the way towards his eye, cheek and nose. His teeth looked almost human except for two large single teeth on either side of the mouth that hung over his bottom lip. They were twisted into a smile that almost sent Greene running. Such a smile was on Newman's face as he unleashed hell upon Exia.

'Vengeance,' the creature said, using the common speech. Whether he meant for himself or Barbatos, Greene wasn't sure.

'Of course,' Barbatos said. 'I believe many of us will gain vengeance from this crusade. You most of all, Doomis.'

'So that's your name,' Shallai said. She seemed in contemplation, glancing between Barbatos and the Fiend. 'It kinda fits.'

'If you think that, ask him about the other name he's known by, especially where we're going,' Barbatos remarked.

Shallai's eyes narrowed. 'So that's where you're taking us first,' she said.

'Wait, you know where we're going?' Greene asked.

'Yeah,' Shallai said, shaking her head. 'Elcaris.'

'Elcaris?' Greene asked.

'Home,' Doomis answered. 'Where my kind lives.'

6

Kyrios

Days passed before Lucifer reached Kyrios, his true home. Old feelings returned as he laid his eyes upon the other monstrous city of metal. His head throbbed, and there was a feeling of bitterness he couldn't shake.

Am I to carry pain wherever I go, leaving only regrets behind? Lucifer wondered. He had never intended to return here. Exia was meant to be his new start, his salvation. He smiled bitterly.

Unlike Exia, Kyrios did not exist alongside a mountain or seas, but was surrounded by the forests of the Darklands. A forty-foot metal wall enclosed it, obscuring most of the buildings except for the great cathedral that stood prominently to the far north. It was a gothic monstrosity, a contortion of metal spikes that warped and stabbed into the sky. Like all the major cities in Ethero, Kyrios was entirely made of metal. However, no vehicles moved around it. The citizens of Kyrios either walked or flew by dragon.

I still can't believe I'm back here, Lucifer thought, before forcing his eyes closed, taking in intentional breaths. His hands shivered, and not from the cold. It occurred to him that his "new start" had done little to change the aspects of himself that may have led to his own downfall.

I focused on the wrong parts, deluding myself into thinking that changing my surroundings would change anything. It fixed nothing within, and I took that brokenness and destroyed everything I touched.

'Well, I'm here, Ven. Just like I promised. And now I wonder, how am I supposed to find forgiveness here?'

No answer came to him, nor did he expect one to. There was no turning back now. He had made his promise to Ven. He would see it through. Despite his body's reluctance, Lucifer forced himself to take a step forward, then another. Before he knew it, he was making the last stretch towards where it all began.

Towards what he hoped would be forgiveness.

Lucifer reached the wall surrounding Kyrios roughly thirty minutes later, snow crunching beneath his feet and a light snowy breeze swirling around him. As he drew close, tension racked his body, and he recalled the words of humans cursing his race. It had been the reason his parents had never allowed him to go outside as a child.

But I am no longer that child, Lucifer told himself. *Now, I just hope I'm not the deluded fool who followed.*

He approached one of the main gates leading into the city and a single light beamed towards him. A human wearing robes was gesturing in his direction while talking to someone, before moving to approach him. Lucifer froze, fighting the urge to run, instead watching as the figure drew close. The approaching man looked like a priest, wearing clothes similar to what Johann Stratos had worn. This man, however, was much older than Johann, and his smile struck Lucifer as odd. He kept his mouth shut as the human reached him.

'Hello there, Hateful friend,' the priest said, his voice courteous, pleasant to the ear. 'Welcome to Kyrios. It's always a wonderful surprise to have visitors brave the treacherous Darklands to make it here. I doubt I could carry out such a journey myself. Have you been here before?'

Lucifer said nothing, stunned. He had never expected such words, especially from a priest loyal to the Divinity. In his eyes, Johann and the likes of Diana Skagen had been exceptions. No one besides them had ever spoken to him that way.

The priest frowned at him. 'Is something wrong?' he asked, increasing Lucifer's bafflement. Beyond them, Lucifer noticed more humans dressed in similar garb to the priest emerging by the gate, appearing as surprised by him as he was by them. But as much as it amazed him to realise it, he could discern no scorn or hatred in their expressions.

'I'm sorry,' Lucifer said, knowing he had seldom ever used the word before, especially to a human. 'I don't understand. I wasn't expecting this conversation to go this way.'

'What do you mean?' the priest asked. 'We always endeavour to welcome our visitors.'

'No, it's not that,' Lucifer said, placing a hand on his chest. 'You see what I am, don't you?'

'Why, yes,' the priest responded, as though such a thing were obvious. 'Please, forgive my rudeness, but what has that got to do with anything?'

Everything, Lucifer thought, but remaining silent.

'Is everything alright, Markus?' one of the other priests called out.

Markus turned, nodding. 'Yes, we're fine. I think our Hateful friend here is a little surprised by our hospitality. I guess he was expecting a different type of welcome.'

I certainly was, Lucifer thought, watching as Markus turned back towards him, placing his palms together.

'My name is Markus Hansin. I'm one of many priests who live here. My duty is to welcome people to Kyrios.'

'I see,' Lucifer said, unsure. He wondered why he seemed to get along with priests, but rather than consider that any further, he decided to ask a more important question. 'Why are you so kind? Why don't you despise me?' he asked.

'Do we have to despise you?' Markus asked.

Lucifer had never expected to hear such words from human lips, and his jaw dropped open.

'But the Divinity's decrees concerning my kind,' he began. 'After what happened in the past.'

Markus nodded, his expression reflecting his understanding. 'I see,' he said. 'I think I know why you're asking. Please, my Hateful friend, consider that times and people can change. At one point, yes, we probably would've responded to your arrival with scorn and ignorance. However, much has changed within Kyrios. The work Silver Wing has done is a miracle. Thanks to them, our kind live and work together in peace. Now, we understand that your kind is not Cursed, but needs more support.'

Am I dreaming? Lucifer wondered, stunned. He couldn't recall anything named "Silver Wing" and he was sure that discrimination didn't just vanish among groups in such a brief span of time. It sounded too good to be true.

Markus half turned toward the gate as his fellow priest reached them, gesturing towards it. 'Please, come inside. Perhaps you should meet Silver Wing. They might explain things better than me. Still, regardless of what you choose to do, please exercise caution while roaming the city. I'd recommend you travel with a group.'

'Why?' Lucifer asked.

The two priests exchanged glances before Markus returned his gaze to Lucifer, sighing. 'Alas, despite the incredible work Silver Wing has done here, a Hateful Killer roams this city, hunting down and destroying your kind. Silver Wing is pursuing for him, but hasn't captured him yet.'

'Is this Hateful Killer human?' Lucifer asked, concerned.

Markus's expression saddened. 'We don't know,' he admitted. 'They emerged a few months ago, hunting only your kind. Many suspect they seek to spread fear among the Hateful living in the city, trying to plant seeds of hatred between us again. Unfortunately for them, I believe Silver Wing, and the efforts of us humans who refuse to return to those days, have prevented such hatred from manifesting. But that seems to have led them to more extreme methods.'

Lucifer's gaze narrowed, while Markus appeared to shudder.

'Make sure you connect with your kind and find Silver Wing,' he said, his expression serious. 'You shouldn't find them too difficult to find. They often travel as a group. Please, don't view the Hateful Killer's actions as representative of the rest of Kyrios. Humanity here does not condone their actions.'

Those words clung to Lucifer as he roamed the snow-covered

streets of Kyrios. It was still waking hours, and the humans on the streets paid no attention to him, amazing him.

He could no longer feel the constant air of melancholy that he was sure pervaded Exia. Neither did he sense apathy among the humans. Rather, humans smiled here; laughed, even. As Lucifer walked along familiar streets, he shook his head, stunned.

Is this what you meant, Johann? Diana? Was this the Ethero you envisioned? Even you, Hela?

Lucifer stopped himself, remembering the haunting sight of Megidra standing over Hela as she died by his feet. Lucifer wondered what had become of Megidra, but painful memories of Vennifer emerged, making him wince. Lucifer didn't want to picture that again. He didn't want to relive that mistake. Still…

'I wish you could see this, Ven,' he whispered, looking up to the grey sky, partially blinding himself from the metal streetlights as his smile grew. Nothing about this place made sense. It was all wrong. Alien. He wanted to believe that it was an elaborate trick, a ruse. Once he was ensnared in their trap, they would reveal their true selves, their loathing of his kind. Yet, that didn't seem to be the case here. The humans were not hiding anything. They didn't seem to care.

It doesn't make any sense. How has this place changed so much?

Lucifer turned towards the western part of the city, wondering if his parents were still there. Despite the discomfort of their memory, he forced himself to keep his gaze west, his head tilting to one side.

Can I face you again? After everything that happened? Lucifer wondered. A familiar sensation arose inside him. He ignored it: it was too soon to speak to the being within him, especially after what had taken place in Exia. Lucifer shook his head, sighing, remembering what the being in the Darklands had said concerning the Fallen.

'I shouldn't blame you. I am responsible for my own actions,' he said. 'I promised her, Korai. I will find forgiveness.'

Lucifer headed to the centre of the city. It was much smaller than Exia, not separated into districts, but more interconnected, lined in neat half circles. They converged towards a single large fountain, built from metal like the rest of the city. It was surrounded by cafes and bars. To the north he saw more buildings, flanking a narrow river that ran from the fountain all the way towards the great cathedral. It stood imperious, far taller than any other building in Kyrios. Lucifer regarded it before examining the humans all around him.

They look so happy, he noticed. They were all wrapped in thick winter clothing, laughing among themselves. Many of them held something in their hands that they almost seemed to treasure against the surrounding cold: plastic cups with steam rising into the sky. A longing filled Lucifer, as an idea manifested in his mind.

I'm doing it.

Lucifer returned to a bench a few paces behind the fountain a short time later, cradling a similar plastic cup in his hands, warming him. He looked down at the cup in amazement, inhaling the scents of coffee and syrup. Vennifer had loved coffee, though he had never understood why. Lucifer thought it was time to try it.

It had seemed like something momentous, stepping into a coffee shop full of humans, standing among them as he waited for his chance to order. It surprised him further still when he was greeted by a smile, before being questioned about his day as the server made his drink. What he said, Lucifer couldn't remember, but the next thing he knew, he was outside, realising that he had not received a single word of abuse. Now, many questions filled his mind.

'What has Silver Wing done here?' he mumbled. Lucifer took a sip of his drink, relishing its sweetness. His eyes widened; he was enjoying every second. He almost chuckled. 'Why did I take so long to try this?' he thought aloud before a piercing human scream interrupted his thoughts.

He turned towards the fountain from where the scream had come. A group formed, pointing out something. He could hear the whimpering of the woman who had screamed as others murmured with concern. His previous contentment dissipated into dread.

There was a body floating in the fountain's basin.

It was Hateful; Lucifer could tell from the silvery-gold hair on its head, which had been stuck on top of a metal cross. From what he could see, the victim's arms had also been separated before being stuck on the flanking spikes of the cross. The bottom spike was where it appeared they had impaled the lower torso. Blood leaked from it, staining the water deep ruby. A metal plate across the centre of the cross had words scratched on it.

Is there beauty in death? it read.

Lucifer regarded the corpse with morbid fascination. He looked around, seeing many shocked humans who appeared as disgusted and fascinated as he felt. Among the murmurs, he could hear many mentions of Silver Wing.

What happens now? Lucifer wondered. Then he froze as an arm wrapped around his left shoulder.

'Move, and I'll kill everyone,' a wispy male voice said.

Lucifer remained still, feeling Korai rise within.

Stay out of this, Lucifer warned, then forced himself to focus on the hand gripping his shoulder. It seemed almost mangled, covered in scars. The fingernails were broken.

'What happened to you?' Lucifer uttered. He was certain this man was the Hateful Killer.

The man sighed, relaxing his grip on Lucifer's shoulder. 'I was born Hateful,' the Hateful Killer said. 'Still, what do you think? Is there beauty in death?'

'That was you?' Lucifer asked, betraying fear as his voice quivered.

He thought he heard a snicker in the Hateful Killer's voice. 'It's one of the first delusions human beings tell themselves. They say that death is something to be treasured, a natural occurrence, as if that is fair compensation for everything that happened before it. So, what do you think? Is death beautiful?'

Lucifer turned to find a cloaked figure studying him. His face was also scarred, as though he had been tortured. Revulsion filled Lucifer, balanced by shame. The Hateful Killer's hair, long like Lucifer's, was unkempt. The man exuded calm detachment, as if examining a specimen.

'Fascinating, isn't it?' the Hateful Killer said, his voice still wispy. It made him sound as though he were being choked. 'You've walked into this city, no doubt expecting to find only hatred and scorn. Yet you've found kindness and joy. I envy you. That drink looks wonderful. It's like we're walking through a dream, one that could turn Hateful at any moment.'

Lucifer frowned before glancing down at his drink. He offered his cup to the scarred man. 'Here, take a sip,' he said.

The man's eyes flickered towards Lucifer's and back down again. He reached for the cup, took a sip, then handed it back.

'That's interesting,' he said. 'You know who I am, don't you? The human outside the wall must have mentioned me. Why did you do that?'

Lucifer didn't answer. He didn't have a reason. He felt an unfamiliar sensation, reminding him of the being who had emerged in the Darklands.

Forgiveness...

The Hateful Killer paused, as though considering. 'You've felt pain because of our race too, haven't you?' he asked. Lucifer figured the question to be rhetorical. 'Yet you showed me kindness. Why? What drives you?'

'Guilt,' Lucifer admitted. 'Because I made a promise.'

'A promise? To do what?' the Hateful Killer asked.

'To find forgiveness.'

The Hateful Killer sneered, making Lucifer think he was about to attack, although he didn't. 'Forgiveness. As if such a thing exists,' he said, shaking his head in apparent disbelief. 'We do not deserve forgiveness for what we've done, for what we are. Our existence is a curse to ourselves and those who surround us. Do you truly believe you can attain such a thing?'

'I... don't know,' Lucifer admitted.

The Hateful Killer smiled. 'Don't worry, I smile to hide my hate, too. You understand what that means, don't you? We all secretly despise them, the masks we create, yet we use them anyway. It's all we've ever known. The mask protects us, shields us from our broken minds. Yet, every smile makes the cracks widen, as your true self despises every step you take, every word you speak. Inside, we're suffocating, longing to be free.'

The Hateful Killer gestured towards the corpse in the fountain. 'I break through the masks. I expose the hatred in our hearts. Silver Wing thinks it has made this city better for us, but all they've done is create a new mask for both ourselves and humanity to use. We're clinging onto it out of desperation, terrified of what lies within.'

The Hateful Killer paused then, his smile growing. 'I am what lies within. I no longer wear the mask, and I sense you no longer do either. What is your name?'

'Lucifer,' Lucifer answered.

'Lucifer,' he said, as though tasting the name on his lips. 'Tell me, how do you think we'll ever find forgiveness?'

'I…' Lucifer began, before the surrounding humans turned to the south, pointing into the sky.

'It's Silver Wing!' one of them called, as relief seemed to wash across the humans.

Lucifer watched the Hateful Killer glance in the same direction, before returning his gaze to Lucifer. He then extended his hand towards the floating monstrosity in the fountain basin, a violet and crimson glow enveloping it. The corpse disintegrated into dust. Inside, Korai stirred, as though stunned by this demonstration of power.

He possesses Vorus, the Fallen said. *The Destroyer.*

'What did you just do?' Lucifer asked.

'What I'm going to do to the mask this society and Silver Wing created,' the Hateful Killer said, dropping his hand. 'I still want to hear your answer. We've run out of time, but we will meet again.'

The Hateful Killer disappeared into the crowd. As Lucifer watched him, someone bumped into him; a Hateful woman, wearing a similar cloak to the Hateful Killer. At first glance she looked like Vennifer, but it soon became obvious that she was not. She looked like the Hateful Killer, but with fewer scars on her face. Her expression was pleading.

'Please, help him. I don't know what to do,' she said.

'What?' Lucifer asked, trying to understand. 'Do you know him?'

The Hateful woman appeared unsure of what to say, looking at the ground and pressing her hands together. 'He needs someone who understands him,' she said, biting her bottom lip. 'You're the first he's ever let go. Please, just help him. I don't know what else to do. He'll never listen to anyone from Silver Wing, or me.'

Anger flashed across her face, then disappeared. She turned to walk away, but Lucifer grabbed her arm.

'Who are you?' he asked. 'What is he?'

'Someone who's misunderstood,' she said. 'I just want to help Gabriel.'

The Hateful woman turned to dissolve into the crowd.

'Gabriel. The Hateful Killer,' Lucifer muttered, then heard footsteps behind him. Lucifer turned to see a small squad of Hateful, three men and two women. Their leader appeared to be in his late thirties. Their attire was typically Hateful: sturdy black boots, leather pants and jackets, and white undershirts. They sported silver wing patches on their jackets, making their identity obvious.

The leader addressed him. 'You must be the one Markus mentioned,' he said, extending his hand to Lucifer, who took it. The older Hateful man flashed a confident smile, eyeing Lucifer up and down.

'Looks like we got another coffee drinker, Setsu,' he said,

glancing at a Hateful to his left, a man Lucifer guessed was around the same age as himself.

He flashed a grin at Lucifer. 'Nice to see he has good taste. Hopefully, his taste in women is just as good,' he remarked, clapping Lucifer on his right shoulder.

'I'm glad we met you before the Hateful Killer did,' the older man said. 'My name is Lionas and I'm the leader of Silver Wing.'

7

New Responsibilities

The Hateful entered the Hearing Room, looking tired and frustrated. At least that's how she interpreted their looks. Diana didn't know what time it was, and she hadn't considered it when she made her impulsive call. However, this couldn't wait. The Hateful needed to hear this, even if they hated change.

Then again, you've all coped so well despite everything that's happened, Diana thought. The last time they'd been here they'd made the most controversial decision in their history: electing a human as their leader. The effects were still being felt. Diana spotted some of the More Cursed being aided into the room by their Less Cursed counterparts - Reni's influence, she was sure. Indeed, she could see Reni being guided along by one student.

You've done so well since that first day we met. I'm so proud of you, Reni.

Diana moved towards him then, stepping over the small barrier that separated the audience seats from the last third of open floor. She made her way along the walkway, gliding past some of the Hateful who greeted her with nods and warm smiles. As she reached Reni, she held out her hands to take his, thanking the students, who glowed as they looked at her. Diana then led Reni along towards the open floor.

Pauli informs me you've had a surge of inspiration, Diana, Reni said, using his Illusionary Blessing.

Diana helped him over the barrier as she smiled. 'I have,' she confirmed. 'But I'll talk about it once everyone is here. I think it'll help a lot.'

I look forward to hearing it, Reni said. *You will always have my support.*

'Thank you, Reni,' Diana said, squeezing his hand back.

The last Hateful were entering the courtroom, before Pauli shut the doors behind them. A nod from him told her that everybody was here.

Diana walked with Reni alongside her, choosing to keep silent until everyone around her settled. When she was satisfied, she felt Reni squeeze her hand again, gaining reassurance from it. Diana took in a breath.

'Thank you all for coming,' she began. 'I truly appreciate it. There's something I wish to discuss with you all. Since taking on the role as your leader, I've realised the enormity of the task ahead of us. Now, I understand why Hela struggled so much with the responsibility.'

'Why are you telling us this?' one of the Hateful asked, not masking their agitation. 'We chose you because we were sure you were the right person to lead us. Are you saying you cannot handle your responsibilities?'

Murmurs of agreement arose from the audience.

'Yes, that's exactly what I'm saying,' she admitted, knowing it would silence the Hateful. 'I cannot handle it all, and

51

neither could Hela. I realise now that's why she rarely saw anyone when she was the leader, which led to the state we find ourselves in. Like me, she didn't have time to progress things for your kind. So, how can we work on progress, especially when we're given responsibility for everything?'

Diana allowed that question to settle in their minds before continuing. 'Right now, I have a responsibility for all of you, the towers, the Education Section, supplies. I doubt that's even a third of the things I have to manage now. Again, how can I work on changing things for your kind when I've got all of this to do? The answer is obvious. I can't, and neither could Hela. I know she wasn't popular among you, and that many of you feel she abandoned you in favour of the children. However, that wasn't true. I know that now. While Hela was not perfect, she didn't know how to free herself. Hela didn't communicate with you all like I am. Instead, she placed her hope in the children, praying that they'd figure out a solution. I won't do the same.'

Diana paused then, letting her words sink in.

'I cannot handle everything expected of me, and all of you have long been neglected. Because of this, we are going to form a Hateful Council. A small group of you will be given responsibilities and domains. This group will also aid me in running the Institute. We will create a system that will provide opportunities, with the goal of freeing me so that I can focus on the mission you all chose me for.'

Excited murmurs arose from the Hateful audience. Satisfied, Diana turned to Reni. He was smiling, despite half hiding his face. When she looked at Pauli, Diana could see his pride; he was practically beaming.

'So, who volunteers to join my Council?' Diana asked. The

room fell into silence once more. Reni squeezed her hand again, while his Illusionary Blessing filled her mind.

I volunteer for a position, he said, as Diana realised he was projecting his Blessing to everyone in the room. *I wish to oversee the needs and care of my fellow More Cursed brethren. I will become an intermediary, someone they can approach to discuss their needs, with the long-term goal of teaching them to communicate, much like myself. This is the burden I wish to remove from Diana. Who else wishes to contribute?*

Pauli stepped forward next.

'I want to take a more active role in the Education Section,' he said. 'I'd be happy to oversee anyone who wishes to help me. I also volunteer myself in tending to those who protect our wall, ensuring that we give them everything to perform their task. I will remove these burdens from Diana, so she can focus on the future of our race.'

'Thank you, Pauli,' Diana said, nodding in appreciation before turning her gaze towards the audience. Who else, apart from her two friends, would volunteer? The doors of the Hearing Room opened and a single Hateful man emerged from them, to the surprise of everyone else. Yet, rather than appear embarrassed by this, the Hateful man smiled.

'Please, forgive my interruption,' he said, bowing. He was a young man, probably in his early twenties. What marked him as very different from the others, apart from his long hair, which reached his waist, was his elegant white robe. It reminded Diana of the human Council, while the man's clean-shaven, boyish face almost gave him the air of an apprentice. Diana sensed that something was not quite right with him.

'We should appreciate the wonderful opportunity Diana is providing us, my dear Hateful,' he began, spreading his hands wide as though to embrace the entire room. 'We can end the madness washing over us as we sit alone in our rooms. We can live with purpose, free from ourselves. We should all jump at this chance.'

The young Hateful man reached the small barrier, smiling at Diana. She frowned, feeling that this was part of some strategy. Unease washed over her, and Reni bristled alongside her.

I sense it too, Diana, he remarked. *There's something off about him.*

'I volunteer for the responsibility of aiding Diana's dream,' the Hateful man said. 'To forge connections between humanity and Hateful. This is where my passion lies, and I believe I could contribute to this Hateful Council. Who else will join us? Who wishes to change the future for our race?'

The young Hateful man's words had the intended effect: all around him, Hateful rose from the audience, ready to put themselves forward. This made the Hateful man smile, confirming what Diana had suspected.

This wasn't an accident.

In one sweep, you've influenced so many of your kind to act, taking the platform I provided. You've helped give me the result I wanted, but what do you expect in return? Was this to prove your prowess, or was it something else? Either way, you're not like the others. Normally, the Hateful struggle with aspects such as influence and human interaction.

'He's different,' Diana whispered, so only Reni could hear her.

What do you mean? he asked.

'What do you get if you take your kind's capacity for devotion and routine, and then focus it to learn about human nature?' Diana responded.

Without waiting for an answer from Reni, she stepped away, moving to meet the young Hateful man who extended his hand towards her.

'What is your name?' Diana asked, taking his hand.

The young Hateful man conveyed complete control. Diana felt concern and admiration in equal measure.

'Valki,' he answered, releasing her grip. 'And I believe I have much to offer you, Diana Skagen.'

8

Johann Stratos

The touch of something damp and cool across his forehead caused the Devil of Anubi to stir, as he groaned in exhaustion and weakness. He'd been out for a while, but he was surprised he wasn't covered in snow or soaked. Instead, he felt warmth from what sounded like a crackling fire to his right. The Devil tried to open his eyes, frowning.

I'm lying on a floor, he realised, his head propped up by something.

'He's awake!' a familiar voice called out, sounding pleased. It belonged to a young boy.

The Devil attempted to open his eyes again, finding only blurriness.

'Hey, can you hear me?' the voice asked, sounding closer.

The Devil blinked before his vision returned to reveal the small black boy he had helped in the streets of Rai, wearing a thick green woollen jumper. Recollection struck him then.

He'll know what I am. They all will, the Devil realised, his eyes widening. He tried to push himself into a sitting position, blocked by a gentle but firm hand to his chest.

'Destin, give him space. He needs to rest,' an unfamiliar voice said. It was an older white woman, who had blocked him from rising. She held a flannel in her other hand. She had tied-up brown hair, with strands that fell across her scalp, and her hazel eyes showed she was fighting tiredness. She wore a thick black coat.

When the Devil glanced at the flannel, she seemed to take this as a hint, raising it to his forehead again. The Devil was stunned.

A human. Helping me...

Barbatos' potion had worn off, so he looked Hateful again. Anxiety spiked through him as he looked around. He was lying in a damaged church, full of human refugees.

Do none of you realise who I am? A Devil lies among you.

'Thanks for saving me back there,' the boy said. 'After you passed out, I got my dad and some others to help bring you here. You're safe now. Johann's a good guy.'

'Johann?' the Devil asked, not recognising the name. He needed to get out as soon as possible, but he felt like he could barely move. He had gone days without eating.

'Destin,' another unfamiliar voice said, this one male and older. A large black man had joined them. He was powerfully built, bald, with a short beard that covered his chin. He seemed agitated, which made the Devil's chest swell in anticipation.

Here it comes...

'I told you not to go outside without me,' the black man said, before gesturing at the Devil. 'He could've died had we not got to him in time.'

What? The Devil almost sputtered, not expecting those

words.

The boy looked away, ashamed. The Devil guessed the larger man was his father. He tried to make sense of what had happened. Humans had saved him, and were now tending to him?

'I'm sorry,' the boy said, appearing to mean it, before turning back to the woman. 'Thanks, Marienne.'

'It's no problem, Destin,' Marienne said, smiling before wiping sweat off her forehead.

Nodding, Destin rose to his feet. 'Give me a shout when you can speak,' he said to the Devil, before turning away, leaving the Devil with Marienne and his father. The large black man lowered himself into a squat.

'Hey, thanks for saving my kid,' he said, extending his hand to the Devil. He knew he should take it but found himself unable to. All the Devil could do was stare at it. After a few seconds, the black man pulled his hand away, nodding in understanding.

'I get it. Must be strange being surrounded by us. We would have taken you to the Institute, but... Still, I never imagined I'd be thanking a Hateful for saving my boy. We're living in strange times.'

The man shook his head then, smiling.

Meanwhile, the woman rinsed her flannel in a bucket, wringing it out before placing it back on the Devil's forehead. Cool water ran down his face. Did he have a fever? Perhaps. Weakness engulfed him; he couldn't move. After a couple of seconds of watching the woman, the Devil looked back at the black man, who was scratching his chin thoughtfully.

'We'll help get you back on your feet, then you can decide what you wanna do. We could use your hands if you got nowhere to go. With all the idiots trying to take advantage, it's nuts outside. Plus, there's the Devil to consider. Some say he's still out there.'

No, he's lying right in front of you, having just saved your child, the Devil thought. Inside, he heard a chuckle from Ryun. The Devil ignored it.

'Anyway, you ain't under any pressure. You helped us, so we owe you. The name's Deion. Give me a shout if you need anything. My boy will want to talk to you later.'

Deion rose to his feet, smiling at the Devil as he turned to walk away. He stopped halfway, as though remembering something. 'By the way, what's your name?'

A name came to the Devil's lips, but he didn't dare utter it. That name caused him shame. His greatest creation. His greatest delusion. The Devil contemplated creating another name. Such thoughts brought back Lucifer's last words to him.

I cannot do that again. I cannot run away from what I've done, repeating the same mistakes.

'Megidra,' the Devil answered instead, refusing to go down that path again. 'Megidra Dionysus.'

Deion nodded and walked away.

Marienne wiped his brow again, her strokes gentle and caring. Megidra allowed his head to fall back on whatever was being used as a pillow, surprised to settle in her presence. It reminded Megidra of how much he loved touch.

'You're calming,' Marienne remarked. He savoured every one of her rhythmic touches. She was smiling at him too.

'Silent type, huh?' Marienne said then. 'My husband was the same. Took some prodding before he'd talk. He struggled with his feelings too.'

'Was he human?' Megidra asked. Marienne's smile grew, portraying a warmth that reminded him of Hela when she talked about the human she had fallen in love with, Philippe. Megidra felt more shame rising from within. He had taken away her love, her happiness. And he had taken her away, too.

'He was,' Marienne said, oblivious as she wrung out the flannel again, before wiping Megidra's face. 'Though, I guess he was a little unusual by human standards. Perhaps he had some Hateful traits too.'

'You make it sound as though you've met my kind before,' Megidra said.

Marienne's warm smile showed some cracks. She paused and seemed to recall something. 'My brother was Hateful,' she commented.

Megidra's eyes widened in surprise. Her warmth returned as she wiped around his head and neck, before working towards the top of his chest. Figuring she didn't wish to discuss the matter further, Megidra left it. That was often the case with his kind. After all, his and Hela's parents had been human. Not wishing to remember them, Megidra focused on something else.

'You remind me of my sister,' he said, causing Marienne to stop in her movements. She sat back on her heels.

'Was she Hateful?' she asked.

'She was,' Megidra said.

A young bald and clean-shaven white man wearing priest robes appeared then, his smile also warm and genuine.

'You must be our Hateful friend who saved Destin,' he said.

Megidra recognised his robes and what they represented.

'You're a member of the Council,' Megidra said, amazed.

The priest smiled, placing his hands inside the opposite sleeves. 'Indeed, I was,' he answered, his voice soft. 'But times have changed. I doubt there will ever be a Council in Exia, not unless peace is established. I sense permanence in these winds of change.'

'You sound as though you accept that,' Megidra said, confused yet intrigued by the priest.

'I accept all that the Divinity charts as our course, though I cannot deny that my belief in the eternal creator has been shaken. If you want my honest opinion, I think we've been staggering towards change for a long time.'

'What do you mean?' Megidra asked, frowning.

The priest smiled. 'Change is already here, my Hateful friend. Despite everything the Divinity sought, even he cannot stop this evolution. These words may sound sacrilegious, but I think that much of Ethero believed our way of living was permanent. It did not surprise me when your kind were the ones to enact change upon us, beginning with the Hateful man I crossed paths with. He influenced my current thinking, as well as bringing me much learning. I don't doubt you will too.'

'When did you meet one of us?' Megidra asked, his interest provoked.

'Not too long ago,' the priest answered. 'Though his intentions had not been as noble as yours. After we conversed, he spared my life before returning to seek aid from me. He then confronted the Devil of Anubi, and I haven't seen him since.'

Coldness washed over Megidra then. He wondered if the priest sensed who he was. It didn't seem so; the priest gave no sign of recognising him. Instead, he maintained his warm smile.

'His name was Lucifer Armedeus. You've heard of him?' the priest asked.

Megidra nodded. 'Yes,' he said, finding it strange to consider Lucifer's full name now. That name had set him on the course that led him to his current position. Before that name, Megidra had been pursuing his dream, his delusion. Lucifer had threatened to ruin all he had sought to establish. Of course, he had never realised the poisoned dream for what it was, a justification for his hatred towards his own kind. Now, he was just a broken traitor. Not wishing to contemplate such things yet, Megidra returned his gaze to the priest.

'He made his impact,' Megidra commented, not sure if he was referring to Lucifer or himself.

The priest nodded in agreement. 'Yes. That we can agree on. Regardless, thank you for saving young Destin. My name is Johann Stratos. As you can probably tell, I'm the priest of this church. I use it as a shelter for people who don't want to be involved in violence, but we are having problems with supplies. Deion is collaborating with other groups to organise a supply run. Until then, I'd recommend staying here and recovering, at least until you're at full strength.'

Johann paused then, appearing thoughtful. 'I should also mention you're welcome to stay here. Although I'll admit that many of my kind were unsure about harbouring you, the words of myself, Deion, Marienne, and especially Destin, seem to have put them at ease.'

Megidra nodded at that, allowing gratitude to emerge on his face. 'Thank you. I appreciate what you've done, even if I don't deserve your kindness,' he said.

'We've only done what we believe to be right, Megidra,' Johann said. 'That's all we ever do. Even behind the most evil of hearts is a soul that believes it's doing the right thing.'

He knows, Megidra realised. He watched as Johann turned and walked away, leaving Marienne, who seemed oblivious.

'What about you?' Megidra asked.

'What do you mean?' she replied.

'Why don't you fear me?'

'I had a Hateful brother,' Marienne answered. 'Besides, you saved a child when you didn't have to. That tells me you're a good man.'

Oh, Marienne, if only you knew how many I've killed, alongside all those who have perished because of my actions. I am not a good man. I'm a monster. A devil.

'Get some sleep,' Marienne said. 'You need to rest. I'll bring you food later.'

'Why? Do you not have anyone else to tend to?' Megidra asked. 'Surely, there are others who need you more than me? You said you have a husband.'

'Had,' Marienne corrected, as Megidra realised how careless he had been in uttering that sentence. Still, his curiosity had been aroused.

'What happened to him?' he asked.

Marienne's smile became sad; bitter, even.

'I'll tell you if you tell me what happened to your sister,' she said.

Despite the pain he knew would come from returning to such a truth, Megidra forced himself to nod in understanding. 'She was killed,' he said, his voice barely audible. 'By the Devil of Anubi.'

Marienne nodded at that. Megidra knew then what words

were about to leave her lips. Ryun stirred in delight, knowing the truth that was about to emerge.

'So was my husband,' Marienne said. 'By the Devil of Anubi.'

9

Silver Wing

Lucifer had only been with Silver Wing for ten minutes, yet he knew he was among a very different type of Hateful. Their moves were fluid. They seemed to possess greater control of their Blessings than he did, floating between the rooftops as they headed west of the city.

I look sluggish by comparison, Lucifer noted, impressed. Lionas was at the head. His jacket fluttered as he moved, darting from rooftop to rooftop as the snow fell.

The others followed in a precise formation behind him, with Lucifer feeling as though he could hardly keep up. He did notice one of the female members of Silver Wing staying close by. From the way she moved Lucifer could tell she was adept with the Physical Blessing. She had a lean and powerful frame, possessing a different elegance than Vennifer's.

But why am I even comparing them? Lucifer wondered, shaking his head.

It almost seemed random when Silver Wing finally deviated from their current path, as every member except for the woman darted towards the network of narrow alleyways, disappearing from sight. Before he could question where they were going, a firm hand gripped his jacket collar and he was pulled down hard. He thudded onto the metal floor of Kyrios a few seconds later. Lucifer gasped as he relinquished his Blessing. He looked up to find the Hateful woman studying him dispassionately.

'Why didn't you just say something?!' he snapped, rushing to his feet while pulling her hand off him. 'I don't like being touched! Only—'

Lucifer stopped himself, seeing surprise on the Hateful woman's face. Despite being Hateful and appearing to be around his age, she looked different. Her face was narrow and her eyes looked as though she had descended from a different segment of humanity. Still, it was clear she hadn't expected his reaction, which added to Lucifer's embarrassment as he realised what he had been about to say.

That only Vennifer could touch him.

Damn it, Lucifer thought, ruing his lapse of self-control. He felt Korai stir in response, as though he were about to speak. Lucifer shook his head, not wishing to dwell further upon that.

'Sorry,' he said. 'I just…'

He wasn't sure what to say. It wasn't like anyone from Silver Wing or among the surrounding humans could understand what had taken place back in Exia. The wound was still deep. The Hateful woman nodded in understanding, before gesturing towards a narrow alleyway.

'Our hideout is down there,' she said, matter-of-factly.

Not wishing for their interaction to become awkward, Lucifer nodded in silence before moving to follow her. They climbed down a small metal staircase. The bright white streetlights diminished in the distance.

'We split up so that others cannot find us,' the Hateful woman explained, without being asked.

Lucifer found that explanation reasonable. Jumping down at different points kept their hideout concealed.

While their numbers protect them.

They moved along the network of cramped passageways and alleyways for what Lucifer guessed was another twenty minutes, heading north-west of Kyrios.

Eventually, they stopped alongside a thick metal door with a single slit across the eye line. The Hateful woman checked both sides of the alleyway, making sure no one else was with them. Satisfied, she knocked on the door then took a step back. Lucifer studied the Hateful woman's nimble yet powerful frame. She reminded him a little of Vennifer, especially her narrow hips and upper torso. When he looked at her face again, he found her staring at him, her look bordering on agitation.

Thankfully, the slit on the door opened.

'Password?' a male voice demanded. Lucifer recognised it from earlier. It possessed a certain mischief, which made the Hateful woman roll her eyes.

'Just let us in, Setsu,' she said, impatient.

The man chuckled behind the door. 'Hmm. That doesn't sound like the password,' he said. 'Try again.'

'I mean it: open the door,' the Hateful woman said, leaning forward. 'I'm not in the mood for this.'

'Ah, wrong again, Mika. That ain't the password either.'

A groan escaped Mika's lips then. 'Setsu, don't you have any human girls to annoy?' she said.

Lucifer frowned. 'Human girls?' he asked, drawing a glance

from Mika.

'Yeah, Setsu here has a rather particular taste,' she said, but then the bolts were drawn and the door opened. Setsu appeared. His hair was long but brushed to one side, and his smile was confident. He wore his Hateful jacket with no shirt underneath, exposing his abs in a way that suggested he wanted people to stare at them.

'That I certainly do,' Setsu remarked, before grinning with a charm Lucifer found infectious. 'I just thought it was important that we show the new boy the ropes. Besides, it's not a bad thing if we get to know each other better, right?'

'Oh, please,' Mika said, stepping past Setsu and knocking him a little on purpose. 'All you need to know is that I got better abs than you.'

'She's got me there!' Setsu said, appearing to take no offence over the shove, continuing to smile as Mika walked past him. The confident Hateful man turned towards Lucifer. 'Don't worry, she's all yours. I'm only interested in human chicks.'

'What?' Lucifer said, stunned. However, before he could offer any further protest, Setsu clapped him on the back. He closed the door behind them, and Lucifer felt Setsu's arm wrapping around his shoulder, much like how Gabriel had done. Unlike him, Setsu didn't convey malice and hate. He acted more like a best friend.

'Once you're done with Lionas, we'll hit the streets! I know all the best spots for human girls. Smile a little more and tie that hair of yours into a messy bun and they'll be fawning over you!'

Lucifer frowned, and after a couple of seconds Setsu's confident demeanour changed, becoming more relaxed.

'Not used to this, huh?' he said, his question seeming

rhetorical. Setsu patted Lucifer's shoulders a few times before unlatching himself, moving to catch up with Mika. 'Give yourself some time. Things are different here. Better.'

'They certainly are,' Lionas agreed, emerging from within the corridor. He gave Lucifer a warm smile, before turning to Mika and Setsu. 'Let's go. I imagine our friend here has much to discuss,' Lionas said, moving ahead of the other two members of Silver Wing.

Setsu glanced back. 'What's your name, by the way?'

'Lucifer,' Lucifer said.

Mika snapped her gaze back at him. 'From Exia?' she asked.

Concern arose in Lucifer. He didn't like the fact that someone here understood who he was. 'Yes,' he confirmed, not hiding his displeasure. 'How do you know that?'

Mika looked stunned then. She changed radically from before. Now, there was warmth to her, a sense of hope as she held her hands together, stepping into Lucifer's personal space.

'You're the one Vennifer mentioned,' she said, a beautiful smile on her face. 'How is she? She was called back a month or so ago.'

Realisation dawned upon Lucifer, and he stopped in the middle of the corridor.

This is where you were. This was where Hela sent you. You ended up with these guys.

Lionas looked back towards them. 'Mika, give him some space. We'll talk about this when we reach the common room.'

They got to the common room a few minutes later. Like all buildings within the major cities, the interior of Silver Wing's hideout was made of metal. It was large and rectangular, with walls lined with bookshelves and multiple seating areas throughout. Between them were large spheres that were ruby in colour, pulsing with a kind of energy. Lucifer wasn't sure what they were.

The members of Silver Wing made their way towards a long table surrounded by chairs.

'If you're wondering, the orbs are Kyrn's latest project,' Lionas said, pulling out a chair and sitting down with the others. 'Though he would describe them as failures, I think they're very useful, especially during cold times. I've even asked him to make more for the other Hateful and humans of Kyrios. They store heat, which I think will prove invaluable in the coming weeks and months.'

Lucifer nodded at that, figuring there was nothing else to say on the matter. He sat down at the table too. He made sure not to look at Mika then, who he had no doubt was still awaiting to hear what had happened to Vennifer. Instead, he focused on Lionas.

'So, what brings you to Kyrios?' Lionas asked, smiling warmly.

'It's complicated,' Lucifer admitted. Figuring he should probably avoid the subjects of Korai and the other being within, he decided to fold his arms and sit back on his seat.

'I'm looking for something,' he began. 'Though, I'm not sure how or where to find it. I'm originally from here, but I ran away to Exia years ago, before I guess you guys all showed up.'

'So things are very different for you here,' Lionas said, appearing thoughtful. 'That makes your reaction to us and this place make a lot more sense. Was this thing you're looking for the reason you returned?'

'Yes,' Lucifer said. 'I made some mistakes in Exia, so I'm back here. I made a promise to someone that I'd find what I'm looking for.'

'Was that Vennifer?' Mika asked.

He regarded her then, ignoring the stirring that came from Korai.

'Yes,' he decided to answer, but adding nothing else. A tension grew between the two of them then, before Lionas decided to speak.

'Well, you clearly have a lot on your mind,' he said. 'I'll not pry. However, you should know that Vennifer did spend some time with us. She was very popular and well-liked, and she became a very good friend to Mika here. I too would like know what's happened to her. She was called back with haste. She declined our offer of assistance, and refused to disclose her reason for returning to Exia. In truth, I've been wishing to make the journey myself, but we have problems here that must be addressed before we do so.'

He's referring to Gabriel, Lucifer knew at once. It was also obvious that Vennifer had not wanted to mention that he was the reason she had been called back. Lucifer wondered what might have been had he not pursued his poisonous dream.

Would we have come here together? Would she have introduced us? he wondered, as ruefulness filled his heart. Of course, he never would have made the journey here, knowing what pain awaited him. No, her death and his final promise were the reasons he was here. There was no use contemplating what might have been. Regret was the torture of memory.

Lucifer realised that silence had fallen, and he was unsure of what to say or do.

Setsu glanced at Mika and Lionas before rising to his feet.

'Let's head out for a bit,' he suggested. 'I know you just got here, but I'm getting the vibe you might need another coffee.'

He nodded towards Lionas. 'That alright with you?' he asked.

'Yes, I think that would be a good idea, Setsu,' he said, as though understanding what Setsu was thinking. 'Enjoy your coffee.'

'Certainly will do,' Setsu said. 'Let's go, Prince,' he said, making Lucifer frown.

'Prince?' he asked, confused.

'Yeah, that's your nickname now,' Setsu said.

Lucifer stood up, moving to follow Setsu. 'I don't get it. Why Prince?' he asked.

'Because you always look gloomy, edgy. So you shall now be known as our Prince of Darkness.'

10

Motives

I t appeared to Greene that the Darklands were much more than the void of nothingness humanity believed they were. The Darklands were the complete opposite: a land of varying terrains and environments, which only added to the sense of mystery Greene felt about Ethero. What didn't help was that the man leading them through this world understood things that he only shared at his own convenience. He remained a mystery in himself.

I still don't know what his goal is.

Greene's face twisted in frustration. He looked up at the surrounding forest, noting how it had changed from lifeless trunks to lush growth. The atmosphere had altered too, becoming warm and humid. Greene could sense this in his new body. Every day unveiled fresh changes. Lately, those changes appeared to be occurring within him.

It's like I'm turning human. How do they even function like this? So much chaos. So much confusion and constant anxieties. I can hardly concentrate. Am I even a Titanius anymore? If not, what am I?

Greene forced himself to focus at that moment, wary of the hole he was about to fall into. At least, despite everything he was feeling, he was sure he could understand humans better now. If their minds were always this chaotic, did it not make sense how they often acted in ways that didn't serve their best interests? Why they sought control and momentary pleasures?

And why they chase dreams, even at the expense of others, he thought, recalling Newman. *I have to be careful. If I don't watch myself, I could end up on the same path. I may dislike humans for what they've done to my race, but at least with these insights, I can understand why. It is easier to control something external to yourself than wrestle with the pain within.*

'You seem thoughtful,' Shallai remarked. She was walking alongside him, seeming curious.

Greene tried to smile, realising how fake it would seem.

Then there's you. You're the one who arouses the strangest feelings within me. I don't understand it, but every time I look at you, I sense longing, a desire to find comfort from you. What does it mean?

'You know, you're giving me a hilarious look,' Shallai said, causing Greene to snap his gaze away from her, aware that both Barbatos and Doomis would hear this conversation. The former was wandering ahead of them, while the latter kept his place behind the group. The memory of the scarred Ethero Fiend's face caused Greene to shudder.

'Sorry, Shallai,' he said. 'I have a lot on my mind. I'm not sure what to make of everything that's happened.'

'That makes sense,' Shallai said. 'I'd struggle if I'd grown a few inches too.'

'It isn't just that,' Greene began, turning to Shallai. The

Cybernetic appeared to be repressing a chuckle, which caused Greene to smile.

'Thank you, Shallai,' he said, meaning it.

'So, what's really going on?' she asked.

Greene wasn't sure how to answer. How could one confine so many confusing thoughts into one sentence? He looked in Barbatos's direction.

'Shallai, what is it like to be half machine and half human?' he asked.

'That's a weird question,' she remarked, before shrugging. 'Though, I think I understand why you're asking. Almost all Cybernetics are blind to their pasts. We wake up like this, often fully developed. There are rarely any kids among us.'

'You just wake up as you are?' Greene asked.

Shallai nodded. 'Pretty much. There's always a feeling inside the first time you wake, like a dream you've had but cannot remember, no matter how hard you try. I've always felt like me. I don't think I've gone through anything like you have. By the way you asked, I'm guessing you feel more human?'

'In a roundabout way, yes,' Greene admitted. 'But it makes little sense to me. I'm a Titanius, descendant of Titans. Apart from how we appear, to a certain extent we share no commonalities with humans, so I'm struggling to comprehend why I'm gaining emotions and sensations. It's like a byproduct of the potion that shouldn't have happened.'

'You realise you're talking about a potion he created, right?' Shallai said, nodding towards Barbatos.

Greene had nothing to say to that. Rather than pursue the matter, he switched focus. 'What do you believe his goal is? What does he stand to gain by me unleashing my ancestors?'

he asked.

Shallai appeared reluctant to answer that question.

'You know something,' he said, intentionally not phrasing it as a question.

'There are rumours,' she admitted. 'But no one knows anything about him. I've seen no one like him. Doesn't it strike you as odd that we can all name times we've seen many humans – Hateful, Titaniuses, Cybernetics, Ethero Fiends and Animus – but we've all only known one Barbatos?'

'Perhaps he's part of a rare race?' Greene ventured.

Shallai shook her head. 'No, I think he's the only one of his kind. He knows about our pasts too, and the oaths we all swore back at the beginning. How does he know those things?'

'I'm not sure,' Greene admitted. Barbatos was surrounded by so much mystery, and possessed motives he kept close to his chest. He described them as heralds of war, representatives of the Eternal Mother, another conundrum to Greene. Until recently, all he had ever known of was the Divinity. He understood there was so much more to uncover now. He was determined to discover the truth.

'Maybe we should ask him?' Greene suggested.

Shallai looked at him, her expression sceptical. 'Do you really think he'll tell us?' she asked.

Then a presence drew near from behind.

'We are drawing close,' Doomis said.

They walked further into the forest, as the overgrowth became thicker and the surrounding air grew dense with moisture. There was no snow here. Greene noticed that Doomis seemed tenser now, and Barbatos continued to lead from the front.

'Are you alright, Doomis?' Greene asked, knowing how stupid such a question would sound. Regardless, he mustered up the courage to at least turn back and check on the Fiend, noting how Doomis walked with an air of anticipation.

Then again, we are heading into the capital of Ethero Fiends. By rights, I should be more tense myself. The prospect of being surrounded by them does not fill me with great enthusiasm.

'Barbatos!' Shallai called out. 'How far are we?'

'Close enough,' Barbatos replied, a smirk rising on his face. He half-turned to them, spinning his sceptre between his fingers before placing it and both his hands behind his back, leaning forward.

'Naturally, our resident Ethero Fiend here knows that his kind sense our impending arrival. I suspect our friend has other reasons for his tension too. This is the first time he has returned here.'

Indeed, the Ethero Fiend seemed to ready himself for battle. His breath left the black void that concealed his face in longer blasts of steam, while he held out his arms in preparation.

'You seem raring to go,' Barbatos commented, words Greene would've thought unwise for someone ready to fight. Yet, Barbatos always exuded self-control and confidence, as if he knew he would never come to harm. The sorcerer seemed to be revelling in what was about to transpire.

'A legend returns – but not the legend they were wishing for,' Barbatos said, chuckling. 'I cannot wait to see you in action, Doomis. I'm glad you're on our side. Perhaps we won't even need others to join us, not when we have you amongst our ranks.'

'Gast kuoll riasha muder,' Doomis growled, reverting to his

native tongue.

Shallai seemed sad, biting her bottom lip. Greene glanced between them, a question forming.

'Shallai, what do you know of Doomis's past?' he asked.

'Nothing, but Barbatos prodding him is cruel. He's on edge.'

'He is unlike other Ethero Fiends, or at least he differs from the few I've seen,' Greene said, recalling his encounters with Doomis's race. Their fangs, unusual powers, and unmatched hatred of everything still sent a chill through him.

'That's because he isn't like the others,' Shallai retorted. 'Greene, Ethero Fiends are unique in that they can choose how they develop as they age. Many other factors can affect the outcome. Whatever happened to make Doomis like this, it has something to do with Elcaris. I just don't like it.'

'Then why did you both come?' Greene asked. The question had been lurking in his mind ever since they had left Exia.

Shallai sighed. 'Because we fear the war Barbatos is trying to start,' she said. 'For reasons we don't know, he wants to drag us back into a war that ended so long ago. I want to understand why, while trying to stop my race from getting involved. Part of me knows something horrible is about to happen. He said it himself. The Fiends know we're coming. If that's the case, what about my kind? What about the Animus? Do they know we're coming too? If so, what are they doing now? What seeds of chaos don't we know about?'

She was asking fair questions. Unfortunately, Greene had no idea of how to answer them. There was still so much they didn't understand, about Barbatos and his plans.

'I guess we'll find out more once we reach Elcaris,' Greene commented, shaking his head as he and Shallai moved to catch up with Doomis and Barbatos. Shallai said nothing in response, which didn't surprise Greene. The situation was developing rapidly, and that didn't even include what was taking place inside of him.

We need to keep our wits about us, Greene thought. *I think we're missing something. Barbatos is using us, but he isn't hiding that. He's taking advantage of our pasts, and what we desire for our races. Doomis and I clearly exemplify that. So, what's your end goal, Barbatos? Why do you want this war? What are you?*

No answers came to Greene, only a rising frustration. A part of his old DFA instinct kicked in, something Greene was relieved to feel. He wasn't completely lost yet. He would solve this mystery.

He would uncover the truth, about himself and about Ethero.

11

Changes

The past few days had worked out better than Diana expected. The stacks of paperwork she usually faced were no longer on her desk. They were being handled by her new assistant, Volsi who sat at a small desk in her office.

Now we're having more of you engaging, mixing with your Less Cursed brethren, Diana thought, smiling. Volsi had been proof of this. Diana had received many inquiries after the hearing and that had led to Volsi's current position, alongside another Hateful Diana had not met, Kalas.

He was one of the Less Cursed, and he had begun engaging with Volsi, displaying patience and a desire to help him communicate his desires. Kalas then guided Volsi to Reni, who pointed them toward Diana, before Kalas asked Diana if Volsi could show what he wanted to do. They then watched as Volsi started organising the piles of paper on Diana's desk. His desire was obvious then: he enjoyed sorting things; organising and putting things in order.

His role had been born alongside one for Kalas, who

jumped at the chance to become an intermediary between the Less Cursed and the More Cursed, working under Reni. They had also found new teachers to help Pauli, while many more willing guards came forward. Other roles had emerged as well. Diana's Council was now established, and their first meeting was today.

Now, I need to fulfil my end of the bargain, Diana thought, gathering another pile of papers for Volsi to organise. As she rose and stepped around her desk to approach him, the Hateful man turned towards her, smiling in a way that warmed her heart.

'You're doing a great job, Volsi,' Diana said, placing a gentle hand on his back while putting the pile of papers alongside him. 'Just don't forget to take a break when you need it. I'm not paying you for any of this.'

Diana chuckled then and turned to walk away.

'Th… Th th th,' a voice said, causing Diana to stop and look back at Volsi. He looked determined, and Diana nodded for him to continue. Volsi faced her once more, stuttering as he tried to get the words out. His body shook as he tapped his own head.

'Th… Th…' he tried again, his shaking intensifying from the sheer effort. Inside, Diana felt a familiar fire emerge, recalling when she first met Reni. She went to Volsi, lowering herself into a squat alongside him so that she was level, her face determined.

'Go on, you can do it,' Diana said.

Her words seemed to embolden Volsi as his body shook with even more intensity, his lips quivering as he sputtered. 'Th… Tha…' he managed, as tears swelled in his eyes. After a couple of seconds, the tension dissipated before he closed his eyes and balled into himself, appearing defeated. Tears ran down his cheeks, expressing his frustration. Diana shed a tear too, but from pride. Diana pulled Volsi into her embrace and they rocked back and forth in a slow rhythm.

'It's alright; you'll get there,' Diana said, releasing Volsi. 'I'm so proud of you. I'm so proud of all of you. The fact you're here and willing to try is amazing. Each day, we'll get closer to our goals. One day, I know you'll speak to me, but even if you can't, I don't want you to worry about it. I just want you to be happy.'

Volsi smiled, which Diana returned. He then nodded and returned to his task, falling into the pattern of deep concentration that Diana knew many Hateful fell into. It often accompanied an activity they loved doing.

I could do with some of that myself, Diana noted, returning to her desk. She had a promise to keep. She reached into her drawer and took out a notepad and pen, opening up the dreaded first page. The start was always the hardest part. Minutes passed, and Diana knew the trap she was heading towards.

The procrastination trap.

I feel like I understand you even more now, Hela. It's so easy to fill our lives with menial tasks and delude ourselves into thinking they're important, using them to distract us from what we should be doing. So, how do I unite our races, especially under these circumstances?

As she pondered that question, Diana found words emerging on the once blank page. She had taken vital steps to address the first point of concern, dealing with the air of melancholy that pervaded the Institute. The Hateful wanted purpose. Giving them purpose solved many issues in that respect.

But what about my race? It's easy to establish order in a place that's surrounded by a giant wall. Everything outside that wall has fallen to chaos.

That was where things became tricky for her kind. War raged on the streets. The DFA was pinned into their headquarters, while the knowledge that Megidra had worked for them had destroyed public faith. No one obeyed them now. The streets had become a free-for-all for chaos and crime.

Leadership needs to be established in Exia again. Many are taking advantage of the situation. Perhaps the next logical step is to uncover all the major players. Despite my kind's tendency for pettiness, anger can only be sustained for a limited time.

Diana shook her head. Megidra's actions wouldn't be forgiven easily. He had caused many human deaths, along with the current state of Exia. Humanity would pin everything on him and the Hateful.

The key is to show that Megidra's actions were his own. However, my kind won't accept that unless it comes from other humans, not me. They'll not trust a human who leads the Hateful. It needs to come from a perceived unbiased source, but finding that source will be hard.

'And it's still too dependent on others, on outside influences,' Diana muttered, drawing a glance from Volsi.

'It's going to be tricky, Volsi,' she said, drawing a nod of understanding from the Hateful man, before he turned his attention back towards his papers.

Diana was pleased she had her Hateful Council. She wasn't alone anymore.

But who of them can understand human nature? Along with the political manoeuvring that await us?

She recalled how swiftly Valki had taken control of the room. He was dangerous, that was obvious. His performance had been intentional in every respect. Unlike so many of his kind, who struggled with the intricacies of human nature, he appeared a complete contrast. Capable. Terrifying.

I need to learn more about him. His past and his motives. Perhaps then I can channel his talents, and focus him in a direction towards fulfilment, Diana thought, glancing at the clock on the wall just above the door. It was 11:34, still hours away from her first Council meeting. It was a small group, with each member preceding over a domain alongside a few Hateful underneath them. It was a simple structure, but that was what they needed. The Hateful revelled in organisation and punctuality.

Still, there's a risk that I'm underestimating the enormity of the task ahead, Diana knew. There was a thin line between success and failure. She couldn't afford to make many mistakes. Diana shook her head.

I'm thinking too much like my mother. I can't act as though perfection is achievable. The last thing I want to give the Hateful is more pressure.

Diana wondered what her mother was doing amid all the chaos, but she silenced her mind. Now was not the time.

A door knock interrupted those thoughts. Volsi shot to his feet, before shuffling towards the door. He opened it slowly, inspecting who was standing on the other side before moving to open it fully. It was Pauli, who smiled at Volsi as he towered over him.

'Hello, Volsi. I didn't realise Diana was beyond answering her door now,' Pauli said, smiling at Diana with a knowing look.

'You've trimmed your beard,' Diana commented, feeling the magnetism emitting from the Hateful man. His beard was no longer long and bushy; it was shorter and more pointed while retaining its thickness. Unable to stop herself, she reached forward and brushed her fingers through it. It was soft, and scented with oil.

'It looks amazing,' she remarked, before pulling her fingers away and turning before he could see her blushing. Then she stepped back to her desk.

'Sorry. I shouldn't have done that.'

'It's alright, Diana. I don't mind,' Pauli said, trying to sound reassuring, and making Diana blush more. She pretended to rummage through her desk, hoping the blush would fade.

I can't believe I did that. What in Divinity was I doing?

'Are you alright there, Diana?' Pauli asked.

Not helping...

Diana forced herself to take in a breath. 'So, who did it?' she asked eventually.

'Sadio,' Pauli said. 'He's been offering free haircuts for everyone. Apparently, he's wanted to do barbering for a long time, sneaking in human hair catalogues and barbering magazines to read, visualizing how to do it. He somehow sneaked in a mannequin head a year ago so he could practice. Now, he's open for business, thanks to your call to action. I don't think he would have done it without you.'

Diana tried to recover herself. 'So, anyway. How can I help you, Pauli?' she asked.

'Honestly, I was going to ask you the same question,' he said. 'Are you alright?'

You're so genuine. I'll feel terrible if I lie to you. Sometimes, I just don't get myself when I'm around you. It's like you bring something out of me.

'Yeah, I'm fine,' Diana lied. Breathing in a sigh, she felt herself settle. 'Encourage Sadio to continue what he's doing. Let him know to inform me if he needs supplies. I don't want him to hide his passion anymore. I want to show that we're encouraging this. Hopefully it will inspire others to follow. You can help me in the meantime. Could you help Reni get ready for the meeting? I think we'll need him for who we're about to face.'

'I assume you're referring to Valki?' Pauli asked.

Diana nodded thoughtfully. 'Do you know anything about him?' she asked.

Pauli shook his head. 'Not really. I hadn't seen him until he showed himself. I didn't like what he did.'

'I know, but I feel so will he. Pauli, you need to be careful around him. Regardless of how little we know about him, his aptitude for human nature is obvious. If he does harbour ill intent, he will plan to use your feelings against you.'

'I understand that,' Pauli agreed, his expression showing his displeasure. 'I'll see if I can find out anything.'

'Thank you, Pauli,' Diana said, watching as the large Hateful man turned, making his way towards the door. With a smile, he opened it and left the room, leaving Diana alone with Volsi. He appeared oblivious to the discussion, continuing to shuffle paper.

Diana considered more about Valki, wondering if his intentions were noble. She wasn't sure. She had never encountered a man like him before. He seemed to represent a different path for the Hateful to follow.

But what path is that? Where will it lead?

12

A New Perspective

Setsu had hardly spoken since they left Silver Wing's hideout. He guided Lucifer to a busy street filled with humans, stalls, and quaint shops. Even then, the confident Hateful man had not uttered a single word, as he headed to a particular coffee shop, before finding a seat and leaving Lucifer on his own. He returned with two drinks a few minutes later.

That had been twenty minutes ago. Lucifer was still adjusting to the notion of their kind sitting among humans, with nothing being said about it.

I wasn't expecting this, Lucifer thought. It was one thing visiting somewhere for a few minutes, like he had while getting his first coffee. However, staying was another matter, especially when the place was filled with humans. Lucifer sensed something wrong about this.

'Silver Wing thinks it has made this city better for us, but all they've done is create a new mask for both ourselves and humanity to use. We're clinging onto it out of sheer desperation, terrified of what lies within,' Lucifer recalled Gabriel saying, trying to

compare what he had seen in their headquarters. It didn't feel as though anything desperate was happening here. There was a genuine sense of comfort and relaxation. The humans truly didn't care about them being here. Hateful lived alongside them.

And Ven was here too. She would've seen all this, but why didn't she tell me? Would I have listened? I once swore that I'd never return here, so why would have I believed her?

'You enjoying the coffee?' Setsu said, speaking for the first time since they'd left the hideout. Lucifer took a sip, wondering if this was the nicest drink he had ever tasted. It was nutty, with hints of caramel. Lucifer looked at Setsu, seeing the Hateful man grinning.

'Knew it. Had a feeling you'd go for a sweeter blend – you know, to counter the darkness inside.'

Lucifer suppressed a smile. Setsu had a certain charm, a tender confidence that put him at ease. Setsu's own cup was tiny compared to his.

'I assume you've tried an espresso shot before?' Setsu asked. Lucifer said nothing, but Setsu pushed his tiny cup across the table, gesturing towards it. There was still steam rising from it, as darker and lighter tones of brown swirled within.

'I would say take a sip, but I'm sure that's committing sacrilege among coffee lovers. You're obviously just getting into the art.'

'The art?' Lucifer commented, reaching towards the small cup and taking a sip. It was difficult to do, like drinking half the cup. Still, the instant hit of concentrated caffeine almost caused him to choke, which drew a chuckle from Setsu.

'I was kidding, man,' he said. 'You'll blow your brains out.'

'That's what it feels like,' Lucifer half spoke, half choked.

'I'm sure you just had a Hateful moment, brother,' Setsu said, causing Lucifer to stare at Setsu. In return, Setsu shot him a knowing smile, as if everything prior had been setting up those words. Yet, Setsu didn't follow it up, as though satisfied with his point, sitting back while taking in the atmosphere.

A Hateful moment, Lucifer considered, ruing his lapse. He reflected on such a clear human flaw, looking around the coffee shop.

It was a small place, buzzing with human chatter and filled with the scents of coffee. There were rows of wooden benches and separate tables and chairs. The designer had been clever, weaving in the metal shell and network of protruding pipes as though they were decoration. Lucifer was impressed.

'You know, this place ain't bad,' Setsu commented. 'I never used to give a shit about coffee. Kyrn always raves about the stuff.'

'So what got you into it?' Lucifer asked.

'I'll show you in a minute,' he said. 'What about you? Ven?'

Lucifer froze at that. If that concerned Setsu, he didn't show it, his expression unchanging as he sat back.

'Cut a little close there, did I?' he said. 'Don't worry, I tried nothing with her. It's like Mika said. I'm only interested in human chicks.'

'Why?' Lucifer asked, relaxing.

'Ah, that's when things get interesting,' Setsu said, grinning before something caught his attention. 'Hold that. You're about to see why I love coffee.'

A human waitress appeared. She was in her late twenties, with amber hair tied into a ponytail. She reached for the two empty cups on their table without a word as Setsu smiled at her.

'I gotta say, your hair is gorgeous,' Setsu said.

The waitress shot him an unimpressed glance. 'I know who you are, Setsu,' she said.

'Perfect. Just means I've got less work to do, doesn't it?' he said, flashing her a huge smile.

The waitress sniffed, more out of amusement than disgust. 'I'm not that easy, I'm afraid,' she said next.

'That's what they all say. Hence the fun begins,' Setsu replied, as though having practised this interaction many times. He leaned on the table, propping his elbows on it while resting his head on his hands.

'My brother here is over for the holidays. I wanted to show him all the best coffee spots in town. Who knows, we might even come back.'

The waitress's eyes fell upon Lucifer, who wondered if she'd fall for Setsu's blatant lie. She smiled at him instead, as though in on it. 'I hope so. I like him better,' she said, offering Lucifer a cheeky wink before spinning on her feet and walking away.

Setsu was left surprised. 'Well, I'll be damned. I might have found me a wing man,' he grinned. 'Imagine all the human chicks we could get.'

Despite his desire to smile at that, Lucifer found himself unable to. It was too close after losing Ven. Emptiness flooded his body. He felt longing, knowing that he could never satisfy it.

To his surprise, Setsu seemed to settle, as though interpreting these thoughts within Lucifer. 'She's gone, isn't she?' he asked.

Lucifer nodded. There was no use lying about it.

'I thought something was up,' Setsu continued, speaking

with more reservation. 'She left too fast, and she wouldn't tell us what was wrong. I'd offered to go with her, but she refused. Said it was something personal. I guess it had something to do with you?'

Lucifer smiled sadly at that, not doubting it had everything to do with him. Shame compounded with guilt and Lucifer had to close his eyes, taking in a breath. The question that had consumed him since his greatest mistake arose again.

'Setsu, what is forgiveness?' he asked.

The Hateful man studied him. 'That's an interesting question. Maybe a little deep for me. Then again, I guess that suits your disposition, Prince.'

'Don't call me that,' Lucifer muttered.

'Sorry man, it's engraved on stone. Can't change it now,' Setsu said.

Lucifer didn't consider it worth arguing, so he fell into silence, hoping that Setsu would at least try to answer his question.

Eventually, the Hateful man shrugged. 'Forgiveness,' he began, before sighing. 'I guess the only experience I can talk about is when I was a kid. Unlike many of us, my parents were both human and they loved me. They didn't care that I was Hateful. They were happy to have a child. I think they'd been trying for years. Now, school… that was different. Course, that was because my loving parents dumped me in a human school.'

'What was that like?' Lucifer asked, curious.

Setsu chuckled. 'Fucking awesome. The human kids and adults hated me. I got bullied, and no one except my parents gave a shit. I guess if we're talking about forgiveness, I'd say they were the first people I forgave, even if I had many reasons to hate them.'

'Did you?' Lucifer asked.

Setsu half shrugged. 'Kinda. I just focused my anger on humour and pranks. If someone got me, I got 'em back harder. Once I got older and my Blessings got stronger, they left me alone. Wanna guess what happened next?'

Lucifer shrugged.

'I got bored. Once the humans started leaving me alone, I started losing my mind. I realised that even shit attention is still attention.'

'What did you do?' Lucifer asked.

'I just showed you,' Setsu said.

When Lucifer frowned in confusion, he smiled back. 'I chased after human chicks!' he exclaimed, as though this should've been obvious.

'Since the guys were being dicks, and I wanted interaction with people, I thought, "Hey, if you're all going to be assholes, I'll just take your girls instead." I've been a happier man ever since,' he said.

Lucifer's confusion only grew. 'I don't get it,' he said. 'Is that related to forgiveness?'

'No idea,' Setsu admitted, 'Just felt applicable. Look, just be careful when you're thinking deep. A pool full of shit is still full of shit, no matter how deep you go.'

Setsu paused then, appearing more contemplative.

'Look, what I'm saying is that I forgave those clowns. I could've got bitter and angry, but I realised it wasn't worth it. Now, especially spending time with human chicks, I kinda understand what goes through their heads. Forgiveness, you gotta find that shit within you, else what are you gonna do? I assume you've heard of the Hateful Killer?'

Lucifer said nothing, not sure if he should reveal his meeting with Gabriel yet. He nodded instead.

'The guy's pissed about something to do with our kind. You ask me, he's probably looking for the same thing as you. I don't know what happened in Exia or to Ven, but you're wrestling with something that's got you fixed on forgiveness. Sometimes, you just gotta find the answer for yourself. I can only give you my interpretation, and that means that's the answer that applies to me. What forgiveness means to me might mean something different for you. There isn't much else I can say.'

'I appreciate that,' Lucifer said, rising to his feet. 'I'm going to have a walk. I'll meet you back here in an hour.'

'You remember I said there's a Hateful Killer around here?' Setsu said, not moving to stop him.

Yes, and I have Korai, Lucifer answered in his mind, offering a smile to Setsu. Despite Lucifer's initial impressions of him, Setsu was clearly someone who cared, more in tune with others than he let on. The Hateful man regarded Lucifer calmly, before shrugging.

'Alright, if it suits you,' he said. 'Gives me more time to chat up that waitress.'

'Thank you, Setsu,' Lucifer said, meaning it, and left.

Lucifer headed south-east, using his Physical Blessing to jump from rooftop to rooftop. He felt sluggish compared to what he'd seen from Silver Wing earlier, but he reached the wall surrounding Kyrios a few minutes later. Lucifer wondered how he got to Exia and back. Recalling what had made him leave caused Korai to stir, and he turned to a set of buildings he hadn't looked at since he had left Kyrios. He found himself flooded with a sense of loss as he focused on one particular building.

The building wouldn't have seemed special to anyone else. To Lucifer, however, it held great meaning.

Home.

Humans walked the surrounding streets, never realising that Hateful eyes were watching them. Yet now, home brought a different meaning. It had driven him, having originated from this very place, from a conversation that Lucifer never forgot. It had led to his decision that changed the course of his life.

You told me everything that was wrong with me, and I cried myself to sleep that night. Yet, so much has changed since that day, Lucifer thought, lowering himself into a crouch on the wall. He allowed the snow to wet his resting knee, while he folded his arms and rested them on his raised knee, followed by his head.

After everything we went through. All the slights. The silences. The lies we kept telling ourselves. Things never changed. Without realising it, we created a cycle we couldn't see, a poisoned cycle that ruined everything for us, and for Mother. Now I see it. We weren't thinking about making things better. All we had was anger. Hatred. Yet, knowing it was making both of us miserable, we still kept repeating the same mistake. Is it any wonder that I did the same in Exia, as if removing myself from the situation changed my part in creating it.

Lucifer recalled Gabriel's words when they met, wondering why they seemed to apply now.

'We do not deserve forgiveness for what we've done, for what we are. Our existence is a curse to ourselves and those who surround us. Do you truly believe that you can attain such a thing?'

'I'm not sure,' Lucifer muttered, his head sinking further

into his arms, accompanying a sense of heaviness that threatened to pull him down over the wall.

'Forgiveness, you gotta find that shit within you, else what are you gonna do?' The words of Setsu echoed in his mind, causing Lucifer to compare them to Gabriel's. They were both chasing the same thing. Lucifer was certain that Setsu was correct.

'But is it that simple?' Lucifer asked himself. 'It's easy to say you forgive, but forgiveness is more than words, isn't it? Is it not something you do in the face of whatever challenges you, regardless of your anger and pain? I'm not sure anymore. I feel sick being here. How can I even consider forgiveness when I feel like this?'

Inside, Lucifer noticed a faint stirring of Korai.

Have you forgiven me, Lucifer? he asked, prompting a smile from Lucifer in return.

'There's no point in despising you, Korai. I realise I know nothing about you. I don't know why you're inside me, or what you even want. I just sense the same emptiness I eventually felt towards my—'

Lucifer stopped himself, noticing a figure in the window of his former home. It was a large man in his early forties who wore glasses, with hair as short as the stubble on his chin, wearing a grey T-shirt and trousers. Lucifer prayed he wouldn't glance up from the street he was observing. Seconds passed before the man reached out and closed the curtains, unaware that his son had been watching him. The old fears and anxieties faded, and Lucifer forced himself to rise, shaking his head in disapproval.

'What did I expect to gain by coming here?' Lucifer wondered, turning to see someone standing a few paces away.

He was frightened for a moment, then amused.

'How long have you been watching me?' Lucifer asked Mika. She wore her Silver Wing garb, her hands in her jacket pockets as the snowy wind flicked her short hair. She was looking at the same building Lucifer had. After a few seconds, she looked at Lucifer, her expression almost unreadable.

'You shouldn't be alone,' Mika said. 'The Hateful Killer could be anywhere.'

'I don't care,' Lucifer said, moving to step past her.

'How did she die, Lucifer?' Mika asked, stopping him. It didn't surprise him she'd figured out why he'd been so reluctant to speak about Vennifer. Lucifer knew it was unfair, though. He needed to say something.

It would be an insult to Ven anyway, alongside what I've been trying to find.

'Ven died trying to save me,' Lucifer said.

Mika's face was a stone mask.

Lucifer sighed, knowing he needed to say more. 'I deluded myself into pursuing a dream I refused to let go of. Knowing I wouldn't listen to her, Hela called back Ven in order to get through to me. I refused to let her in. Scared of my feelings about her, I pushed her away. Ven still saw what I was doing. I neglected her, yet she still loved me, fighting for me until the end. I didn't deserve it, Mika. Ven deserved better than me.'

Mika became more thoughtful, which surprised Lucifer a little. He had expected at least some anger, but his words appeared to give her some clarity, some closure. After a few seconds, Mika turned her eyes back towards him.

'Makes sense,' she said. 'Vennifer was a good person. I didn't open up to the others until she came. Before then, I think most of Silver Wing just tolerated me, but she helped me see it was okay to trust others with my feelings. I owe a lot to her.'

'She'd appreciate hearing that,' Lucifer said.

Silence fell again, and Mika looked at his old home. He expected the obvious question, but it didn't come. Instead, Mika joined him.

'You're hurting,' she said. 'Though I don't know why, you're here for a reason. Maybe it's something to do with that building, and that man you were watching. Or, it's about what happened in Exia, perhaps even both. I won't ask. It's none of my business, and I figure you'll talk about it when you're ready. Either way, I believe you should be with us. The Hateful Killer could be anywhere.'

'I don't think he intends on killing me. Not yet, anyway,' Lucifer said, putting his hands in his jacket pocket, mirroring Mika. 'I met him before you all showed up. He was intrigued by what I'm searching for.'

Mika nodded, not prying. She turned and tapped into her Physical Blessing, her lean body growing with more muscle.

'Mika, what is forgiveness?' he asked.

Mika stopped to look at him, her mask unblinking as she appeared to consider that. 'I'll tell you if you can answer a question for me,' she said.

'Alright, what question?' he asked.

'What do you think it means to be Hateful?'

Before Lucifer could answer, Mika launched herself off the wall, leaving behind a burst of mist-like snow, before bouncing from building to building.

'What does it mean to be Hateful?' Lucifer asked himself aloud, remembering a conversation with Megidra on the same subject, amid a burning Exia and many dead humans and Hateful.

Another time when I'd fooled myself. I was so ready to end it all, to be done with our accursed race. So was he, and we no longer cared who got hurt in the process. Oh Divinity, I don't even know what I think about our race anymore. Even here, Gabriel contrasts so much with Silver Wing. How do I find the answer to that question? Is that why you asked it, Mika?

Lucifer looked at his old home once more, before tapping into his Transformative Blessing. He summoned large black feathered wings, then launched himself into the sky. Mika had stopped and was standing watching him. Knowing it was the best choice he could make at that moment, Lucifer followed her.

13

Kindness

Marienne had hardly left Megidra's side in the days since his arrival at Johann's church. Megidra was sure she was channelling the pain of her loss through him, not knowing that he was the very reason for her pain.

Do I tell her? he often asked, especially during the moments he'd stare at her, watching as she smiled back at him. Guilt and self-disgust would arise then. He found himself unable to speak about what had happened in Anubi. The past burned every time his mind touched those raw wounds. Megidra would look at Marienne and see only Hela.

Oh Hela, I'm so sorry, he thought, unable to stop his tears. Marienne would wipe away his tears without question, making this worse.

I don't deserve your kindness. Why are you helping me? Megidra wanted to ask, but didn't. The Devil of Anubi lurked in his being, in every thought. That was his punishment. This pain. This guilt and suffering. He deserved it.

But not as much as the pain I've inflicted upon others, he thought. Ryun chuckled at that, seeming to take pleasure in watching this unfold.

'Without your dream, what are you now?'

'I don't know,' Megidra muttered.

He looked around at the surrounding humans. Most were silent, sitting bunched up in blankets. Fires burned in different sections of the church, which also served as social hubs for those who wished to talk. Megidra caught a few cautious glances his way before they turned away, unsure.

I can't blame them, Megidra thought. Few talked to him, mostly just Destin, Deion, and Johann. Marienne was always there, which Megidra found comfort in. She was busy now organising first aid supplies. After watching her for a few minutes, it surprised him to see her smiling, as though she understood what he was thinking.

'You don't know what to think of us,' she said, before casting a glance in his direction. 'You ready for another wash?'

'No, I think it's time I tried to move,' Megidra said, then tried moving his body for the first time since waking up in Johann's church. His weakness hadn't abated, as though the effort to prevent the transformation a couple of days ago had drained him. Still, Megidra tried, his face straining from effort as he turned onto his side, exhaling once he stabilised.

'You're gonna need my help,' Marienne said, as Megidra flickered a glance towards her. She was resting on her knees, palms on legs. It surprised Megidra to discover that he found her rather beautiful, a notion that disturbed him. After all, she was human, while he was Hateful. It made little sense for him to find anything about her attractive. Despite that, he offered no refusal as Marienne reached towards him, using a surprising amount of strength to help him onto his feet.

'I'll help you to the shower,' she said, as Megidra stood on his own two feet. His legs buckled beneath him, and he started falling. He was caught by Marienne, who once again showed great strength despite her diminutive stature. She reached underneath his arms and held him up with no struggle. Then Megidra realised.

'You're a Physical,' he said, seeing her enhanced muscles expanding through her jumper. Marienne said nothing to this, swinging herself around so that she was by Megidra's side, gripping his back while draping his right arm over her shoulder. She guided him forward, heading towards the main floor of the church, drawing gazes from all the surrounding humans.

'They're not gonna bite,' Marienne said, no doubt sensing the way Megidra's body bristled. Embarrassment washed over him, and he tried to relax. Marienne was guiding him towards the curving staircase that led to Johann's room. The kind priest had given it to the children while he slept with the adults on the main floor. His room had the only shower.

Although, I don't know how I'm going to clean myself. I may have been overambitious.

Marienne knocked before they entered, knowing the children were in lessons with Johann and the other adults. Once they reached the bed inside, she helped Megidra to sit, before taking a step back and moving to close the door.

'Take off your clothes,' Marienne said, shocking Megidra.

'I'm sorry?' he asked, unable to hide his bafflement.

Marienne rolled her eyes, folding her arms. 'How do you expect to wash unless you do?' she asked.

'Well, yes, I understand that,' Megidra said, 'But—'

'If it's because I'm here, please don't worry. I've been

101

cleaning you the past few days. Besides, I've seen a naked man before.'

'I'm aware of that, but—' Megidra said, protesting, only to find Marienne step towards him instead, reaching for his boots.

'Megidra, just take off your clothes,' she said, already undoing his laces.

Megidra obeyed. He began by removing his jacket and unbuttoning his shirt. He could see how much weight he had lost in the past month; he was skinnier than he ever remembered himself being. What had happened in Rai had affected him.

Ever since that night, I've barely slept or ate, walking for days, not knowing what to do. Is it any wonder why I fell unconscious?

His train of thought stopped as he realised Marienne was undressing in front of him. Megidra's eyes widened before he tore them away, shielding them with a weakly raised arm.

'Marienne,' he began, trying to gather his thoughts. 'What are you doing?'

'Did you think I'm going in there with you clothed? I haven't had a shower in days, so I'm going with you.'

'What do you mean go in there with me?' Megidra asked, confusion adding to his sense of shock.

'How else are you going to wash?' Marienne said. 'You can barely hold yourself upright.'

'I'll go on the floor. Marienne, I don't—'

'Megidra,' Marienne interrupted, silencing him. She made no effort to cover herself. Her frame was slight, including her breasts. Still, Megidra sensed a strength in her that contrasted with this vulnerability.

'Do you even think I look good enough for that?' Marienne

asked, the frankness of the question surprising Megidra so he relaxed.

Marienne, appearing almost embarrassed, breathed out a loud sigh.

'I'll not deny it because I know you sense it. I've been putting off my grief by helping you since you got here. After what happened to Felix... You've helped me feel needed when I wasn't sure what to do. It's not just Exia that's falling apart. I'm fighting to keep myself from falling apart. So please, this isn't anything like that. I just want a warm shower so I can clean myself, and I'm happy to help you while you're here. Nothing has to happen.'

Megidra nodded at that, taking in a deep breath before removing the rest of his clothes. The two of them stood naked, while Megidra found himself more confused than before. Despite this, Marienne's smile only drove his guilt, seeing the state they were both in.

I did this to her. I've ruined her life. What right have I to judge her? Still...

'Marienne, I'm struggling with all this. You're human. I'm Hateful. Although I spent years working with your kind, this is the first time humans who haven't cursed me have surrounded me. Seeing you like this... I don't deserve your kindness. I don't deserve the care you've shown me.'

'Then I guess you know how it feels to struggle with pain,' Marienne said, shivering. 'I'm cold, Megidra. I just want to feel warmth again.'

So do I, Megidra thought, not daring to utter the words as he reached towards Marienne's outstretched hand. They walked side by side into the bathroom together.

Marienne helped Megidra dress around twenty minutes later, having dressed herself first. Deion had given Megidra some of his own fresh clothes, although they were a little big on him. Megidra appreciated the gesture regardless, now finding himself revitalised after sharing the shower with Marienne. It had fulfilled something Megidra had neglected, a sense of intimacy. Sharing in a moment of vulnerability, being able to hold another with no desires getting in the way. It had been perhaps the most wonderful moment of Megidra's life.

But what does that mean? Megidra wondered, unsure. He knew he would recover soon, which meant he would have to face the question he'd been avoiding these past few days: what next? He couldn't just return to the Institute, or to his home. Both were filled with reminders of his failure and pain. Besides, the latter was Lieutenant Newman's home, not Megidra's, and especially not the Devil of Anubi's.

So what do I do?

Megidra walked alongside Marienne as they headed for the staircase once again. Deion came up to meet them, smiling.

'Nice to see you on your feet, Megi,' he began, flickering his gaze between him and Marienne. 'Looks like she's been treating you well.'

Megidra and Marienne said nothing. Deion's smile waned, as though recognising that they had caught his small talk out for what it was. He gave an awkward sigh as he scratched his head.

'Look, I know you're thinking about getting out of here soon, but before you do, I need your help. I've been organising a joint supply run in Seraphu with some other groups, and we could use your help. Despite the snow, things are heating up out there. Groups like ours are banding together to fight for diminishing resources. Having someone who's Hateful could give us the edge, especially over the bandits.'

Megidra nodded, having expected this conversation at some point. Still, he sensed Marienne stiffening alongside him.

'When are you thinking of going?' she asked. 'Megidra's in no condition to be leaving now.'

'Yeah, I'm aware of that,' Deion said. 'But we're running short of food, Marienne. That's already after rationing, so I figure we have days left. If I'm being honest, I've been delaying the supply run so we could have Megidra with us. His power with all four of the Blessings gives us great defensive and offensive options. That could make the difference between us getting a few months of supplies, or only weeks. We don't know how long this will last. We need to think long-term.'

It was all sound logic. Megidra couldn't fault it. Though he was sure Deion was trying to arouse guilt in him, without these people, he'd be dead. Then there were the likes of Marienne. She had helped him, and Megidra knew he was the reason Exia was this way. He was indebted. He had no other choice.

'Yeah, I'll help you, Deion,' Megidra said, drawing a surprised look from Deion, and a concerned one from Marienne.

'You cannot seriously intend to go out there in your current state?' she said, angrily. 'You've only just started walking. You need more time to recover.'

'We don't have the time, Marienne,' Megidra said, giving her a calm smile. 'Besides, I can do this for you.'

'I get that, but just give it a few more days,' Marienne said, frustrated.

'I'll be fine, Marienne,' Megidra said. 'You've helped me so much. Please, let me return the favour.'

'If it's any consolation, I can wait until tomorrow,' Deion said, gratefully. 'That gives me time to make sure everything is ready, and more time for you to gather your strength. I'll ask the cook to give you a bigger portion of food. We'll leave during the early hours.'

'No problem. Wake me up when you're heading off,' Megidra said.

Deion nodded and made his way back down the staircase. Megidra wondered how he'd gone from slaughtering humans to seeking to help them. What surprised him was how Ryun didn't respond to this either, knowing the Fallen would be watching. Megidra turned to Marienne and saw sadness in her eyes.

'You don't owe us,' she said. 'Especially considering what your kind has gone through.'

Marienne, what my kind has gone through isn't justification for what I did, Megidra almost replied, glad that he didn't. Instead, he tried to express warmth in his smile, looking into Marienne's hazel eyes and finding them beautiful.

'You have wonderful eyes, Marienne,' Megidra said. 'I'd love to know what they see. A Hateful monster, or a creature worth pitying?'

'Neither.' Marienne said, her expression hardening. 'I see someone wanting to do the right thing.'

14

The Forbidden Path

The snow hadn't reached every part of Ethero, Greene noticed as they went further into their jungle-like surroundings, gentle steam rising from the trees and overgrowth. Still, Greene regarded the terrain with concern, unsure of what to make of it.

What is this world? It seems so much is unknown, or unsaid. Yet, the mysteries keep coming. Why is everything like this? What made everything this way?

He doubted he would get any answers from Barbatos; not unless it suited him. Indeed, the sorcerer had hardly spoken, consumed with leading the group towards Elcaris with purposeful steps. What drove this pace, Greene didn't know. He was sure it didn't lead to anything good.

Instead, it led towards ruins.

From out of nowhere, a giant wall of stone emerged in the steamy jungle. A circular metal door stood within it, shrouded in overgrown vines and moss. From the few patches that weren't covered, Greene could see engravings of unreadable text, along with tiny illustrations that formed into monstrous creatures. Greene did not recognise them. Still, he sensed something ancient and forbidden behind that door, something that was telling them to turn and walk away.

'Here we are,' Barbatos said. 'It has been far too long. I hope you're ready for what we're about to face. Once this door opens, there is no turning back.'

The Fiend lowered his hood to reveal his scarred head and gazed at the giant door. *'Guasha elch omnias,'* he said.

'What did he say?' Greene asked Shallai quietly.

'I don't know. I don't speak his tongue,' Shallai said.

Doomis half-turned towards them, freezing Greene on the spot. 'I said I made a promise,' the Fiend said. He reached down towards his cloak to pull it off overhead. His body was ghostly white, with a powerful physique covered in scars similar to those on his head. Gigantic boulders for muscles bulged, whole veins spread all over as though he had undergone some kind of mutation. A giant broadsword was strapped to his back, as wide as Greene himself, while standing almost as tall as Doomis himself.

The Fiend reached for his sword, unsheathing it before holding it in his right hand. He appeared a great and terrifying warrior, his scars showing how many battles he had fought.

'What happened to you?' Greene asked.

'Hell,' he said. 'Greene. Shallai. Once we pass this door, stay far from me. There is only one thing my kind respects, and I shall give it to them.'

'And... what is that?' Greene asked, despite the tremble in his voice.

'Fear,' Doomis responded. 'Barbatos, open the door.'

'By all means. I'd hate to interrupt your reunion,' Barbatos said, aiming his sceptre towards the door. Doomis turned and grabbed the sorcerer by the neck, lifting Barbatos with little effort.

'Do not mock me, Barbatos,' the Fiend seethed, as Barbatos choked in his grasp.

The sorcerer still smiled somehow. 'Touched a raw nerve, did I?' Barbatos said. 'Why don't you focus that rage upon those who wronged you, Doomis?'

The smile faded, and a look of absolute hatred appeared on Barbatos' face. 'Remember, you're not the only one with a score to settle. We've only just begun. Soon, we'll make them all suffer.'

Doomis revealed a cruel smile of his own then, amused. 'Now we see the real you,' he said, before throwing Barbatos on the ground with a loud thud. 'Open the door.'

The sorcerer chuckled, showing no signs of intimidation. 'Oh, Doomis, you confuse my good nature for leniency. If I were you, I would proceed with caution if you ever consider handling me like that again. After all, you know what I'm capable of.'

Despite the palpable tension in the air, Doomis's smile never faded. He went down on one knee and leaned towards Barbatos, as though welcoming the threat.

'You mock my pain, and expect me to just stand and take it. No, you foolish child. I do not care who you are, or your strength. They gave your power to you. I earned mine. I hope you don't expect to make allies here, Barbatos, for they made the same mistake. Many will fall until Greene finds the piece of the core. Until then, stay away.'

Doomis arose then, still looking down towards Barbatos.

'Open the door,' he commanded.

Barbatos made no move to do so. 'You don't know me, Doomis. You aren't the only one who's experienced pain.'

'No, but pain comes in many forms, doesn't it?' Doomis retorted. 'I see what guides you, Barbatos. Mine is the pain of loss. Greene, the pain of subjugation. Shallai, the pain of identity. You, the pain of rejection and loneliness.'

'Well, aren't you perceptive one,' Barbatos noted, his expression relaxing as he closed his eyes. When they opened again, his smirk returned, and he raised his sceptre toward the door, causing its emerald orb to glow.

'Then go, avenge your pain,' he said.

There were sounds of mechanisms turning. A few loud clicks followed, then the sounds of bolts unlocking. The door moved inward before spinning to the left, moving inside the rock wall. A void awaited them, which Doomis appeared to welcome by stepping inside. Barbatos rose to his feet, dusting himself off.

'Sorry you had to see that,' he said. 'This place holds many unpleasant memories for our friend. Heed his words. Once he gets started, I doubt he'll stop.'

'But what was that about?' Greene asked.

Barbatos shrugged. 'I'll let him tell you in his own time. Either way, I hope you're both ready for what we're about to face. A lot of Fiends are about to stand against us, much to their peril.'

'Their peril?' Shallai said, frustrated. 'What do you mean?'

'I would've thought that was obvious,' Barbatos commented, regarding Shallai with a distasteful look, before turning to follow Doomis.

Greene, compelled by his new instincts, moved to intercept the sorcerer. 'Barbatos, what Doomis just said about our pain:

what did he mean about yours? What did he mean about rejection and loneliness?'

'You and Shallai mentioned it before, did you not?' Barbatos said. 'You've only ever seen one of me. Why do you think that is?'

Neither Greene nor Shallai replied.

'You think your kind were the only ones the Divinity betrayed?' Barbatos asked. 'Everything you know about Ethero is a lie, Greene. I told you that. You're only just realising how deep the lies run. I promise you, the ones responsible for those lies will suffer for what they've done.'

They went through the door, which led to a series of caverns and caves. Greene followed Barbatos alongside Shallai, finding that his transformed body illuminated part of the path ahead, as the violet lines over his body seemed to glow even brighter. Ahead, the claustrophobic caverns declined slowly, and all Greene could hear was their echoing footsteps. He had half-expected to hear the hisses and shrieks of Doomis's kind.

Greene wondered what Elcaris would look like. The prospect of a city full of Ethero Fiends filled him with dread.

They emerged into an expanse in the cavern that even his light could not fill. Summoning his Life Essence in his palms, Greene raised his hands, realizing that a significant drop awaited them should they take a wrong step.

He looked ahead: Doomis seemed to walk with a sense of readiness that brokered no interruption. Whatever had happened to him was affecting him now. Greene wanted to talk to him, but he was sure Doomis didn't. So, he remained silent, wondering what awaited them.

Then he heard hissing up ahead, accompanied by guttural growls.

Doomis stopped, moving his head from left to right, loosening his neck. His muscles bulged as he did so.

Barbatos stepped alongside him. 'They won't wish for us to get to the core,' he said. 'They will put up stern resistance.'

'You talk as though I should care,' Doomis remarked. 'They will die.'

'That I know,' Barbatos said, before turning towards Greene and Shallai. 'I want you to focus on retrieving the piece of the core. Doomis and I will take up most of the Ethero Fiends' attention. If you encounter anyone, do not let them stop you. Kill them if you must. We cannot afford to stumble here, so close to the beginning. Assume all who stand before you are enemies.'

'You assume they'll find a way past me,' Doomis said, before sounding a guttural growl of his own.

Barbatos turned towards him. 'Oh, I doubt that. What I'm counting on are those smart enough to hide. They know why we're here. It would make sense for them to leave protection behind.'

'Unless we give them a threat to make them respond,' Doomis countered, his body bristling, ready for battle.

Barbatos conceded this with a shrug. 'Well, I don't doubt you'll give them that,' he said, folding his arms and nodding to the dark path ahead. 'Have fun.'

Doomis said nothing to that. Greene and Shallai moved to follow him, but Barbatos held out his arm to stop them, as the sounds of hissing and growls grew.

'Wait,' he said, not averting his eyes. 'We'll let him get ahead of us.'

A cacophony of shrieks accompanied roars ahead. Greene shivered, hearing the screams as slashing and hacking followed. No Fiend rushed to meet them. Instead, the sounds of slaughter and death seemed to grow distant, as though indicating Doomis's advance.

'What is he?' Shallai asked, her voice small.

'He is their Executioner,' Barbatos replied. 'They created their monster, and now that monster has come for vengeance, as have we all.'

They moved forward to witness the carnage and death Doomis had inflicted upon his kind. Bloody and dismembered corpses lay, with no one alive to tell what had befallen them. Many were sliced, others hacked, and some even crushed. The sounds continued in the distance; it seemed Doomis had no intention of stopping.

What fuels this hatred? This is slaughter. What promise led to this?

Greene understood that his fear of the Fiend was warranted. Such death and bloodshed reminded him of the path the lieutenant had chosen; a path he didn't wish to replicate.

So what is the right path? If I don't wish to exact revenge on humanity, what do I intend with the release of my ancestors?

'Greene, your body,' Shallai then said.

Unsure what she meant, he looked at his hands. A strange steam was rising from the violet lines across his body.

'What is this?' he asked.

The sorcerer smiled. 'A byproduct of my potion,' he said. 'I released you from the Divinity's bounds with the power of chaos. We must continue on our mission, unleash my… no, the Titans. Then, they will trample all who the Divinity loves.'

Greene looked on the dead and dying, remembering the

human screams that had followed Newman's monstrosities. 'I don't want this,' he said, shaking his head. 'I may wish to release my ancestors and my kind, but not at this cost. Death will not compensate for what they have inflicted upon us.'

'Then what do you suppose we do, my dear Titanius?' Barbatos asked, his expression darkening. 'Go back? Allow things to resume as usual? Let everyone get away with what they've done? Do you wish to remain ignorant of the truth?'

'What truth would that be, Barbatos?' Greene retorted, allowing some of his anger to show. 'The truth you constantly dangle before my eyes? Smirking with mocking abandon?'

Barbatos stepped towards him then, his gaze menacing. Much to his own surprise, Greene stood strong, staring into the sorcerer's eyes.

'It would seem that Doomis has emboldened you, Greene,' Barbatos said, his voice venomous. 'Don't make the same mistake.'

'No, I won't,' Greene said, remaining still. 'But neither will I make the same mistake as Newman. I may despise humanity for what they did to my race, but I will not follow this path either.'

'Really? Then why are you standing on it with me?' Barbatos retorted. 'Whether you like it or not, you will still continue to follow me, my dear Titanius. You've already begun this journey. You cannot avoid the bloodshed that it has unleashed, and the lives that we will take. The Fiends and all those who stand before us won't give you the same courtesy, so let's see how long your noble stance lasts.'

The sorcerer moved in the same direction as Doomis. Despite the darkness, Greene could still see remnants of shadow coming from the sorcerer. His form seemed to grow and shift, turning into something Greene didn't recognise.

'Remain here,' a voice commanded, one that sounded like Barbatos but younger. The shifting form continued to change. Barbatos's sceptre glowed as it assimilated into his body, disappearing along with his hat while his hair grew longer, reaching down to his lower back as he grew in height. His black leather outfit seemed to morph into his body too, becoming skin-like before he disappeared into the darkness.

'Now the war begins,' the younger-sounding Barbatos said, then laughed.

Greene wasn't sure who sounded more terrifying: the new form of Barbatos or the monster known as Doomis.

15

The Hateful Council

Diana was first in the Hearing Room ahead of the meeting of her Hateful Council, pacing as she waited. The Council was small: Pauli, Reni and three other Hateful. The oldest by some distance was Heimval. He was the archivist and held an excellent reputation among the Hateful.

Then there was Artemi. A promising young student recommended by Pauli, she was a proactive organiser and speaker. Pauli believed she had the makings of a future leader. Diana wanted to cultivate that, so she had invited her. Diana knew Artemi was going to face competition for the future Hateful leadership from the third and final Hateful: Valki.

Pauli's research had uncovered little, only that Valki had rejected the offer to join the other students in the Education Section, choosing to remain alone. Diana didn't understand why. Mystery surrounded the young Hateful man. It was like he'd come from nowhere. No one knew anything about him.

I doubt that's accidental, Diana thought, scratching her chin as the doors to the Hearing Room opened. Valki was the first

Hateful to join her. That didn't surprise Diana. Nor did his chosen attire of a white robe, which reminded her of the garb worn by the members of the human Council. Valki moved with confident grace, placing his hands behind his back as he smiled at Diana, while making his way down the walkway.

'Hello, Diana,' he said, stopping before the barrier that separated the open space of the floor from the audience section. He stepped over it gracefully and resumed the same pose as before.

'I wanted to thank you. With each day that passes, you make decisions that further dissipate the differences between humanity and Hateful. I appreciate the work you've done.'

Diana nodded in acknowledgement. Her response seemed to amuse Valki, his smile turning wry.

'You believe my praise to be idle flattery. I assure you, it is not.'

'I'm not sure how to interpret your words, Valki,' Diana said, figuring that honesty was the best course of action. 'You're tough to read, and I feel that is intentional with you. You strike me as a man who can wield words like a Transformative wielding claws, arming and retracting them as you see fit.'

'That's quite a colourful comparison,' Valki said, still smiling, unfazed. 'But you've put too much stock in your initial interpretation of me. That is my fault. When I performed during the hearing, it was because I wanted to create a failsafe in case my kind rejected your proposal, at least without considering how it benefited them.'

'But you somehow knew what I was planning,' Diana said. 'How?'

'It was a rational deduction,' Valki said, seriously. 'To me, Hela's failings were clear. She was overburdened and overworked, hence why she buried herself deeper, unable to see that the solution lay in going in the opposite direction. Seeing how you spoke and engaged with us, while also being detached, I figured you would uncover the solution. Then, the urgency and randomness with which you organised our latest hearing showed to me you'd finally worked it out. I took a chance on you, and you proved me to be correct.'

'I see,' Diana said, unsure of what to make of this conversation.

I need to figure out what he wants. Although I know I should be wary of him, he could make a powerful ally, Diana thought.

'You're wondering what my goal is,' he said. 'And why I mentioned nothing to Hela.'

I hadn't considered that, Diana thought, knowing it was a good point. However, that brought with it a sense of suspicion.

'Why didn't you?' she asked.

'She was entrenched,' Valki replied. 'Sometimes, when someone is set in their own ways, they are beyond saving. They cannot be moved or told otherwise. Hence they lead themselves towards their own destruction.'

'So you waited until Hela was gone before putting yourself forward,' Diana said, not masking her displeasure.

'Yes,' he answered, appearing unaffected by her insinuation. 'Because from the moment I heard of your legend I knew you were going to become leader, Diana.'

'What?' Diana asked, stunned.

Before Valki could elaborate, their conversation was interrupted by the doors of the Hearing Room opening. Pauli entered alongside Reni, followed by Heimval and Artemi.

'Ah, hi everyone,' Diana said, smiling.

Pauli regarded Valki with a displeased look. In order to distract him, and because she wanted to, Diana reached to take Reni's arm from Pauli. Reni flashed her a smile that warmed her heart as she felt his Illusionary Blessing emerging within.

Hello Diana, Reni whispered in her mind. *How long have you been speaking to Valki? Blink for each minute.*

Diana considered that, then blinked five times. Reni nodded in understanding as he hummed to himself, tapping his head.

We'll speak later, he said, taking Diana's hand as his Blessing faded away. Diana then nodded towards Heimval and Artemi. Heimval was an old man with a wispy beard and receding hairline, his posture stooped. The latter was young and carried herself with controlled grace. She wore her Hateful hair in a single thick braid that reached the bottom of her neck, while her features were narrow and somewhat pointed. They greeted Diana, then she looked at Pauli.

'Thank you, Pauli,' she said.

'It's no problem at all, Diana,' Pauli replied, not taking his eyes off Valki. 'How long has he been here?'

'Not long, Pauli,' Valki said smoothly, as though knowing just how much Pauli disliked him. 'Don't worry, I won't be stealing your precious Diana from you.'

Diana forced a cough then, trying to end that conversation as quickly as possible. The group moved to congregate around the elevated wooden platform, forming a circle. Once everyone was settled, Diana took a moment to survey her Hateful Council, the first of its kind. This was the beginning. This was the first step to succeeding in her dream.

'Thank you all for joining me,' Diana began. 'I must

begin with matters of the utmost importance. I've been contemplating how to unite humanity and Hateful, and the problem I keep facing is how to make the first contact with my kind. Megidra's actions have made things difficult. Even if I argued that he should not be thought to represent all of the Hateful, and that some of you moved to stop him, I doubt that humanity would listen. Then there's the matter of what Lucifer did to the human Council.'

Diana paused then. 'So, I'm asking what you think we should do? My kind are still fighting in the streets, while others camp outside our walls, attacking us. Though our defences are strong here, that doesn't solve the issue. I'd like to hear your opinions.'

Pauli and Reni appeared thoughtful, Heimval seemed troubled, and Artemi seemed unsure. Only Valki kept his air of confidence, of calm and ease.

Diana turned to him. 'Valki, I would like to hear your perspective on this. The floor is yours. What do you think?'

'We should begin by analysing the current situation, especially with humanity. Exia has become a battleground, and it has been so since Megidra's massacre. I find it suspicious how quickly things deteriorated in the aftermath, especially in how the DFA lost control so easily.'

'They had the entire city turn against them,' Pauli said. 'They can only maintain law and order as long as groups agree to obey them. It's the flaw in human thinking with societal and social discourse. We invented the systems out of thin air, yet our minds give them the life that sustains them.'

'Exactly,' Valki said. 'But we're missing the bigger picture. The fall of Exia happened too fast. Someone is taking advantage of what Lucifer and Megidra did. The chaos presents the perfect opportunity for those who see the possibilities.'

So you think someone is seeking power by taking advantage of the chaos among humanity? Why? Reni asked.

'It's quite simple,' Valki said. 'I believe someone may wish to reestablish order, but in their image. It wouldn't take much, especially if this current state continues. Supplies will become scarce, meaning that the various human factions will fight more intensely just to survive. Once they do, I doubt it would take much for someone to sweep in and present themselves as heroes seeking peace. Humans would probably accept whatever cost comes with that peace.'

'So you think we're dealing with a hidden entity playing a game of patience?' Artemi asked. Valki nodded.

Pauli sighed. 'It still doesn't bring us any closer to solving the problem Diana is trying to solve,' he said. 'We could discuss reasons and possibilities behind the current state of play all day, but none of them bring a solution to the dilemma. We're here to figure out how to unite humanity and Hateful.'

'Indeed,' Valki retorted. 'However, what if we are the solution? What if we became that faction?'

'What do you mean?' Pauli asked, his eyes narrowing with suspicion.

'Look at us. We're hunkered down here, safe, our supplies coming either from ourselves or from means that humanity hasn't clicked onto yet. We're in the best position to deal with the current situation. All we're doing is defending ourselves, wasting little in the way of energy and resources. Rather than trying to figure out who's fanning the flames of this conflict, we could take advantage of their work. We can sit back and wait for them to reveal themselves. Then we can make our move, utilising our power and superior position to sweep in with coordinated attacks and take control of the city.'

The group appeared struck by his suggestions, not just because of what they entailed, but also how logically sound they were.

'There may be fewer of us, but we're in a much stronger position than humanity,' Valki said. 'Megidra's and Lucifer's recent actions are still prominent in their minds, and it wouldn't take long for us to reestablish control. Then, with Diana as our leader, they'd have no option but to gravitate towards collaboration. We can present ourselves as the bringers of order and peace. We could restore a new Council of Exia, but one with all races, including ourselves alongside humanity. Once established, we'd offer the order both sides crave, while paving the way towards a better future.'

Valki stopped then, satisfied with his argument. The rest of the group remained silent, contemplative. After a minute, Reni's Illusionary Blessing drew their attention, as he hummed to himself, covering his face with his hands. It was a technique he used for self-soothing.

Your deductions are well considered and calculated, Valki, he began, *But I must ask the obvious question: How would that make us any better than Lucifer or Megidra? What you're suggesting is to take advantage of humanity's fear in order to subjugate them, to force change upon them. Isn't that what Lucifer sought to achieve with his poisoned dream?*

Reni regarded the rest of the group in silence, which Diana knew required a great effort from him, before his gaze settled on Valki.

Your idea would work, Valki. I don't doubt that. However, I believe it would come at the cost of sacrificing the very thing we seek to achieve. Nothing would change, and both humanity and Hateful would continue to harbour resentment towards each other. We cannot repeat the same mistakes both sides have been making since the beginning. We must follow Diana's example and find a better way.

'But what is the better way?' Heimval asked, directing the question more to the group than to Reni. 'Because that means we've gone around in a circle. We're back to where we began.'

The group fell into silence, while Diana reflected on what had just taken place. Valki had shown his mental prowess in its terrifying beauty. By doing so, it had forced Reni to prove why this group was important, to ensure all ideas were checked and vetted. It proved how great the task was. There would be no simple solution.

Which I don't doubt Valki has already calculated, Diana thought. *We may regard ourselves as different races, but the Hateful are human at heart. That means they can possess their own agendas, while being vulnerable to influence and manipulation. Valki will know that, which is probably why he revealed his plan so early. What is his goal? What is he after?*

'There has to be a way,' Pauli said, saying what most of the group were thinking. Then they all turned to her, their gazes questioning. It was time for their leader to offer her perspective.

'Our goal is to unite humanity and Hateful,' she said. 'While Valki is correct that his plan would get us the result we want, I side more with Reni. It would only sow deeper seeds of hatred within humanity. Control and order need to be reestablished, not for our domination, but for peace.'

'But how can we establish that, Diana?' Pauli asked. 'We recognise that to seek a peaceful solutions bring with it the risk of humanity wishing to use us to their advantage.'

'No matter which action we choose, there will be risks involved. If we're going to succeed, then we must begin discussions with humanity. That opens the door for manipulation. That is a facet of human nature,' Diana said.

I am prepared to face that, Reni said. *However, I refuse to resort to any means that include violence. We cannot repeat the mistakes of those who came before us. We must show humanity that we desire change. While I disagree with most of Valki's proposal, I agree with the idea of a future Council of Exia with humanity, Hateful and even Titaniuses involved. It is vital for our futures. I would like to hear the thoughts of everyone else.*

Diana felt immense pride in Reni, remembering the man she had met when she'd just arrived at the Institute. Not only did he have the courage to speak his mind, but he also embodied everything of the future she desired for the Hateful.

'I agree with Reni,' Artemi said. 'We have to be different.'

'I too concur,' Heimval said. 'There must be understanding and peace. It is the reason we chose Diana to lead us, and why we're here.'

'Exactly,' Pauli agreed.

It seemed then that most of her Council agreed, except for one.

'Valki?' Diana asked.

'An admirable sentiment,' Valki said. 'I'll support the decisions of this Council regardless of whether I agree with them. However, I would like to ask what you're willing to accept to achieve the peace you seek. A non-violent solution is noble, but what if humanity rejects that? What happens if they decide to turn violent towards us?'

Valki paused then, as though allowing his questions time

to settle.

'Diana is a wonderful example of what kind of relationship we could build with humanity. No one denies that. However, has it occurred to you she could be an exception to the rule? An outlier?'

'You've never struck me as the cynical type, Valki,' Pauli said, drawing a dark glance from the young Hateful man.

'You don't understand me, Pauli,' he said, keeping a smile despite a strange shift in his tone. Diana sensed a crack in the mask he was wearing.

'You don't even understand yourself,' he continued. 'And that's part of the problem we face. Humanity. Hateful. We're all similar in how we comprehend what we are that we spend most of our lives fighting those outside us, just so we can discover who we are. We use stories and theories, and even then, there are aspects that remain consistent. Neither of us desire change in our lives. Emotion and irrationality guide our every move, even when we delude ourselves into thinking we're calm and detached.'

Valki paused, his expression unreadable.

'Both sides pursue vengeance for actions that took place so long ago that neither of us knows if they happened or not. Never do we question that history, especially if it suits our agenda. Whether it comes from someone's lips or letters on a page, we choose what serves our reality. Without this, our perception of ourselves would be shattered.'

'What is your point, Valki?' Pauli asked.

'We created this world, Pauli,' he answered. 'And we delude ourselves into thinking that going in the opposite direction will change anything. Our future exists on a continuum, and all we do is slide across that continuum. The future is predictable, for every path has already been trod. So, how do you think this avenue of non-violence will be different?'

Valki fell into silence, his expression expectant. No one had an answer for him. As though expecting this, he relaxed before moving to step over the barrier to leave.

'Valki,' Diana said, stopping him. 'Something has to change. I swore before all of you I would do everything in my power to break down the wall that separates us. I don't know if non-violence is the key to that, but we've all seen what happened when Megidra and Lucifer chose the opposite path. We have to be the ones who end it, Valki. If either humanity or Hateful are to have a future, we must stop the routes of pain, hatred, and frustration. The cycle must end.'

'Indeed, it must,' Valki agreed. 'And yet, those words strike me as familiar. I've heard something similar before. Ah yes, I remember now. They came from Lucifer Armedeus.'

16

Differences

Lucifer awoke in Silver Wing's hideout. He was struck by the difference from the Institute. There, he remembered a tiny box-shaped room, dank and barely lit, and the agonised moaning coming from his More Cursed brethren. A feeling of depression dominated everything. There had been no hope there. Nothing worth living for.

Now, Lucifer woke up to the warm amber light of his bedside table, in a spacious room full of wooden furniture. A fake fireplace stood glowing near the foot of his bed, with a carpeted floor beneath. He wondered if this was a Hateful Dream, and shivered at the memory of the dreams Korai once gave him.

This isn't a Hateful Dream, and this isn't Exia.

Lucifer pushed himself up, glancing at the bedside table on his right. He was surprised to see a set of neatly folded clothes that hadn't been there before. Lucifer guessed Mika had put them there.

'What do you think it means to be Hateful?' Her question rang

through his mind. His eye was drawn to the jacket at the bottom of the pile, to the patch of a silver wing. He shook his head.

'I'm not one of you,' he murmured. He got up and went to shower in the small adjoining bathroom. Ten minutes later, he was fully dressed.

Lucifer emerged into a corridor that had a single red carpet running across its centre, lying over a metal floor. More warm amber lights illuminated it, contrasting with the memory of the dimness of the spaced candles he remembered from the Institute. Paintings hung on the walls. One depicted a strange black-cloaked figure wearing a white mask, wielding a sword while white-powder-faced women danced around him.

'That's one of Claire's favourites,' a familiar voice said.

It was Setsu, looking tired. He was wearing yesterday's clothes and his hair was ruffled.

'I think she called it *The Sleep Token,* or something like that,' he continued, before stretching his arms in the air, a great yawn following. He realised Lucifer was looking at his chest, where faint lipstick marks could be seen. His confident grin returned.

'She's already gone, my brother. Doing the good ol' walk of shame.'

'The walk of shame?' Lucifer asked.

Setsu didn't answer, instead wrapping his arm around his shoulder, encouraging Lucifer to walk with him towards the common room.

'You never came back, and I got bored. So, I became a sacrificial second place.'

Setsu leaned towards Lucifer. 'Don't worry, I'm not mad.

I'm happy to be someone's consolation prize, especially if I get what I want. Besides, I knew the waitress was playin' hard to get.'

'The waitress from the coffee shop?' Lucifer asked.

'Oh yes,' Setsu said, looking up at the ceiling, as though recalling a fond memory. His smile deepened as he glanced back at Lucifer.

'You were her first, man. She was asking after you.'

Lucifer hoped his awkward embarrassment wouldn't show.

'Don't worry about it. Remember, you're my wingman now. I think we can work on the edgelord thing, but maybe that's your shtick. Besides, you can't pull off being our Prince without the edge. Still, at least tie your hair in a messy bun or something. The human girls will love it.'

They entered the large common room, and Setsu guided him towards the long table at the centre.

'Take a seat. I'll scramble us some breakfast,' Setsu said, before releasing Lucifer from his embrace.

He headed to a door alongside some closed metal shutters to his left. The kitchen, Lucifer guessed. He turned to examine one of the strange ruby orbs that sat throughout the common room. He noticed what looked like a tiny flame flickering within them. When he raised a hand to touch one, he felt heat emitting from it.

'What are these things?' he asked.

'They're conduits,' a stranger replied. The man who spoke was much taller than Lucifer and Setsu, with short Hateful hair. He wore glasses, which seemed to focus his gaze within them.

'I wanted to build a heat source that the Elemental Blessing could fuel. Unfortunately, these only solve part of that ambition. While the glow is a nice byproduct of their design, it soon became obvious that they are volatile. If one places too much heat within them, the results are explosive.'

'I'm sorry?' Lucifer asked.

'To put it another way,' the man continued, 'they store heat by absorbing heat and expanding. If one were to exceed the orb's absorption point, the subsequent expansion would cause the orb's crystal-like compound to crack. This means, if expanded further, the cracks would shatter with the aforementioned explosive consequences. The devices become almost weaponised, and downright dangerous if one is not careful while using them.'

He won't stop, will he? Lucifer realised, as the Hateful man continued, enthralled. It was a common characteristic of their kind, but it could be difficult to deal with. Thankfully, a saviour appeared: an older Hateful woman. She reminded him of Hela, especially in her voluptuous body shape. Her face glowed with excitement.

'I've been meaning to catch up with you!' she said, her clear happiness infectious. She rushed towards him, grabbing his hands.

'How are you?!' she asked, while Lucifer glanced towards their touching hands.

'I,' Lucifer tried to begin, but the Hateful woman released his hands and turned to her next victim. Her face somehow glowed even brighter upon seeing the constantly talking Hateful man, who was still muttering about his orbs. To Lucifer's amazement, she rose on her toes to kiss him.

'You left without waking me up, Kyrn,' the woman said. The Hateful man, Kyrn, only smiled back.

'You two need a room, Liesa?' Setsu came out of the

kitchen's swinging door with two plates.

'Hello, Setsu,' Kyrn said. 'I was explaining to our new companion the various intricacies of the heat orbs, before Liesa snapped me from my trance.'

'That's probably a good thing,' Setsu put the plates on the table. 'You probably overloaded him.'

'Perhaps,' Kyrn replied, glancing slyly at Lucifer, who figured it was better not to say anything. He sat down and reached for the plate closest to him.

'I got us sausage, bacon and eggs,' Setsu announced. 'I'd say that's a pretty nutritious meal, though Mika would disagree. She can stick with her shitty protein shakes. After the work we've done, we've earned a good meal.'

'What work is that, Setsu?' Liesa asked, pulling a chair alongside. Kyrn sat next to Lucifer. 'Have you not slept with all the human girls yet?'

There was a deviousness to her expression that made Lucifer shift uncomfortably. Still, if it affected Setsu, he didn't show it. He just shrugged.

'I keep tryin', but there's just too many of 'em…' he said, before he grinned at Lucifer. 'That's why I'm glad we've got Prince over there. He's my new wingman.'

'Prince?' Liesa said, her gaze questioning as she flickered between Lucifer and Setsu.

'Yeah, Prince of Darkness,' Setsu said, as though the title made complete sense. 'He's got the edgy thing goin' on. Brooding. I know they'll be chicks that'll buy that shit. Still, I keep tellin' him to tie up his hair in a bun or somethin', then he'd even rival me for some of the hottest human chicks in the city! If I hadn't already gone through them, of course.'

The confident Hateful man shot a cheeky wink towards

Lucifer, who said nothing in return. The way the members of Silver Wing spoke to each other stunned him.

They're so strange, Lucifer thought, deciding to focus on his food. Looking up after a while, he found Liesa staring at him with Hateful abandon, smiling dreamily. His discomfort rising, Lucifer matched her gaze.

'What?' he asked.

'You're not comfortable around us, huh?' she asked, causing a spike of anxiety to shoot through Lucifer, stunned at how simply she'd reached his core with one sentence. He felt obliged to answer, but he wasn't sure how to. Lucifer sensed Liesa wasn't pursuing an answer, however, as though she understood what was going through his mind.

It's not just that, Liesa. I don't understand how you all act like this. So happy. So positive. It's like you don't even see yourselves as Hateful, just humans with differences.

Lucifer considered that, contrasting what he was seeing with the likes of himself, Megidra and Gabriel. Between them, there was so much anger. So much hatred. Pain had changed them, shaped them into what they were. Lucifer remembered what Setsu had told him of his past.

But is it that simple? Lucifer thought, feeling Korai stirring at the question.

'You know,' Liesa said. 'I think you'd go for a Hateful girl. You don't strike me as a Setsu type.'

'Excuse me?' Setsu said, his mouth half-full of food before swallowing. 'There's only one of me.'

'That we can agree on,' Liesa remarked, propping her elbows on the table, while resting her head on her palms. 'By the way, what do you think about Mika?'

'What?!' Lucifer exclaimed.

Liesa smiled. 'I was just asking. I think you two would look cute together.'

Lucifer was too amazed to speak. It was too early to think of anyone after Ven. He shook his head. 'Look, I don't doubt Mika's told you all what happened to Ven. I don't want to talk about this right now.'

'So you're saying maybe?' Liesa asked.

In return, Lucifer shot her a glare.

'Liesa, give him some space.' It was another unfamiliar voice.

Lucifer was amazed at the sight. *A human?*

Indeed, it was: a thin black woman with raven hair tied into a long ponytail, wearing a plain white T-shirt slick with sweat and a pair of black shorts. There was a small towel draped across her shoulders.

'He's been through a lot,' the woman said, pulling a chair alongside Liesa before smiling at Lucifer.

'I know that,' Liesa retorted. 'I just wanted to gauge his interest in Mika. I think she likes him.'

Lucifer ignored that, reflecting on how the members of Silver Wing acted nothing like any Hateful he had ever seen before. Not only that, but they also had a human living among them.

Then again, Hela allowed Diana to live in the Institute, Lucifer remembered, before turning his gaze towards the black woman, who didn't seem surprised by his response. It was as though she had expected it.

'You're surprised to see me here,' she said, phrasing the words as a statement.

'I think Prince is having trouble with everything here,' Setsu remarked, drawing a raised eyebrow from the human.

'Prince?' she asked.

'Prince of Darkness. That's his nickname,' Setsu elaborated.

The human woman chuckled at that, turning back towards Lucifer.

'My name is Claire,' she said. 'You'll probably see me a lot more if you choose to live here. I am the only human and—'

'Hang on, that's not true,' Setsu interjected. 'Humans come through here all the time.'

'Alright,' Claire conceded. 'I'm the only human who sticks around here longer than a few hours.'

Claire glanced at Setsu then, who seemed to nod in approval.

'I shall accept that,' he said, causing Claire to shake her head.

'Take as long as you need,' she continued, directing her words at Lucifer, 'There's no pressure for you to leave. Besides, it would seem you're settling in here. Setsu evidently likes you, and it would appear that Liesa and Kyrn do, too.'

'And Mika,' Liesa added, causing Lucifer to shoot a glare towards her.

'Yes, Mika too,' Claire said. 'She was talking about you this morning, Lucifer. Though not in the way Liesa hopes.'

The table chuckled at that.

Then Lionas appeared, wearing full Silver Wing attire. He went to Claire, leaning down to share a kiss with her. Lucifer was stunned at this, and Lionas noticed.

'Ah. None of you have told him, have you?' he said. 'Claire is my wife,' he explained, sitting down next to her. 'You probably have her to thank for Silver Wing's existence.'

'What do you mean?' Lucifer asked.

'We're both from the city of Virtue, so we share in your experience of braving the Darklands,' he said. 'Life in Virtue isn't too dissimilar to what I expect you encountered in Exia. Hateful and humanity are enemies there.'

'And I come from a minority group, even if I am human,' Claire added, before reaching for Lionas's hand. 'Though I didn't face persecution anywhere near as bad as Lionas, I know what it feels like to not belong. We met as children and became friends, understanding how it feels to be an outsider.'

Lionas continued: 'Our friendship soon turned into love. But neither our families nor humanity in Virtue would tolerate what we wanted, so we left Virtue and started somewhere else.'

'That led us to Kyrios,' Claire said. 'But we wanted to enact change. Hence, Silver Wing was born. It began with us doing acts of kindness, helping all humans and Hateful that needed it. Since there isn't a DFA presence here, we sort of became the representatives of law and order. However, we wanted to distinguish ourselves from the DFA, so we launched the aim of encouraging Hateful and humanity to mix.'

'In time, this city changed,' Lionas said. 'And once both sides realised the foolishness of our old beliefs, the attitudes between humans and Hateful changed. Now, you've seen the results of our work.'

The leader of Silver Wing fell into silence then, reminiscing. 'We've added quite a few members since then. I wish you'd been here to see it. Perhaps the struggle you feel now wouldn't exist.'

How can you know that? Lucifer wondered, suppressing memories he didn't want to face. While everything Lionas said made sense, there was still one outlier that the leader of Silver Wing hadn't mentioned. It was him Lucifer wanted to understand more about.

'What about Gabriel?' he asked.

Lionas frowned before shaking his head. 'He's a rather unique case,' he began. 'He comes from a place that not even we understand. Hatred has corrupted his soul, poisoning him into believing that everything we've built is a lie, and that the humans and Hateful here are lying to themselves. I don't know what kind of situation he came from. I don't know what twists someone so much that they turn into a monster that hunts down and kills their own kind.'

'Why haven't you stopped him?' Lucifer asked.

'We can't,' Lionas admitted, allowing some frustration to show. 'He possesses a strange power. I don't think it's part of a Blessing, but he can degrade things into dust by raising his hand towards them. It makes fighting him impossible. Plus he has an elaborate way to hunt down and kill his victims.'

'Yeah, I remember,' Lucifer said, shivering as he recalled the horrific sight in the fountain.

'To make matter worse, he seems to be adept with the Transformative and Illusionary Blessings,' Lionas continued. 'Both are excellent for evasion. We also believe he has an accomplice.'

'Please, help him. I don't know what to do,' Lucifer recalled, remembering the woman who he'd seen after Gabriel. Lucifer didn't think it was a good idea to mention her yet. There was something about her, her desperation and loyalty to Gabriel. It reminded Lucifer so much of Ven, which made Gabriel's current state so much more difficult to untangle. It was like encountering a previous version of himself, but one who had gone one step further.

Then again, I killed humans. I killed...

Lucifer recalled Megidra's horrific "Final Truth" then,

shuddering at the realisation of what his monstrosities had been. Lucifer wished to expel those memories from his mind, realising then that his mission made that impossible. How could he find forgiveness if he ran away from his past? Even knowing what they'd done? He knew the path that thinking would take him.

Mika appeared, wearing workout clothes like Claire. She wore a sports bra, revealing defined abdominal muscles. A myriad scars ran across her sweat-soaked body. Lucifer realised she was looking at him strangely. She then turned to Lionas, whose phone was ringing. He answered and then looked concerned at what he was hearing.

'I see. Yes, we'll send someone at once,' he said, before hanging up and addressing the group. 'The Hateful Killer's struck again. Setsu. Mika. Take Lucifer and head to the cathedral. A body has been found.'

17

A New Mission

The snow had intensified over the past few days. It was almost impossible to tell where they were in the thick fog. Snow crunched beneath their feet, making their movements slow and staggered. It exposed just how much weaker Megidra was as he followed Deion, as blistering wind pelted them from every side within the narrow alleyway they found themselves in.

I doubt I'll be able to use my Blessings for long. Not like this, anyway, Megidra thought, looking ahead towards Deion, who almost appeared drunk as he struggled to walk.

They were on a mission to recover enough supplies in Seraphu to last the next few months.

And protect them, no matter what happens. I owe Deion and Johann for what they've done for me, and Marienne.

Memories of her flooded him then, a rare source of peace in his otherwise scattered mind. Megidra pictured her beautiful nakedness, along with the intimacy they shared in the shower. There was nothing sexual in it, but Megidra remembered longing for closeness to her, to another human being. As though sensing this desire in him, she had smiled at him, before reaching forward and taking him in her arms. There was warmth, and Megidra had savoured the contact. It had been wonderful. Too fleeting. Too undeserved.

Megidra exhaled, hearing his own breath quiver in a mixture of pain and fear.

No, I don't deserve it, not after what I did to her. I'm the reason she suffers, and I don't even have the courage to tell her. Besides, I'm Hateful. Marienne's human. Who am I to wish for such things? I took away Hela's lover. What right do I have, wishing for any comfort from another?

Megidra closed his eyes, trying to prevent the thoughts from flooding in. He sensed a familiar stirring that caused him to freeze. An inner snickering followed.

Ryun. What do you want?

Hmm, the voice of the Fallen came through, taking his sweet time in answering. *Entertainment,* he answered, forcing Megidra to remain silent. As though interpreting something in this, Ryun's presence swirled in smug amusement.

You're struggling, aren't you? the Fallen asked. Again, Megidra refused to answer. Ryun didn't seem to care either way.

You should know they're coming. I sense them, he said, ominously.

'Who?' Megidra whispered, seeing only the metal monstrosities he knew were buildings, along with Deion, who was facing him.

'You alright, Megi?' he called out.

Why, those who have waited thousands of years for this, Megidra. The ones who wait silently for humanity's brink, the threshold that you created.

139

'What are you talking about?' Megidra muttered, before a hand landed on his shoulder. Megidra snapped his gaze ahead in fright, resisting the urge to switch his arm into a blade and stab forward. He realised it was just Deion.

'You alright?' he asked, his voice muffled by the large coat covering the bottom half of his face. Megidra nodded. Deion seemed to accept this, turning away and continuing ahead. Megidra allowed the human to gain some space on him before focusing on Ryun.

'What did you mean before?' he asked. 'What's coming, Ryun?'

The Fallen didn't answer, but Megidra could sense his amusement. Despite his frustration, Megidra knew if Ryun didn't talk, there was nothing he could do. He had learned that early on when he discovered the Truthseeker lived within him. Still, he squeezed his fists, before deciding to accept what he had been told.

It doesn't matter. I know what I must do now. Nothing changes that. I will protect them. I will ensure that they get what they need to survive.

Megidra followed Deion for the next twenty minutes as they struggled through the snow. Eventually, Deion turned back towards Megidra and waved, showing that they had reached their meeting point.

'This is the rendezvous!' Deion elaborated, gesturing to a door to his right. He went to open it, but Megidra blocked him.

'Can you trust these guys?' Megidra asked.

Deion nodded immediately. 'They were friends of mine before all this shit happened!' he said. 'We can trust them!'

But how can you trust me? Megidra almost asked, but let

Deion proceed.

They opened the door to the building. It was a storage facility, plundered long ago and almost empty, except for a few wooden crates that stood under a single dangling light. Deion headed for them, and Megidra held out his arms in nervous preparation, checking out the building, unable to escape the feeling that something was wrong.

This feels too much like a set-up. Did he realise who I am?

'You're still not comfortable around us yet, are you?' Deion asked. The large man pulled the zip of his coat down to reveal his mouth. Megidra saw the sadness on his face, which drew guilt from him.

'Yes,' he admitted.

'We put your kind through some shit; I get that,' Deion said, before his expression hardened. 'I don't think any of us said sorry.'

Megidra was unsure what to say. He wished he'd realised the same thing before committing his "Ultimate Hateful Dream". He sighed with regret.

'You don't have to apologise, Deion. You had nothing to do with them.'

'Most of us weren't better. I didn't exactly trust your kind until you saved my son,' Deion said, causing Megidra to smile at the irony.

'I wanted nothing to do with your kind until I saved your son,' he said. 'I guess I've got much to thank Destin for, especially for bringing me to your people. I appreciate everything you've done for me, Deion.'

'Yet you don't know where to put yourself around us,' Deion said. 'Even now, you're acting like you're expecting me to betray you. Half the time you act like you don't even deserve kindness.'

'That's because I don't,' Megidra said. 'You don't know what I've done. How many I've hurt and—'

Megidra stopped himself, realising how close he was to revealing the truth.

Deion's expression become more intent. 'What did you do?' he asked.

'I betrayed my kind, Deion, before hunting them down as part of a poisoned dream. I deluded myself into believing that I'd save them, only to realise that I was the traitor they all believed me to be, and worse.'

Megidra allowed the words to settle, watching as Deion appeared contemplative.

'We've all done things we regret, Megi,' he said, as though that justified everything. 'We all got demons within us. I'll not pry any further. I just want you to know that I appreciate you. Without you, this wouldn't be possible.'

Without me, you wouldn't have to, Megidra almost retorted. *As for demons within us, don't give Ryun any ideas.*

His Fallen chuckled at that.

Then the door slamming open behind them caused Megidra to jump, summoning a weapon he hadn't wielded since Anubi. His right arm shifted into a large curving blade that tore his jacket sleeve. He sensed urges he never wanted to face again.

The desire to slaughter every human around him.

'Megi! Wait!' Deion called out, the panic in his voice snapping Megidra out of his monstrous trance. Megidra looked at his bladed arm, eyes widening. He realised what he was about to do, then looked at the group of humans still standing by the open door, allowing the howling wind and blizzard to enter the building.

What am I doing? Megidra wondered, turning away and relinquishing his Blessing, letting his arm revert to normal.

'I'm sorry. I just panicked,' he said, the shock obvious in his voice.

The other humans came in, albeit hesitantly.

'Thanks for coming,' Deion said, nodding in appreciation to the group. Many of them cast wary glances at Megidra, filling him with shame.

'I know this is a big gamble,' Deion continued. 'But if we succeed, we can last a few more months. However, I doubt we'll be the only ones. The plan is simple, but it will paint a large target on our backs. We need to be quick, especially when we move in a truck. The snow reduces visibility, but that also means it slows us down. Thankfully, we have my friend Megi here to help.'

'What makes him so special?' one human said, suspiciously.

'Megi was a specialist before Anubi happened,' Deion answered. 'Worked for the DFA before turning against them. He didn't agree with their practices, especially when they hunkered down to protect themselves.'

Megidra suppressed a laugh, wondering what Deion would think if he knew he actually had worked for the DFA. Either way, it seemed the rest of the group accepted his cover story, relaxing. Deion seemed almost impressed by his own lie, nodding before turning to one crate, removing its lid and reaching down into it. He pulled out a machine gun.

'Everyone take a weapon if they need one,' he said. 'We set off in five minutes.'

The journey to Seraphu was slow and arduous. Under

normal conditions, the walk would've taken an hour, but the snow tripled that time. They also needed to navigate the narrow streets and alleyways with caution, increasing the time. They encountered no other human factions as they walked. Megidra was thankful for that, noting how little his body had recovered. His breath was laboured and he was bringing up the rear.

Still, it's been too quiet, Megidra noted, his old DFA instincts kicking in as they reached Seraphu with no incident, approaching the tall metal walls that surrounded most of the warehouses.

I hope you know what you're doing, Deion.

Deion led them towards a wall to their left. He then rushed for the customary gap at the centre of each wall alongside the road. As they moved, Deion burst into a sprint, heading to the first warehouse, for one of the smaller side doors to the right.

Once there, he shot the lock off before kicking in the door. The others stormed into the warehouse. There they found boxes of canned food, ready to ship. An excited fervour enveloped the humans as they moved the boxes closer towards the door. Megidra remained standing guard at the open side door, feeling awkward as the humans buzzed among themselves. To distract himself, he turned outside, watching the thick snow continue to fall. As he did so, an obvious question entered his mind.

Why have none of you taken advantage of this? Megidra wondered, before shivering at the prospect of Ethero Fiends flooding the streets, preying on unsuspecting humans who thought them merely legend. Inside, he felt Ryun snicker at the notion.

The truth, Megidra, is waiting to be discovered. It will be fascinating to watch the shattered reality of humanity. I cannot wait to see how you'll respond.

'What do you mean?' Megidra asked aloud without realising, but it seemed none of the humans had heard him. He turned back towards the world outside once more.

Ryun, what did you mean by that? What's coming?

You'll see, soon enough. I do hope you enjoyed your time with that human. It's truly beautiful to witness another truth blossom before your eyes. Again and again, you keep giving me more to relish.

Megidra's mind returned to the shower he and Marienne had shared. He couldn't deny her beauty, and he remembered wanting to be held. Megidra forced himself to confront the simple truth: he wanted to be loved and to feel appreciated.

Of course, it's easy never to consider things that others struggle with, especially if you don't struggle with them yourself. But what if you're born incapable of something other human beings find innate? What if your design is so broken that even if you try to become more human it's never enough? That you're made in such a way that you cannot be fixed.

Megidra raised his hands to his head, feeling heaviness drawing it down. He forced himself to focus on his breathing, trying to regain control.

'What am I doing?' he muttered, before leaning back against the door frame.

'You alright, Megi?' Deion called out.

'Yeah, I'm fine. Just a little dizzy,' Megidra said.

Deion nodded, before continuing to help the rest of the group organise the supplies.

Glad that the human didn't pursue the matter, Megidra

sighed, closing his eyes.

'The more I pursue truth, the more confused I become,' he murmured, before turning to look outside once again.

He found himself staring at a group of figures that had no business being there.

Ah, and here they are, Ryun said from within.

Megidra froze in silent horror; he recognised them at once. They were looming black figures with chalk-white skin and long black hair; the fierce wind caused their hair and their long black jackets to flutter wildly around them. Megidra could see something like a smile on the one closest to him, as two teeth curled over its bottom lip. It held out its hand, stopping the others behind it from advancing.

'*Gaskill shivial goust tririal,*' a voice growled, and it lowered its hand, tilting its head as its smile grew.

We won't hide anymore, Megidra translated, now understanding why everything seemed so quiet in Seraphu. The creatures believed to be myth had revealed themselves. Everything was about to change forever. This was what Ryun had meant.

And I gave them the opportunity they were looking for, he realised.

'Deion, we got company,' Megidra said.

18

The First Relic

Greene and Shallai followed the creature that was supposedly Barbatos. He seemed to blend into the darkness, emitting wisps like black waves. The sorcerer exuded a forbidden power now, something so corrupting that it could cause whatever touched it to wither and die. Greene sensed death all around him.

He realised the corpses were decomposing as Barbatos drew near them, disappearing from existence. The sorcerer's hands dangled like mangled claws by his sides, ready to strike. Beyond him, Greene heard Doomis' massacre, as the haunting shrieks of his brethren continued. Greene lowered his gaze, frustration filling him, knowing what was taking place.

'Whether you like it, you will still continue to follow me, my dear Titanius. You've already begun this journey. You cannot avoid the bloodshed that it has unleashed, and the lives that we will take.'

It was true. He hadn't tried to stop Doomis when he had begun his carnage. He hadn't stopped Newman before he had slaughtered countless humans. And he understood there was nothing he could do to stop Barbatos now.

Why do I end up in these situations? Surrounded by beings that don't hesitate in taking others' lives? Beings who I cannot stop?

Greene scowled and his body tightened.

I despise my weakness.

Though he wanted to protest his thoughts, to deny them and call them foolish, Greene knew he had put himself in this situation. Barbatos had been right. He had chosen this path. The death would be meaningless if he walked away.

And my kind would continue to be slaves. Still, this is wrong. Does it have to be this way? Do others have to die for my kind's freedom?

A white light trailed into an opening, appearing to come from a single source. Barbatos reached it, and took in the sight ahead. He smiled and turned to Greene and Shallai. His blue skin had gone, leaving behind an almost demonic creature of black, with a glowing emerald core and eyes. Only his mouth was white, which made his smile more prominent as he regarded them, extending one arm out to whatever lived beyond the opening.

'I welcome you both to the city of Fiends: Elcaris.'

Greene emerged out of the opening. The city appeared to be held within a similar dome-like expanse, akin to The Place That Doesn't Exist. It was roughly the size of two of Exia's districts, with interconnected buildings that ran alongside a single road, illuminated by white streetlights. It weaved and curved through the city, heading all the way towards a sight that seemed strange to Greene. He narrowed his gaze.

'Is that a—'

'Yes, that is a tree, Greene,' Barbatos confirmed, 'And where you and Shallai will head for next. The relic should be there. Only you can access it.'

'Only I can access it?' Greene said, surprised. 'How?'

'I'm prevented from doing so,' Barbatos said, his expression darkening. 'By he who defeated your ancestors, and allowed the world to become this way.'

Greene didn't wish to pursue that matter any further. He observed the tree in the distance. Its thick trunk and branches appeared to be silver, hung around with golden leaves. It almost looked as though Elcaris had been built around the tree.

'I'm surprised you don't question what I've just said,' Barbatos said.

Greene gave him a stern look, saying nothing.

Barbatos shrugged. 'Suit yourself, but wait until I've joined Doomis before making your move. We should be enough to distract the Fiends, especially while they haven't realised I already have the nobles on my side.'

'The nobles?' Shallai said.

'Don't worry, Shallai,' Barbatos grinned. 'All you need to know is that those who would cause us concern have given me their word that they will not interfere, thus making our task much easier.'

'What makes you think they'll listen to you?' Greene asked, though not understanding what Barbatos was talking about.

'Because they believe in what we're trying to achieve, and him.'

Barbatos gestured towards the open space between themselves and the city, and they finally saw Doomis.

The Fiend, standing alone, was tearing through what looked like an endless horde of his own kind. He swung his giant sword, roaring with rage and fury. He was an unstoppable force. Still, his kind tried, or at least many did, only to meet their deaths.

This shouldn't be happening. Why do so many have to die? Why?

'I knew we should fear him,' Shallai said, stunned at the sight.

'It's magnificent, isn't it?' Barbatos commented, revelling in the sight. 'So much fury. So much rage and hatred. It is a wonderful thing, chaos in its purest form, spitting in the face of destiny. He alone represents the fallacy of those who believe fate is predetermined. He stands as a lone bastion against the society that believed their caste system was correct. Now, they meet their fate at the hands of the monster they created.'

Barbatos turned towards them, his smile fading into a line. 'Anyway, can't let him have all the fun, can we?' he said. 'Wait until I've joined the fighting, then advance towards the city. Keep going until you reach the tree. Unfortunately, that's as much as I can tell you, for I am prevented from interacting with it.'

The sorcerer flickered his emerald eyes towards Greene. 'I understand this isn't what you wanted, Greene. This is the only way to free your kind. All of us, Ethero Fiends, Cybernetics, Animus and even me, have been brought up to believe that we're just mistakes. Imperfect blots in an already broken world. This war is for our freedom, to live unashamed of what we are.'

He paused then, and spoke with resignation. 'Many will not see that. They will only see death and chaos, and they will stand against us. Those who are perishing at our hands are not innocent, and neither are we. But we are the future, while they are relics of the past. They represent the notion of the one who created them, of him who abandoned them long ago. Why should we continue the legacy of a father who discarded us as though we meant nothing to him? We are all born sentient, free of will. This world has done nothing but make others believe they don't deserve free will, making them into slaves. You understand this most of all.'

'Why are you telling me this?' Greene asked, confused.

Barbatos didn't answer at first, looking at the tree in the distance. 'I just have a feeling,' he said eventually. 'Knowing who created it, he would've expected me to lead a Titanius here. It wouldn't surprise me if there were other defences, or at least, ways in which he might communicate with whoever I send to retrieve the piece of the relic. Either way, do not trust whatever is told or shown to you, Greene. You do not understand how valuable you are in this war.'

You mean how valuable my ancestors are, Greene almost corrected the sorcerer, only to decide against it. He turned his gaze towards the tree too.

I am tired of beings telling me what they wish to tell me, as though I were some ignorant child. I am a tool to him, nothing more. Nothing he says will change that.

'Are you ready?' Greene asked Shallai

She nodded. 'Yeah, let's get that relic.'

Barbatos and Doomis proved perfect distractions for the Ethero Fiend horde. They gave Greene and Shallai the opportunity to enter Elcaris by descending into the narrow alleyways that ran through the city.

At least the Fiends have taken to the roofs to get to Doomis and

Barbatos, Greene noted, feeling a surge of dread whenever they heard footsteps clanging on the metal rooftops, accompanying hisses and shrieks. Still, that was nothing compared to the sounds of Doomis' rage and Barbatos' satanic laughter in the distance.

What is he? Greene wondered, concerned.

Shallai picked up on his unease. 'What's wrong?' she asked.

'Apart from running in a literal city of Fiends… not much,' Greene said, hoping his attempt at humour would come across. When Shallai's frown grew, he knew it hadn't worked. Rather than dwell on that, he concentrated on the alleyway they were passing through. There was an opening up ahead, leading to an open street. The steady incline told him they were heading towards the tree. Greene dreaded being out in the open. He had hoped they could hide in alleyways all the way there.

'Shallai, I assume you favor a stealthy approach?' Greene asked. He needed to know if the odds of a fight were getting more likely.

'In this place, absolutely,' Shallai said, 'We're lucky Doomis and Barbatos are so much of a threat that they're occupying the horde.'

'Yes, but we're about to enter an open street, so there's a stronger chance of us being seen.'

'Maybe,' Shallai said, though her tone suggested otherwise.

'What is it?' he asked.

She smiled confidently. 'Let me go ahead,' she said.

Greene pushed himself back against one building so Shallai could squeeze past. As she did so, Greene sensed a strange stirring. It was like a desire for their temporary closeness to last longer, which only increased when Shallai stepped ahead, smiling as she looked back.

'We continue forward,' she said, raising her mechanical arm and switching it into a small cannon. 'I'm the next distraction if need be. You're the one who needs to get the relic, so whether I'm with you doesn't matter.'

'But where will you go?' Greene asked.

'I'll join Barbatos and Doomis. I figure if I get close enough to those two, any Fiends chasing me won't be much of a problem anymore.'

Greene nodded at that. Shallai had proven herself a capable fighter when they first met. Besides, he didn't like how his new instincts gravitated towards wishing to protect her. That seemed wrong, and Greene doubted Shallai would welcome any kind of coddling.

Shallai advanced with Greene in tow, moving stealthily from alleyway to alleyway. Greene noticed little details: the buildings here were covered in a withered moss-like substance. They gave the city a slightly abandoned feeling, alongside what looked like the remains of ancient machinery, long unused. When he considered that, along with the size of the city in relation to how many Ethero Fiends had mobilised, it seemed low. That struck Greene as odd. Surely, if you intended on defending your city, you would use more numbers?

I know nothing about them. I only know bits and pieces from their perspective. Perhaps one day I could return to this place when we stand together in peace and harmony.

'Greene, we're almost—' Shallai began, but then froze, as though something horrific were happening to him.

'What is it?' Greene asked, frightened.

'It's that steam again,' Shallai said.

He could see it – the strange steam emerging from the violet lines over his body. Then he felt power flowing through him, along with something else.

Other presences in his mind.

They were faint, but Greene could sense them. It was like hearing multiple voices, unintelligible, sleepy, but all the same. It reminded Greene of the voices of his kind he had heard during his visions back in Exia, when he had first gazed upon the majesty of his ancestors. As soon as he tried to concentrate on them, the presences faded. With it, the steam rising from his body diminished.

'How far are we from the tree?' he asked.

'Not far, I think,' Shallai said, appearing to scan his body. She turned and continued forward. The alleyways became steeper, leading up stairways where Greene could see strange golden spores floating down all around them, like falling leaves.

As they reached the next opening, Shallai paused and allowed Greene to stand alongside her.

They had arrived at the tree.

It was beautiful. Tranquil and graceful. It was silver with golden leaves, shaped with a thick curving trunk, and the height of a three-story building. All around it, the spores continued to fall.

'It's so peaceful,' he remarked.

Winding silvery roots expanded almost to where they stood. In the tree's centre was a small metal object, cube-like, sitting among the golden leaves.

One of the four pieces of the Titan core.

Greene stepped into the nest of winding roots. Shallai had her head tilted upwards, as though listening to something.

'Can you hear that?' she asked. Greene listened, surprised to find that he couldn't. The sounds of battle, shrieks and hisses were absent. It was like they had left Elcaris. Looking beyond, Greene noticed a faint shimmer to the surrounding buildings, as though they had walked through some kind of portal.

But where did it start? Greene wondered. He thought back to when they first noticed the spores falling, remembering how Barbatos said the tree had been made to protect the relic from his interference.

Is that what this is?

'Greene. I'll wait here,' Shallai said.

'Why?'

'I'm feeling something, like I'm not supposed to be here,' she said, her gaze flickering all around her. 'I think I'm only allowed here because I'm with you.'

'How could you know that?'

'You're telling me you don't hear him?' she asked.

Before Greene could ask what she meant, something gripped around his ankle. The roots were moving, wrapping around his legs.

Ah, finally, an unfamiliar voice said, sounding as though whoever had spoken it encased him.

Greene didn't panic, raising his arms to maintain his balance. 'Are you talking to me?' he asked.

Indeed, the voice answered, sounding ancient and wise. *I have been waiting for you, Descendant.*

'Descendant?' Greene asked, concerned at being called the same name as the monsters Megidra had unleashed. He was being dragged closer towards the tree. Then, more roots rose and wrapped themselves around his body and arms. He could no longer hear Shallai.

No wonder no Fiend protects this tree. It protects itself.

That is one way of putting it, the voice answered.

The tree lifted him then, moving him towards the small metal cube it protected.

'Are you going to give me the relic?' Greene asked.

The tree stopped him mid-air.

Yes, but before I do, there is something I wish to show you, Descendant. I was created along with the others for this reason: to show you the truth kept from you and your kind. The origin.

'The origin of what?' Greene asked, as he was turned towards Elcaris.

But the city behind him was not Elcaris.

The world had turned into a hellscape. Everything had turned blood red. The surrounding city, wherever it was, had become a warped metal monstrosity, a contorted ruin filled with monsters Greene didn't recognize. Most of them resembled black shadows, with burning crimson eyes and jagged teeth.

Are they the original Ethero Fiends? Is this what Ethero used to be?

In the open plain beyond the city, a sun bled in the sky in mourning. Beneath it, an army stood, ready to face the creatures that surrounded him.

'What is this?' Greene asked. Colossal shapes appeared in the distance beyond the army, beneath the bleeding sun.

Oh Divinity. Those are the Titans.

There were four of them. Four great beings of mechanical horror. As the ground trembled beneath their feet, Greene found himself sure of one thing.

They signalled the end of everything.

The monsters of the city rushed forth, meeting the assembled forces in battle. From there, bloodshed ensued, as dust flew and screams and roars meshed with the clashing of blades. Beyond it all, the four Titans continued their march, not caring what faced them.

'Is this the future?' Greene asked with dread.

No, the voice answered. *This is the origin, the past. This is the ultimate battle, that which threatened to ruin everything.*

'It looks like it succeeded,' Greene remarked.

It almost did, the voice agreed. *If not for a single decision.*

Beings of violet and crimson clashed with beings of gold, fighting in the sky while the armies battled below. The Titans marched ever closer. One being of each colour stood alongside each other, emerging between the two armies. The fighting reached an impasse. The two at the centre reached towards each other, fusing into one, creating a single blinding light.

A new being emerged in their wake, one of silver, radiating hope.

'Who is that? The Divinity?'

No, it is a child that possesses the essences of the Divinity and the Ether. It is the hope that must rise again, to finish what it started. It is the progenitor to what Ethero needs if it is to heal.

'And what is that?' Greene asked.

Forgiveness. The one who must come after the fall, who precedes the final stage. However, that can only be possible when the Child of Healing rises from his sorrow, and blesses another with the forgiveness he seeks.

'I don't understand,' Greene said. Inside, he felt something akin to calmness and tranquillity, as though understanding.

It is the same thing you seek, Titanius. You seek freedom for your kind, but freedom is a choice. Forgiveness is freedom from hatred. Soon, you will have a decision to make.

Or else, Ethero will perish.

Greene snapped from his vision, blinking. He was still standing, facing Shallai, who seemed frozen in time. He watched as the roots unwrapped themselves from his ankles, before retreating back into the tree.

The relic was unveiled before him.

19

Changing Landscape

Diana stood on the giant wall that surrounded the Institute. The world had changed drastically. Monsters now roamed the streets of Exia. Creatures like ghoulish versions of the Hateful had emerged from Seraphu, with paler skin and black hair, shrieking and roaring. War erupted within the snow-covered city again in their wake. Diana shivered, watching, as the monsters moved to attack the humans in the camps below, as they rushed to defend themselves.

'Do you know what they are, Diana?' one guard asked alongside her, a young female Hateful who appeared as though she had recently left the Education Section. Her voice wavered.

'No, I don't,' Diana admitted, forcing herself to regard the situation as calmly as her mind would allow. The creatures were using hit-and-run tactics, driving the humans to panic and shoot wayward shots. They struggled to bring the creatures down, and it was difficult to see why.

'What should we do?' another guard asked, a young man.

He was clean-shaven, with hair in a messy man-bun. Unlike the other guard, his expression was focused yet intense, as though he were holding himself from acting. It occurred to Diana that was why he had asked his question.

'I'm not sure, but we cannot stand here, else those creatures will come for us. Pass the message along to be on high alert, and to resort to long-range weapons. It looks like they prefer close-range combat. Don't give them the chance to do that with us.'

'And the humans?' the young Hateful man inquired.

Before Diana could answer, someone landed alongside her. Pauli had arrived. He regarded the chaos beyond, his expression dark.

'What in Divinity is happening here?' he asked.

'That's what we're trying to figure out,' Diana said. 'These creatures emerged from Seraphu then started to attack my kind. I think everyone thought they were more Hateful, but it's obvious they're something else. This has derailed our plans. Maybe Valki was right.'

'Shadows are moving towards us,' Pauli said, pointing ahead. 'They look like black mists.'

Diana looked where he was pointing. She could see them too: five misty black shapes flying towards them.

'Guards! Get ready!' she bellowed.

The surrounding guards readied themselves for combat.

Beneath them, the humans seemed to take this as their cue to prepare themselves, not aiming at the Hateful for a change. The sight gave Diana an idea.

'Pauli. What would you say if I asked a guard to help them?'

'The humans?' Pauli asked, his concern obvious in his tone.

Diana nodded. A pause followed.

'Do you think they'd let us help?' Pauli asked. 'What if they take advantage?'

'Then send me,' the young Hateful guard said. 'If one of us goes, there's less risk, right?' he said. 'Besides, I've been watching those things. Gunfire doesn't seem to work against them, so I want to try something else.'

'Why do you want to go, Eren?' Pauli asked.

'Diana took the chance with us, so I figure we gotta do the same,' Eren said. 'If this works, maybe we can stop them attacking us too.'

Diana smiled at that, appreciating the compliment. His logic made sense, even considering the risk. The mist-like shadows veered toward the human camp, drawing gunfire, which did nothing to thwart them. That made up Diana's mind.

'Go for it,' she said. 'But stick to ranged combat.'

'Don't worry, that's what I intend to do,' Eren said, his expression hardening with focus.

The shadows continued to shift and weave, evading the human attacks with ease.

Eren waited. He remained still, disciplined.

Below, the gunfire stopped as more humans emerged, armed with different Blessings. As though sensing the opportunity to kill them, the shadows surged forth before manifesting physical forms, holding out claws in readiness to strike. They let out their horrific shrieks.

Then Eren moved into action.

The young Hateful man dived off the wall, holding out his arms as a powerful gust of wind emerged from him. He landed alongside the humans, not hesitating for a second before flames erupted from his hands. Eren held them up, directing a burst of fire at the creatures. They shrieked and backed off, before reverting into shadow forms and shifting away, ending the engagement in one swoop.

Eren relinquished his Blessing, before turning to face the humans he had saved. He lowered his hands, before moving to approach them.

'Eren's confident,' Diana observed.

'He's a good kid,' Pauli said. 'Eren was one of my first students when Hela recruited me for the Education Section. He's always had confidence, but was a bit of a hothead. He's calmed down since. His dream was to explore the human world when he grew up.'

'That's why he's doing this,' Diana realised, feeling inspired by him. Eren represented what she was trying to achieve. Diana prayed that this worked. So far, she could see that her kind weren't attacking him, but engaging in a conversation that they couldn't hear from their distance.

Minutes passed before the shadowy forms returned, drawing Eren's attention. Two humans stood alongside him, readying Blessings of their own.

'He's done it,' Pauli said, stunned. The shadows rushed forth again, facing another eruption of fire from Eren. The two humans fought back with smaller walls of fire of their own. Still, the creatures didn't retreat, manifesting physical forms before shrieking.

'Diana,' Pauli said, pointing beyond the engagement below.

More ghostly forms were approaching. Fear arose in her.

'Shit! He's gonna need—' she began, watching as the new shadowy forms, five of them, appeared just behind the others. However, the creatures fighting Eren and the humans turned and roared at the ones that had joined them. They then shifted into their own shadow forms, before retreating.

Eren and the humans relinquished their Blessings before the new group of creatures. Eren said something to the humans before heading to the creatures. These ones appeared to have no interest in attacking.

Does that mean they have different goals? Diana wondered.

Diana followed her instincts to trust in Eren and stepped off the wall to join him. She copied Eren's manoeuvre, landing on the surface alongside him. Seconds later she heard feet land behind her, causing some humans to shift behind Eren.

'Hold your fire!' one human alongside Eren barked, a colossal mass of a man who was bald with light stubble on his chin.

Diana nodded in appreciation before examining the group of creatures that stood a few yards away. It was easy to understand why they were confused as the Hateful, but the differences were obvious. While their chosen attire was similar, their skin was a more literal milk-white with thick black veins, possessing an almost undead quality to it. They had long black hair, and their eyes were giant pools of black. Diana shivered at their icy silence, while Eren gestured towards her in introduction.

'This is our leader, Diana Skagen,' he said, causing the human man to study her, his expression unchanging. Some of the other humans behind him murmured among themselves, no doubt recognising her name.

'Skagen, huh?' the man said, unimpressed. 'So this is where the Darling of Exia's daughter ended up. How did you become their leader? You're human.'

'So are they,' Diana remarked. 'It's time we stopped treating them like they're not.'

'And Anubi?' the large man countered.

'That had nothing to do with them,' she said, maintaining her calm. 'Only one, and we banished him. The Hateful here don't want violence. Surely, it's apparent to you all that we've been acting in self-defence the entire time you've been here? Besides…'

Diana turned back to the creatures that were still standing there, watching them.

'I think we've just proved that if we wanted to hurt you, we could have. It looks like the situation has changed, hasn't it? Am I right in assuming you're not our enemy?'

One creature stepped forward then, smiling in a way Diana found disconcerting.

'*Acruza giamasu daska,*' it growled.

Diana frowned in confusion. 'I'm sorry,' she said. 'I don't understand. Can you understand me?'

'Yes, and it means that we are not your enemy.' The creature stopped before her, glancing at the others. 'Though many of us are.'

'Why?' Diana asked. 'What are you?'

'Beings that are not supposed to exist,' the creature answered, becoming rueful. 'Or, at least not in the eyes of your kind, and the Hateful.'

'What do you mean?' Eren asked.

'War is coming,' the creature said. 'A division has erupted among my kind, between those who desire peace, and those who seek retribution. The Eternal Mother is coming. Soon, so will he.'

Diana nodded, not understanding, but knowing that they were on the verge of a potential precipice. That could wait until later. What mattered was that it appeared the creatures were friendly, and that they had managed to engage with her fellow humans. The latter needed addressing first.

'Do you and your friends have anywhere to stay?' she asked, knowing that everyone would stare at her. Even the creatures behind the leader seemed unsure.

'Not now,' it admitted, before looking down, its smile fading. 'We have made our decision. Our customs will now cast us as traitors.'

'Then, will you stay with us?' Diana asked, before turning towards Pauli. 'Would that be alright with you? After all, you're part of my Council. You have every right to challenge my proposal.'

Pauli nodded in appreciation at that. 'I wish we had more information. Still, we don't have the luxury of time. Granting them asylum might be our best option.'

'I agree,' Eren said, surprising Diana with his forwardness. 'Though I'm not part of your Council, I think they could help us understand what we're facing. The situation has changed.'

'Indeed, it has,' Pauli agreed. 'I guess that decision is a lot easier.'

'Still,' Eren said. 'What about them?' He gestured at the large man and his companions, his insinuation obvious.

'We should bring them with us. If creatures are attacking them, then surely we should offer them the same protection?'

'You're kidding?' the large human man said, scowling. 'You want us to join you, in the Institute?'

'I've been living here for the past few months,' Diana said. 'I've found it a wonderful place to live, perhaps more so than anywhere I lived in Exia. I've never felt more comfortable.'

The large man and his human companions exchanged glances, mystified. 'How do we know the Hateful won't just slaughter us as soon as we get inside?' he asked.

Diana contained her desire to sigh. 'Again, I'm right here. I'm human, and they chose me to become their leader. Do you know why?'

The question was rhetorical, but Diana allowed her fellow humans to consider it.

'Because they realised things need to change between us,' she continued. 'They realised previous generations have blinded us, believing that we're meant to hate each other. Ever since I took the chance to meet them, I've confronted how much we've lied about them. They didn't have to give me a chance. However, they did, allowing me into their world. Now, I understand why things have become this way.'

Diana paused then, letting her points settle.

'We allowed ourselves to become afraid, arrogant, believing what we're told and that our way of thinking is correct. We created divides among ourselves. Like Eren did with you, the Hateful took a chance on me. So please, let them show you what they showed me – that all they want is to be treated like you.'

20

Monster

Megidra cackled as the snow fell around him, leaving gore and corpses in his wake. He felt something like an out-of-body-experience as he looked down at his blood-soaked metal claws. Violet and crimson wisps flowed from his body, as the detachment gave way towards the presence of Ryun within.

And the sense of elation and ecstasy.

'I'm free,' he chuckled, watching as the once snow-filled sky turned scarlet and fires burned all around him.

The sounds of human screams intermixed with the cackling roars of his Descendants.

Megidra froze, his eyes widening in horrified realisation. The bodies, once appearing human, returned to their true Ethero Fiend forms. Megidra staggered forward before collapsing to his knees. He relinquished his Blessing, and wrapped his arms around himself, tears streaming down his cheeks as his body convulsed.

'No! I've done it again. I allowed myself to become that monster.'

'Megi!' he heard a distant voice call to him.

Megidra looked at the bodies once more, sure that even for a few seconds they'd returned to their human forms. He wondered if one of them had been Marienne's husband.

'I'm so sorry.'

'Megi!' Deion's voice finally cut through, and powerful arms reached under him before lifting him to his feet. The people reverted to Ethero Fiends once more, while the snow returned. Inside, Megidra was sure he could sense Ryun's satisfied snicker.

Did you enjoy that, Megidra? the Fallen asked. Megidra didn't speak: the answer was obvious. *Tell me, when you were slaughtering them, did you picture them as humans? Or were they something else?*

The Truthseeker laughed, while Megidra felt hollow. It took a light slap from Deion to break him from his trance.

'Megidra! You there?' the large human asked. Thankfully, none of his human companions were hurt. They regarded him in silence now, their fear palpable.

'I...' he began, before stopping himself. What was there to say? What reason could anyone give for what he had just done? Worse still, how could he deny the flurry of emotions swirling all around him, fuelling the thrill?

Yes, fear me. Whisper my name in terror. The Devil of Anubi.

Megidra shook his head, his mind heavy. He almost collapsed in Deion's arms then, weakness flooding him.

I thought I was getting better. He glanced at his hands. Even if the black blood of Ethero Fiends faded, Megidra wondered if he'd ever be able to wash them clean, especially after all the lives he had taken.

But why now? Why are they here?

'We won't hide anymore...'

Megidra shivered. The situation had changed. Now, Ethero Fiends roamed the streets of Exia. That could only mean one thing. He needed to regather himself. The humans needed to know what they were dealing with.

'Deion,' he said, cringing at how weak he sounded. 'We need to go back inside. The mission has changed. I need you all to leave this place.'

'Alright,' Deion said, nodding, even though he must have had many questions. Megidra moved to step around the large human, only to find an extended arm blocking his path. Fear spiked through Megidra as he looked at Deion.

'Megi, you alright?' he asked, tension obvious in his voice.

Megidra smiled. 'Yes, I'm fine now,' he lied.

Deion didn't appear convinced, but he dropped his arm, turning to walk alongside Megidra as they rejoined their companions.

Within minutes, Megidra was surrounded by them, as they either sat or stood, staring at him with a mixture of fearful silence and icy determination. Megidra acknowledged the awkward air between himself and them. There was no point in delaying or sugar-coating what he needed to say. The mission had changed.

And I caused it, Megidra thought, allowing himself to smile. He looked at the ground, sighing.

'Alright. There's not much time to explain everything. However, the situation has changed; not just here for us, but for Exia and your entire race. The bodies outside belong to a race your kind was never meant to uncover, along with my kind too.'

Megidra paused. He reached towards his hood, pulling it

down to reveal his Hateful hair.

'So, as you've probably figured out by now, I'm Hateful. The corpses outside belong to a race known as Ethero Fiends, who until now were just tales you used to scare your children. You should be terrified of them. They may look and dress somewhat similar to my kind, but we're very different.'

Megidra stopped then, trying to gauge their response. They didn't seem to react at all. Figuring this a delay that often overcame humans as they faced a shift in their reality, he continued.

'The best way to tell an Ethero Fiend is their ghostly white skin, black hair, and almost entirely black eyes. They cannot use the Blessings, but they have unique abilities. They all share a propensity for violence, while also feeding on blood. As for their weapons of choice, they prefer close-range combat. Blades. Claws. Any form of stabbing weapon. Besides this, almost all Fiends can shift into a shadow-like form, making them almost untouchable, while giving them great manoeuvrability. Bullets are almost useless against them. You'll have to use your Blessings. Now, we no longer have any choice. We must abandon this mission and return to the others.'

Megidra fell into silence then. He wasn't sure how the humans would respond. After all, he'd just revealed truths they'd never known, and that they were all in danger. Megidra knew it wouldn't take long for the Ethero Fiends to spread throughout the city, if they hadn't done so already.

A human who appeared in his early twenties stepped forward, blond-haired with a little stubble, holding a rifle with which he gestured towards the supplies behind them. 'We can't go back now. We need these to survive. Our friends and families won't last long without them.'

'I understand that,' Megidra said. 'But everything has changed. The Ethero Fiends swore an oath never to reveal themselves to you, yet they've broken that now. If that's the case, then none of you are safe.'

'I get it,' the young man said. 'But it doesn't matter what we end up facing if we don't have food and water. Without those things, we're done for anyway.'

The rest of the group nodded in agreement.

Megidra understood he was fighting a losing battle with them. Part of their plan involved hijacking a truck to transport the supplies, which meant they'd turn themselves into a beacon that would attract unwanted attention. While Megidra had no qualms when this originally meant other human factions, Ethero Fiends were a different proposition. They were close to The Place That Doesn't Exist; they were already deep within enemy territory. Their options were dwindling.

Unless you use me, Ryun chimed in. Megidra ignored the Fallen, not wishing to allow the Truthseeker to walk in Ethero again. Ryun was amused.

You think you can contain me forever, Megidra? Let's see how long that lasts.

'Hey, Megi, was it?' an unfamiliar voice said; a well-built gruff white man. He had greying short hair and stubble, while his expression appeared a permanent scowl.

'That was a lot like a DFA briefing. I know that because I worked for the DFA myself before defecting. Last time I checked, the only DFA Agent who was Hateful was a guy called Megidra. Then there's the nickname Deion's given you. You and him both had thick moustaches. I assume you're the same person?'

Megidra nodded; there was no point in denying it. Around them, the other humans shifted, sensing something within the conversation taking place.

The gruff white man nodded. 'You went missing,' he said, before appearing to weigh his next words. There was only one logical question that Megidra thought might follow.

Are you the Devil of Anubi?

'Nobody could find you. Word was that the Captain had sent you to the Institute to detain Lucifer Armedeus, the Hateful killing all those Council members. Nobody knew what happened after that.'

The human's gaze fell upon Megidra then, asking the silent question.

Where were you?

But Megidra said nothing, his gaze dropping. He didn't doubt where this conversation was heading. Still, knowing that another DFA Agent was among them brought questions to his mind. Had he been one of the many to call him "Cursed", treating him like the monster he was, the monster known as Lieutenant Newman? Even that name felt distant now. It almost felt as though he could never understand why he became that person.

Yet I can't even run from him now, can I? No matter what I do. No matter what I say. I can't escape Newman. I can't escape from what I've done. Humanity will learn who I am. They will uncover what I've done and will never look at me again. It all points to the one truth I'm trying to run from: that I cannot be forgiven.

'I ran away, like a coward,' Megidra admitted, looking the former DFA agent in the eye. 'My failure was my shame. I knew I couldn't face any of you, knowing that I'd failed.

My dream was to show that our races could coexist. After what happened at the Institute, I understood how much I had deluded myself, so I ran. I didn't know what to do.'

'*I hate everyone and everything,*' he recalled saying. Megidra shivered as he remembered everything that had led to that moment, and what followed.

To his surprise, the former DFA Agent didn't appear to wish to pursue the matter further, looking away as though embarrassed.

'Look, I wasn't one of the ones who treated you like shit, but I'm no better since I did nothing about it. Honestly, I don't think you were wrong back then. Only you were willing to change things for the better.'

The large human stepped forward then, extending his hand. 'I want us to work together,' he said. 'Regardless of how anyone else here feels, we need you. You know what those creatures are. Besides, if Deion trusts you, that's enough for me.'

Despite himself, Megidra reached up and took his hand, shaking it as the surrounding humans moved a little closer.

'I think you know that we ain't leaving here without those supplies,' the former DFA agent said, smiling. 'So let's figure out a plan to get these things back home.'

Megidra nodded, figuring that the human reflected the feelings of the rest of the group.

The large human folded his arms. 'By the way, the name's John. John Milton.'

'Megidra,' Megidra replied, amazed at what he was about to do, especially in front of a group of humans: revealing his full Hateful name. 'Megidra Dionysus.'

21

Broken Cogs

Lucifer followed Mika and Setsu as they raced through the air, heading towards the grand cathedral of Kyrios. The building looked like a barbaric metal altar, an amalgamation of metal spikes built on top of each other, rising as high as the Institute's towers. In its centre was a black clock with white hands, forever locked on the time of 12:30. It was one aspect of Kyrios that hadn't changed since he had left and returned, but Lucifer knew that was nothing compared to the rest of the city.

I barely recognise this place anymore.

He took in the shifting ground and buildings beneath them. He caught the glances of many humans as they passed. Some of them seemed to smile.

But how? Change doesn't occur that quickly. How has Silver Wing done this, flipping this entire city on its head?

No answers came to him. What Lionas and Silver Wing had achieved should not have been possible. Still, one problem remained.

Gabriel.

Lucifer tried to consider his perspective, recalling the brief conversation they had shared alongside the fountain. Was it all a lie? Were humanity, Silver Wing and Hateful deluding themselves? Were they the Cursed beings Gabriel claimed they were? Lucifer remembered feeling such thoughts himself, and where they had led him. Now, he wasn't so sure. Were things so absolute?

With these uneasy thoughts, Lucifer landed before the cathedral alongside Mika and Setsu. Metallic statues flanked the walkway that led towards the doors, one side depicting what Lucifer guessed were the Divinity's Angels. The other side depicted evil versions of themselves. Though Lucifer doubted the sculptor knew of the Fallen, it made him wonder, which led to a familiar stirring.

Korai.

Lucifer held himself, becoming contemplative as he allowed the Fallen to emerge.

There are things you aren't telling me. You know who lives within Gabriel, and you understand who the other is within me. Soon, we need to talk about that. When that happens, I want answers.

Korai seemed to consider that, his presence becoming thoughtful. At one point, Lucifer knew this would've frustrated him, but he kept himself collected and calm. The Fallen filled him with amusement.

You have changed, Lucifer, he said. *Matured.*

Lucifer shook his head at that, watching as Setsu and Mika moved towards the cathedral's metal doors.

No, I haven't. All I feel is more confusion, Korai. There are humans that accept us now. Hateful who appreciate and love themselves despite their flaws. I wonder – was this what you

175

wanted me to see, Ven?

'Hey, Prince!' Setsu called. 'See any hot chicks up there?'

Lucifer barely repressed the smile, coughing into his hand.

'Made you laugh. I'm taking that victory,' Setsu said, before turning towards the doors and knocking on them with three hard strikes.

The doors swung open, revealing a priest and a priestess, looking concerned.

'We're glad you're here,' the priest said, an older balding man. 'The body is still... suspended from the ceiling. We haven't touched it.'

'Didn't realise it was that kind of party,' Setsu muttered, shrugging before motioning for the two priests to lead them.

Mika hung back with Lucifer. Her gaze was still difficult to read.

'Is something wrong?' he asked.

Mika allowed her gaze to shift, becoming awkward. 'Before, you were looking at my scars,' she said.

It surprised Lucifer that she brought that up now. 'Sorry. They're none of my business,' he said, hoping to placate her.

Lucifer followed Setsu and the humans into the cathedral, Mika's footsteps trailing behind him.

The cathedral expanded into a giant hall, leading to a section containing rows of benches. They led towards an altar, although there was no procession taking place.

All around them were thousands of flickering candles, releasing a soft incense that provided warmth and a pleasant smell.

'It just fell out of nowhere,' the priestess said to Setsu. 'We were in the middle of a service, and–'

She froze, as though recalling something horrible. Setsu

didn't urge her to continue, displaying another example of his strange ability to understand people. Lucifer admired it. Eventually, the priestess shook her head, gesturing towards the ceiling. There they saw it.

A body hanging on a chain, swaying back and forth.

'Mika,' Setsu said.

Mika moved ahead of Lucifer, positioning herself beneath the body. Setsu tapped into his Transformative Blessing, changing his right arm into a strange projectile-firing weapon with a wide barrel, raising it towards the body. The weapon launched a bladed disc that spun quickly in the air, cutting through the chain with ease. The body dropped into Mika's arms as she caught it with her Physical Blessing, before lowering it with care. Setsu relinquished his Blessing, and the disc vanished. He approached Mika.

'One of us?' he asked. Mika nodded, before lying the body down flat on the ground, her face cringing.

'Oh, damn,' Setsu murmured, tearing his gaze away, appearing to blink as though wishing he could erase what he had seen from his mind. He looked at Lucifer.

'I'm warning you, Prince. This is a bad one. He's seen better days.'

And you have no idea what I've done, Lucifer answered in his mind, glad that he had kept the words there. He moved to inspect the body. Rather than look away in disgust, his expression darkened.

'How is that not messing with you?' Setsu remarked, as though amazed. 'I get you're the edgelord type, but jeez.'

Lucifer said nothing, studying the corpse. The face was skinned, revealing muscle and tendons. His clothes were a parody of Silver Wing's, but wrapped in barbed wire, all the way from the lower torso to the neck. The head was still attached, and there was a small folded note tucked within the biting wire. Lucifer leaned forward and took the note.

"How can you fly, Silver Wing, when your mask keeps weighing you down?"

'I don't get it,' Setsu said, while Mika looked up with a questioning glance. Lucifer handed the note to Setsu, who turned it in his hands, holding it out so Mika could read it. Once she did, she nodded, offering no comment.

Setsu looked over to Lucifer. 'Any ideas?'

'This is my first day doing this. Why would I?' Lucifer asked.

Setsu shrugged. 'You got me there, Prince,' he said, before folding the paper back up and sticking it in his pocket. He straightened himself while looking around the cathedral.

'Don't allow humans to see this. It will traumatise them. They won't need any more details.'

'Should I wrap it?' Mika asked.

'I'd say he's already wrapped enough,' Setsu commented, drawing a frown from Mika.

'That's not funny,' she said.

Setsu shrugged again. 'Just tryin' to make light of a fucked-up situation,' he said.

There were multiple floors throughout the cathedral, each possessing a giant rectangular gap at the centre, allowing one to see all the way towards the top.

'You two know he's here, right?' he said.

Lucifer felt haunted. It hadn't occurred to him before, but he was sure Setsu was right.

'He might've escaped while the humans waited for us,' Mika countered.

Setsu shook his head. 'Na, he's here. This is a deliberate message. I'd guess he's on one of the upper floors.'

'Should we call for backup?' Mika asked.

Again, Setsu shook his head, serious. 'No, that'll take too long and attract too much attention. I don't want the humans to panic. One of us can stay here while the others search the cathedral. If we find nothing, we'll meet back here and call for backup then. By that point, I'll accept he's gone.'

Mika rose to her feet, reaching into her jacket to reveal what looked like a foil blanket. 'Who do you want to stay?' she asked.

'Prince,' Setsu answered. 'We've faced the Hateful Killer a few times, plus he can protect the humans we'll be sending down as we search.'

Mika nodded in agreement, before handing the blanket to Lucifer. As he unfolded it, Setsu smiled. 'Alright, let's do it. If anyone runs into him, conjure something from the Elemental Blessing. The other two will join you once you do. No one is to engage with Gabriel alone. We fight him together. Understood?'

'Yes,' said Lucifer.

'Got it,' Mika said, before a strange twist on her face almost appeared like a smile.

Setsu frowned. 'What?' he asked.

'Oh, it's nothing,' Mika said. 'It's just that you sound a lot like Lionas when you put your leader head on. It's weird not hearing a comment about beautiful women or some kind of joke every three seconds.'

'Now, now. You're just being mean, Mika,' Setsu said. 'I'm still the same me.'

'Unfortunately,' Mika remarked, before walking away.

'She wouldn't joke like that before you joined us,' Setsu commented to Lucifer.

Lucifer frowned, not liking where he was going. However, Setsu didn't add anything, just giving Lucifer a knowing look before following Mika.

Lucifer was left alone. He began by unfolding the strange material Mika had given him before wrapping the body with it. Remorse and guilt filled him, imagining the pain the victim must have endured before Gabriel killed them.

Why did he do it? What makes someone want to do this?

Lucifer shook his head, not wishing to know the answers. Footsteps pattered all around him, along with concerned whispers that reflected the fear and confusion he had sown by this one action. Lucifer remembered a time he would have revelled in such fear, especially from humans, and then he felt shame and regret.

This fear. The dread. I wanted them to feel it all, along with my pain. How selfish I was. Only concerned with my own feelings and emotions. Is that what he sees? Is he just another soul who's so self-obsessed that they cannot see beyond themselves, like me and Megidra?

'Why do we do it?' Lucifer whispered, confident that none of the nearby humans could hear. 'What do we want? Love? Happiness? Forgiveness? Why do we do this? To what end?'

'I would've thought the answer was obvious, Lucifer,' a familiar voice said from behind him, freezing Lucifer to the spot.

Gabriel.

He wore a thick black cloak that covered everything but his face and he was looking down at the victim he had created. The Hateful Killer seemed impassive as he lowered himself to the same level.

'What did you think of it, my latest piece?'

Lucifer looked at the body. He had tapped into his Transformative Blessing, switching his left hand into a bladed claw and his right into a giant revolver, which he aimed at Gabriel's face.

'Why?' he asked. 'What did he do to deserve this?'

Gabriel's expression remained unchanged. After a couple of seconds, he closed his eyes, taking in a breath as he shook his head. 'You already understand why, Lucifer. I told you: we're broken by design, and then expected to function in this already fractured world. We deserve punishment. What else could deter the Hateful condition?'

'But we don't have to think that way,' Lucifer countered. 'Silver Wing—'

'Created the mask for both humanity and Hateful to live by. I know. I told you that too, Lucifer. However, such masks only paper over the cracks. We are broken cogs within the machine, a machine called human society. Anyone not made for its design, or born a broken cog, can never fit into the machine, Lucifer. It makes all the perfect cogs see which ones are broken. And what happens when the perfect cogs see the broken ones?' Gabriel asked.

'I…don't know,' Lucifer admitted, relinquishing his Blessings. 'I don't understand what you're trying to tell me.'

Gabriel smiled, as though expecting that answer. 'Let me show you,' he said. Gabriel reached towards the folds at the front of his cloak, pulling them apart to reveal a bare torso covered in scars, even more than Mika had; a mixture of burns and jagged scar tissue. Lucifer's eyes widened, unable to comprehend the pain he must have endured.

'Where does hated come from? Rejection, separation, isolation. The broken cogs are told to fix themselves, do whatever they can to fit in, or at least act in ways according to the machine that guides them. Never do they question the machine itself. Never do they question the notions that govern their minds. If they did, they'd realise a horrific truth, Lucifer. It's such a truth that beings like us cannot run away from.'

Gabriel's smile became sad then, as though recalling the pain it had taken to come to his conclusion. 'Everything we've been told is merely convenient to those who wish to view the world in a certain way. Problem is, we don't align with that vision, with the instructions that guide the machine. We are faulty at birth, so we copy Silver Wing, wearing masks that make us appear like the other cogs. However, a broken cog, even if masked, still harbours the same scars you see on my body. The mask is the lie, and the machine forces us to act this way. We lie to ourselves, and the lie is convenient to those who live in the machine, both perfect and broken cogs alike. Soon, I will expose that lie, Lucifer. I will break those who believe compliance is freedom from our Curse.'

Gabriel rose to his feet. He looked down at Lucifer, who noticed the faint dashes of violet and crimson emanating from his body, causing Korai to stir within.

'Hatred comes from those born into a world that was never meant for them. It grows from those Cursed with our affliction, the affliction that brings pain and suffering to everyone around us. Only two solutions remain: find a piece of the machine that we can work in isolation, or, destroy the virus that the machine created. The former has failed in Exia, has it not? Is my solution not the only one?'

No, there's Silver Wing's way, Lucifer almost said, glad that he didn't. He rose too. Along with Korai, Lucifer felt another sensation, emerging from the other being within. It reminded him of what Gabriel was after, the same thing he was pursuing.

A solution to the Hateful problem.

Lucifer could feel the distinct realities of what his kind endured: the two extremes of Gabriel and Silver Wing. One side sought peace, the other ruin. It wasn't so simple to just discount the latter. Just because one side could be viewed as a collective "good" for the majority, one had to assess the cost the minority had to pay.

But I understand where that leads. What you end up telling yourself. And, who you ignore in focusing on your own pain.

'Gabriel, I know the path you're walking. I know where it leads. You think it can heal your pain by removing what you perceive causes our problem. However, the cause is inside us. It is within our very beings. Harming and killing the others won't remove our problems. It just inflicts the same pain and hurt onto others.'

Lucifer paused. 'That is where we differ, Gabriel. I've seen this path all the way to the end. I know what happens. Believe me, this isn't what you want. All you're doing is prolonging your own pain, believing that everyone around you is to blame. You ignore the words of those who care about you. You're blind to what's before your eyes.'

Lucifer recalled the moment he rested on his knees, holding Vennifer in his arms. Pain flooded his body, forcing him to close his eyes.

'There has to be another way, Gabriel. This cycle has to end. We need to stop what has led us to this point, or we're fated to continue to repeat the same mistakes.'

'I guess you're referring to forgiveness?' Gabriel asked.

Lucifer opened his eyes. He could see it then, the hatred concealed within his fellow Hateful's smile, while the dashes of violet and crimson intensified around him. Lucifer could hear the nervous chatter of the humans behind him, no doubt seeing what he was seeing. Inside, Korai's presence rose, as though interpreting what was about to happen.

Lucifer, call forth the Sword of Greyr, he said. Lucifer didn't, instead narrowing his gaze. Gabriel seemed to regain control over what was happening, exhaling to relinquish the power that had been emerging from within him. He forced himself to smile.

'It would seem that my Fallen wants to play,' he said. 'But not yet. You claim you know where my path leads, that there's a way we can find forgiveness without wearing the mask. Why don't we test that? Let's see if these humans can forgive us once we slaughter an entire building full of them.'

Gabriel turned, throwing his arms out by his side so that he could slip his cloak off his body. Lucifer could see the full extent of his injuries and scars. Along with his dishevelled hair, the look was almost horrifying to witness. As though sensing this reaction from Lucifer, Gabriel's smile grew.

'Don't worry, I still smile to hide my hate, Lucifer. These humans will understand what that means. Please, stop me if you can. After I break you and everything you care about, let's see if you can forgive me then? Show me if even a creature like me can find forgiveness. Vorus...'

The Fallen aura returned then, as Gabriel's muscles strained with effort. Lucifer held out his right hand, deciding to go with Korai's earlier suggestion. He summoned the weapon he hadn't handled since Exia, manifesting the sword he had won from killing Hannibal Desmarti, with its lightly glowing black blade and golden inscriptions.

Tapping into his Physical Blessing, Lucifer grew and enhanced his muscles, kicking off his feet to launch himself at Gabriel. Lucifer covered the ground between them in less than a second, swinging a heavy fist at Gabriel's gut. The blow sent his fellow Hateful flying, sending him hurling through the air before he crashed into a wall at the opposite side of the church. Humans screamed then, and Lucifer remained standing with his blade in one hand, watching Gabriel laugh while struggling to his feet.

'Now that was unnecessary,' he remarked, spitting out blood and grinning as he pushed himself off the wall. 'You didn't even let me get started.'

'Wish I could feel sorry for you,' said Setsu, landing to Lucifer's left, with Mika landing a few seconds later to his right. 'How about we make it up to you? How does a good beating sound?'

Gabriel chuckled, staggering a few steps before recollecting himself. 'You read my mind,' he said.

'Made him laugh, too. Though I'm not proud. There's only enough room for one Prince. Nice sword, by the way.'

'Setsu,' Mika said, trying to make him focus.

Setsu shrugged. 'I was just sayin',' he said, going towards Gabriel. 'Let's get 'em. Then perhaps I could borrow that cool sword to pull some more human chicks afterwards.'

Lucifer shook his head despite his smile, doubting that the ensuing battle was going to be that easy.

22

Hidden Power

The cathedral shook as Gabriel unleashed his power. He channelled his Fallen as his aura exploded. Lucifer thought that he might have unleashed his Demon. He hadn't, but waves of violet and crimson emitted from Gabriel's body now.

The power was strong and sudden that it forced Setsu and Mika to step back.

Lucifer tapped into his Physical Blessing to enhance his muscles, opting for density and strength rather than size, and launched himself at Gabriel. He charged forth with the Sword of Greyr, bringing it down with a heavy two-handed slash that would force Gabriel to respond.

Gabriel stepped to his left, avoiding the blow. Lucifer struck the floor instead, causing a strange chime to sound as the sword glowed. Pressing on with the attack, Lucifer strode forward, this time slashing the Sword of Greyr sideways. Again, Gabriel simply stepped aside, then lowered himself into a crouch, extending one hand towards Lucifer.

Lucifer! Korai bellowed within, and Lucifer looked down,

seeing a strange violet and crimson orb appear in Gabriel's palm, inches away from making contact.

'Game over,' Gabriel remarked, but something struck him hard from the side, sending him flying back towards the wall.

Humans screamed as they scrambled to get away, and Lucifer was surprised to see Mika standing with him, bulkier than before. She'd used her Physical Blessing to strike Gabriel.

'You alright?' Mika asked.

Lucifer nodded, lowering his sword. 'Thanks,' he said

Mika nodded, smiling in a way that Lucifer found attractive. Her smile faded as she focused on the battle. Gabriel was stumbling off the wall. Although in obvious pain, he still appeared amused.

'I wasn't intending on killing him, you know. I just wanted to see what he'd do.'

He means he wanted to know if I'd use you, Korai, Lucifer deduced. His Fallen signalled his agreement.

If it comes to it, will you emerge? Lucifer asked. Korai seemed uncertain.

Lucifer frowned. *What is it? Why are you so apprehensive now? You were never like this in Exia.*

I'm just surprised you'd be willing to use me, Lucifer. Especially after what happened last time.

Then what is the point of forgiveness? Lucifer argued back, his agitation growing. *Nothing changes unless I seek to understand it. I may despise you for encouraging my poisonous dream, filling my head with delusions, telling me everything I wanted to hear. However, I won't repeat those mistakes. I won't let the same hatred that drives Gabriel fill my heart again!*

As though responding to those thoughts, the Sword of

Greyr glowed brighter, especially the strange runes etched across the flat of the blade.

Hmm. I feel something from that blade, and from you, Korai said.

'Lucifer,' Mika said. 'Your hair: it's changing.'

'What do you mean?' Lucifer asked, his face twisting in confusion. Inside, he could feel Korai's presence growing, alongside another that felt familiar. It reminded him of the being of silver he'd seen in the Darklands, standing as a beacon of hope in this broken world, radiating peace and tranquillity.

Forgiveness.

Lucifer. I can feel him, my–

The power faded, along with the other presence. Still, the Sword of Greyr glowed, filling Lucifer with a strange power. Inside, Korai seemed to question it, finding it a strange phenomenon that shouldn't be occurring.

I never experienced that when I used it. It's as though the sword is awakening, responding to you.

So what does that mean? Lucifer asked, watching as Gabriel remained enveloped by violet and crimson wisps. It was as though he had tapped into a unique form, a precursor to reaching his Fallen state, while still barely keeping control. Gabriel smiled before drawing his arms back, his muscles contorting, filling with more power. As he did this, his short hair rose, as though he were attempting the full transformation, his body convulsing.

'I said I would use your strength, but that doesn't mean you get to take control of me,' Gabriel growled, straining while veins appeared over his body. Lucifer knew what was happening, even though Mika and Setsu wouldn't understand it.

Gabriel was fighting against his own Fallen.

Lucifer tapped into his Transformative Blessing, summoning his favourite giant revolver in his right hand. He raised it towards Gabriel, taking aim. He fired, the blasts echoing throughout the cathedral, with some rounds striking the wall like a hammer.

Gabriel was still standing, one hand raised towards them, unharmed.

'Thanks, Lucifer,' he muttered, his voice distorted, as though the two entities were still fighting for control. 'You shut him up long enough for me to get control. Was that intentional? Or is it because you understand what's happening and tried to stop Vorus?'

Lucifer didn't speak. Instead, he lowered his revolver, as Setsu joined him and Mika. He looked confused. 'What is he talking about? What is that power he's using?'

Lucifer wanted to keep Korai a secret from them, but he knew what Gabriel was doing would be difficult to explain away. Sometimes, the truth couldn't be avoided.

'I'll tell you later,' he said, resigned. 'Just stop him, and if he calls out the name Vorus, run. I'll deal with him.'

'Why?' Mika asked, confused. 'We'll be better if we work together.'

'True, but if he reaches for that power you can't do anything to stop him. I'm surprised he hasn't used it against you yet.'

Lucifer approached Gabriel. 'If you possess a Fallen, why won't you use him? You said it before. Your mission was to destroy the machine, along with all those wearing masks. With him, you could, so why haven't you used your Fallen already? No one could stop you, and it would do everything within minutes, so why prolong it? Why wait?'

Gabriel didn't answer, his expression darkening. Lucifer relinquished his Transformative Blessing, but kept the Sword of Greyr by his side.

'You could level this place in seconds,' he continued. 'Yet, you're delaying. I see it now. You want us to stop you, don't you? You want me to find forgiveness.'

A flicker of anger crossed Gabriel's face, as though that word held a very different meaning for him. Wisps of violet and crimson rose off his body, making Lucifer hesitate. He sensed an imminent attack, or at least the emergence of a Fallen.

'You presume to understand me, Lucifer,' Gabriel said. 'Just like you did before. What do you think this is? Me pretending to kill my kind, before pulling away the curtain and act like it was all one big joke? No, now you overstep your mark. Forgiveness doesn't exist for beings like us. Our state is one of constant punishment and nothing more. We are examples of what awaits those who are never good enough for the Divinity, or the Eternal Mother.'

'Eternal Mother?' Lucifer asked, frowning. This grabbed Korai's attention from within, his presence flooding Lucifer's body. The term clearly meant something to the Fallen. Lucifer felt a strange sense of recollection, though he wasn't sure why.

His Fallen is whispering in his ear, Lucifer. Those words, they are both him and Vorus talking. Gabriel's slipping.

What did he mean by that? Who's the Eternal Mother?

The Fallen fell silent, as though deliberating.

You said to them you'd explain about me and the others later. Allow me the same privilege in this matter.

Lucifer nodded, turning while raising his sword. Gabriel tilted his head forward, opening his arms and smiling.

'You think he has control of me? No. I will always hold dominion over my body, Lucifer. Here, let me show you.'

Slits opened across Gabriel's upper body and tiny metal blades emerged, along with strange crimson strands that looked like a cross between tendrils and whips. Two monstrous wings sprang from his back, something between a bird and a dragon, half scaled and half feathered. Blood seeped from every open wound as this transformation took place.

Lucifer realised what he was doing. Gabriel was tapping into multiple Blessings at once, while in his Hateful form.

He'll kill himself, Lucifer thought, watching as Gabriel's hideous new form grew jagged teeth, growling as it unleashed shards of ice from its fingertips.

'Yet, I am still in control,' the monster that Gabriel had become seethed, his voice almost unrecognisable.

'Prince!' Setsu called out. The Hateful man flew past Lucifer, launching a hard Physically enhanced kick at Gabriel's face. But he kicked at nothing, as the attack flowed straight through Gabriel.

'Thought I would repeat the same mistake?' Gabriel said, smiling as his body shimmered out of existence.

Lucifer turned back in panic; they'd fallen prey to his Illusionary Blessing. Gabriel's real body appeared behind Setsu a second later, still in the same monstrous form. He raised one arm towards Setsu, shooting tendrils that wrapped around his body.

Setsu screamed.

Lucifer and Mika threw themselves into the fray, the former leading with his glowing sword, the latter with a Physically enhanced fist. With her boosted legs, Mika reached Gabriel first, landing a hard fist into his face. The blow launched Gabriel across the main hall of the cathedral, crashing against multiple columns as he did so. Lucifer swung his blade at the tendrils that grasped Setsu, slicing through them to free him.

'You alright?' Lucifer asked once he was released.

Setsu chuckled. 'Yeah, just wish you were a beautiful woman crouched over me with such concern,' he said. Lucifer smiled, shaking his head. But then Setsu's face darkened, and he struggled to turn himself onto his side.

'Don't get caught by him. Whatever Blessing he's tapping into, it burns like some kind of acid. I've encountered nothing so painful in my life.'

'Can you move?'

'Yeah, I should be alright,' Setsu said.

A plan came to Lucifer. 'Get the humans out of here. Mika and I will deal with Gabriel. Get Lionas and the others.'

Setsu considered that, before nodding. 'That's not a bad idea, Prince. You think you two can handle him?'

Lucifer looked over at the fighting between Mika and Gabriel. Mika was still utilising her Physical Blessing, but using speed over power, darting between columns, and walls to land blows against Gabriel. She seemed not to be causing significant damage, but would probably serve as a distraction.

'We should be alright. Mika looks like a good fighter. If it comes to it, I'll take care of him. I have a last resort.'

Lucifer felt Korai's amusement, but ignored it.

Setsu struggled to his feet. 'Alright, I'll get the humans out of here. Just keep that monster away from us.'

Lucifer nodded, turning back to the fight. He relinquished

the Sword of Greyr, tapping into his Transformative Blessing to summon his large revolver. Timing it so Mika landed her last blow before darting out of the way, Lucifer fired. The bullets struck Gabriel's arm, making him screech in pain as he reeled back. Lucifer fired multiple shots again, forcing Gabriel to defend himself. The goal wasn't to harm Gabriel. Instead, he was counting on Mika to take advantage.

'Lucifer!' she called out, landing before Lucifer before relinquishing her Physical Blessing in favour of the Elemental. Mika's hands and upper arms glowed with a radiant light and, as Gabriel turned to engage her, she unleashed two golden beams at him. Gabriel leapt aside with unnatural speed, landing to Mika's right. Knowing what was coming, Lucifer trapped further into his Transformative Blessing, changing his hands into bladed claws, before throwing himself in Mika's direction.

He clashed with the diving form of Gabriel.

They tumbled on the ground, snarling as they fought for dominance. Lucifer recognised Gabriel had the momentum, as the monstrous Hateful rose, right arm pulled back, ready to land a killing blow. Lucifer brought his knees to his chest and kicked Gabriel hard in his stomach. He gasped and stumbled as Lucifer got to his feet.

Mika came in next, landing a hard Physically enhanced kick in Gabriel's face. Unable to defend himself, Gabriel was thrown back onto the wall Mika had hit him against before. His nose exploded with blood.

'Now!' Lucifer bellowed. He dashed towards Gabriel, while Mika maintained her own Blessing. She reached him first, pinning Gabriel with hard blows to his body and face. Lucifer arrived seconds later, jumping into the air with his claw raised. This blow Gabriel moved to deflect by raising both his arms, which was exactly what Lucifer wanted.

'Mika!'

Mika threw herself at Gabriel again, launching into a spin as she kicked his rib cage. She struck true, making Gabriel gasp, his eyes widening as he spat out blood and spittle. Gabriel fell to his knees, shocked, his monstrous form fading. He coughed violently.

'Now I know why you never fought us together,' Mika remarked, as though unimpressed, relinquishing her Blessing. 'You're strong, but you cannot fight more of us, especially if we're suited to combat.'

'To be fair,' Lucifer said, smiling as he relinquished his own Blessing, 'I don't think many can fight like you.'

Mika seemed embarrassed, snapping her gaze away while folding her arms. 'Well, I wouldn't have done it without you.'

'Thanks,' Lucifer said, nodding in appreciation before moving over to Gabriel.

'It's over, Gabriel,' he said. 'We're bringing you in.'

Gabriel seemed to collapse in on himself, choking on the ground.

Lucifer contemplated whether to step in and help him. Then he realised Gabriel wasn't choking. He was laughing.

Lucifer and Mika frowned, confused to why Gabriel would laugh in this situation. Surely he was defeated?

'I expected better,' he said. 'You're nothing. Not even close. Did you really think I'd leave it all here? Against you two? In this place? Oh, no. I've only just begun. Silver Wing and humanity, your mask will shatter. I will show this city the lie for what it is. Humanity. Hateful. We're all cursed beings, and I will free us from our curse. The only salvation from life is death.'

'That's tough talk from a guy barely breathing on the ground,' Mika remarked, unimpressed.

Gabriel chuckled. 'That's a tough-sounding statement from a fool who's been spending the last five minutes fighting an Illusionary Blessing.'

'What?' Lucifer said, looking at Mika in alarm.

There was a loud finger click, and the crumpled form of Gabriel by their feet vanished in a haze of violet and crimson. Lucifer turned in the click's direction. There, leaning against one of the many metal columns throughout the cathedral, was Gabriel. His torso was still bare and he seemed almost bored, with his arms folded.

'Had your fun?' he asked, making Lucifer shiver. Gabriel then shoved off the column, unfolding his arms.

'Did you not think it was too easy? That I was acting differently from normal? Since when do I talk like I did on the floor? Is it that easy to fool you?'

Gabriel shook his head before turning to walk away. Lucifer tilted his head in confusion before Mika stepped ahead, her anger obvious.

'You think we're just going to let you walk away?'

'I doubt either of you could stop me,' Gabriel said, not bothering to look back. Mika gritted her teeth, tapping into her Physical Blessing once again. Lucifer realised what was about to happen.

'Mika! No!' he called out, but it was too late. Mika had already launched herself at Gabriel, her right leg back, ready to swing another hard blow. The authentic version of Gabriel smiled, turning his head.

'I was hoping you would do that,' he remarked. He then

faded out of existence again, before reappearing in mid-air, just before Mika. Gabriel seized Mika by her neck, then slammed her hard into the ground.

'Mika!' Lucifer called out, half stunned by this turn of events.

Gabriel kept his grip on Mika's neck as he leaned over her, his smile almost smug. 'I'll give you some credit. You're a decent fighter, just not that good. Your problem is that only one of you can defeat me.'

He looked up to Lucifer then, as faint stirrings of violet and crimson emerged around him.

'You know, you were right before, Lucifer. I have been delaying my mission. Do you want to know why? It's because I promised Krista that I wouldn't.'

Krista? Lucifer wondered, frowning. He then remembered the woman who emerged after he first met Gabriel.

"Please, help him. I don't know what to do."

'You mean the woman that was with you?' Lucifer asked.

Gabriel's smile faded, along with the violet and crimson wisps. 'So you saw her. Or, more accurately, she saw you. That's interesting,' he said, rising to his feet, releasing Mika's neck. Her body went limp. 'She's still trying to find help. I've never understood why.'

'Because she cares about you,' Lucifer said, knowing how close this was to his old dynamic with Vennifer. 'She sees things you can't. That's what I was trying to tell you earlier. I know where your path leads, because I've already wandered this path, and the consequences of doing so.'

Gabriel didn't respond, appearing to consider his words. 'Your Krista, she died, didn't she?' he then asked.

At first, Lucifer didn't answer, his gaze downcast, regret

filling his heart. He sensed another presence, this one like Korai and the silver being, but different.

Lucifer, a female voice whispered in his mind, filling him with warmth and love. Lucifer frowned, then the sensation disappeared. After that, he felt empty.

What was that? he wondered, half asking Korai as he felt the Fallen stir from within. *I just heard a woman's voice, he elaborated, Like you and... whoever the other one is.*

Korai seemed to consider that, filling Lucifer with confusion.

Could it be? he asked, more to himself than Lucifer. *No, it can't be. That would mean...*

Then, clarity emerged from Korai, as though he was stunned.

What? What is it? Lucifer asked.

Before Korai could answer him, Gabriel began walking away.

Lucifer followed him. 'Where are you going?' he asked.

'Home. I want to talk to Krista,' he said, stopping just before he reached the doors of the cathedral.

'This isn't over. We shall resume our conversation,' he said, stepping out of the door. Lucifer watched him leave, then went back to Mika. He was relieved to see that she was still alive, just unconscious. As Lucifer reached to pick her up in his arms, he felt as though they'd lost this encounter.

Yet, there had been developments too.

Before, what did you realise, Korai?

His Fallen seemed reluctant to say anything, leaving Lucifer annoyed. However, he did not pursue the matter any further. Mika was the priority now. He needed to get her back to Silver Wing.

Like I said before, we will talk, Korai. There's much I wish to understand.

23

A Father's Honour

After finding the relic, Greene and Shallai searched for Barbatos and Doomis, eventually finding the Fiend waiting for them at Elcaris' entrance. He had been alone with his giant sword sheathed, arms folded. The sorcerer had left a message with Doomis.

That he'd catch up later.

When asked where Barbatos had gone, Doomis didn't answer. It added to Greene's suspicions. The other Ethero Fiends had cleared the streets, allowing them to walk back without disruption. It was as if they no longer wanted to stop them from leaving with the relic.

He doubted Doomis would speak any further on the matter.

That left them to navigate the vast cavern network that surrounded Elcaris. Thankfully, they had Doomis to guide them, which he did, having put on his giant black cloak. He seemed to revert to the state he had spent most of the journey in, giving no hint of his power and ferocity. Greene walked farther behind, unsure of how to act around him.

Then again, it's not like I could stop him should he decide to turn. *I doubt there'd be many who could stand against Doomis, maybe even Newman.*

The second relic, the next piece of the Titan core, was in the city of Cybernetics, a notion that made Shallai much quieter as they began the journey. They travelled via the long winding tunnels. Greene wasn't sure where they led, or why they existed. The tunnels, lit by tiny electric lights, remained a mystery like so many other aspects of Ethero.

For the first time, I don't feel a desire to uncover that mystery. The more we travel, the more we discover hidden truths. However, now I'm uncovering the reasons behind that. Forgiveness. The Child of Healing.

Greene became contemplative, trying to recall the details of the hellscape the being had shown him. They must have shown him the vision for a reason, but he didn't yet know why.

Perhaps as I uncover more pieces of the Titan core, I'll be able to communicate more with that being. He seemed willing to answer questions, but can I trust him? What makes him any different from Barbatos, even if he himself said the trees were safeguards against him? There's something else going on here, something beyond the simple mission we've set for ourselves. There is a reason they have kept us from the truth. If I'm not careful, I could tear this world apart with one choice alone.

"Or else, Ethero will perish..."

What did that mean? Greene wasn't sure. He was distracted, and walked into an unmovable object: the great mass of Doomis. The Fiend responded by turning to look behind, making Greene step back.

'Sorry,' he said quickly. At once, images of Doomis' power emerged. He had slaughtered all those who crossed him, especially those from his kind. Greene wondered if Doomis saw the same thing his ancestors must have seen in others as they roamed the world.

'Apology unnecessary,' Doomis said, surprising Greene. His voice remained a growl, but without the rage that he had carried throughout Elcaris. It still made him sound terrifying.

'You fear me,' Doomis said then; a statement, not a question. 'Why?'

How does someone answer that? Greene wondered.

'Before you changed, I always knew you were strong, but I didn't realise how strong until I saw you back there. Still, I know what it's like to hold anger towards my kind, and I've seen how such rage can turn into hatred. The Lieutenant taught me that. Yet, you... I've seen nothing like that before. I just–'

Doomis went down on one knee, towering over Greene. He kept his gaze fixed on the void where Doomis' face was.

'Greene. Tell me, what does it mean to despise your own race?' he asked. 'Why do you seek to unleash the Titans?'

Greene's lips parted in surprise, unsure of how to answer. Still, despite his fear of Doomis, he was sure that his life wasn't in danger; not yet anyway. He answered as honestly as he could. 'I'm not sure why you're asking, Doomis, but I despise my race for what it's allowed itself to become. I want to understand what happened; why my race ended up imprisoned in Exia.'

'How do you know unleashing the Titans will give you the answers?' Doomis asked.

Greene considered that. 'I don't know,' he admitted. 'It just feels like I need to do this. I want to free my kind. Why are you asking me these questions?'

'Because I made a promise, Greene,' Doomis said. 'Because we all have our reasons to make this journey. The war for Ethero has begun, and I must honour that promise.'

'What promise is that? Why do you hate your kind so much?' Greene asked.

'Because I want to change my kind too. Unlike you, I hold only contempt and hatred for my kind. I am not loyal to them. Their ways are outdated, and my life is proof of that. What you saw back there was me honouring my promise, and showing to my kind the monster they created.'

Doomis rose to his feet then, reaching towards his hood and pulling it down. Greene found himself amazed that the Fiend was smiling, a look that, despite his monstrous appearance, seemed genuine, with a warmth that looked almost wrong on his face.

'Before, I told you that the only thing my kind respects is fear. For one to fear you is to show no weakness, only power and dominion. My kind is always searching for the opposite within others, leading to a cycle in which we're scrambling to tear each other apart. It is barbaric, unforgiving and hateful. To stand, to crush all around you until they tremble before your presence, that is survival. That is my goal. That is the promise I made.'

'But why? To who?' Greene asked. 'I mean, I'm terrified of you as it is. I doubt the others feel any differently.'

'But that is the problem, Greene. I don't want you to fear me. The only ones I want to fear me are my kind, and Barbatos. That is all.'

'Why is that important to you? What difference does it make whether Shallai and I fear you?'

'Because my promise wasn't to inflict that fear on either of you,' Doomis said, before sighing. 'I pursue survival against my kind because I was born to be weak,' he said, resigned. 'Though we can all somewhat decide how our bodies grow and evolve, my kind has always been born into three classes: those who are noble, those who are servants. Then, those who are weak.'

He paused then, before resuming his walk. Greene and Shallai followed.

'My mother was born weak, so she died giving birth to me. My father was also born weak, but he tried to protect me as best as he could. This is a rarity among my kind. They cast aside most children, but he felt emotions for me that were not normal. Unlike so many fathers, he wanted his child to live, to survive in this cruel world. Those who are born weak almost always become fodder. The servants are destined to become enslaved to the nobles, but they can live long lives. Nobility rule over us all, and are powerful.'

'More powerful than you?' Shallai asked. Greene meanwhile recalled what Barbatos had said about the nobles, leaving the others to perish as they fought to stop Doomis and Barbatos.

Is that why he stayed back? Is he meeting with the nobles now?

'No one is more powerful than me. Or, at least among our kind. I made it so.'

'How? You just said you were born weak. How can you become more powerful?' Greene asked.

Doomis smiled. 'As I told you before, I made a promise,' he said. 'My father died to protect me. Often, it is a custom for the weak born in Elcaris to serve as entertainment for the others. We know one such form of entertainment as the Bloodbath. A place where weak destroys weak, while servants and nobles come to inflict pain.'

'You mean like some kind of fighting ring?' Greene ventured. He recalled his early days in the DFA, when many of his missions had been to take down illegal human fighting pits in Exia's underground. That was before Newman. Greene felt sadness and regret in that memory.

'In a way,' Doomis confirmed. 'But entering the Bloodbath meant death for all but one. However, as soon as a victor is crowned, they are forced to keep fighting, until they too perish. The servants tried to force me to partake in the Bloodbath, but my father didn't wish for me to die in such a cruel fashion. His love for me was uncommon among my kind, and he wished to find another solution, a way to save me from that horrific fate.'

'So he offered himself, didn't he?' Shallai said.

Doomis didn't deny it, but Greene noticed the Fiend bristling, before he forced himself to relax.

'They did not give him a choice. At least, that's what I realised after the fact. They told him if he offered himself to the Bloodbath, then they'd spare me. So, he went in of his own accord. I watched as they slaughtered my father before my eyes, smiling in the belief that he'd saved me.'

'He'd been lied to, hadn't he?' Greene said. He noted pain and sadness in the Fiend's expression, before that pain turned into something harder that almost made him fear Doomis would turn against them.

'Yes. As soon as he died, they threw me into the Bloodbath, where I had to face the one who had just killed my father. Crying, I crawled to his mangled corpse, wondering why he had to die. The audience jeered and mocked my show of love, while my father's killer circled around us, taunting me. It was while holding onto my father's body that I realised something that would change my fate. A purpose that drives me.'

He stopped, reaching over his shoulder to unsheathe the giant sword. Greene could see his rage returning, the unrestrained fury and hatred that he had used to slaughter his own kind without hesitation.

'I stopped caring about being born weak, Greene. I swore that I would honour my father's love for me, by destroying everyone that stood in my way, by surviving in this cruel world.'

He towered over Greene as his stance showed his readiness to fight. However, he sheathed his sword once again, the burning fires of rage dissipating.

'I tore him apart, Greene. I found strength in my pain, in my hatred. Once it was done, I demanded more. I needed them to fear me, to tremble at the sound of my name, a name I would forge with blood. They came, one by one. Soon every one of them knew they wouldn't be walking out of the Bloodbath alive. Soon, I created that name, as my reputation spread throughout the city of Elcaris. I became the punishment for those who lied, cheated, and committed crimes. I turned myself into what you see today, the Fiend known as Rukshai.'

'Rukshai?' Greene asked.

'Executioner,' Doomis said.

Greene recalled Barbatos using that name, but now he understood where it came from. Despite his fear, he felt pity for Doomis.

To have so much pain driving you. But to what end? Until someone takes you down?

'How did you get out?' Greene asked.

A strange sound came from the Fiend then. Greene realised

that Doomis was laughing.

'Why are you laughing?' he asked, stunned.

'Because I know what you're expecting, Greene,' The said, showing a rare moment of happiness, or perhaps just irony.

'You're expecting a grand conclusion to my story. An ultimate battle. A deal with which I earned my freedom. Unfortunately, one day I realised they couldn't hold me. After slaughtering my kind for years, it occurred to me that no one in Elcaris could stop me if I left, including the nobles. I defeated my last opponent before reaching towards one of the cage panels that enclosed us and ripping it away. Then I left, and no one tried to stop me. I decided to leave for Elcaris for Exia, learning of the oaths that my kind had sworn to keep. There I became guardian of The Place That Doesn't Exist until a certain Titanius crossed my path.'

Doomis smiled again. 'And so here we are. I aid you in your mission, because I believe you have survival in mind, not just for your kind, but for all of us hidden races. You see inequality, and you wish to change that for all. With you, I see a cause beyond just hatred and rage. However, I can also see where such hatred and rage could corrupt your own mission, so I also serve that purpose. When you find the relics. When you see the dreams you don't share with us, I want you to remember the path I've chosen and where it leads. Salvation can turn to destruction. Before you know, you've ruined all that you wished to build.'

'Why are you telling me this?' Greene asked, trying to understand. 'What do you see in me that I don't?'

'A being that wishes to know and sways between two different paths. You have so many opinions around you, so many motives and desires. They have their own intentions for you, and soon you'll find yourself unsure of where to turn. It's from there that you'll move towards instinct, but not all instincts should be trusted. I see my hypocrisy, and it's because of that hypocrisy that I help you, so you can make your own decisions.'

'And which way do you think I should decide?' Greene asked.

'Whatever way you won't regret,' Doomis said. 'Whether you decide to destroy this world, or save it, I don't care. You are free to choose. That freedom is all Shallai and I wish for you. Barbatos seeks only vengeance and destruction. Remember, you always have a choice, no matter what he or anyone else tells you. Don't forget that, especially as we close upon our goal.'

Doomis fell into silence, while Greene felt gratitude towards him. Even if forged in blood, it was the first truly helpful perspective he had received. Greene opened his mouth to speak, only to be stopped by Doomis.

'Barbatos,' he growled, his aggression returning. 'I didn't realise you brought more of my kind to die.'

Emerging in his normal form, Barbatos approached with his customary grin, spinning his sceptre between his fingers. Greene realised what Doomis meant: behind Barbatos were three Ethero Fiends.

'Now, now, Doomis. Is there any need for such hostility?' one of them said, striding ahead of Barbatos. He had a particular look to him, with black boots, pants and a jacket with chains and studs. His black hair was dyed gold, while his eyes looked as though they were outlined in black eyeliner. The Fiend emitted a strange charisma as he strode up to Greene, slapping his chest with the back of his hand.

'Nice to meet you, Titanius. I hear you're the harbinger of Ethero's imminent death,' he said.

Greene looked down towards the hand, not taking it.

The Ethero Fiend shrugged. 'Suit yourself. I know our kind can be a little harsh, but–'

He didn't get the chance to finish that sentence. Doomis moved with his unnatural speed, grabbing the Fiend's neck before crashing him into the cavern wall. No one moved to stop him. Greene doubted anyone would dare to, yet the Ethero Fiend he now held by the neck was laughing, despite his struggle.

'I knew the Executioner was strong, still...'

'You're one word away from death,' Doomis growled. That silenced the Fiend.

Meanwhile, another of the three Ethero Fiends came up to them, a woman dressed almost entirely in black, who appeared delighted by what was transpiring.

'Please, do it. I want to see his blood,' she said, touching her lip as though imagining the taste. Doomis didn't look at her, keeping his gaze fixed upon the Fiend in his grasp.

'Step any closer, and we'll be seeing yours,' he said.

'Please, don't do that,' the third Ethero Fiend said, stepping around Barbatos with a slowness that struck Greene as odd. The Fiend wore a cloak like Doomis, except his was white and showed a much slimmer frame. He caught Doomis' attention.

'Who are you?' Doomis asked, releasing the Fiend in his grasp.

'A reject,' the female Ethero Fiend said. 'The Tortured. I–'

'I don't care who you are,' Doomis cut her off, before looking towards the first Fiend. 'Nor you. If either of you step out of line, or dare utter my name, I'll rip you both apart.'

'Hmm,' the female Fiend said, more curious than fearful. 'I like you. I am Escara. The fool you despise is known as Yuvi.'

'Hmph,' Yuvi muttered, straightening himself.

Doomis kept his gaze on the third Fiend. 'And you?'

'I am the Tortured,' he answered, sounding as though he didn't want to elaborate.

Barbatos stepped forward. 'So nice to see all of you getting along,' he said, before addressing Doomis. 'We will require their services, and they were kind enough not to intervene in Elcaris. Surely, you can give these three nobles a chance.'

'I have said my warning,' Doomis said. 'I will honour it.'

'Then I guess we agree,' Barbatos said, nodding in satisfaction. He took his place at the front of the group, smiling at Greene.

'Did you miss me, my dear Titanius?' he asked.

Greene scowled. 'Barbatos, we need to talk,' he said.

'Oh, I know about that,' the sorcerer said, his smile never fading. 'Did you run into my old friend, Forgiveness?'

24

Inner Struggle

Diana had been preparing herself to meet the strange beings they now harboured in the Institute, before Pauli ran into her office, reminding her there were others to whom they'd granted asylum.

'Diana!' he gasped as he staggered through the door.

Diana forced herself to remain calm, as the large Hateful man gathered himself.

'The other humans... They've entered a standoff with my kind. Eren's trying to deescalate the situation, but it's fractious. We need you.'

Diana rose from her seat and went to Pauli, placing a reassuring hand on his shoulder. 'Take me there, Pauli,' she said.

The two of them headed towards the bottom floor. She noticed the tension in the building as they drew close to the dining room, noticing many nervous Hateful along the way.

At least they find my arrival assuring, Diana noted, pleased with this as their faces relaxed at seeing her.

'Everyone, please go back to your rooms,' Diana said,

sounding cool and authoritative. The Hateful around her turned and obeyed without question. As she reached the entrance to the dining room, she understood what had happened.

The idea was for humanity and the Hateful to eat separately. To make both eat together would've been foolish, with the distrust between the two groups. But tensions had arisen, and there was a standoff between her kind and the Hateful, both armed with Blessings and ready to fight. Only Eren stood between them, arms raised towards both groups.

To his credit, Eren looked as calm as one could, despite the obvious tension. All eyes fell upon Diana as she entered the room. She wondered if she appeared like her mother, commanding respect and authority. Disgust arose.

I am not my mother. I will never become her.

Diana forced herself to ease. She walked over to Eren, the young Hateful relieved to see her.

'Thank you for handling this, Eren,' Diana said.

He lowered his arms, taking a step back as Diana positioned herself between both groups. Diana kept her arms down, folding them across her chest instead. She cast an expectant gaze between both humans and Hateful.

'What is the problem here? I've had to walk past many scared faces, so what's going on?'

'It's these bastards!' one human snapped, an older man Diana didn't recognise. In fact, it became obvious to Diana that none of the humans who had been around them during their talks outside the wall were here. This made the situation more likely. Diana studied the man, seeing the fear hidden within his anger. A quick glance behind him revealed a small girl, who seemed terrified.

'They tried to hurt my daughter!' the human man yelled, pointing an accusatory finger at the Hateful contingent.

'That's not true!' one of the Hateful said, armed with a Transformative shotgun, appearing in his mid-thirties with short hair. 'She dropped her toy! I was trying to give it to her!'

'Bullshit!' the human man retorted. 'You were going to attack her!'

'But why would I do that?' the Hateful man snapped back, as though astounded by the human man's claim. 'She panicked when I approached!'

The human man said nothing, instead sneering at the Hateful. Diana looked nervously at the handgun in his right hand, which shook. Thankfully, he didn't seem likely to use the weapon, but Diana thought she understood why things had escalated.

Fear, from two groups that didn't understand each other, having absorbed dogma and lies all their lives.

'Alright, that's enough,' Diana said, glancing between the two sides. 'Lower your weapons.'

A brief pause followed, as both sides regarded each other, before lowering their weapons.

Eren breathed out a sigh of relief, scratching his head as Diana turned towards him.

'Eren, where are the humans we spoke to earlier?' she asked.

'I don't know, Diana,' Eren said. 'If you ask me, one of them should be here during mealtimes.'

'I agree,' Diana said, nodding. 'But right now I'd like to take that idea further. I'm removing you from guard duty, effective at once.'

'Wait, what?' Eren stammered in shock, as though he were

being punished.

'I'm creating a new role for you, Eren. You'll be a liaison between humanity and Hateful. You will also put together a small group of Hateful who you trust, before introducing them to our human companions. Once that's done, I want you or one of your representatives to attend them during mealtimes.'

Diana paused, allowing these new instructions to sink in not just for Eren, but also for her kind and the surrounding Hateful.

'In addition,' she continued, 'I want you to organise sessions for both humanity and Hateful to mix and engage with each other, giving each side the opportunity to learn about each other. Also, I will open a seat on my Council for you. When you believe the time is right, I want you to put forward a representative from my fellow humans, so they can add their perspective to our Council.'

Diana stopped there, not surprised to find that everyone around her was looking stunned. The confusion and amazement was helping ease the tension.

The human man frowned at her, confused. 'So, we're to be monitored like children?' he asked.

Despite her initial desire to roll her eyes, Diana kept her face level, shaking her head instead, before gesturing towards Eren. 'No, not at all,' she said. 'In fact, the reason I'm implementing this is that Eren clearly cares about you, just as much as the Hateful. This is the second time he's stood in to help you, so I can't think of anyone better to help us work towards trust. By working with those Eren chooses, you'll see that most of the Hateful don't wish to harm you. In fact, I think many of you will come to the same realisation I did.'

'Which is?' the man asked, making no effort to hide his doubt.

'That the only difference between them and ourselves, Blessings and looks aside, is that our minds work differently. That's all. We need to stop treating the Hateful like a dirty little secret. They're human, and once both sides attempt to understand each other, you'll realise we've been lied to. So no, I'm not trying to treat you like children. I'm trying to create an opening for both sides to interact. You're going to be staying here for a while, unless you wish to return outside the walls.'

Diana knew they wouldn't say anything, knowing what was happening in Exia. It also reminded her of the next pressing business she needed to attend to. The situation now resolved, Diana nodded towards both sides, before turning to walk out of the dining room. The dynamic had changed, and everyone needed to accept that.

But do I accept that? I thought our problem was engaging with my kind, but now...

According to her scouts, monsters had flooded the streets of Exia, emerging from Seraphu. More fighting had followed, along with gunshots and explosions, before eventually giving way to an eerie silence. Knowing that the situation was evolving each second gave Diana more concern. Everything seemed to head towards something that Diana wasn't sure she could stop, something she knew would change Ethero forever.

I need to uncover what's happening, Diana thought, as she entered the corridor. She was riding a fine line now, especially in trying to handle everything around her. It made her more grateful that she had her Hateful Council now. They could run most things within the Institute. However, one wrong step, and everything would be over for both humanity and Hateful alike.

'Diana,' a familiar voice said.

Pauli was approaching. At once, she interpreted shame in his expression, along with frustration. Diana realised how much she was putting him through, alongside the Hateful. It was easy to forget that they struggled with change, which filled her heart with guilt. Thankfully, she knew Pauli wouldn't read this on her face, instead appearing more awkward as he seemed to struggle to maintain eye contact with her.

'I'm sorry, Diana,' he began, though she wasn't sure why he was apologising. 'I panicked. I should've handled the situation better.'

'Pauli,' Diana said, understanding, before turning her gaze towards the floor. 'I'm asking so much of you,' she said. 'Of all of you. I keep forgetting how much change I'm forcing upon your kind.'

'That's still no excuse for the way I acted, Diana,' Pauli said, his hands reaching out to her before he stopped himself. Pauli shook his head, as if realising what he was about to do. The corridor they stood in seemed to grow smaller. Diana realised how much he was trying to contain himself around her, fighting against feelings she knew all too well.

A tiny smile appeared on Pauli's face, knowing he couldn't hide this from her. 'I want to be better for you,' he said. 'Diana, I just want...' He stopped, as though realising his next words.

Something stirred within Diana, something that reminded her of what she had sensed around him when they first met, the feelings that stirred whenever he was around her.

Longing. Desire. Need. They would sweep through her, and still she would hold herself, despite despising herself for doing so. That reminded her of only one person.

Her mother.

Oh really? Him? She could hear her mother's voice, speaking with such mockery and disgust that Diana cringed. *Diana, you're a Skagen. You're meant for power and domination. He won't give you any of that. He's Hateful. Cursed...*

Just shut up, Diana responded in her mind, forcing her eyes closed for a couple of seconds before opening them again. She forced herself to smile at Pauli then, unable to deny that the feelings she always had around him were swirling again.

I want him so much, yet I keep running away. It's all I've ever done. I know what will happen if I just take the first step.

'I'm sorry, Pauli,' Diana said. 'It's been a strange time for your kind. For all of us. I'm so proud of all of you.'

That drew a smile from Pauli, one that Diana wanted to melt into. Yearning fell upon them once again, as words threatened to leave her lips, words she could never take back if she uttered them. Diana grimaced.

I must deal with this sooner rather than later. If I hold myself back any longer...

'Pauli, I'm going to meet our new guests. Do you want to join me?'

'Shouldn't the Council be involved?' Pauli asked.

It was a fair question, though Diana felt some disappointment.

I wanted to go with you, she thought, before forcing herself to acknowledge his point. The Council had to be involved.

'I don't want to overburden you all,' Diana said, as Pauli shook his head.

'No, but neither will I accept you overburdening yourself,' he said. 'I care too much about you to-' Pauli stopped himself, his face twisting as though realising his words and what they meant.

'I mean...' he began, before embarrassment fell upon him.

Diana bit her bottom lip, her longing returning.

'You're allowed to care about me, Pauli,' she said, trying to assure him. 'I want you to.'

That drew a look from Pauli. Knowing things were getting a little close, Diana left the subject, returning to the previous discussion.

'Could you get Valki for me?' she asked, as Pauli frowned in surprise.

'You want Valki?' he asked. 'I would've thought you'd want Reni in this situation.'

'Normally I would,' Diana admitted. 'But on this occasion I think Valki is the best option.'

'Even if we're not sure of his aims?' Pauli asked. Diana knew he didn't like the young Hateful man, and Diana was unsure of him too. There was something within him, a deep-seated anger that differed from what she had seen in Lucifer and Megidra. There was a cold rational detachment in it, forcing her to consider every thought she had, and every action she took. Considering that, Diana folded her arms.

'We need to watch him, that I agree with. He's after something. Though I'm not sure what that is, he's clearly very calculating. Whether that means he's on our side, I'm uncertain. However, he's an asset we need to utilise. Valki has unique strengths that your kind doesn't usually have.'

'Maybe so,' Pauli conceded, 'But at least bring Reni. He seems to have a good grasp on Valki.'

'That's true, but I don't doubt Valki has already learned much from our meeting. He will have already come up with strategies to deal with Reni.'

'And you don't think Reni will have done the same?' Pauli asked, a fair counter, which Diana acknowledged with a smile. She turned and made her way along the corridor again, considering her next task.

Meeting creatures that weren't supposed to exist.

25

Regret

Megidra led the group of humans from warehouse to warehouse, praying they wouldn't run into any of the beings born of the Ether.

They had yet to encounter any. But that didn't mean they weren't there. They were no longer hiding. That left only one question.

Why now?

Megidra could hear the bestial growls of the Ethero Fiends in the distance. The longer they remained here the more likely they would be trapped. Megidra moved quickly, knowing they needed to leave as soon as possible.

Something is happening here, Megidra noted, as he glanced over at the humans, seeing occasional hesitation as they looked back, before they followed him. It fuelled the growing respect he held for them, in being able to confront the fear he didn't doubt they felt. They were facing creatures that had been myths and fairy tales.

They're doing well, all things considered.

It reminded Megidra of when he'd first encountered the

beings of the Ether, early in his career as a DFA Agent. He had been patrolling these very warehouses, having received reports of his kind being spotted stealing. However, the suspect caught hadn't been Hateful, but an Ethero Fiend. The same Fiend had then guided him to the settlement no human knew existed beneath their feet, changing his world.

Oh, how things have changed, Megidra thought, moving along the walls that ran alongside the warehouses, approaching the gap that would reveal if they had found what they were looking for.

A truck to load the supplies, and get them out of Seraphu.

None of the warehouses had yielded a truck, meaning they had to continue further into Seraphu, which meant moving further into enemy territory. Megidra was thankful the continuing blizzard was shielding their movement.

He looked at the next gap in the wall of what was the eighth warehouse they had searched. There were no enemies there.

But neither was there a truck.

'Shit!' Megidra muttered, gritting his teeth. With reluctance, he raised his right arm, before waving it forward to show there was nothing here and they had to continue forward.

They had to take a chance. But that meant dealing with streetlights.

They were spread quite far apart, but every time they stepped under them it removed the protection the weather gave them, exposing the footprints they left behind. As Megidra considered the next burst of a sprint that it would take to traverse this obstacle, he prayed the humans wouldn't get spotted. After all, it was easy to care for yourself in this kind of situation. It was harder when you needed to protect an entire group. The strange part was Megidra realising how much he cared about them.

They're changing me, but what will happen once I've served my use to them? Or, what will happen once I'm done and I realise I don't want to leave them?

Megidra shook his head, knowing that fear was guiding his thoughts. To counter this, he forced himself to rise so that he was standing, then burst into a sprint that the humans would follow without question. As they passed under the streetlights, Megidra was anxious, waiting for a roar or a shout to inform others of their presence. None came, which filled him with relief as they reached the next opening in the walls. As he waited for his companions to catch up, Megidra closed his eyes, relief washing over him. They'd survived another pass.

Then he opened his eyes and noticed footprints leading to the opening. Megidra froze, his eyes widening as he held out his right hand, forming it into a fist that told the others to hold position. He forced himself to take a breath, considering. A firefight would draw unwanted attention, so he needed to contemplate his next move. Of course, he could go in himself and kill whoever stood on the other side. The other option was to avoid conflict and move on to the next warehouse.

That means we have to go even further into the district, Megidra knew. He tapped into his Transformative Blessing, changing his right arm into a large curving blade. Behind, he heard guns being cocked in readiness: his human companions were ready for a fight. Megidra swallowed, before stepping around the gap in the wall.

Two Cybernetics stood on the opposite side, their postures lowered with cannon-like arms held to their sides.

'Move and you die,' Megidra said, cold and detached.

Much to his surprise, the two Cybernetics sighed in relief.

'Thank the Ether,' one of them said, a large Cybernetic with black skin and a mechanical upper body. 'Please, don't panic. I thought you were one of us, or worse, one of the Fiends.'

'Huh?' Megidra retorted.

The large male Cybernetic rose into a standing position as he switched away his weapon. Behind him, a sleeker female Cybernetic stood, with white skin and blonde hair.

'Are you alone?' she asked nervously. They obviously harboured no violent intent.

Megidra trusted his gut instinct and relinquished his Blessing, before holding out his left hand, waving it up and down to show to the humans that they could relax.

'No,' he answered the Cybernetics, waiting to see what they'd say next.

The two Cybernetics looked at each other, then the large male turned towards Megidra. 'Are you willing to talk?' he asked.

Megidra glanced at his human party, aware that this could be a trap. Still, he sensed these Cybernetics weren't a threat. Maybe they had information to help them understand what was happening. Megidra decided based on that. 'Yes,' he said. 'But if you make any move against my companions, I will tear you both apart.'

'Very well,' the male Cybernetic said. He pointed towards the warehouse inside the walls. There was no sign of a truck. 'Let's go inside. I don't want the others to discover you or your companions while we talk.'

Much to Megidra's surprise, the humans didn't hesitate to

follow him and the Cybernetics into the warehouse. Once inside, the female Cybernetic closed the door behind them, then stood alongside the male. Glancing at his human companions and seeing their expectant looks, Megidra turned to the Cybernetics.

'So, what's happening here?' Megidra began. 'Why have you all started coming to the surface?'

The two Cybernetics looked at each other, surprised.

'So you know what we are?' the male Cybernetic said, turning back to Megidra.

'Yes. I also know of The Place That Doesn't Exist,' Megidra said.

'What's that?' Deion asked. 'I've never heard of it.'

'It's where they all live – in Exia, anyway,' Megidra said. 'A city your kind doesn't know about. What made you break your oaths?'

The Cybernetics hesitated, unsure.

'We have little time to talk. Either tell us what's happening, or we're going,' Megidra insisted.

'We're not hiding anything,' the female Cybernetic said. 'It's just that we would've thought it was obvious why our races have broken our vows. The Ether's children have risen and have cast humanity in disarray. She returns.'

'You speak as though you've been waiting for this,' Megidra said, conscious of how close this discussion was getting to his actions in Anubi.

'We have,' the male Cybernetic said. 'War is coming; that's why so many of us have mobilised. The shamed races have waited for this. Though, I doubt many expected there to be such a divide among us. The war has begun.'

And we're in the middle of it, Megidra thought, considering this new turn of events.

Everything is changing. No longer are other human factions the threat. They need to unite. To–

He interrupted those thoughts then, as realisation dawned upon him.

'I'm sorry to have to say this, but if we don't find a truck in the next hour, I'm making us turn back. The mission has changed, far beyond what I could've ever imagined.'

'What do you mean?' Deion asked.

'I mean that the church will no longer be enough, Deion. We won't be able to protect the others. We'll have to find a new place for them, a place that we can defend, somewhere like…'

Megidra froze, realising what words were about to leave his lips. An icy chill ran through his spine, as he pictured the one place he understood would be the best to protect the humans. He couldn't risk taking them there, not after what he had done.

Besides, how can I even dare think of taking them there? It's bad enough that I stand along them, pretending that I can redeem myself for what I did. Now, I'm even have the gall to think of bringing them there… Home…

'We'll find somewhere,' he said, seeking to sound confident despite himself. 'Together. All of us. We'll need to join and fight as one. It's the only way I can protect you all.'

Megidra turned back to the Cybernetics. 'Where do you stand in this?'

The Cybernetics exchanged glances, unsure.

'We want no part in slaughtering innocents,' the female said eventually, the male nodding in agreement.

Megidra took that as a good sign. 'Does that mean you're

with us?' he asked.

This time, the Cybernetics showed more hesitation.

'I'm assuming neither of you has anywhere to go. You broke away from the others. Am I right?' Megidra asked

'Yes,' the large male Cybernetic said. 'We were just debating whether to return to our capital.'

'I thought you said there was fighting there?' Megidra asked.

The male Cybernetic's expression darkened. 'Yes, but I believe there's fighting everywhere, no matter where we go. You don't realise what's transpiring here, Hateful one. What's happening in Seraphu, this is the Ether making her move. We're establishing ourselves here, setting up and taking control of the district. Then, we move to take the city.'

'Oh shit,' Deion said behind Megidra. 'You mean those things out in the streets now aren't even the primary force?'

'No, unfortunately,' the male Cybernetic said, his gaze lowering. 'They're just scouts, sent to strike fear into your kind, human. If they kill anyone along the way, that's just a bonus. No, the true fighters, the ones you should fear, are coming next.'

'We need to leave here, now,' Megidra said. 'Is there a truck anywhere near here?' he asked.

'Did you not hear what he said?' the female Cybernetic replied.

Megidra nodded. 'If we don't bring back supplies, all their families will die. So, are there any trucks nearby?'

The female Cybernetic said nothing.

Megidra shook his head, looking back towards the humans. 'John, contact your groups. Tell them to meet us back at

Johann's church. As soon as we return, we'll figure out a new place to go, somewhere we can stand together.'

'Got it,' John said.

Megidra nodded, tapping into his Transformative Blessing. He shifted his right arm into a sniper rifle, turning towards the Cybernetics while cocking the weapon.

'So, are you with us?' he asked.

The blizzard outside had intensified. Megidra led from the front, racing towards the surrounding wall. The humans followed, along with their new Cybernetic companions. Despite the raging weather, Megidra could still hear high-pitched shrieks and roars everywhere around them. There were other, less obvious, sounds among them too. The animal-like calls of Animus. The shifting mechanisms of Cybernetics. Megidra doubted any of them would be friendly, and he made it his mission to spot them.

The Cybernetics had told them about a truck, just alongside the next warehouse.

It filled Megidra with relief to know that, especially as he emerged onto the opening in the wall. Ahead he could see faint black shapes moving on the road towards them in the distance. Thankfully, they wouldn't have to engage them; not yet, anyway. Megidra knew what would happen when they switched on the engine of the truck. The priority was getting to it.

With that in mind, Megidra burst forward into a sprint, running along the wall towards the next gap, the humans and Cybernetics following. It didn't take long to reach the next gap in the wall, which Megidra rushed straight into. He was confident that, since the Cybernetics knew of it, none of the

Ether's beings had searched it yet. Thankfully, that turned out true, alongside something else that gave Megidra great relief.

There was a small truck next to the warehouse, covered with snow.

They rushed towards it as a group. Megidra noticed some humans breaking away from the formation, running beyond him as they headed towards the truck.

'Oscar! Enji! Get that truck started so we can get out of here!' Deion bellowed, taking command. 'Everyone else, surround the truck and keep low. Give us a heads up if you see anything!'

The group formed a tight formation around the truck, while the two humans Deion specified moved ahead. First, they broke into it, before attempting to switch on the ignition. As they waited with nervous anticipation, it occurred to Megidra that someone could use the warehouse alongside them to hide in. He moved to the side door, listening for any sign of activity. There was none, but he felt a strange sensation.

Wait... What is this? he wondered, as though recognising the door. Lowering his rifle and relinquishing his Blessing, he stepped towards it, frowning deeply. Though he couldn't understand why, he felt pulled towards it, as though his body refused to turn away. Megidra saw something on the ground covered in snow in front of the door, and he understood what this warehouse was.

And what was inside.

'Megi? You alright?' John called to him. Megidra said nothing, raising a single hand towards the door he knew would open as soon as he pressed his fingers against it.

Why am I doing this? I should pretend I know nothing about this place. I shouldn't be here.

Still, he proceeded, pushing the door and finding only darkness awaiting him. Of course, that was a lie. So much more lived within that darkness. Regret. Shame. Hatred. Pain. They all lived in that darkness, and Megidra understood his body wouldn't allow him to run away from it. Inside, he felt Ryun stir, responding to what was happening.

Megidra could feel the Fallen snickering.

Oh, so we've returned here, he said, as though amused. *What? Did you think you could forget, Megidra? Pretend that everything you've ever done could be swept away. No. That's not how this works. After all, I am the Truthseeker. I won't let you run.*

'I think you confuse what's happening here, Ryun,' Megidra muttered, lowering his hand as he walked inside. 'I want to run, but I won't allow it. If I'm ever to redeem myself, I must face this. I must face everything I've done.'

Does that mean you'll tell them who you really are? Ryun asked, knowing that was the question he wrestled with most. Megidra didn't answer, knowing that needed to be dealt with sooner rather than later. The only question was how, and—

A hand grasped his shoulder, forcing him to turn until he regarded John. Hesitation appeared on the human's face then, as though seeing the shame and horror on Megidra's.

'What's going on?' he asked. 'Do you know this place?'

'Oh yes,' Megidra said, nodding. He could smell it now, chemicals, along with the sound of humming tanks, tanks that would emerge into view within another few steps.

Tanks that once held his abominations.

Megidra moved without a word, not caring if John followed him. Megidra recognised the dull emerald glow ahead, as he reached the console that overlooked it all. He heard John gasp, seeing the same thing he was now. Beyond, expanding into the rest of the warehouse a few feet below, were the tanks in which he had created his Descendants, standing upon a grid of many rows and columns.

'What in Divinity is this?' John asked alongside him. Again, Megidra did not answer. Stepping to his left where he knew a metal staircase awaited him, he began the slow climb towards the tanks.

'Megi,' John said, sounding spooked. Megidra turned, seeing the concerned human standing at the top of the staircase.

'What is this place?' he asked, in disbelief. 'What are those things you're heading to?'

My greatest shame, Megidra almost answered, finding himself silenced by the memories of gargled shrieks, human screams and seething flames.

And of Hela, smiling as she died.

'I'm sorry, John,' he said, meaning it. 'But I need this. This is something I have to do before I leave.'

Megidra walked among the tanks. He looked inside each one through their glass panels, knowing that only bubbling water remained within them, containing the liquid potion Barbatos had given him. He didn't know their contents, just that it would transform his kind into the monsters he'd called "Descendants".

I turned you into slaves, Megidra thought, staring into one particular tank, recalling a time when he believed he was doing the right thing, that he was giving them a gift.

Only to guide you towards more suffering. Oh Divinity, why did I hate you all so much?

There was no answer. Instead, all Megidra could hear except for the bubbling tanks was John's approaching footsteps.

The human was staring at the tanks. 'What is this place?' he asked, quietly, as though afraid of disturbing some kind of monster. 'What were these used for?'

'To conceal just how far I'd fallen,' Megidra answered, no trace of emotion in his voice.

John nodded. 'There's something you're not telling us,' he said. 'Since we met up with you and Deion, there's something you've been afraid of.'

Megidra smiled despite himself. He didn't deny it. Instead, as Ryun's presence filled his body, he found his smile growing.

'You were the Devil of Anubi, weren't you?' John asked. 'When you went missing, it was because you broke down, and because you were alone, you turned to those monsters. These tanks… this is where they were held, isn't it?'

'No, John,' Megidra answered. 'These tanks held victims, victims of only one monster. That monster's biggest mistake was believing he could become human.'

He stopped before John, unblinking. John moved next, nodding again as he turned to walk away. However, just as he reached the metal staircase, he turned back.

'That's funny,' he said, smiling. 'Because from where I'm standing, that monster sounds more human than the rest of us.'

26

Love

Gabriel can't sleep tonight, and he knows it's because of his Hateful mind. So often fixated on unimportant things, and sometimes his fears and desires. They all mesh to create the same result, more tossing and turning, more exhaustion. This is a part of his curse, of his everlasting nightmare. There is only one escape.

Death.

But he cannot allow himself that mercy. Not yet. The same thing stops him from taking that step. It's the reason Gabriel despises her more than any other being, except one.

Why can't you just let me go, Krista?

Gabriel never questioned her when he returned home after facing Lucifer. There was no point. Krista's been asking for someone to help him for years.

Never realising that she's the only one he needs.

Gabriel shifts to the side of his bed, curling into himself as he pictures a tiny box appearing near his stomach. He wraps his hands around it, praying that Krista gets the right combination. The only problem is that he knows that too many swallowed keys will make him bleed internally someday.

Might be for the better, Gabriel thinks, finding himself gripping that box a little tighter, shaking as coldness and pain fill his mind, manifesting as a throbbing in his head. Tears stream from his eyes.

It is a cruel thing, hope, that tiny part of us that despite our pain still clings to our soul like a tiny life-support machine, still giving us precious seconds.

Which we then waste, dreaming of the things we fear most. But why am I thinking about this?

Gabriel recalls the image of a small child wandering one of Kyrios' whorehouses, looking up towards the myriad human women who smile back at him. He knows why now, especially as they knew he couldn't understand why humans kept coming and going into their rooms, causing strange moans to reverberate throughout the corridors. Gabriel remembers thinking that they were in pain. It had been worse when he'd heard his mother make the same sounds. Eventually, humans would leave her room, all looking at him, all asking the same questions.

"Why is there a Hateful child here?"

Often, a look of pity followed, or contempt or disgust. Only one thing would remain on Gabriel's mind as he'd watch them leave.

I didn't choose to be Hateful.

As Gabriel grew older, he realised he could never remove this affliction, his disability. No matter how much he wished it would go away, it didn't. Whatever his condition was. Wherever it came from. It was always there. There was nowhere to run.

And you expect me to forgive this, Lucifer? After what it forced my mother and I to do? You deluded fool. There is no forgiveness. There is only–

Destruction, the other voice spoke from within, filling Gabriel with his presence. Opening his eyes a little, he can see the faintest violet and crimson wisps rising from his body. He knew what came next. Memories of his mother dying, almost appearing relieved to be removed from her Hateful problem. Of a father he'd never met. Of monsters that whipped and tortured him for their own entertainment. The latter causes him to shake again, but this time in anger and hatred. Gabriel understood what needed to be done to end it. One way to ensure that none of his kind would endure the same fate.

Destroy them, and the delusion the likes of Silver Wing had created for them.

Yet, I can never destroy you, can I? After everything. After seeing what a monster I am. You still stay with me. Why?

The thoughts ended then. Exhaustion would strike him, rendering him unable to move. Krista would come to nurse him back to health, another fact that shamed him beyond anything else. Yet, tonight he feels something different from exhaustion, especially thinking of her now. He had always considered what would happen to her if she lost him. However, never had he considered what he'd do if he lost her.

Despite having never said it, he understood Lucifer knew what it meant to have someone stay by your side, despite everything you've done. One person who still cared about you. A fear grips Gabriel, one he is not familiar with. Though he isn't sure why, he rises, shifting onto his hands and knees, realising that he'd been sweating profusely. The fear compels him to move off the bed, naked.

Why am I moving now? Why am I so afraid?

No answer comes, as Gabriel finds his feet and his body moving despite him. His steps lead him to his bedroom door, as weakness threatens to crumble him. However, Gabriel refuses that notion, gritting his teeth as he opens the door. He enters their cold bare living room. Goosebumps prickle across his skin. His gaze turned towards the only chair in the room. Piles of books sit alongside it. He was never taught to read, but he loved listening to Krista telling him her favourite stories.

But what if that was gone?

A haunting shiver travels through him, as Gabriel finds his breath turning into light gasps. He's so tired, but he refuses to stop. The fear drives everything. Gabriel cannot leave it. His Hateful mind won't let him. Heaviness permeates every step. Gabriel shifts towards Krista's door, knowing that she's in there.

And that he needs her.

Disgust rises from within as he steps closer, while his Fallen emerging causes him to wince. He knows Vorus is watching, that he's probably about to laugh at the pathetic state he's in. Still, Gabriel moves forward, embarrassed by his last attempt to kill himself. Only now, he realises what pain he was about to give her, along with the pain he knows he gave her after she discovered him. Gabriel imagines how he would've reacted had he caught Krista doing the same thing.

Oh Divinity. How selfish have I been? Without even knowing it, I have hurt you so much. I shouldn't be doing this. I should let her sleep, enjoying precious seconds without having to worry about me.

Still, Gabriel finds himself outside her door, within a single movement of getting what he knows he needs most. He freezes, now questioning whether he deserves that or her. Moments pass, and a painful throbbing fills his mind once more. It causes more tears. It creates more guilt.

'No. I'm better off alone,' Gabriel mutters, his tears falling as he slumps against the wall, his steps heavier than before. He goes back to his own room.

'Gabriel?' someone calls out behind him. Krista. More shame and regret fill his heart, despising every part of his being. Alongside that, he also senses a certain vulnerability and stupidity over his nakedness, over the impulses that brought him here. It's then he hates himself, as he wraps his arms around his body.

'Are you alright?' Krista asks next, her words cutting far deeper than any blade. For reasons he doesn't quite understand, the image of the small box around his stomach appears again, forcing him to wrap around himself just a little tighter.

'I'll be fine,' Gabriel lies, as every part of his being cries out in agony. Inside, he longs to be held, to be touched, to feel anything resembling affection.

'I'm so sorry, Krista,' he stammers, before somehow finding the strength to return to his room. It doesn't surprise him she says nothing to this, as he finds a way back, reaching his bed before collapsing onto it. It is there Gabriel releases his tension, breaking down into uncontrollable sobs, wishing that everything would just end.

But this will never end, will it? Now while we're like this. Not while we're so broken...

It surprises Gabriel then that he hears his bedroom door opening, causing his sobs to cease as he freezes in fear. The sound of soft footsteps follows, before the bed lowers on one side, accompanying the sounds of shifting alongside him. Krista has joined him.

'What are you doing?' he asks, hearing how afraid he is and hating it. Krista doesn't answer. In response, Gabriel reaches for his bed sheets, gripping them towards his body. Yet, she's somehow able to pull the quilt away from him, without having to use any strength. Soon, there's nothing between them. All movement ceases. A fearful pause washes over the two of them. For Gabriel, it represents a moment they've replayed many times, in which they remain silent, finding solace in each other's presence, but too fearful to take the fateful next step. For Krista, it represents the very thing she's always wanted, ever since she's met Gabriel.

The prospect of them finally exchanging their boxes.

Problem is, Gabriel knows that. He also knows that she's given away her love far too often, only to find it taken advantage of before being thrown away, discarded as though it meant nothing. Krista told him this during the first time.

"And that's why I know we're meant for each other. Why I'll wait until you're ready for me," Gabriel recalls, a simple showing of faith and devotion he's never known how to deal with. He wonders why she remains by his side, despite everything he's done. Now, despite his desire to push her away once more, another desire is far stronger. Gabriel inches closer to her, his body shaking uncontrollably. He's so close now, repressed needs and longings are threatening to be unleashed.

'Krista,' Gabriel murmurs, almost sure he can hear her holding her breath, as though realising how close they are.

But why? I don't deserve you. I don't deserve...

Gabriel holds himself, knowing that there's something he

wants to say.

'I'm so scared of losing you…' He speaks, inching that little closer. 'I'm so sorry for what I've put you through.'

Gabriel holds out his hand, not sure what he will find. Skin. Bone. Hair. Something. As his fingers graze what he's sure are hers, a jolt runs through his body, and their fingers dance, touching before linking. The burning furnace Gabriel knows lives within ignites further, guiding him ever still closer to Krista. He's one step closer to losing the locus of control his kind has always feared beyond all else.

But now a new desire and courage takes hold of him. Gabriel reaches his other hand forward, finding hair, Krista's beautiful Hateful hair, which he's always loved. Before Gabriel realises what he's doing, they pull each other closer, as their breaths grow shorter, more panicked, excited.

What is this? Gabriel asks, not understanding what is happening. Of course, he has theories. Everyone has theories. The closest logical one in his mind is abstract, something he's always believed wasn't capable of their kind. Yet, as he feels the warmth of her breath, he cannot deny what his instincts tell him this is – the freedom of the unknown.

The phenomenon known as love.

'Krista, I…' he begins, only to fall silent. Words cannot describe the myriad emotions that flood his mind. Instead, he cups her face before stroking it with a tenderness he never knew he was capable of. So often, those two hands caused only hurt to himself and others. Now, he realises he can do something else, that he was wrong about himself and his kind. Rather than sense anger or pain, Gabriel wishes to give everything to her, to see if he can do what he's always feared.

But, if I can love, does that mean I can also forgive? he wonders.

Before his mind answers, her hand reaches to cup the back of his neck, and he senses the radiance of Krista's love, ready to mesh with his own. His mouth, keeping the last defence he has, opens to speak one last time.

Before her lips stop them.

Krista can no longer hold back her hunger, throwing herself at him. He does not push her away. Instead, he takes her in, as desperation and passion flood between them. Time loses all meaning, skipping moments while focusing intensely on others. Gabriel does not remember when she removed her dressing gown. Nor does he remember the moment their bodies truly meet, connecting in ways he never thought they would. Another skip happens, and then he remembers the two of them crying as they throw every emotion into their joining, creating a storm they cannot stop. They can only hold on to each other for safety, for the storm doesn't end until they both do.

By the time that happens, his mind reverts to reality, finding himself lying with half of her on top of him. As Gabriel opens his eyes, he sees her face in the moonlight entering his room. Gabriel can recall nothing that ever looked so beautiful, as fear and intense love feed her every expression.

'I love you,' Krista stammers, and wiping tears from her eyes, giving him a smile no one has ever given him before. 'I love you so much.'

'I love you too, Krista,' Gabriel replies, knowing it's the first time he's ever said it. They stop shaking, allowing themselves to settle before she moves and finds a spot underneath his arm where she can lie her head, draping her arm over his chest. Understanding what this means, he looks for her eyes, radiating warmth but also exhaustion, as though finally allowing herself to be so.

'Can I stay?' Krista asks, knowing the last hurdle between them both. Despite himself, Gabriel finds his mind at ease, as though everything he had once thought in the past no longer mattered. Naturally, he knows this isn't the case. Gabriel knows he must meet Lucifer again, to talk to him, to understand why this is happening to him. Until then, the words that leave his lips surprise him, for they reflect a new truth he can no longer deny.

'I want you to,' he says.

27

Scars

Days had passed by the time Mika stirred from her unconscious state, which had consumed Lucifer's attention in an almost Hateful fashion.

Still, I'm not sure how she'll react to me being here.

No one in Silver Wing protested when he offered to watch over her. In fact, he was sure some had welcomed his proposal. Either way, he sat next to her bed, spending most of his time looking around her room, even if it made him uncomfortable to do so.

It's like I'm peering into something personal here. A part of Mika I shouldn't see, Lucifer thought in frustration, knowing there wasn't much else to be done except wait.

Lucifer shook his head; he needed to consider what had transpired in Kyrios' cathedral, especially with Gabriel.

He's a walking contradiction, like we all are. Yet, as soon as I mentioned that woman, Krista, it was like he realised something. Did I make him see? Did he understand what I meant when I told him about the path he was walking, about Ven?

Lucifer cringed, shifting as he folded his arms over his chest.

It still hurt to think of her. It brought painful memories and feelings of longing.

'I miss her so much,' he murmured, exhaustion gripping him as tears ran down his face. Something stirred within him then, a presence that wasn't Korai, nor the silver being. Lucifer's eyes widened, his mind pulled away from the possible comfort of sleep by a jolt of realisation.

You, Lucifer recalled, sensing the new presence swirl inside.

Lucifer, it said, once again speaking with a female voice, ancient. Lucifer held his breath. In response, the presence seemed to acknowledge him more.

You have little time, she said. *You must forgive, Lucifer. It's the only way to heal the hatred that has permeated Ethero. Still, I fear he may not be enough. You must unleash the Healing.*

'What is that?' Lucifer asked aloud. He glanced in Mika's direction, praying that she wasn't conscious. She wasn't, so he rose to his feet, pacing around her bed, waiting for an answer. Still, it was as though the presence hadn't acknowledged it, fading. Desperation rose in Lucifer.

'Please. Who are you?' he asked. 'How many of you are there inside me?'

Three. And there are three stages you must undergo if you're to unleash the Healing.

'What does that mean?' Lucifer asked.

The end, with your own healing. It begins with the fall. Then, you must forgive.

'And the third part? The part I assume you represent?' Lucifer asked. The beings within him were always cryptic, as though waiting for him to uncover things on his own, rather than telling him. Korai seemed the most receptive.

I still need to have that conversation with him. Can you sense him? And the silver being?

No, for we are independent souls. We cannot interact with one another directly, only through you, she answered. Lucifer nodded, even though he wasn't sure. He was sure that Korai had sensed something during their encounter with Gabriel.

Why me? Why are you all in me?

The presence didn't answer. Lucifer shook his head.

What do I need to do next? he asked. *The being of silver. Who is he? Why is he important in all this?*

He is my son, the presence within answered, *Forgiveness.*

The presence faded away, leaving Lucifer feeling empty once again. He scratched his chin, considering what she had said.

'Forgiveness… So that's your name,' Lucifer whispered. 'Tell me, Forgiveness, can you hear me now?'

Lucifer waited, feeling no stirring arise from the mention of his name.

'There's something I'm missing,' Lucifer said. 'There's a realisation I need to uncover. If I do that, will you arise?'

No answer came.

It was at that moment that Mika stirred. She groaned as though her entire body ached. Lucifer went over to her, sitting alongside her on the bed.

'About time you woke up,' Lucifer said, causing Mika to flicker her eyes open.

'What are you doing in my room?' she asked.

'I…was looking after you,' Lucifer said, realising how strange that might sound.

This seemed to placate Mika as she nodded, pushing her bed sheets down her legs. She sat up. She was wearing one of her training vest tops, revealing her well-defined muscles and abs, as well as the many scars over her body. 'You're doing it again,' Mika said.

Lucifer frowned. 'Doing what?' he asked.

'You're staring at my scars,' Mika said.

Lucifer pulled his gaze away, realising that it was true. 'Sorry,' he said.

Mika reached over him towards the bedside table, taking a hairband with which she tied her hair into a messy knot. Lucifer watched her, and her eyes flickered towards him, once again compelling him to look away from her.

'Sorry,' he repeated, embarrassed.

Mika's gaze fell on *him,* before she pulled the band off her head, undoing the knot. 'Would you help me with this?' she asked.

Lucifer frowned, but he shifted closer, moving to be more behind Mika. As she waited, Lucifer reached for her hair, running his fingers through it. He gathered as much as he could, pulling it back so he could tie it into a knot. Lucifer remembered doing this for Vennifer. It had been one of his favourite things to do for her. He felt calm as he repeated the motion a few times.

'I knew it,' Mika said, breaking Lucifer's meditative trance.

'Huh?' he said.

'You like hair, don't you?' she asked.

Lucifer had an impulse to protest, but didn't. Instead, he allowed himself to smile. 'Ven used to let me massage her head, but yes, I do like hair. How did you notice?'

'You looked at it when we first met,' Mika said. 'You always look at it.'

'You're observant,' Lucifer said, half impressed.

'Yeah, I see things like that,' Mika said.

Lucifer brought all of her hair together, only to be stopped by Mika reaching towards his hands. 'You can keep going,' she said. 'I don't mind.'

'Are you sure?' Lucifer asked, surprised.

'Yeah. Though my hair is nowhere near as long as Ven's, I still like what you're doing. You're gentle.'

'Erm... thanks,' Lucifer said, unsure. Still, he began the process he used to do with Ven, moving his fingers through Mika's hair by starting at her head, before gently pulling the hair back. As he found a rhythm in repeating this, Lucifer felt himself lulled again.

'Thank you,' Lucifer said eventually.

'It's alright. You looked stressed before. Besides, it's not like I don't get something nice out of it.'

'I guess that's true,' Lucifer agreed, finding a pleasant surprise to see this side of Mika, appreciating it as he continued to work his hands through her hair.

'You don't let yourself indulge in your Hateful tendencies, do you?' Mika asked, the randomness of the question catching Lucifer off guard.

'I guess not,' he admitted.

'Why?' Mika asked. 'I do with my book collection.'

Lucifer looked around at the many book shelves that surrounded them. Hundreds of books were stacked on them, small paperbacks, organised with Hateful precision and detail. Lucifer marvelled at them.

'What books do you like?' Lucifer asked, smiling, appreciating every second of this.

'Tankobons,' she said. 'I love the stories and the characters, the transformations and the deep philosophical subjects.'

'Sounds cool,' Lucifer said, meaning it.

'What's happened to you?' Mika asked.

'You helped me stop thinking about all the shit running through my head,' Lucifer said. 'Thank you.'

Mika nodded thoughtfully before brushing her hair back. 'You do it better than I do,' she said, looking sad. 'Lucifer, why do you hate yourself?'

'Because I'm Hateful, Mika,' Lucifer answered, his smile fading, despite the calmness in his voice. 'Because this condition makes everything confusing. I have to keep fighting it. I'm so tired of fighting.'

'But you enjoyed what you did before, didn't you? Was that not because of your Hateful parts?'

'Maybe,' Lucifer admitted. 'But I've done horrible things, Mika. I've hurt so many trying to become something more than our condition, only to lose the person I should've realised meant more to me. All I saw before I met you was broken Hateful, struggling with a condition we never asked for. Shouldn't we despise it? When it causes so much pain and suffering for us?'

Mika considered that before allowing a smile to emerge on her face.

'Is it just us, though? Is it just us who suffer because of our condition?' she asked, before gesturing at the scars on her body. 'These were from my mother. When I was a child, she would come into my room, looking at me as though I were her curse. My mother despised every part of my Hateful being. I guess she wondered if she could beat the condition out of me. Yet, no matter how hard she tried, I remained Hateful. Once she realised the beatings weren't working, she'd start throwing things at me instead, every time she saw me.'

Mika paused, tears brimming in her eyes. Lucifer wished

to reach out to her, unsure of whether he should. In that instance, his hand inched towards hers.

'She would throw anything at me, screaming that I was a monster, and that she wished I was dead. The only reason I left my room was because she wouldn't feed me. Every journey beyond my cold room was a test of survival. Father left us when he realised what I was – or at least that's what she used to tell me. My existence ruined her life, so she wished to ruin every second of mine. My scars reminded me of what I was, and why I was punished for it.'

The tears ran down her face, and she squeezed the quilt by her legs tightly, her body shaking. Lucifer didn't know what to do, his own body tensing in response to her pain. His hand inched closer to hers again.

'I lived like that for years, Lucifer. Then one day, someone knocked on my door. No one ever did that, and I braced myself for more hurt, more pain. Yet, the door opened, and rather than my mother, it was another human: Claire. She stepped in, and I remember cowering away, so scared of another person being near me.'

Without warning, Mika released the quilt and put her hands on Lucifer's face, cradling it.

'Claire touched me like this, the first time anyone had ever touched me without hurting me. Do you know what she said next?'

Unsure, Lucifer shook his head. He didn't dare say anything, sure that she needed this. Her expression was softening, as though relieved to tell this story.

'Claire told me I didn't have to hate what I am anymore, that I could forgive myself. That my pain could allow me to help those who suffer, because I understood what it means to hurt, to hate. To be Hateful.'

Mika allowed her hands to fall, her head tilting to one side.

'That's what forgiveness is to me, Lucifer. It's something you choose, despite everything you are, and everything you've ever done. I can only change so much. My condition. Your condition. We cannot run from it, for it creates so much of what we are. Forgiveness is choosing to accept that, despite our condition. By doing so, we end the pain we spend so much of our lives trying to run from.'

Mika closed her eyes, relief emerging across her face.

'We're the same, you and I. All the things that you think are wrong with you are the exact reasons I like you, Lucifer. You're so Hateful. If we're broken, then what's wrong? We can be broken together, a scattering of pieces that don't need fixing.'

Mika paused, allowing her warmth to carry through in her expression. Lucifer stayed silent, recognising something about Mika that he hadn't before. Something he couldn't deny as he stared into her eyes.

That she looked beautiful when she talked like this.

'The world is broken like us. How are we supposed to fit in it? We don't need to. Who gives a shit when we have each other?'

Lucifer didn't have an answer. Just like Setsu. Just like Gabriel. Mika gave him much to ponder, a perspective that made sense. However, especially as Lucifer kept his eyes on her, he felt something he hadn't expected to feel with anyone, especially after losing Ven.

I don't want to leave her, he realised, confused, *I want to stay here. It's almost like...*

'Lucifer,' Mika said then, saying his name so softly he almost didn't hear it.

'Yes?' he asked.

'What are you thinking?' Mika asked.

'Things I never expected to think again,' Lucifer said. He stood up and headed to the door.

'Why are you leaving?' Mika asked, as though sensing his desire to stay.

Lucifer turned towards her, smiling. 'Because I fear all the different thoughts and emotions running through my head, Mika.'

'You could spend some more time stroking my hair,' Mika offered, running her hands through her head to emphasise her point. 'Maybe that'll help.'

'Or perhaps you just want me to stay too?' Lucifer said.

Mika made no move to deny it, but she looked away.

'Would it embarrass you if I said yes?' she asked.

Lucifer almost chuckled, before moving back to her. Mika turned and repositioned herself, giving Lucifer a similar angle as before. He ran his hands through her hair once again.

A little indulgence won't hurt, Lucifer mused, while allowing the almost meditative trance to return. Both Lucifer and Mika remained silent, not feeling the need for pointless chatter, which was exactly what Lucifer wanted. Ven knew not to speak, and the fact that Mika understood meant so much to him.

She gets me, Lucifer understood. *And, this time, I'm letting someone in.*

28

The Origin of Ethero

Diana moved through the illuminated halls of the Education Section, about to meet creatures she knew shouldn't exist. Monsters that reminded her of the beings she feared most as a child.

Ethero Fiends.

Diana recalled the stories of the monsters said to stand seven feet tall, with claws and sharp teeth to suck the blood of their victims. She had spent many nights with a light on, afraid of one creature emerging from under her bed. What she imagined their demonic growls sounded like melded with the sounds of whatever was going on outside, making her shiver.

Diana forced herself to consider the stories. There were many untrue stories told to kids. More often, they sowed the seeds that would become issues later in life.

We were told to fear the Hateful too.

Whatever she and her Council were about to face, it would change everything they understood about Ethero, and of the situation in Exia. Diana was sure about that. The creatures were still emerging from Seraphu, spreading through the city like a plague. She stilled her mind. She needed to prepare herself.

Pauli was rounding up the members of her Council, and Diana had arrived alone. She approached the classroom their new guests were occupying, Classroom 1-A.

Diana took a controlled breath and went inside, finding the lights switched off in what seemed to be an empty room. She listened for any sign of life, hearing nothing. Frowning, she reached for the light switch but paused before flicking it on.

'The light won't harm you, will it?' Diana asked the room, recalling the creatures' ability to shift into a shadow-like form. She saw a black smoke-like substance hanging over the floor. A scent like a burnt-out candle filled her nose, and she was sure she could hear soft breathing. Had she not had her experiences with Reni, this situation would've terrified her. Instead, she remained calm, even when she felt something emerging to her left.

'*Duash skula,*' a wispy voice said, right alongside her. Diana looked to her right, but saw only wisps of shadow.

'I'm sorry, I don't understand what that means,' Diana said.

The wisps of shadow stirred, manifesting physical forms.

'You may turn on the light, human,' the same voice said.

Diana did so, and illuminated five human-shaped shadows. They looked somewhat similar to the Hateful, but with ghostly white skin and black eyes. Clawed hands extended from their black cloaks, and the one closest to her gestured.

'You are the human female who spoke before,' it said. 'Why are you among the Hateful?'

'I'm leader of the Hateful,' Diana answered, calmly. 'They

chose me after the previous leader passed away.'

The five beings, Ethero Fiends if her gut instinct was correct, glanced at each other, before returning their gazes towards her.

'You're tolerant of others, human,' the one who spoke before said, lowering his clawed hand, tilting its head slightly. 'Why?'

'I don't know,' Diana admitted, before moving to sit at Pauli's desk. 'It's just who I am. I've always questioned what others have told me, especially about those I've been told to fear or distrust.'

Diana considered that, wondering if that was indeed the truth. She leaned back against the chair and folded her arms. 'No, that's not right. I think it was because of my relationship with my mother. I didn't like the way she looked at the world, or how she treated others. You could call it a rebellion.'

'Interesting,' the Ethero Fiend said. 'You differ from the rest of your kind. Even now, I don't sense fear from you, considering how momentous this meeting between our races is. It would seem that our previous knowledge of human nature is incorrect.'

'Oh, I'm nervous,' Diana admitted, appreciating the openness of their dialogue. 'But I figure treating you with respect and honesty is my best move. After all, none of you had to approach us. However, I have many questions. I remember you saying that your kind was not supposed to exist, at least to humanity and the Hateful. Why?'

The Ethero Fiend was about to answer, only to be interrupted by Pauli and the rest of her Council coming in. Artemi guided Reni from the rear, just behind Heimval and Valki.

Diana rose to her feet, gesturing towards them. 'Sorry, I should have asked. Would you mind if my Council join us?'

The Ethero Fiend shrugged, a sign that Diana took to mean yes. She nodded before going back to her seat, while the rest of her Council positioned themselves alongside her. When everyone was settled, Diana resumed the conversation.

'Why are your kind supposed to be unknown to ours? I assume you're Ethero Fiends?'

'Indeed, we are,' the Fiend confirmed. 'We have remained hidden for so long because we swore an oath to remain in secret. After the Eternal Mother's defeat and the Divinity's resignation, this was the price we had to pay.'

'You mentioned this "Eternal Mother" before,' Diana said, remembering it from outside the wall when they first met. 'Who is she? You said she was coming, and someone else. Did you mean the Divinity?'

The Fiend appeared reluctant to answer that, before nodding. 'She is the true creator,' the Fiend said, glancing back at its companions, as though unsure to continue. They nodded in silent agreement. The Fiend returned his gaze to Diana and her Council.

'The Eternal Mother is chaos and creation. By creating the Divinity, she created order. That is, she created the thing she needed to achieve permanence in the world. However, order and chaos are contradictions, always destined to fight each other. It is in that contradiction war emerged between both entities, which dragged humanity and all the other races into it. As you humans say, when the strong wage war it's the weak who die.'

'So the other races are of the Eternal Mother?' Pauli asked. Diana sensed the Fiend didn't wish to answer that question. They were touching on something taboo.

'I'm sorry, but despite breaking our oath of silence, there

are other oaths we swore to uphold. We cannot reveal to you the truth behind our origin, or of the other races or the Hateful. The only thing I'll tell you is that the Divinity created a single child among his creations. This child would eventually betray him and join the side of the Eternal Mother, becoming known as the Child of Chaos.'

The Fiend paused, its expression darkening. 'The Child of Chaos created her Demons, otherwise known as the Fallen. They were the ones to fight the Divinity's Angels, until a chance meeting changed everything, including the outcome of the war.'

What do you mean by that? Reni chipped in, drawing a glance from the group, including the Fiend.

'One of the Fallen encountered one of the Divinity's Angels. From their desire to end the war a miracle was born, a being who defeated the Child of Chaos and his creations. However, he failed to defeat the Eternal Mother and the Divinity. Something was missing. With that, he placed the Fallen and the Angels within special beings. As for himself, he insisted on our race swearing oaths of secrecy, while creating other conditions that would ensure we would postpone the war. This created the state of Ethero prior to the Eternal Mother's children rising again. It began with the Fallen known as Korai, the Guardian. He defeated the Angel of War before a second Fallen unveiled themselves. The Truthseeker. It was he who plunged Exia into chaos.'

'Wait,' Pauli interjected, trying to take all of this in. 'That was Megidra.'

'The Hateful that possessed the Truthseeker,' the Fiend elaborated.

Diana was amazed. 'Are you saying these Fallen exist within

the Hateful?' she asked. The Fiend made no move to deny it, so Diana figured it was true. Stunned by this revelation, she sat further back in her chair, shaking her head.

'That's what corrupted Lucifer, isn't it?' Diana asked. 'He possessed one of these Fallen too, didn't he?'

'The Guardian, Korai,' the Fiend said.

Diana reflected on the reports Hela received from the Hateful who had gone to confront Lucifer in Anubi, in her mother's estate. Things clicked in her mind.

'Hannibal Desmarti. He was the Angel of War,' Valki said, in a thoughtful pose, sitting back with his legs crossed.

The group looked at him then, as he regarded the Fiends. 'When Megidra sent this city into chaos, you all decided that this was it, a premonition, the herald of the Eternal Mother. Correct? You took his emergence as a signal to mobilise,' he said.

'Well deduced, Hateful,' the Fiend said, though he didn't appear impressed.

Valki smiled. 'Makes sense,' he said. 'After all, it is the perfect opportunity. Perhaps I can express it best: *Duas cryu feavur.*'

The Ethero Fiends stepped back in shock, snarling at Valki.

'How do you know our language?' the leader asked, his tone hostile.

Valki's smile never wavered. 'I know much more about your kind than you think. I know that all of you live underground, within a city that is not meant to exist, at least to humanity, ourselves and Titaniuses. The Darklands are a front to hide the hidden races.'

'So you know of Elcaris too,' the Fiend said.

'I do,' Valki confirmed. 'As did our traitor, and a few others who lived outside the Institute.'

'Wait, you mean Megidra knew of this place, and of these races?' Pauli asked.

Valki nodded. 'Yes. It surprises me that none of the humans ever discovered it. After all, a monster guards the entrance.'

Valki, Reni's voice emerged. *You've been withholding information from us, vital information. What else do you know? How do you know?*

Valki's face contorted in contempt. 'Do you believe the likes of Megidra and Lucifer were the only ones who dared venture outside the walls?' he asked, the question rhetorical. 'Like many of us, I was abandoned as a small child. I doubt this will surprise you, but I wasn't popular within the Education Section. I preferred my company. I wanted to understand things. I was driven to seek answers to the questions that burned within me, such as what lived beyond those walls. Naturally, most of my reading and self-education had prepared me for engagement with the likes of humanity, so I chose a disguise and finally ventured outside for myself.

'My curiosity led me towards Seraphu, where I came upon a strange warehouse guarded by a creature far bigger than any human. He was protecting something. I visited the guard, and he would speak back to me in a language I didn't understand. It fascinated me. Although his words were a warning, I stayed and tried to communicate with him. I think he realised I wasn't human, and that I possessed an open mind. He then spoke in our language and I learned how to speak in the tongue of Ethero Fiends. I would like to believe my show of respect endeared me to him, so he allowed me to descend. I saw the world hidden in plain sight. *Yallic gulas vishva.*'

'You use our tongue too lightly,' the Fiend who had spoken

said, eyeing Valki as though in chastisement.

Valki looked at him. 'And you aren't telling them the most important details,' he said. 'You haven't told them the entire of truth of what's coming. You haven't mentioned the Cybernetics or the Animus. Neither of you have mentioned your noble, the one we should be most afraid of.'

All the Fiends except the one who had spoken hissed in retaliation, but Valki didn't shrink. He appeared in total control of himself.

Diana decided it was time to join. 'What noble?' she asked. 'What does that mean?'

'They split their race into three castes,' Valki answered. 'First, are those they describe as the weak. Second, the servants who represent the majority. Then, they have their nobles, the most powerful of their castes. I'd like to guess that Exia's the main reason they've mobilised.'

'That's enough, Hateful one,' the Fiend who had spoken warned, his tone seething. 'You do not have the right to utter her name.'

'No, but I bear responsibility to my kind, to inform them and my leader of what we're about to face, especially when none of us will fight them. We have a bigger problem if they are behind this. If your kind wishes to maintain this alliance, I believe a show of trust is in order.'

The familiar smile returned to Valki's expression. 'Besides, you need us,' he continued. 'You and your friends here will have been marked for death among your brethren. You cannot return to them, and word of your choice will spread to Elcaris. Your only negotiation ploy here is the inside information you can bring us.'

'Valki,' Diana cut in, not liking the way this conversation

was going. 'You may be part of my Council, but I remain leader. I will not have you threatening our allies into working with us. That is not grounds for a relationship. I believe the Council agrees with this.'

'Absolutely,' Pauli said.

'Yep,' Artemi added.

Heimval nodded in affirmation, while Reni soon followed.

Yes, but we must share our information. While I agree that threatening is no basis for a working relationship, I also believe withholding information applies to this. I would like our allies to disclose the name of the noble who Valki believes is leading the forces against us.

'Did you project that to them?' Diana asked, nodding towards the Fiends.

'Yes, we heard his words,' the Fiend who had spoken replied. 'And as much as I dislike the underhanded position we hold, I appreciate your honesty and intentions. Hence, I will give you her name of my volition. Our noble is Helenia Acratis.'

29

The Second Relic

'It has already begun,' Shallai said, her mouth agape as she looked on at the sight in horror.

In contrast, Barbatos appeared delighted.

Greene scowled, feeling Barbatos was out of line, making no effort to empathise with Shallai. It was worse than Elcaris, a great giant city in the middle of a desert, amid war. Laser fire, cannon blasts, and rockets arose from behind a wall that reminded Greene much of the Institute's, while many standalone towers rose from within it. Even they appeared damaged, showing how long the fighting had been taking place.

That just leaves the question of who they're fighting for, Greene thought, his gaze pulled towards the great battle taking place. *The Ether, or the Divinity?*

Alongside him, the Ethero Fiend known as Escara had her hands clasped together, a gleeful look on her face. It was as though she were watching a beautiful fireworks display, revelling in it. Yuvi, who had almost met his end by Doomis, appeared nonchalant. As for the Tortured, Greene couldn't tell what he was thinking. He remained concealed within his cloak, apparently fearful of others seeing his true form.

'I hope you are seeing this, father,' Barbatos murmured under his breath, causing Greene to glance towards him. As though sensing this, Barbatos turned and grinned.

'I wonder, did Forgiveness expect this when he created his delusion of peace?' he asked, scornful. 'What things he must have showed you, my dear Titanius. Tell me, do you believe what he achieved was truly peace? Or did he admit he was wrong?'

Greene said nothing, figuring the questions were rhetorical. He had yet to talk to Barbatos about what had happened in Elcaris. He doubted the sorcerer would say anything of truth. Greene sensed Barbatos knew what he had witnessed.

And he acknowledged the existence of Forgiveness, the one who had ended the previous war, who had spoken to Greene.

If my instinct is right, Forgiveness will have placed another defence around the relic, which means Barbatos has to use me to retrieve it. Then, I can ask Forgiveness the questions I harbour, and understand what purpose me bringing about the Titans serves.

Meanwhile, the war continued. It was Doomis who resumed their journey, appearing unaffected by what he was seeing.

At least he's on our side, Greene thought, still terrified by the Fiend.

'Doomis,' Barbatos said, stopping the Fiend. Greene noticed that the sorcerer had dared utter his name.

'For this part of our journey, I believe it would be wise for the group to hold back. Two of us shall enter Cybara.'

'Obviously Greene,' Doomis said, not shifting his gaze. 'But who else?'

Barbatos looked over to the other cloaked Ethero Fiend, who seemed to know the sorcerer was referring to him. The Tortured stepped forward, keeping his head down as he moved to the front of the group and beyond, before Greene realised the Fiend was leaving without him. A strange emotion rose within him then that compelled him to move with haste. He glanced behind to Barbatos, seeing his expression darken, the mask slipping once again.

'Remember, my dear Titanius, is what you see peace? Is your kind truly free, after what he and the Divinity did?'

They approached the city across the wide plain of sand, Greene feeling a sensation he was sure humans described as awkwardness while walking alongside the Ethero Fiend. There was no conversation. The Fiend hardly acknowledged his existence, never looking at him or speaking.

Why did Barbatos choose you? What is it about you that gains Doomis' respect?

He didn't dare ask those questions.

They moved over the sand dunes and stretches of flat terrain in silence, watching the vicious battle taking place in the city of Cybernetics.

'Titanius,' the Tortured said eventually, his voice soft. It was as though he were containing himself, from the way he clung onto his cloak, to how his tone seemed restrained. 'Tell me, what do you see?' he asked, sounding old, possessing the wisdom that could only come from suffering.

Greene looked at the walls. Among the laser fire and missiles, he could see the towers crumbling.

'I see pain,' he finally answered. 'I see two sides fighting a war for reasons I don't know. The problem is my ignorance.

I cannot tell what is true and what is deceit.'

'Why do you believe that is?' the Tortured asked.

The question made Greene think of the sorcerer responsible for this journey, and his expression turned scornful.

"I can explain who created those barriers. That distinction belongs to the Divinity," he recalled Barbatos saying to him, mere seconds after breaking through the barrier he didn't know imprisoned his kind. It brought with it the old sensation of anger.

'I don't know,' he admitted. 'But I will uncover the truth.'

'Has it ever occurred to you why the truth was kept from you, Descendant?' the Fiend asked, surprising Greene with the name Forgiveness had called him. Still, being kept from the truth filled him with anger.

'It doesn't matter,' he responded, trying to keep his voice calm. 'What gives anyone else the right to keep that truth from us? My kind were once great beings.'

'And terrible,' the Tortured said, his words conveying foreboding that made Greene shiver. As much as he wished to contest such words, the vision Forgiveness had given him kept him silent. Though the Titans were his Descendants, they did possess a terrible power.

And the desire to destroy everything.

'Conflict arises within you,' the Tortured said. 'You saw them. You know what they will bring to Ethero.'

'Yet I see you make no moves to stop me,' Greene said, walking alongside the Fiend. 'You support Barbatos and the Ether.'

'Is that so?' the cloaked Fiend replied, amused. He regarded Greene. 'You pursue a terrible power, now knowing what you are, understanding that Barbatos seeks to use that power for terrible means. Though I sense guilt within you, I think anger drives you forward.'

Greene said nothing to that. The Tortured, whatever he was, possessed something that suggested he could see much within Greene, to the extent he couldn't hide it if he wanted to. If the end was going to be terrible, what good were the intentions?

But I don't have a choice, do I? Greene wondered, remembering what Doomis had said to him about choice, and Forgiveness. *If I do not do this, then my kind remain enslaved, ignorant. Is that a price worth allowing humanity to maintain their dominance over us? Should I choose the greatest good, even if my kind continue to suffer as a result?*

Steam started to rise from the violet strands across his body. Greene allowed this, concentrating on it. It was another mystery, yet it brought another insight. He did not believe its emergence was coincidence.

'You know something about this,' he said.

'I know many things,' the Tortured said. 'You're wrestling with the dichotomy of the cost of truth. The effects of the irreversible. You question why you're the one to make this painful choice, and why they chose a Descendant. I would weep for you, Titanius, but I ran out of tears long ago.'

'Why?' Greene asked.

The cloaked Fiend stopped then, turning towards Greene. He opened his arms from his cloak, exposing long, narrow, ghost-white limbs covered in scars like Doomis was. Yet, the Tortured's arms seemed longer, his hands more claw-like. He reached towards his hood and pulled it back, revealing a face without eyes, just a small nose and mouth.

Greene stared at the Tortured in amazement. 'You're...' he

began, toying with the word "blind", but having no eyes was not blindness. It meant the Tortured could never see.

The Ethero Fiend smiled, as though reading Greene's thoughts.

'Not expecting this?' he asked. 'Do not confuse my name with one meaning, when many can apply. Doomis has probably explained to you how my kind grows and develops. However, what I imagine he's neglected to tell you is that growth comes with a price. To gain strength, one must sacrifice. This is the lesson I learnt as a child, and what I wish to impart to you now, Titanius.'

The Tortured half turned then, somehow giving the impression of looking towards Cybara's walls, leaving Greene in silence.

'This world is cruel, full of lies and hatred. To change that, one must first understand that reciprocation leads to empathy. One cannot understand another without first enduring what they've been through. Titanius, I am not known as the Tortured because someone tortured me. I tortured myself, as we all do, every single day. With that, I gained a power that even Doomis respects. Now, it is time we entered the city. The relic will be unprotected.'

'How do we get in?' Greene asked, feeling foolish asking for directions from someone without sight. However, the Tortured held out his hands and motioned them upward.

And Greene floated alongside the Ethero Fiend.

It was as though the Tortured had somehow reversed gravity, levitating them high into the air. Greene felt cold running over his body before their momentum shifted forward.

Then they were flying.

How are we doing this? Greene wondered. He looked back, trying to see the rest of their party. He couldn't, and he wasn't sure what they would think. Still, he could see they were being pulled towards Cybara, the city of Cybernetics.

The city was in chaos. Many Cybernetics were fighting against each another. Unlike Elcaris, whose structure and buildings followed a seemingly intentional arrangement, circling around the tree that protected the relic, Cybara's buildings and towers formed a sprawling metropolis, mismatched and veering off in different directions. Skeletal bridges connected many of the buildings at different levels throughout, which meant the fighting took place at different heights and hardly ever on the ground. Greene couldn't see a tree anywhere, but the Tortured guided them towards a single tower, which leaned to one side, independent from the others.

'Why there?' Greene asked. The Ethero Fiend either did not hear or chose not to answer. Rather than try to force the issue, Greene looked at the city beneath them, wondering how no one had spotted them yet. That wasn't the only thing Greene considered, as he focused on Cybara's strange formation, noticing other buildings among the mismatched metal sculptures the city seemed to represent. Greene tried to narrow his gaze on them.

Then the Tortured's power released.

Greene landed hard on a metal surface. When he realised where the Tortured had landed them, he pushed himself up, agitated.

'You could've done that more gently,' he said.

To his surprise, the Fiend smiled, before approaching the edge of the tower. Greene moved alongside the Tortured, looking over to the area he was staring at. Towards the north, looking like an independent district, Greene could see golden buildings with glowing aqua-coloured domes. Canals ran from the domed towers towards the rest of the city.

From this vantage point, Greene saw that Cybara sat on top of what looked like ancient metal gears, which glowed underneath from the substance the domed towers contained. Greene wondered if the liquid was the city's power source. That could explain the presence of the canals. Either way, it seemed the city possessed the capability to shift and change sections of itself.

But why? Greene wondered, frustrated with his limited knowledge. Something else occurred to him then, reminding him of what had transpired at Elcaris.

'The fighting. They're keeping it away from that section of the city with the domed towers. Is that where the relic is?'

'Perhaps,' the Tortured replied, sounding thoughtful. 'It would make sense for the tree to live alongside the Conflux generators.'

'Conflux generators?' Greene asked.

'The source of the Cybernetics creation,' he answered.

This intrigued Greene, knowing that Shallai had been unsure of the origin of her race.

'Where do the other races come from?' he asked.

'That is a question I cannot answer,' the Tortured said.

'Cannot, or will not?' Greene countered.

'Whichever suits your preference, Titanius,' the Tortured said, his voice a little icy, enough to end the subject there. 'We may have broken some oaths, but not all. Not all truths should be discovered.'

'What gives you the right to decide?' Greene challenged.

The Fiend smiled at that, as though respecting his boldness. 'There is a price for truth, Titanius. You will discover that soon enough.'

The Tortured carried them towards the site of the Conflux. Once again, Greene was surprised that no one had seen them, nor launched anything in their direction. Amid the domed towers, he stared down at the glowing canals that contained the supposed source of the Cybernetics' creation.

Why won't you tell me about them? About yourselves? Is it linked to the past?

These questions filled him. Greene hoped his next encounter with Forgiveness at his guardian tree would give him more insight.

They landed in the centre of the gear on which the domed towers sat. Greene was surprised to find it void of any Cybernetics. He wondered if the tree was the same as it was in Elcaris, capable of defending itself. He didn't sense it anywhere around them.

'You must go beneath the towers, towards the source of the Conflux. There you will find the tree, Titanius,' the Tortured said.

'Are you not coming?' Greene asked.

'No, I cannot,' the Tortured said. 'Only the Descendant may enter and retrieve the piece of the Titan core.'

'But Shallai–'

'Is lucky the tree didn't destroy her,' the Tortured finished for him. 'Forgiveness created them for a specific purpose. I do not wish to lose my life just yet, Titanius. Find the tree. I will remain here to ensure that no one interrupts you.'

Greene nodded and headed towards one of the domed towers, guessing they'd lead him towards the tree. The architecture was grand: a giant glass column ran from the domed top through the entire building, filled with Conflux. Surrounding it, a golden metal staircase ran underground, and Greene noticed a faint change to the air around him as he walked inside it. There was a whiteness to it, shimmering with some kind of ethereal essence.

Have I entered the barrier? Greene wondered, before making his way towards the glowing column of Conflux, following the staircase down. From there, Greene continued, mere centimetres away from the source of all Cybernetics.

The staircase led to a tunnel, in which tiny streams of Conflux emerged and streamed away. It reminded Greene much of the violet Life Essence that ran through his own body. With that, Greene noticed a strange steam rising from it, and his body responded by doing the same. Unlike before, the steam flowed more consistently, and accompanied the sound of multiple voices. Dizziness overcame Greene then, though he wasn't sure why. Still, he continued forward, hearing a distinct thrumming that sounded like the activation of generators all around him.

'Forgiveness, can you hear me?' he asked, as an opening emerged within the tunnel, revealing a single silver tree with leaves of gold. It looked like the guardian tree in Elcaris. Upon seeing it, goosebumps broke out over his body, and his vision shook. Greene fell to his knees as though in a drunken stupor.

What is this? he wondered, before crawling forward. Beyond, the tree wove and shifted, changing.

Then Greene fell unconscious.

At least, that's what he thought. He was certain he was still present in his body despite everything being black. He groaned, while the sound of thrumming and steam leaving his body continued. Despite the weakness threatening to overcome him, Greene forced himself onto his hands and knees, trying to regain control over himself.

'What is…happening to me?' he croaked, fighting the desire to collapse again. He gritted his teeth and rose to his feet. He opened his eyes, seeing a new being before him.

It looked like a bigger Titanius. Standing at least twenty feet tall, this being appeared powerful and imposing, yet there was a calmness to it. It possessed the same streaks of violet veins as he did.

Hear me, all Titaniuses.

Greene froze. The voice sounded like his own, but stronger, more authoritative. It was as though it had matured, evolved, carrying great power.

'Are you a future representation of me?' he asked.

The being looked down at him. Then, it shifted into one of the colossal beings he had grown to fear and appreciate in equal measure: a Titan.

My name is Greene. I am speaking to all of you, using the power of our ancestors, of the Titan core that has granted me control of the Titan known as—

The voice did not complete its sentence. Greene rose, his vision blurring, shifting. The image of the Titan, huge as it was, shook as debris and bodies fell from the sky. Human bodies, Greene realised.

'What is happening?!' Greene exclaimed, listening to the chilling sounds of their screams. It made little sense. Why were they falling? Was it because the Titan had picked them up before dropping them? Or was it something else? Greene didn't know, but the screams reminded him of his failure, of

Megidra unleashing his own Descendants upon humanity.

We have risen. The voice that sounded like Greene continued speaking as though addressing a large audience. *I have exposed the lie, and I present to you the truth behind our kind, the truth that has led to us being imprisoned and forced to serve as slaves. My goal is to liberate my kind and make humanity pay for what it has done to us. The beings of the Divinity and the Ether have lived under sworn oaths to protect the truth from our kind. Now that I am speaking to you, they will stop at nothing to exterminate us, knowing the power we possess.*

I won't let them have their way.

I will begin my march, to trample and destroy all the settlements that the other races occupy. Then, I will awaken my brothers one by one, those who humanity has mocked for so long, never realising what lies beneath their feet. Together, we will obliterate all life, until Titaniuses are all that remains on Ethero.

Greene screamed as the vision of his ancestor faded, leaving only swirls of silver wind. Then he felt a strange calmness. Eventually, those slivers swirled before him, fusing into a silver being, its hair rising towards the sky.

'Forgiveness?' Greene asked. The being, Forgiveness, dropped to one knee, nodding.

'You saw it?' he asked, his voice ancient and wise. Despite the weakness flooding his body, Greene nodded.

'Was that a premonition of what I will become? Should I choose to continue down this path?'

'It is a possibility, one I wished to show you,' Forgiveness said. 'Truth always comes at a cost. The cost of my truth left me no choice, Descendant. Ethero had to become this way.'

'Why?' Greene asked.

'Because I wasn't strong enough, missing something of vital

importance,' Forgiveness said. 'I could not defeat the Divinity, nor the Ether. All I achieved was a suspension to the war, not a solution. In return for that truth, I realised another.'

'The missing piece?' Greene ventured.

Forgiveness nodded again. 'Yes. I realised that destroying those who created the world would not heal it. That is what Ethero needs, Descendant. It needs a power known as the Healing to heal. However, the Child of Healing must undergo his path to unleash it. You have to make a terrible choice, but you are part of that path.'

'What is the other choice?' Greene asked. 'Is there not another way?'

'No. You cannot erase centuries of hurt and oppression from the minds of those enslaved. By uniting the relics and creating the Titan core, you will carry the hatred of all Titaniuses. That hatred will make you want to destroy everything, but it will also unlock your true power. With that, you can free your race, show them they have always held the power to choose.'

Forgiveness rose to his feet.

'Descendant, the cycle of healing begins with the downfall, before one can seek forgiveness.'

'But you said it wasn't enough,' Greene said.

Forgiveness considered that. 'No, they aren't. Both are precursors. They both lead to the last step of healing: acceptance.'

Greene's eyes flickered, and he realised he had returned to the world of Ethero, of Cybara. A glowing object flickered on his chest. It was the Titan core, bigger now. It dawned upon Greene that the second relic had already combined itself with the first.

'Acceptance,' he murmured.

30

Escape From Seraphu

It surprised Megidra when John said nothing to the others as they left the warehouse. The infamous Devil of Anubi walked among them. The one who had made Exia this way, ruining countless lives in the process, stood in their midst. Megidra knew he'd scream the truth from the top of his lungs if it was the other way around.

Or, perhaps that's because a part of me wants this done, because I know what I deserve.

Inside, Ryun seemed amused by that thought, watching along with Megidra as Deion greeted John from the truck, his rifle ready in hand.

'Anything in there worth taking?' the large human asked.

'Nah, nothing important. Just some old fuel tanks,' John answered. 'Nothing we could fit on the truck ahead of the other supplies.'

'That's a shame,' Deion said. 'Thought Megi had been onto something.'

'Yeah, so did he,' John said, looking back at Megidra, his expression impassive. 'We should get going.'

Why aren't you telling him the truth? Megidra frowned. He wondered if it was because John was being smart, knowing that they'd need him for this crucial part of their mission. It made more sense to tell everyone the truth later, when they'd at least gained their safety. As Megidra considered that, Deion turned to him.

'We contacted the other groups,' he said. 'They'll meet us at Johann's church. I hope you know what the next plan is, Megi. Our friends think more monsters are on the way.'

Those monsters, meaning Ethero Fiends, were the major threat they had to worry about for now.

'We need to leave here now!' the female Cybernetic insisted, standing with her male companion.

Deion turned to them and nodded, before looking back to Megidra.

'Let's do this!' he said.

The humans cheered, and someone switched on the truck's engine, the lights beaming to life.

Deion had already planned a strategy for their escape. First, Megidra and the Cybernetics would guard the truck, sitting on the roof, ready to intercept whoever or whatever came their way. The rest of the humans would use their guns and Blessings to keep enemies away.

To think I was expecting to be the only guard, ready to deflect other humans, Megidra mused. By his reckoning, the Ethero Fiends would be the biggest threat, followed closely by the Cybernetics. The former would likely prefer close engagements, while the latter would use long-range weaponry. This would not be a straightforward mission.

To reduce the likelihood of combat, Deion and the humans

would drive the truck slowly, with no lights. Then they would head towards the earlier warehouses that they'd marked for collecting supplies. Once they filled the truck, they'd get out of Seraphu, using the narrow streets to get to Rai.

Overall, it was a simple plan, largely based on hope and confidence.

Megidra had his own plan if things went wrong. As a last resort, he would use Ryun, while making the Cybernetics take control of the truck, forcing the humans to return home.

Hehehe... I'm always here if you need me, Megidra, the Fallen said. Megidra forced himself to ignore him, despite knowing that they'd need to talk sooner rather than later about how to proceed. That, of course, depended on how he proceeded himself. Megidra was sure John would tell the others the truth about him soon enough.

Resignation washed over him, but Megidra forced himself to concentrate, tapping into his Physical Blessing and jumping on top of the truck, along with the two Cybernetics. It would at least give him the speed to respond to threats as they arose. The truck moved then, slowly. Still, that meant little when they moved under streetlights. Megidra chose not to focus on that, instead listening to the drowned-out sound of the truck, muffled by the heavy blizzard.

'What are your names?' he asked the Cybernetics.

'Odeon,' the male Cybernetic said.

'Ilara,' the female Cybernetic said.

Megidra nodded. 'Megidra,' he said. 'Can you alter your sight to see at range?'

'Yes,' Odeon said, 'I've scanned the area. There's no sign of anything. I don't like it.'

Megidra didn't like that either.

'Keep looking. Be ready,' he said.

The truck reached the first warehouse of their reverse order around ten minutes later to no sign of resistance. That was suspicious to Megidra, but he was sure that Odeon and Ilara weren't guiding them to an ambush; he could tell they were as anxious as he was.

Besides, they'd have no reason to, he rationalised, allowing his DFA instincts to help him reach his conclusion. *There's nothing to gain from a sneak attack. We have nothing of value to them. So, either we're incredibly lucky, or...*

Megidra pondered this, knowing it was also a part of his Hateful nature to fixate and become anxious while considering things. Still, the humans were quick despite their efforts to be quiet, finishing their first collection in minutes. They returned to their positions before the truck moved again. They emerged onto the single road that ran through the district, and Megidra could find no sign of movement. It was like Seraphu was empty.

But they must've discovered the bodies I left behind? Where are they?

It surprised Megidra further when the second collection went the same, as the humans collected the next batch of supplies without issue. They headed towards the main road once again.

'I don't like this. Something's wrong,' Odeon said. 'This all seems too intentional. It's as though they're waiting for us to reach a certain point.'

'I know. I'm just not sure what they'd gain from that,' Megidra said, relieved someone shared his thoughts. However, if the Fiends were going to spring a trap, the most likely spot would be the first warehouse, where he had slaughtered the group of Ethero Fiends. As the truck turned into the warehouse, he braced himself for attack.

But the signs of his slaughter had disappeared.

Megidra was stunned. The bodies were gone, along with any trace of their black blood.

'What is it?' Ilara asked.

Megidra threw himself off the truck as it stopped, going to where the bodies should've been. There were still indents in the snow.

'This is wrong,' he muttered. 'Their bodies are gone. They should be here, waiting for us.'

'Megi!' He heard Deion call out to him. A few seconds later, an arm wrapped around his shoulder. 'They're gone,' he murmured.

'Yes. I don't like this, Deion,' Megidra said, rising to his feet. 'Make the next collection.'

'Got it,' Deion said, breaking off to join the others.

Megidra jumped back onto the truck, joining Odeon and Ilara.

'Keep your senses sharp,' he said. He tapped into his Transformative Blessing, summoning his curving arm blade on his right hand, a machine gun on the left. 'If they're going to hit us, it'll be now.'

But nothing did, which only further fuelled Megidra's anxiety as he watched the others load the last of the supplies. He realised how much these humans meant to him, despite the little time he had spent with them. That amazed him, wondering what they had done differently compared to others he had known in the past. Then it became obvious.

You've treated me like one of you, neither human nor Hateful.

Despite his growing fear for them, Megidra smiled in

appreciation, before feeling a wave of bitterness.

But why did it take so long for me to feel these things? Why this situation, and my horrific mistakes? Now, I want to stay with you. I don't wish to be alone anymore.

Megidra felt melancholy, not wishing to indulge in it. Knowing he needed to focus, he surveyed the surrounding area.

Then he saw the woman behind him.

Megidra froze in horror, noting the peculiar black garb the woman wore despite the weather. It was a thin dress, black and embroidered with complex patterns that matched her tights and ruby sleeves, which also matched the colour of her long flowing hair. Had Megidra not seen the black eyes of her face, or the crimson sword she held by her side, he would've considered her an exquisite human in her late twenties. This explained why they had encountered no resistance during their journey.

She's a noble.

'Oh, you're not my Hateful,' she said, as Ilara and Odeon turned in their direction. Megidra prayed they wouldn't make any sudden moves, realising what she was, and what her arrival meant.

'Odeon. Ilara,' he said, his voice small, while Ryun laughed from within. 'Get the others. Tell them we're leaving, now.'

The two Cybernetics obeyed, and Megidra forced himself to rise. He turned to face the noble Ethero Fiend.

'Are you planning on taking me alone?' she asked, as though this amused her. 'I guess I have you to thank for the mess we had to clean up earlier. Still, do you really think I'm going to let your little human friends escape, Hateful one?'

She looked over to the humans. Megidra doubted they

would understand what was about to happen.

The noble turned back to him, her amused look never fading. 'I'm surprised. I would've thought you'd be fighting alongside us. After all, you killed so many of their families and friends. Do you not harbour one of her children? Why do you support them now?'

'Because I made a grave mistake,' Megidra answered. 'I regret everything I've ever done, so I'm going to change. I will not become that monster again.'

'The monster is always within,' the noble replied. 'Is that not the nature of all sentient beings?'

Megidra moved, throwing his curved arm blade up in a single slash. Unfortunately, his attack struck only a black mist, which flowed past him, reforming on the other side of the truck.

'Do you know what I am?' she asked, her tone sinister.

Megidra held strong, raising his Transformative machine gun towards her. 'A noble Ethero Fiend,' he replied. 'And I guess I have you to thank for drawing the others towards the surface.'

'No, that honour belongs to you and my lover. You paved the way through blood, and he convinced me it was time to break the oaths. We will no longer stand as inferiors to humanity.'

'What are you talking about?' Megidra asked.

The noble smiled. 'You will find out soon enough. Either way, we're going to capture your human friends, and we're going to do what we should've done years ago. Besides, it's not like we can produce more of ourselves, is it?'

Megidra's expression narrowed. Though he didn't understand what the noble was talking about, he understood that she and the others were a threat he needed to stop. He scowled. 'Not while I'm here,' he muttered.

The noble grinned. 'I hoped you would say that,' she said.

Before Megidra realised what she meant, his instincts told him to shift his head towards his right. A radiant crimson blade was inches away from his face. He opened fire with his machine gun, doubting it would hit the noble. That didn't matter. It would at least alert the others that they needed to move now.

He spun on his feet, shifting his Transformative machine gun into another curving arm blade. He extended his arms and threw himself forward, spinning as fast as he could, hoping that he'd force her off the truck. Megidra hung in the air for a few seconds, before his momentum shifted over the truck. He completed the spin and landed on the snowy surface. He lowered himself into a crouch, keeping his blades raised, ready to face the noble.

But she was nowhere to be seen, and Megidra felt a sudden pain in his chest.

He looked down. There was a straight line across his cloak, seeping blood.

'How did you do that?' he asked, listening as the truck pulled away behind him, its engine roaring into life.

'What a wonderful sight,' the noble Ethero Fiend said.

Megidra turned to see the truck pulling away. He looked back at the noble, noting her hunger as she eyed him.

'You are the first of many who will bleed from my blade, Hateful one,' she said. She raised her crimson sword towards her mouth, licking off the blood that had yet to evaporate. The sword glowed as though it were hungry for more blood.

Megidra took a step back while shifting his Transformative

Blessing, switching both blades for a short cannon on his right arm, with a handle he held on his left. He charged a blast, which appeared to amuse the noble.

'You still wish to proceed, knowing you cannot win?' she asked, a sentiment Ryun agreed with from within, stirring.

She's right, Megidra, he said. *You cannot defeat her, not without me.*

The noble stepped forward, whipping her sword out by her side. 'Tell me, why do you care about them? You despise humanity, and your race. Why do you stand for them now?'

'Because there's one thing I despise even more than either of them,' Megidra said, his expression darkening as the cannon reached full charge. 'Myself.'

He fired then, and the brilliant ball of energy rushed towards the noble. She stepped to one side, as though to show how easy it was for her. As Megidra watched it race ahead, the emitting light finally exposed all the other Ethero Fiends.

They were sitting on the wall, like vultures awaiting the feeding.

'Do you see it now?' the noble asked.

Looking around, Megidra understood what she meant: Cybernetics emerged from the warehouse roof, while Animus emerged from the sky. He was standing before an army of those who stood for the Eternal Mother. He knew that Deion and the others wouldn't see what he was facing.

I have to protect them.

You have no choice, Megidra, Ryun said, chilling him to the core. *Release me, and I shall lay waste to every one of them.*

Megidra considered, feeling an urge to agree to Ryun's suggestion. He looked at the gathering races, picturing them not as the forces of the Ether, but as human beings, unaware of the slaughter about to befall them. He shook his head.

Not today, he replied to Ryun. *To use you again would mean that I have not changed, that I resorted to you to hide my own fallacies. I cannot do that. Only when I say my truth can I use you again. Until then, I stand alone.*

To his surprise, his Fallen did not protest, nor mock or condone him. The Fallen seemed more thoughtful.

You have discovered a truth, he said, impressed. *However, you know the cost that befalls that truth.*

'Yes,' Megidra muttered, raising his head towards the sky. 'I will tell them, once I've seen them safely returned.'

Very well, Ryun said. *Then at least utilise one of my gifts to ensure you survive this long enough to tell them.*

'A compromise I'm willing to accept,' Megidra said. He relinquished his cannon, switching it to his favoured curved arm blade.

'You already used that, Devil of Anubi,' the noble said. 'It didn't work.'

'Maybe so,' Megidra agreed, feeling Ryun's power filling him. 'But after this, you will know me as a different Devil. Tonight, your kind will remember me as the Devil of Fiends.'

Megidra held out his arms, allowing Ryun's power to flow outward as violet and crimson smoke. The smoke began to change, forming into human shapes.

They shifted into replicas of Megidra himself.

Megidra could not quite believe what he was seeing.

Yes, perfect copies of you, each possessing your knowledge and experience, Ryun said. They can fight on their own. Where do you think Barbatos got the idea of the Descendants from?

So you've always been capable of this? Megidra asked.

Yes. Each Fallen has a specific power. This is mine.

Megidra nodded, deciding that any further questions could wait until later. He knew his copies could handle the rest of the creatures, while he could deal with the noble.

He tapped into his Physical Blessing, enhancing his muscles while keeping them as lean as possible, and kicked off the floor to launch himself at the noble. She didn't expect his attack, and Megidra easily brought her down to the ground. Then he launched himself into the air, raising a giant fist upward before throwing it down to crush her face.

But the noble threw a punch of her own, striking Megidra in the face and sending him crashing into the warehouse. Megidra looked up to see the noble rising to her feet. He blinked and somehow she traversed the distance between them in that time, her sword ready to strike.

'Die, Devil!' she cursed, stabbing the blade forward, only to find violet and crimson smoke. Not understanding, the noble looked towards the battlefield, seeing her kind along with the Cybernetics and Animus fighting the copies of Megidra. She frowned.

'Look behind you,' someone said, and Megidra kicked her hard in the ribs. 'Now burn,' he hissed, summoning a barrage of flame that appeared to swallow the noble. Even her fellow Fiends stopped fighting. Their mouths hung open in disbelief as they watched their noble consumed by flames. However, Megidra remained on guard.

'Enough!' the noble shrieked, extinguishing his flames with a swipe of her arm.

Megidra took a step back, raising a curved blade and a large shield, ready for the next engagement.

We've pissed her off, Megidra noted, noticing the menacing aura that surrounded her. A shimmering of red encapsulated her body, causing her eyes to glow, while her hair floated in a way that looked like the Fallen form. Her sword changed, dripping blood from the blade.

'We're coming for your city,' she said. 'And we will take every one of your precious humans. We will slaughter every one of you.'

Her power faded, and the noble jumped onto the wall behind her with an effortless bound. She disappeared. The others followed suit. Megidra watched them leave, while relinquishing his Blessings. Alongside him, his copies faded back into violet and crimson wisps.

'I have to tell them,' he said. 'We have little time left.'

31

The Healing

Lucifer left Mika's room an hour later, having watched her drift into a peaceful sleep. It didn't surprise him. She was drained from her battle, and they'd discussed elements of her past that must have been difficult. Still, like so many from Silver Wing, she had also given him viewpoints he wouldn't have considered before.

Or, perhaps it's more the case I would've refused to consider them. The more I consider my past self. The more I look at beings like Gabriel and Megidra. I wonder if we're the ones causing our own struggle?

Lucifer knew he was a different person now. Part of this had been because of Silver Wing, and part because of his confrontation with Gabriel. It was time to talk. It was time to understand what was going on.

'I guess there's no better time than now, Korai?' Lucifer suggested. The Fallen stirred from within, becoming contemplative.

So you're ready? Korai said. Lucifer nodded, glancing either way down the long corridor in Silver Wing's hideout. No one was present, so he headed back to his room.

Lucifer noticed the bareness of his room now. The shelves had nothing on them, and he knew the wardrobe was empty. The bedside table had a single light, and it was this Lucifer found himself drawn to, half turning to sit on the bed. He looked around again.

I could do a lot with this place, Lucifer considered, thinking of Mika's room. Then he chuckled, realising. 'It's like I want to live here now,' he whispered.

Korai emerged then, filling Lucifer with his presence. *You're changing,* Korai said, sounding almost impressed. *Your interactions with Silver Wing and Gabriel have affected you.*

'I guess,' Lucifer admitted. 'It's just another path. Both Setsu and Mika had awful things happen to them, Mika more so, yet they've all chosen a path different from my own. They don't look back with hatred. They've chosen to move on. I wonder if I could do the same thing.'

Can you? Korai asked.

'That's what I'm trying to figure out,' Lucifer said, staring at the ceiling. 'It's like I'm on the periphery of something, but there's just one thing holding me back. There's something I need to do.'

Face your past, Korai answered.

'The question is, can I do it?' Lucifer asked, more to himself than Korai. The Fallen didn't have an answer either. It had to be him who decided. Lucifer kept his gaze on the ceiling as he considered that.

'Alright, Korai. Who are you? What are you? And why are you in me with the silver being?'

That's a lot of questions, the Fallen remarked, though he didn't seem agitated by this. *Very well. I was created to destroy the Divinity's Angels, to serve as a Demon in Ethero. After the Divinity failed in his duty and scorned many of his creations, they turned on him, and the war for Ethero begun. The Eternal Mother against the Divinity.*

'Who is this "Eternal Mother"?' Lucifer asked, lying back on his bed.

The progenitor of all life, Korai said. *She created this world, and the Divinity himself. After the Divinity's last creation turned against him, he joined with the Eternal Mother. They declared war against the Divinity, and they created me and four other Demons to serve as their power. They called us the Fallen.*

The war never ended. Years passed, and many lost their lives, yet the rage and hatred that sustained it never faded. It only grew stronger. Eventually, fate led me towards a chance encounter, to face an Angel named Orphani.

The Fallen said the name as if he missed her. Lucifer reflected on the female presence that lived within him.

Yes, I sense her too, Korai said. *Which makes you a very particular case, Lucifer.*

'She called me the "Child of Healing", that I can unleash this thing called "The Healing". What are those things? How are they linked?'

I can only guess. I do not know nor understand much about us, Lucifer. When I met Orphani, I believed I had found someone, a being that I found myself not wishing to harm. Both she and I wished for an end to the war. It was with this desire we had a child, Lucifer, a silver being known as Forgiveness. We believed he had the power to end the war.

But he didn't.

Forgiveness revealed to us he was incomplete, that he needed one more aspect to heal the world. He required both our powers alongside his own. Unfortunately, all three of us were separate entities, incapable of combining our strength. Back then, I didn't understand what he meant by that.

Until you revealed you had him inside of you.

And so, we used our power to call a ceasefire to the war, forcing the scorned and their leader to go into hiding. We tried to help them, but the damage had been done. Soon, both Orphani and I perished, but we believed that Forgiveness could keep this world at peace.

He didn't. Forgiveness shared the same fate as us, which I figure led to this world's deterioration. Years passed, and all I remember is awakening, trapped inside your body. Believing this to be a punishment for my actions in the past, and missing my love Orphani, I turned to hatred, and flamed the hatred within you.

'Leading to what took place in Exia,' Lucifer said. Inside, he sensed Korai's regret.

Yes. And words cannot express how sorry I am for what happened, Lucifer. We were both blinded by hatred. We were a perfect match until I felt Forgiveness within you. I've come to realise what he meant all those years ago. I believe this is the destiny he's chosen for you, Lucifer. To undergo the journey to heal, so you can use our power to unleash the Healing.

'So you were the beginning,' Lucifer said. 'As was Exia. The representation of the downfall, my failure.'

Yes, so you could continue towards the next step: forgiveness.

'So if we're right, and Orphani is the third being within me, she represents the last step.'

That would be my theory, Lucifer, Korai said. *That doesn't mean it's a certainty. We could misinterpret all of this, stipulating our desires on this. However, the next question, knowing all this, is what will you do?*

'Isn't that the question,' Lucifer remarked, sitting up. 'If I'm going to find forgiveness, or at least understand it means, I need to face my past. I cannot run from it anymore. So, I guess it begins with telling Silver Wing what happened in Exia.'

Knowing it was the right answer, Lucifer nodded before rising to his feet.

'I guess today's the day for some important conversations,' he said, moving towards the door, hoping Silver Wing was in the common room.

They weren't, but Lucifer continued with his plan anyway, sitting at the long table at the centre. He looked over the tall bookshelves that lined the walls, and the glowing red orbs that Kyrn had invented. Lucifer imagined Ven sitting here reading. She loved books, and nothing made him happier than to watch her at peace. No words needed to be said. No forced notions. Only love.

I wonder, Ven. What were your times like here? How did you interact with Silver Wing? How did they interact with you? So many questions... I miss everything about you.

A shiver ran through him, and he had to take in a breath. He realised he was crying. He felt no shame. This only opened the floodgates further, and Lucifer wept without restraint, realising he hadn't cried since Vennifer's death.

'I miss you so much,' he said.

And still he wept, as Lucifer felt a great weight upon his temple, resting it in his hands. He hadn't realised how poorly he had slept, and how tiredness was creeping through his body.

Lucifer allowed himself to look upward to see the radiant presence of a woman on the other side of the table. She glowed like Korai and Forgiveness; her aura was gold. She wore a gown of white silk. Upon her back Lucifer could see two giant white wings. Her pale skin made her golden hair stand out, contrasting with her blue eyes.

Lucifer regarded her in stunned silence. 'Orphani,' he said, knowing it was her, Korai's love.

Orphani smiled. 'Indeed, I am,' she said. 'I'm sorry you had to endure this, Lucifer. Still, you're walking on the path towards healing, so then you can unleash the Healing upon Ethero.'

'But why me?' he asked. 'Why do I harbour all three of you? What makes me any different?'

'You're wondering why you're the Child of Healing?' Orphani asked. 'Lucifer, do you know why the Hateful are persecuted?'

Lucifer's lips opened, about to utter the answer he always devolved to. Yet, it seemed wrong. It couldn't just be a case that it was because they were Hateful. That answer was petty, too bitter. It lacked consideration, truth.

As though sensing this within him, Orphani smiled again. 'In the beginning, the Divinity sought to create beings in his image. He wished to build what he viewed as perfection. Unlike the Eternal Mother, he believed all his own creations would follow a similar fate to himself. The Divinity vowed they would be better than anything she created. But they weren't. The animals were too primitive, too rash and impulsive. They did not possess the intelligence to align with the Divinity's ideal. So, he created us next, his Angels. While we were closest to his perfection, we were still not enough. He made us his loyal subjects, signs that he was drawing closer to that which he sought.

'Next, he resolved to do something more radical, an experiment to see if he could mass-produce his next creatures. By doing this, he hoped to find the perfect one among them and then replicate them. This is the origin of humanity, Lucifer.'

'But none of them were perfect, were they?' Lucifer asked.

Orphani didn't disagree. 'They were his next failure, and the Divinity felt only fury. After all, his dream had begun by creating perfect beings in his own image, yet every single time it would fail. His beings would make the same mistakes. I ask you, if you were someone seeking perfection in your own creations, and every single time all you received was imperfection, what would that say about you?'

Lucifer said nothing, feeling tingles running through his own being. He remembered the very people that had helped him form his own dream, and everything else that followed.

His parents.

'You understand now, don't you?' Orphani asked.

Again, Lucifer didn't answer. He didn't need to.

'Dismayed with what he found in humanity, the Divinity grew desperate. In that desperation and outrage, he extracted his next attempt upon humanity. While their physical forms were exactly as he wished, their minds were not. He began to tweak and alter their brains, while bestowing more of his power upon them. He was sure this final alteration would create the perfect being.'

'But he created us instead,' Lucifer said. 'Instead of creating perfection, he created disability.'

'Yes,' Orphani answered. 'And it was your kind that caused

the Divinity to break. Your kind were the failures that represented everything that was wrong in his eyes. The Divinity cast you all aside, blowing the sun out of the sky and condemning your race as failures before humanity. Humans being humans, they accepted this judgement, and hence the persecution against your kind was born. From there, the Divinity in his rage continued in his barbaric experimentation, creating more and more creatures, beings who had remained in hiding from you. The beings were led by one, the last creation of the Divinity. I assume Korai has already told of what happened then.'

Lucifer nodded.

'When our son, Forgiveness, realised he wouldn't be enough, he suggested we required someone with all our strength. He proposed giving it to the races that gained the scorn of the Divinity. I convinced him of another way, of bestowing our power upon one, a child who could heal the world of the hatred and pain that created it. We decided not to tell Korai, for we needed his anger to spark the path that would lead you towards the rest of us.

'Now you're on the path to forgiveness, Lucifer. You're so close. But you must take the last steps. You must forgive those who you once perceived to have wronged you, and you must face your own past and forgive yourself. Once you've shown that you embody forgiveness, my son will grant you his power.'

'But how do I do that?' Lucifer asked, confused. 'What do you mean by embodying forgiveness?'

'You will know, soon, Lucifer,' Orphani said. 'Because attaining something isn't embodying it. However, you are close, Lucifer. You will tell Silver Wing the truth of what happened in Exia. Then, despite your reservations, you will revisit your past and confront it. During this time you must choose to embody forgiveness, or embrace your downfall.'

Orphani faded then, shimmering into golden sparkles. 'I am so proud of you, Lucifer,' she said faintly. 'You are so close to the final stage, that which I embody.'

'And what is that? Please, tell me!' Lucifer said, rising to his feet, stretching his hand over the table towards Orphani, whose form began to shift and change.

She became Vennifer.

'Acceptance,' she said, smiling, much like the way she had done before she died.

'Acceptance,' Lucifer whispered, haunted, before he fainted.

Lucifer awoke sometime later. He wasn't sure how long he had been unconscious. Cooking smells caused him to stir, and the sounds of laughing and happy voices. Groaning a little as he moved, Lucifer realised that he'd fallen unconscious slumped over the table. There was a plate of cooked sausages, bacon, eggs, beans and toast before him, still steaming from warmth.

'Looked like you needed it, Prince,' Setsu remarked. The confident Hateful man was already tucking into his own food.

Lucifer started eating, and energy returned to him, his stomach groaning in a sign that he hadn't eaten for some time.

'Thanks, Setsu,' he said. Lucifer felt his fellow Hateful's studying gaze.

'You've changed, Prince,' he observed.

'Yeah? How so?' Lucifer asked.

'Your tone for a start,' Setsu said, smiling. 'You sound

calmer, more comfortable. Damn, I'm gonna have to be careful around you when I'm bringing human chicks home. If I thought the edgelord thing was powerful, a calm, composed Prince might cause me serious trouble.'

'I doubt that,' Liesa said, from the opposite side of the table, a smug look on her face.

'Oh yeah,' Setsu said, as though understanding her meaning. He continued eating while Liesa stared at Lucifer.

'Still, I think you should tie your hair, man,' Setsu said. 'I'm tellin' ya, that calm, suave demeanour you've got now, crossed with that kinda look; you'll have all the ladies after you.'

'Shut up, Setsu!' Liesa said. 'He's been looking after Mika these past few days. She's the only one he's interested in.'

'You're obsessed with them getting together,' Setsu remarked.

'Yeah, and you're obsessed about getting me to tie my hair and chasing women,' Lucifer said, a response that caused Setsu's eyes to widen in surprise.

'You might be correct about that,' he conceded. 'But c'mon! Lionas already has Claire, and Kyrn has the charisma of one of those orb things he's made.'

'What's that supposed to mean?' Liesa asked, defensively.

Setsu took a long, hard look at her before his customary smile returned. 'Dull,' he answered.

Liesa opened her mouth to retaliate, before falling to silence as though she couldn't deny it.

Lucifer found a chuckle escaping him.

'Did you just laugh out loud?' Liesa said, watching as embarrassment washed across Lucifer's face. Setsu rose from his seat, throwing his hands in the air in celebration.

'Yes! I did it again!' Setsu said, cheering as though he had

293

accomplished something grand. 'I made Prince laugh!'

'Well done, Setsu,' Lionas commented, coming in with Claire.

Mika followed closely behind. She smiled at Lucifer, a smile that warmed his heart. She sat next to him, while Lionas and Claire sat alongside Liesa.

'How are you?' Mika asked.

'I'm alright. You?' Lucifer asked.

'Aww… They're so adorable!' Liesa remarked.

'It's good to see you two appearing so calm,' Lionas remarked.

Mika said nothing to that, and neither did Lucifer. Instead, he shifted his plate across so that it sat somewhat between them, deciding to focus on Mika.

'I assume you're hungry?' Lucifer asked. Mika shifted sightly, as though embarrassed by his gesture. Realising what he had done, Lucifer turned to the rest of the table.

Then they all laughed.

Mika did not laugh, her face beaming red, but even Lucifer found himself chuckling. After a couple of minutes, the laughter faded, and Kyrn came out of the kitchen, holding two plates of food. He brought them to the table and kissed Liesa before sitting down.

'That's so typical of you, Kyrn,' Setsu remarked. 'You always miss the good stuff.'

'That's alright,' Kyrn said. 'Hearing your happiness is enough for me.'

'And that's why I love him so much,' Liesa fawned, stroking Kyrn's back.

Lucifer looked at Lionas then, who was staring at him.

'It's wonderful to see you like this, Lucifer,' he said. 'I hope you can see why everyone here wants you to stay.'

'Yes,' Lucifer said, nodding. He realised that he wanted to stay too, to become a part of Silver Wing.

'Everyone,' he began, knowing he would grab everyone's attention. 'There's something I want to talk to you about.'

32

Typically Hateful

Diana had called the emergency meeting with her Council after hearing reports that the forces of the Ether had mobilised from Seraphu. Fighting had erupted throughout the city. They didn't have much time.

I have to save everyone, Diana thought, walking into the courtroom, wearing some of Hela's clothes. A decision had to be made. They needed to save as many humans as possible, by allowing more into the Institute.

The walls that kept the races apart was about to become a bastion to save them.

Eren joined her. 'Diana, I've been told we're increasing security on the wall. May I join them?'

'It's alright Eren,' Diana said. 'It's just a precaution. I need you on the Council.'

Eren nodded.

The large human they had encountered before was there too, and Diana welcomed him. 'Thank you for coming too. I wanted your input for the talks we're about to have.'

'I appreciate that,' the human man said, appearing more

relaxed than when they first met. 'I just wanted to say thanks. To all of you. I see how much we've accepted what we're told. The Hateful are good people. Eren proves that.'

Diana beamed internally at those words. She had only dreamed of progress. She noticed Eren scratching his head while looking away.

'You've done an incredible job, Eren,' Diana remarked.

The young Hateful man blushed . Before he could reply, the doors to the courtroom swung open again.

It was Artemi, alongside Reni, followed by Heimval. Diana stepped towards them, knowing that she always felt calm when Reni was there. Artemi seemed to sense this, holding out Reni's hand. Diana nodded in thanks, before turning with Reni in tow and heading back towards Eren and the human man.

Ah, another human. I see there's been more progress, Diana, Reni said, speaking to her through his Illusionary Blessing. Diana smiled at him.

Then Reni did something she didn't expect. He ceased tapping on his head, and went to the large human, holding out his hand.

Hello there, I believe we are yet to meet, Reni said, projecting this towards the entire room as the human took his hand. *I am Reni, representative of the less fortunate of us.*

'Erm… pleasure to meet you?' the human said, his face contorting in confusion. Though he didn't understand what was taking place, Diana lips parted in amazement, not believing what she was seeing.

'Reni's been working on that since he became part of the Council,' Artemi commented. Diana glanced back and saw that she was smiling with a certain smugness. 'He asked me to help and keep it secret. Reni wanted to give you a surprise.'

'He's certainly done that,' Diana said. To see him now... It defined the mission she had sworn when they first met. She shed silent yet happy tears.

I'm so proud of you, Reni.

'Diana?' Eren asked, causing all of them to turn towards her. Diana didn't turn away from Reni, who was smiling back at her. She allowed herself to savour this moment.

Before her inner fire burned again.

I will save you all. I will find a way, Diana resolved, and Eren appeared to understand too, glancing between them. Relaxing, he stepped towards Reni.

'Pleasure to meet you, Reni,' he said, extending both his hands towards him. 'You've done so much for us.'

As have you, from what I've been told, Reni said, accepting Eren's gesture as they held hands. *You've been an important factor in us establishing connection with the humans.*

This time, it was Eren's turn to step back, stunned. Clearly, the young man wasn't used to receiving praise, so he distracted himself by turning towards the human.

'Delson, Reni's being polite. It was he who recommended Diana to become leader of the Hateful. He's an inspiration to us all. It's a tremendous honour to meet him.'

'Really?' Delson, said, impressed. He glanced between Reni and Diana. 'Funnily enough, that was a question I wanted to ask you, Diana. How did a human become leader of the Hateful?'

Diana became the leader because she was the correct choice, Delson, Reni answered. He turned towards the human.

Eren flatters me. It was all of us who voted for her. All I did was tell my story to my kind, before making my case why I believed

Diana was the right choice. Look at us now, Hateful and humanity, working together. Before her, this was a dream that neither side considered possible. I believe our decision has been vindicated. We have hope. Now, we must arrive at a consensus, which means we can spread that hope towards the rest of humanity, and the Titaniuses.

'Oh shit, I forgot about them!' Delson said, concerned. 'Where did they go?'

'What do you mean?' Heimval asked.

'I haven't seen a Titanius since Exia fell to the Devil of Anubi. It's like they've gone into hiding.'

'But where did they go?' Eren asked.

'I've heard rumours they come from Exia Mountain, but no one's ever been able to prove that,' Delson said before the doors opened again. Pauli and Valki came in, the last two members of Diana's Council. Diana hoped the latter had uncovered more information from the Ethero Fiends, while the former stepped towards her, smiling in a way that made her heart flutter.

'Diana, you're wearing our attire,' Pauli said, making her flush.

'I was in a rush,' she said quickly.

Pauli smiled in response. 'I think you look wonderful,' he said, forcing Diana to turn away from him to hide her blush. She folded her arms and turned towards the rest of the Council.

'Alright, we should begin,' Diana said. 'It would seem that the forces of the Eternal Mother are mobilising, moving out towards the rest of Exia. We have a decision to make.'

'A decision?' Delson asked, confused. 'What do you mean?'

'War is coming,' Valki answered, sending a chill throughout

the room.

Diana turned to him. 'Did you get any more information from our friends?'

'Yes,' Valki said. 'Their noble is the reason behind their emergence from Seraphu. In the wake of Megidra's actions, they sensed the same thing I did when we first convened. Humanity is at its weakest in Exia, so they intend to take the capital of Ethero before the other cities. They seek to establish control of the other districts before moving to us.'

'Why leave us last?' Eren asked.

'Because we have a giant wall that protects us,' Valki answered. 'Those who serve the Eternal Mother also acknowledge our power, and after what Megidra did, they also know what we're capable of.'

'So we have some time,' Diana remarked, drawing a nod from Valki, before he appeared amused by something.

'What is it?' Pauli asked him. 'What's so funny?'

'Sorry, but I cannot help but see the irony of the wall that's kept us segregated from humanity being the reason we're in the best position to defend ourselves.'

'We're still outnumbered, even with the wall and our power,' Artemi said. 'If they take control of Exia and surround us, we'll not last long.'

'That's true,' Valki admitted. 'However, I managed to uncover a potentially vital detail from the Fiends. They say the forces of the Eternal Mother are avoiding Greyr. They refuse to go near the district. That presents a great opportunity.'

'What opportunity?' Heimval asked. 'There's nothing there but ruins and Heaven's Gate.'

'You're missing the bigger picture, old man,' Valki said.

'It removes one potential spot of attack, while giving us an avenue that we could use to escape.'

'So you intend to guide everyone of all three towers out there, Valki?' Pauli said, his point obvious. However, rather than appear angered, the young Hateful smiled, as though he had already thought of this.

'Oh, I apologise, master strategist,' Valki said.

'Let's not start,' Diana warned. 'We don't have time to fight amongst ourselves. Valki, do you believe there's any way we could talk to Helenia?'

'Possibly,' Valki said. 'But it would be a gamble. The Fiends don't trust us that much. It may not lead to anything.'

'Still isn't a reason not to try it,' Pauli said. 'We can only last so long, and we're facing an army.'

'It would seem that we're in a rare moment of agreement, Pauli,' Valki said. 'If the Council decides that is the best option, then I propose myself to lead such attempts at negotiation. They would slaughter our friends, while Diana is too important to risk. If we're going to choose that course of action, it makes sense if I did it.'

Yet you almost seem too keen to do it, Diana noted, frowning. 'That puts you at a lot of risk, Valki,' she said. 'Are you willing to accept that?'

'We're beyond the point of choosing what we're willing to accept, Diana,' Valki said, measured and calm. 'If we're going to survive, I don't believe I have much choice.'

'What do you think?' Diana asked Delson, who was silent. She couldn't blame him. He hadn't yet met the Ethero Fiends. There was a reason they were referring to them as their "friends". Delson gave himself a moment before addressing the group.

'Look, I barely understand what's happening here. However, you guys didn't have to save us from those monsters. Neither did you have to allow us to shelter here. I guess what I'm saying is that I trust you. If you believe negotiation for a peaceful solution is the best option, go for it. If you believe fighting is the best option, then we'll help you however we can.'

'Alright then,' Diana said. 'Valki will see if negotiations are possible. Once he returns we'll meet in my office and take it from there. Any objections?'

There weren't, and Diana returned to her office an hour later, having walked Reni back to his room before running some checks around the Institute. Diana wanted something to distract her from the stress and fear.

Every decision had an element of life or death. Knowing that, it took much more effort now to push past those emotions. Diana crashed onto her chair. She leaned back while her head throbbed in pain, exhaling.

Oh Divinity, when am I going to be revealed for the fraud I am?

She was almost sure she could hear mother's cruel laughter, forcing Diana to shake her head. She needed no more reasons to doubt.

I have to keep pushing forward. I cannot stop now.

A door knock brought her back. She contemplated saying she was busy.

'Diana, are you in there?' Pauli called. Diana knew she couldn't turn him away. She was relieved to hear his voice again. She didn't have to pretend she was the leader of the Hateful. With Pauli, she could just be Diana Skagen, the flawed human.

'Yeah, I'm here, Pauli,' Diana said, noting the exhaustion in her voice as she spoke. The door to her office inched open then, and the large Hateful man stepped inside. He seemed tired too, and sad when he saw her, regarding her with care.

You've always been able to do that with me, haven't you? Diana thought, relaxing before him, placing her elbows on her desk, while propping her head on her hands. *You're the only one who I've never been able to fool.*

'Are you alright?' Pauli asked, with so much care that Diana almost melted. She wanted to crumble, but she kept herself upright.

Pauli frowned. 'You're doing it again,' he said. 'You're fighting so hard to be strong for us.' He shook his head, half turning and sitting on the desk alongside her. He looked sadly at his hands.

'You know, I just wish,' he began, hesitating before frustration emerged from him.

It was Diana's turn to frown. 'You wish what?' she asked.

'That you could be yourself around me, Diana,' Pauli said. 'You have so much on your plate. I just wish I wasn't so useless to you. Every time I walk inside this office, seeing how much stress you put on yourself, I feel like it's my fault. I had no right to put you in this position. Every time I see you here, I feel like I make you suffer.'

Pauli shook his head again. 'Things are changing in this world, Diana,' he said, 'And I don't know if we're going to survive. I just wanted to say how I feel. You're the only person who I can talk to like this. The only one who I…'

Pauli froze then, realising he was about to say. Diana's heart skipped, her mouth opening in amazement.

'I'm sorry. I'm saying too much, putting more on you than

you need.'

Pauli rose, turning as though moving to leave the room. Despite herself, Diana rose to her feet.

'Pauli,' she said, seriously, stopping him. 'Finish what you were about to say.'

'I just wish I could be more to you, Diana. Divinity knows what's about to happen, but I wanted to tell you how I feel. How I've always felt, from the first time I saw you when you met Reni.'

Pauli paused then. 'I love you, Diana. I always have.'

He stopped and appeared unsure of what to do.

Diana moved around her desk, moving to meet him as tears ran down her cheeks. 'Oh, Pauli,' she began. 'I don't need you to be anything else. I just want you to be Pauli.'

To her surprise, Pauli looked devastated, before nodding in acceptance as he headed to the door.

'Of course. I understand,' Pauli said, offering a brave smile, which confused Diana even more.

Then Diana realised what had happened. *He's taken what I said literally. He thinks I meant...*

Diana chuckled, and that chuckle evolved into a laugh.

Pauli, about to leave, turned to frown at her, causing her laugh to grow.

'You're such an idiot,' Diana said, as she went to him. 'That was so typically Hateful.'

'I don't understand,' Pauli said, unsure as Diana took one of his hands in both her own.

'Yet, that's the reason I love you so much,' Diana said, an immense pressure lifting from her shoulders. 'I didn't mean that I didn't want you to be something more to me. I meant you didn't need to be anything else to be with me.'

Diana considered that then, flickering her eyes towards his, wanting to convey the warmth she felt. 'Pauli, I don't know what's about to happen. I don't know if I will succeed in my promise. But, I want to be selfish. I want to enjoy someone I've loved ever since I saw them. Everyone else expects something from me. You just want me to be Diana. That means a lot to me, so please, don't go. I want to know that I spent my last moments with the man I love.'

'As I do, with you,' Pauli said, pulling her towards him. She could feel his love flooding into her, while she allowed hers to flood into him. All fear and insecurity diminished then, as they held each other.

'I love you, Diana,' Pauli whispered.

'I love you too, Pauli,' Diana said, as their lips met in a kiss.

Firm hands clasped around her backside, and Pauli lifted her to his level. Lust and longing filled her as the kissing between them intensified. Pauli then placed her down on the desk. Before she knew what she was doing, her hands were moving around his body, removing his jacket while his large hands fumbled at the buttons of her shirt. Diana giggled, causing Pauli to stare at her questioningly.

'Just rip it off,' she said, and Pauli seemed to consider this before obliging. The swift demonstration of power thrilled Diana, urging her to claw him into her embrace. This further ignited their desires, as hands moved, caressed and fumbled their way through clothing before touching skin. Another knock on the door caused them to freeze in horror, while Diana held a finger to her lips.

'Please don't come in!' Diana said, fighting to stop herself from laughing at how breathless she sounded. 'Can you come back later?'

'Yes, of course,' the voice said.

Diana didn't recognise it.

'Valki has left the Institute.'

'No problem. Keep me posted.'

'Will do. Do you need me to inform Pauli?'

Diana had to suppress another chuckle, especially as Pauli's eyes widened at the mention of his name.

'No, I'll inform him myself. Tell the rest of the Council to meet me at the wall. In the meantime, do not disturb me for the next hour. I have very important documentation to deal with.'

'Very good. Thank you, Diana,' the other voice said.

She looked back at Pauli, seeing confusion in his expression.

'What?' Diana asked.

'Well, obviously you distracted him from me because I'm here, but why an hour?'

Diana allowed a devious smile to emerge on her lips then, before moving her hands towards his lower half.

'Well, we have business to attend to, don't we?' she asked.

Rather than question any further, Pauli obliged her once again.

33

The Third Relic

Greene roamed the caverns with the Tortured once again, having returned to the Ethero Fiend with the half-complete Titan core. The Tortured had levitated them out of the city of Cybara, leaving it to its war. The Cybernetics never knew they were there.

It didn't surprise Greene when the Tortured said they'd be walking alone until they reach the Animus territory, with Barbatos and the others going somewhere else. He didn't mention where. They descended into the network of tunnels and caverns under Ethero.

Greene recalled everything he had seen in the vision. He had a choice to make between hatred and forgiveness, and it would decide the fate of Ethero.

But why do I have this burden? What makes me this Descendant?

Greene wanted to ask his companion about it, but he was sure the Tortured wouldn't speak. The Ethero Fiend was as mysterious as he was terrifying.

Greene noticed writing inscribed on the cavern walls in a

language he didn't understand. Maybe they were remnants of old rituals and mythology.

'Who built these caverns?' he asked.

'The Eternal Mother,' the Tortured said in a hoarse whisper, saying her name reverently.

Greene nodded. 'Why does time move faster here? We traverse distances in here that should take days.'

'These caverns aren't bound to time, Titanius,' the Tortured said. 'You know what the Ether represents.'

Greene decided against pursuing the matter further, doubting he would get more information.

The more one learns, the more they realise how deep the lies go, from the ones they're told by others, and especially the ones they tell themselves.

'I sense your inner conflict, Titanius,' the Tortured said. 'You fear the truths you are uncovering.'

'I fear the truths I am yet to uncover,' Greene said. 'And the truths kept from me.'

'You only need to ask, Greene,' the Tortured said.

Temptation rose in Greene. 'How can I be sure you're telling the truth?' he asked.

'How can you assume I lie?' the Fiend replied. 'You possess an innate distrust of others, Greene. I understand why.'

'Everything I know is lies. It's the whole reason Barbatos convinced me to join him on this journey.'

'So it has nothing to do with unleashing the Titans?' the Tortured asked.

Greene chose to remain silent.

'What did you see in the vision?' the Tortured asked next. 'Whatever it was, it has shaken you. Is Forgiveness showing you truth?'

'That depends how you frame the question,' Greene re-torted. 'Do you mean that in the sense that Forgiveness is actually showing me truths, or that you're asking if his truths are true or not?'

'You trap yourself in logical fear,' the Tortured said.

'Logical fear? Isn't that a contradiction?' Greene asked. He fought to keep the confusion off his face.

'Not at all,' the Fiend answered. 'Have you never tried to use logic to such an extreme degree that you paralyse yourself? That is logical fear, analysing to the point of becoming afraid of what you rationalise. It is the flaw of all logical beings. They believe in absolutism and black and whiteness, never realising that the primitive emotion of fear grips such a mindset. After all, if things are black and white, they are simple, deducted, safe. It is a foolish belief. Beings are never rational, not truly. Emotion, however small, still influences most actions.'

'What is your point?' Greene asked.

The Tortured turned and aimed his eyeless face towards Greene, smiling.

'To pursue truth is to pursue what is rational, to believe in something comprehensible. Yet, it is emotions that guide it. Hatred. Pain. Love. Fear. They are single pieces of a nexus that intertwine, creating a psychological system that creates our very being, while guiding each step we take. You. Me. Barbatos and all the others. We are not so different. The difference is that we acknowledge what guides our steps. Your struggle comes from not accepting what compels you.'

'And what do you believe compels me?' Greene asked.

The Tortured's smile turned more sinister. 'Anger, and the desire to make humanity pay for taking advantage of your kind. Yet, it conflicts with the part of you that wishes to create peace, to choose what Forgiveness represents. That is where your conflict lies, Titanius.'

He walked on. Greene remained standing, one question remaining on his mind.

'So what about you? Barbatos? What compels the two of you? Why are you doing all this?'

The Tortured stopped once more, glancing back.

'My motivation is simple, Greene. I wish to tear this world apart. Why, you'll discover that soon enough. For Barbatos, why don't you ask him yourself?'

Greene understood there wasn't a single word of the Ethero Fiend's that he could deny. It had all been correct.

But what does that make me, then? What decision should I choose?

Greene stopped that train of thought. He needed to keep moving. He would face the decision soon enough and ask Barbatos the one question he feared most.

Why was he doing all this?

They reached the end of the cavern a few hours later, approaching a giant stone door.

The Tortured raised his hand. *'Bavista,'* he growled in his native tongue. The cavern shook, as though he had caused an earthquake. The door rolled open, causing dust and debris to fall before it stopped. The Tortured stepped forward. Greene followed.

They were in another part of Ethero that defied all logic.

Prior to this journey, all Greene had known was Exia. He imagined the other major cities of Ethero to be similar, surrounded by the infamous Darklands. Now he understood that was a lie. The journey to Elcaris had brought them through the jungle. Cybara had brought them through the desert.

Now, islands floated before him, at different heights in the sky, connected by rope bridges.

The Tortured was standing on the periphery of where Ethero's mainland ended, alongside one of the rope bridges.

'This is the land of the Animus,' he said. 'We should find no struggle here.'

'How so?' Greene asked.

'Animus tend towards peace. The other scorned races harbour more hatred.'

'Scorned?' Greene commented. 'You mean those who stand with the Eternal Mother?'

'Naturally,' the Tortured said. 'But why do you think they're the scorned ones?'

Greene didn't answer, sure the question had been rhetorical. He looked at the first of the floating islands above them.

'Where are the others?' he asked next.

'Heading to our last destination,' the Tortured answered. 'Towards the last relic.'

'Is that what Barbatos organised with you back on Elcaris?' Greene asked. 'Why you're with me?'

'What do you think?' the Tortured said. 'Or perhaps you wish to ask the question in your mind.'

Greene glanced at him, his eyes narrowing in suspicion. It had occurred to him that each of the different races had possessed a piece of the Titan core, tasked to protect it from getting into his hands. With the hidden races now known to have possessed relics, an obvious question remained.

'Who holds the last piece?' he asked.

311

The Tortured smiled. 'Humanity,' he said. 'Dynames.'

That surprised Greene.

It was then the strange power of the Tortured took hold of him, making them weightless, before they floated upward. As they passed one island and another, the Tortured continued to make them rise.

They reached the last island.

Small segments of forests filled it, and there was a stream that fell down through the other islands, before falling into the ocean that surrounded them. He could see the next tree, which held the third relic.

It was like the others, a tree of silver with golden leaves, possessing a small fragment of contorted metal, which Greene knew was the third piece of the Titan core. It surprised him that there was no Animus around. There were no sounds either. It was like the lands of Animus were uninhabited.

'Where are they?' Greene asked, as the Tortured touched them down on the island, just before the tree's glistening white protective field.

'They hide,' the Tortured said. 'They know what we bring.'

The end of Ethero, Greene thought, somehow knowing that was the truth.

It was time to retrieve the third piece of the Titan core. He stepped into the field, while a hum hung in the air alongside warmth, encasing his body, forcing the strange steam-like substance to emerge from the violet crevices.

Why does this keep happening? What does it mean? Greene wondered, looking at his hands, gazing at them as they emitted the same steam. Then he noticed something.

His shadow was growing.

'What the…' Greene stammered, before the roots of the tree wrapped around his legs, then his arms.

And he fell unconscious once again.

Everything became dark around him, as though swallowing him into an infinite void, no longer present anywhere, but everywhere at once. A stirring came from within, one he didn't recognise. The sound of steam was still present, along with the warmth and the hum. Not understanding this, Greene looked around himself, seeing only darkness.

Voices emerged in his head.

It started with one, unintelligible. Others joined it. They were also incomprehensible, but they seemed to keep multiplying. As Greene struggled to hear his own thoughts, the many voices continued to multiply, as though thousands were inside his head now, all speaking nonsense he couldn't understand.

Until he did.

'Avenge us!' a voice called out. Greene froze. They all stopped then, but Greene could still sense them.

Then they all spoke.

'Humanity should suffer for what they've done!'

'Free us!'

'Break our shackles!'

'Kill them… Kill them all.'

Despite himself, despite not wishing to engage with those words, or thoughts, Greene felt hatred, genuine hatred, fill every crevice of his being.

What is this? Why am I experiencing all of this? Anger. Hate. Misery. I feel it all… I cannot stop it.

'Free our ancestors!' another voice shouted. 'Find the last relic! Then…'

'DESTROYYYYYYYYY!!!' a last voice emerged, a low growl that shook him. Human screams followed as Greene dropped to his knees, fighting to prevent himself from crumbling.

'Is it enough?' a voice he recognised asked; Forgiveness. 'Is destroying this world enough for you? If not, what then? What will remain?'

Greene was unsure if they meant him to answer those questions, so he chose silence, feeling the pressure and the thousands of voices disappear, returning his mind to normal.

Greene allowed himself to crumble then, and he lay on the ground, panting.

'What… was that?' he stammered, sure that Forgiveness could hear them now.

'What awaits you when you collect the last relic and form the Titan core,' Forgiveness said. 'Decide, Descendant. Destroy the world, or save it.'

'But I don't wish to harm others,' Greene said. 'I don't want to repeat the Lieutenant's mistake.'

'Then you will never gain the power to free your kind,' Forgiveness said, sounding sad. 'You started this journey because you believed freeing your kind would come from gaining the Titan core. It will, but not without significant cost. Faced with overwhelming anger and hatred, can you control it? Can you say no to your deepest desires and that of your entire race? Can you show them another way? That another path exists for them?'

Greene shook his head, unsure of what he'd just experienced. Still, he could feel Forgiveness all around him, waiting.

'I'll try,' he stammered. 'I don't know if I can, but I'll try.'

'Then that is all I ask, Descendant,' Forgiveness said. 'Your battle means so much more than you realise. If the war is to end, we will need your kind and the power you possess. However, none of that will be possible without accessing your power as Descendant, without creating the Titan core. All that I ask is that you do not stop fighting, no matter what faces you. If you can do that, I can help you, and together we can liberate your kind.'

'How?' Greene asked.

'My conduit, he is close to achieving my power. He just needs time. I know much of this is vague, Greene, and I understand how little you trust the words of everyone, including me. However, you must keep moving forward, stand for something more than the hate and suffering those around you wish to inflict. Those things won't heal the world. It can only heal by forgiveness.'

'And acceptance,' Greene muttered.

Forgiveness said nothing to that, but his presence remained. Greene knew this vision was about to end.

'I will fight,' he said, rising to his feet. 'I will free my kind!'

'And you will, but not without significant cost. I'm sorry, Greene, but before forgiveness there must first come the downfall. Your downfall.'

34

The Truth

Megidra returned to Johann's church to find the truck sitting next to the cemetery gates, relieved to know that they'd made it back from Seraphu. Still, this didn't mean they were clear. The noble had said it herself; they were coming. Megidra needed to get the humans out. He needed to take them to the DFA's headquarters.

He paused as he reached the large doors leading into the church. Inside, he could hear many voices and much movement. Deion and the others had relayed his message. It made sense to return once he had cleared the place for them. Unfortunately, he remembered what he'd promised to Ryun back in Seraphu.

He would tell the others the truth.

Fear gripped him. Ryun stirred, intrigued. Megidra was relieved to feel that. He was accountable to the Truthseeker. He had to step on this path, to rid himself of the monster that he'd allowed himself to become.

'I'm scared, Ryun,' Megidra admitted. 'Even if this period of my life was just a taste, I don't want to lose it. I want to see where it goes, and who I can become.'

But you'll never experience that, not when you live with this burden of truth within, Ryun said.

'Exactly,' Megidra agreed. 'Which is why I have to prove that I've changed, that I embrace what I've done. These people I love can make their choice. They deserve that right, and I won't run anymore.'

Megidra knocked on the door, then heard steps approaching. Deion met him, relieved to see him.

'Megi,' he said, pulling him into a tight embrace. After a few seconds, the human released him, patting his shoulder. Deion then glanced back towards the main hall of the church.

'I'm so happy you made it,' he said. 'Without you, we would've been dead, and so would everyone else here. Words cannot describe how much I'm indebted to you.'

'Please, you owe me nothing,' Megidra said, embarrassment mixing with shame. He looked at the floor, scratching his head. 'Deion, there's something–'

'Megi!' a boyish voice called out, and he looked up to see Destin running towards him. Deion's child threw himself at Megidra, hugging him just as tightly as his father. Megidra saw a smiling Marienne approaching too. His heart fluttered at the sight of her.

Oh Divinity, I'm about to reveal who killed her husband.

Megidra felt hollow as Destin released him. Deion smiled, gesturing for Megidra to follow him as he moved into the church. Destin and Marienne followed. Megidra couldn't bring himself to look at them. He wondered if he could do this.

'We're almost ready to go,' Deion said, oblivious. 'Though everyone's concerned by what we told them, they trust you. I think our account of what happened in Seraphu has quickened their steps – that and Odeon and Ilara. They're just waiting for your word now.'

Megidra didn't speak. Even as Marienne came up to him, still smiling. Megidra could only glance at her, unable to speak. Deion drew him towards the centre of the room, while the surrounding humans moved to create space. Megidra felt their eyes on him, seeing unwarranted smiles greet his presence. Only two among them knew the truth, and Megidra saw one of them approaching, much to his horror.

Johann Stratos.

The young priest extended a hand to Megidra, his expression appreciative as everything fell into slow motion between them.

'You've done well, Megidra,' the priest said, shaking his hand as the surrounding humans applauded. Everything about it seemed wrong, undeserved. Inside, a void appeared where his happiness should've been. Megidra stood on the edge of two paths: the path where his lie would lead if it continued, and the path of truth. He feared both.

'Please, stop clapping,' he muttered, lowering his gaze.

'What was that?' Johann asked.

'I said stop clapping!' Megidra growled, tapping into his Transformative Blessing and shifting his right hand into the weapon he felt was appropriate for the situation.

Lucifer's favoured giant revolver.

Megidra raised it towards the ceiling, firing a shot that silenced the room. Megidra lowered the weapon and looked up again, his anger shining through as he examined everyone around him. They were shocked by this turn of events.

'What are you doing?' Megidra asked, addressing the

humans. 'Why are you applauding? I don't deserve it. This isn't over.'

'Megi,' Deion said, his voice low yet harsh. There was a flash of anger in his expression. 'What's wrong? They're just showing their appreciation.'

'Appreciation for what?' Megidra snapped, turning to him, relinquishing his Blessing as he did so. 'We need to leave. Blood has to be shed.'

'What are you talking about?' a member of the audience asked. It was man in his late forties, wearing thick winter clothing that revealed only his confused face. 'Whose blood?'

'The DFA's,' Megidra answered, allowing the words to sink in. 'That's where we're going next. It's the only place where we can defend ourselves. However, I doubt they'll let us in, so we're going to make them.'

'How?' Deion asked.

'I'll have to kill them. Every one of them.'

He swept his gaze over the crowd again. 'So, will you applaud me now? Knowing what I'm about to do. Knowing the monster I have to become in order to save you.'

'Megidra,' Marienne cut in. 'I wish you'd stop regarding yourself as a monster. None of us think you're a monster. You're just Hateful. And whether you like it, you're one of us now. You do not have to kill anyone to keep us safe. We'll find another way.'

'No. You're wrong,' Megidra said. 'None of you know what's coming, and what it's going to take. Only I do, and only I can become the monster required to stop them.'

His face tightened. 'I'm not one of you. That was the lie I told myself, as I sacrificed everything in pursuit of a poisonous dream that led only to pain and hatred. I put you in this situation. I am a monster, the devil you all fear. When this is done, I will become the devil they fear too.

'This monster that I will unleash again, I will do it for you. For all of you. You gave me hope that the world can become a better place. I know now that Hateful can stand alongside their human brothers and sisters, free.

'However, that world can never exist if the Fiends and their allies succeed. I will not let that happen. I won't allow them to touch any of you, even if it means you all have to despise me in order for that to happen.'

'Why would we despise you?' Marienne asked.

Megidra shook his head, before heading to the doors of the church, throwing them open, allowing the angry wind to whistle through. He turned back.

'Because I am your Devil of Anubi, and not a single day goes by where I don't regret what I've done.'

Megidra landed on one of the stone columns surrounding Heaven's Gate around twenty minutes later. There was nothing here but darkness and silence. Such darkness and silence filled him now, knowing that he had lost those he cared about forever.

It doesn't matter. If they survive this, then I'll die in the knowledge I tried to redeem myself.

Megidra looked over to the DFA headquarters, which was near the bottom of the district. It was a heavily bunkered fortress that looked like a smaller version of the Institute, a cube-shaped building with a wall surrounding it. Something struck Megidra as odd. No lights were on, nor could he see any patrols or vehicles.

His old DFA instincts kicked in, telling him to be cautious.

He tapped into his Transformative Blessing, summoning his favoured arm-blade. Then, he leapt off the column and began walking towards the base.

Soon, the reason behind the apparent silence became obvious. Megidra could see two corpses of humans wearing DFA armour, both of them struck by some kind of bladed weapon across their necks and stomachs. There was no trace of blood. Megidra headed down the ramp that led to the entrance, knowing what he was about to find.

More bodies, each killed by bladed weapons and drained of blood. The lighting above flickered, while equipment, bodies and weapons lay on the floor. An eerie silence permeated throughout, but Megidra moved forward, keeping his Blessing armed.

They've already been through here. Megidra knew he couldn't take the humans to this place. Smartly, the Ethero Fiends had slaughtered those who were the best equipped to stand against them. Time was even shorter than he'd hoped. The last option he dreaded was appearing the most viable.

What difference does it make now, anyway? he thought, lowering his head as he wondered the corridors, resignation filling him. *Once this is over, I will roam alone again.*

Megidra ascended toward the Captain's office, wondering what had become of the man who had given him the opportunity to pursue his dream. By the time he reached the last floor, he relinquished his Blessing, sure that no Ethero Fiends remained.

But where are they now? Megidra wondered, as he headed into the final corridor that led to the Captain's office. Blood was splattered across the wall, while dismembered bodies lay on the floor. Megidra frowned, not doubting that the Ethero

Fiends were moving through the city. Leaving now would be the best course of action. Still, curiosity grasped him. He needed to know.

He reached the final corridor, seeing a strange golden light emitting from the window of the Captain's office, and from the narrow line underneath the door. Surprised to see this, Megidra tapped into his Transformative Blessing, doubting it was coming from an Ethero Fiend. His old instincts warned him of a trap, but Megidra ruled this out after considering the fact that they'd be no reason for one. The fighting was done. What remained?

Still, he was cautious. As he drew closer to the door, the golden glow seemed to shimmer. There was no response to his approach. Megidra opened the door and walked inside.

He was met by a being unlike any other.

A large figure sat in the Captain's chair, wearing silver and sapphire armour covered in gold embroidery and a tall mask that sat like a crown. Eight feathered wings fluttered in response to Megidra's entry.

'Well, this is unexpected,' the being said, sounding much like the Captain. Megidra closed the door behind, relinquishing his Blessing, sensing no danger from the being. He stepped towards the desk.

'I wondered where you had gone,' the being continued, his voice possessing a certain wisdom. 'Especially after what happened in Anubi. I assume it was you that fought with Lucifer Armedeus?'

Megidra said nothing, watching as the being regarded him for a few seconds, before shaking his head and rising to his feet. As he did so, his golden radiance seemed to fade, and his armour shifted and changed. He was the Captain once again.

'What was that?' Megidra asked.

The Captain smiled. 'My accomplice's form,' he said. 'He says it's been a long time since anyone has seen him. You should be honoured, if only you didn't harbour a demon.'

'What are you talking about?'

'I'm talking about the truth, Megidra,' the Captain said. 'That beings who existed long ago live within us, and have chosen this time to emerge. The war is imminent. Soon, I fear the Ether will draw out the Divinity for the ultimate battle, to decide who owns life itself. Chaos? Order? Perhaps even both?'

'So you harbour one of the Fallen as well?' Megidra asked, a question that was rebuffed by Ryun, his disgust apparent.

That was not one of us, he hissed angrily. *That was Seraphu, Angel of Wisdom.*

'Enjoying a chat with your demon?' the Captain asked.

Megidra narrowed his gaze. 'He says that was Seraphu, but I don't understand,' he said.

'Is it that complicated?' the Captain asked. 'Your kind harbours her children, her Fallen. Meanwhile, the Angels of the Divinity live within us humans. To me and Seraphu, it was obvious, but our mistake was in keeping silent about our theory of where the Demons had gone. After all, they had to be somewhere. It was only coincidence that you emerged, a perfect subject to test our theory, a disgraced Hateful who wanted to save his race.'

The Captain moved towards his window, his hands behind his back, shoulders raised.

'That was my first mistake. My experiment was to see if your treatment could provoke the Fallen. I should've known what it would take to unleash him. Even then, Lucifer beat you to it, and because of my negligence, we lost Greyr. What we failed to account for was that your relationship to the Fallen would cause them to gain more power, giving them the strength to kill the Angels with ease. Still, I should've devised a much cleaner method to test. We should've realised what it would take to make you snap.'

The Captain sighed then, glancing at Megidra in the same way he always did. This would have felt like any other conversation without the subject in hand. The Captain was revealing things Megidra never expected to hear, words that he realised now changed everything of what he had once thought of their relationship. Within a few sentences, coincidences now made sense to Megidra. Yet, there was something that pointed towards a new realisation, a truth that made everything the Captain was saying make sense, especially when he considered his time in the DFA.

'You set me up to fail,' he realised, stunned. 'They didn't hate me at all, did they? The others, you made them treat me like shit, never giving me a chance to show what we could be. All because you were trying to expose who lived within me, taking advantage of my self-hatred, convincing me to hunt down my race, to pursue Lucifer Armedeus.'

Megidra paused then, as tears ran down his cheeks. 'I killed and hurt so many. I became the monster I believed I was.'

'Yes, you did,' the Captain agreed.

Megidra reflected on the new truth. However, despite that, such clarity brought with it a new truth that Megidra couldn't deny, and he nodded despite the pain in his heart.

'But that changes nothing, does it?' he said. 'I still committed those actions. Even if you manipulated me. Even

324

if you took advantage of my broken mind. It doesn't remove what I did, and that I have to change.'

Feeling Ryun's presence fill him then, Megidra's face tightened, remembering the humans who had brought him here, the ones who had cared enough to regard him as one of their own. As he considered them, he remembered why he was here, and the promise he had made to himself.

'I will be better,' he said, strength filling him. 'I want to save those who I have wronged. Until I've done that, I can never atone for what I've done. Unlike before, there's something you cannot take away from me, Captain. I will no longer run from the truth.'

He considered that, knowing what had to be done.

'I have to atone to the people I've hurt. I will face them now, and I will save those I love. Thank you, Captain. I'm no longer a DFA Agent. Newman is no more.'

35

Facing the Past

Lucifer landed on a rooftop an hour later, knowing what he needed to do. After telling Silver Wing everything about his past and Exia, he felt somewhat liberated, no longer hindered by the fear of what they thought of him. It seemed what he said hadn't surprised them, especially Mika, who had already heard a version of the truth.

Of course, there were lowered gazes, moments of awkwardness. A few tears falling, especially when he recalled Vennifer's fate, for which Lucifer still blamed himself. Now, he understood he had been responsible for bringing about his own downfall, understanding what Orphani had meant about the next stage.

Forgiveness.

I can never truly forgive myself or the past, not unless I do this, he knew. He tapped into his Transformative Blessing, summoning black feathered wings. He launched himself into the air, moving into a spiral before expanding his wings. He caught the wind, then fixed his direction for south-east Kyrios.

The weather was intensifying: snow, sleet and hail blew all around him. It was driving many indoors.

That meant those he intended to see would be at home.

It didn't surprise Lucifer to see Gabriel standing on the wall near his parents' home. Though Korai stirred, Lucifer quelled this with a simple inner calmness, landing beside his fellow Hateful with no desire to fight. Gabriel simply looked at him.

It's almost as though he's been through some moment of clarity himself. He's calmer now, Lucifer observed, landing on the wall before relinquishing his Blessing. Gabriel was dressed in the same attire as during their battle at the cathedral, and his Hateful jacket flapped open and closed in the wind.

'I thought you would come here,' Gabriel said calmly. 'After I first met you, I kept an eye on where went next. You landed here, and I knew it wasn't random. You chose this place for a reason. After all your talk on forgiveness, it made sense to me. This is where it began, isn't it? This is where you learned what it meant to hate.'

'It was,' Lucifer admitted. He turned to the building, feeling cold and numb.

Even now, I'm afraid, Lucifer realised.

'Tell me, do you genuinely believe forgiveness is possible, despite everything that happened, knowing that it led towards everything you've done since, leading to who you are now?' Gabriel asked.

Lucifer smiled at that, knowing that question brought him here. He was no longer anger-driven. He was different. Loss had changed him, and he understood what he was becoming.

'I'm not sure,' Lucifer said. 'That's what I've always been afraid of, Gabriel. I guess that's what we're always afraid of, especially as we try to navigate through the complexity of life. Whether we're trying to answer a question that lives within our hearts, or we want to find out if we'll succeed, what we fear is never knowing. Yet, we never know until time has passed, beyond the point you can do anything about it. We have only one choice: forgive or hate. I can't guarantee what I'm about to do will change anything. I don't even know what you expect from me, Gabriel. There are no guarantees in this world.'

'Then why subject yourself to the pain?' Gabriel asked. 'If you know there's no guarantee, why try?'

Lucifer smiled.

'Why try indeed? he said. 'If life is an exercise in futility, why bother?'

'Is that meant to be rhetorical?' Gabriel asked, his expression unchanging. 'Do you have an answer?'

'Do you?' Lucifer countered, keeping his gaze level on Gabriel.

The fellow Hateful looked over to the window Lucifer had been focused on.

'That's why I'm here, Lucifer,' Gabriel said, after a long pause. 'I've changed. Your words got through to me. Things have happened since, but something's gnawing at me. I've been waiting for you, knowing you would come here, seeking the thing you told me about.'

'Forgiveness,' Lucifer said.

'I want to see if it's possible,' Gabriel agreed. 'If you can forgive, especially the past and those who planted the seeds of hatred that guide you. I want to watch you look them in the eye, and tell me afterwards if you truly have forgiven them, and yourself, for what happened.'

Lucifer nodded, understanding. He took in a breath, before rising to his feet.

'Let's find out, shall we?' he said, then tapped into his Physical Blessing and stepped off the ledge of the wall.

Lucifer landed on the ground with a thud, kicking up a powdery cloud of snow. He relinquished his Blessing as Gabriel landed behind him.

Lucifer stepped forward, heading for the narrow alleyway where the door stood. A mixture of dread and anticipation filled him. He regarded the door to his right, knowing Ven had meant for him to reach it. It had been his last promise to her in Exia.

Well, I'm here, Ven, Lucifer thought, then knocked on the door with a few brisk strikes.

He waited, not sure what would happen next.

Time seemed to slow. The sound of wind and snowfall evaporated. It was almost easy to forget that Gabriel was with him. Lucifer allowed himself a fraction of the time to close his eyes, focusing on his breath, knowing that it was all he could do to keep himself standing upright. When he opened them, a warm light was emerging before him.

A man he thought he would never see again came into view.

He was a few inches taller than Lucifer, a heavy-set human man with hair that matched the light stubble across his chin. He wore glasses and was dressed in a polo shirt and jeans. The men looked at each other. Lucifer froze, and he felt a fear he realised would be worse than anything.

The fear of being unable to speak.

Thankfully, the man standing before him nodded, resigned as he half turned, allowing more of the warm amber light to wash across him.

'Mary, there's someone here who I think you'll want to see,' he said, gesturing to Lucifer to enter.

'It's nice to see you again, son,' he said, turning and walking back inside the house.

Lucifer found himself paralysed. Despite his desire to move, to continue down this path, it seemed like his body refused to entertain the action. A deep fear gripped him, dread returning, believing that hurt and pain was all that awaited him.

Please... Move, Lucifer instructed his body, as tears fell. The human man, his father, turned to look back, halfway through the hallway, frowning as though expecting Lucifer to follow him.

'Are you alright, Lucifer?' he asked.

Lucifer almost burst out laughing. He almost considered the question a joke. Still, as his mind burned with the desire to proceed, his body refused to cooperate.

I have to do this. C'mon. I cannot let it end this way. I must–

'Move, Lucifer,' a scathing voice said in his ear: Gabriel's.

The dread evaporated, allowing Lucifer to turn his head to look at his fellow Hateful. To his surprise, Gabriel looked enraged, glaring at Lucifer as though he would tear him apart if he remained where he stood. To emphasise this, he leaned towards Lucifer, their faces mere inches apart.

'You're not done yet. In case you've forgotten, you have your own reasons for coming. You're going to show me what it means to change, to forgive. You sounded so assured before, but now I see your fear. Well, I won't allow you to stop here. You're going to move forward. Even if you die. Even after you die. You're going to show me what it means to forgive. After all, this whole story started with you.'

Lucifer now understood why Gabriel was here. How critical these moments and the following minutes would be. He was serving a purpose for Gabriel, showing him two paths. Either he found forgiveness, which would show Gabriel it was possible, or he didn't. If he realised the latter, he didn't want to imagine what would happen. Still, a part of Lucifer couldn't deny what Gabriel was saying. It had started with him.

And that changed everything.

'You're right,' Lucifer said, feeling calm. Gabriel relaxed somewhat, but intensity burned in his eyes. This meant everything to him, and Lucifer needed to treat it with respect. Lucifer looked over to his father. A woman had joined him. She had short black hair, a little shorter than Mika's. She, too, wore glasses, and was dressed in a thick jumper and jeans. When she saw Lucifer, she brought a hand to her mouth and her eyes widened in shock.

'Lucifer?' she gasped, as though the name haunted her. A swell of emotions that danced between that old fear and the desire for connection arose in Lucifer. Yet, he ignored them, choosing instead to take the first step and enter the corridor.

'Hello, mother,' Lucifer said, trying to smile as he stepped forward, knowing that he never intended to see his parents again. However, here he was, so long after promising he would never return, finding his arms opening without his permission, enough so that his mother could walk into him. She wrapped Lucifer in her own arms as he moved his towards her. There, they shared an embrace that caused them to break down, crying as neither had cried before. A few minutes passed before Lucifer noticed his father reach towards his mother, patting her on the shoulder.

'Lucifer said he wanted to talk, Mary. We should let him speak,' he said. The words alone showed how much his father had changed. He wouldn't have said them years ago. Lucifer was sure he wouldn't have cared. As his mother released him, it surprised Lucifer to see relief washing over her, as though she had dreamed of this for years, and was grateful to share it. Lucifer understood that, for it had reminded him of a dream he had once had, not affected by Korai's Hateful dream.

In it, he had imagined a moment like the one he had shared, and it had preceded him following his parents into the living room. It had a log burner, which he was sure had cost his father a lot of money. Lucifer bet it was paying dividends now. It had two leather chairs, a television and bookshelves on which were a variety of unique books, along with statues of animals.

I used to sit in that room for hours, reading books, watching the television. I forgot so much, Lucifer realised, before other memories returned to him. Times when he'd played with robot toys with his father, while his mother cooked. Lucifer smiled at those memories. Until that moment, all he remembered was the conflict, the hate and everything else that was wrong with his parents.

Then he saw Gabriel standing there, leaning against the wall with his arms folded, and he realised it wasn't a dream. This was real. Lucifer turned towards his parents now, seeing a mixture of fear and anticipation on their faces. They didn't think this would happen. Lucifer breathed in that feeling, knowing what needed to be said.

'You know, I'd dreamed of this… Imagining what I'd say, what you'd say, and how we'd go back and forth. The anger. The guilt. They would drive the desire for us to understand

and reach a common ground. Of course, we'd never find that common ground, or perhaps I never believed that we could.

'I understand how selfish such thinking was now. I'd created the script, and without giving either of you a chance, I'd already decided what you'd say. I'd push you to it, just like I knew you'd push me. The result was predictable, safe, and I was in control. I could end our chapter the way I wanted.'

Lucifer paused then, before gesturing towards Gabriel.

'But he was right. This story, it all began with me, a Hateful child that neither of you asked for, facing a world that believed my existence was a curse. How could I expect you to react? How could I decide to forget the moments in which we were a family? No, I focused on everything that was wrong. Everything that would enable me to hate both of you.

'I never tried to think about what you were going through, trying to raise a child with complex needs. I never considered all the times you sacrificed yourselves for me, compromising. Finally, I never asked the most important question: If I had been you, with your own upbringings and personal life experiences, would I have acted differently? Would I be any better?'

Lucifer paused and nodded.

'I don't need your answer to any of this,' he said. 'You don't owe me anything. I'm just thinking aloud, reflecting on everything that's happened to me since I walked out of this door all those years ago. Now, I understand the point to it, what I needed from coming here.'

Lucifer looked at Gabriel, who seemed stunned. He had expected this interaction to go differently. Lucifer understood why, knowing what he had once sought was no longer necessary, and for a simple reason.

'I've made my decision, Gabriel. Forgiveness is a choice. Everything else doesn't matter anymore, because I choose how to proceed, and how to view what happened in the past. It doesn't own me, Gabriel. I don't need it anymore.'

Lucifer looked back to his parents then, smiling.

'So I'll listen to whatever you have to say, truly listen, because how we proceed is your choice and mine. I no longer need anything from either of you. What I've chosen is enough, and-'

Both his mother and father stepped forward, silencing Lucifer, taking him in their arms, holding on as tightly as they could.

'We need nothing from you either, son,' Lucifer's mother said, appearing relieved to say those words as they separated. She glanced at his father, who nodded in agreement. Then Lucifer's mother reached for his hands, taking them in her own.

'We just want to be in your life again, Lucifer,' she said.

Lucifer smiled again, about to speak.

But he was interrupted by a violet and crimson explosion.

Lucifer was thrown across the room, taking his mother and father with him. They landed near the window on the other side. Lucifer was dizzy, his head spinning. He had a vague idea of what had happened. He looked up. Gabriel was standing in the middle of the room, his Fallen aura encasing him, his hair floating.

'That's it?' he said, disgusted. 'That wasn't how it was supposed to end. You were supposed to make them hear your pain. They were supposed to understand, apologise, face what they've done. I cannot accept this!'

Lucifer rose to his feet then, glancing to either side behind him, thankful that his mother and father were alright. He had little time to act.

'Gabriel… I'm sorry,' he said, meaning it. 'But none of that would change anything. All I'd end up doing is hurting them, when it's already obvious how much they're hurting. By doing what you said, all I'd do is continue the hurt. I cannot do that, not anymore. I have been down that road before. We both know where it leads, and I don't want to spread pain anymore. I want to heal. I want us to heal.'

'ENOUGH!' Gabriel screamed, silencing Lucifer. He watched as his Fallen power took hold, his Hateful jacket disintegrating to leave his torso bare. His short hair flickered towards the sky, while the surrounding building collapsed around him. Korai emerged, filling Lucifer with the desire to act, to save his parents from the threat.

Lucifer, if you're going to save them, you'll need me. Call my name.

You'd do that? Lucifer asked, surprised to feel his Fallen's desire to help. Inside, Korai filled Lucifer with affirmation. Lucifer could tell he meant his intention. Korai wanted them to work together.

You forgive me, and I now understand the path you walk. Let me help you until you can call upon my son and my love. Please, Lucifer, let me do this! Let me side with you!

Lucifer nodded before holding out his hand.

Please, just let me try…

He could see it, the tears running down Gabriel's face, swirling amid his show of power.

'Gabriel–'

'I said shut up!' Gabriel snapped. 'You don't understand.

How could you? You were my catharsis, the one who made me believe I could find forgiveness, especially from my mother. What you have done is not something my mother would have allowed. She suffered because of what I was.'

He stumbled then, on the verge of falling. Lucifer could feel his pain now, and it almost consumed him. The only thing that stopped him was the fact that the ceiling and roof had collapsed with Gabriel's power, letting snow in.

'I was the bane of her existence, Lucifer. She had to spend almost her entire adult life working in a whorehouse, where monsters enacted their fantasies upon her. I couldn't save her, because my existence was the reason she had to work there. I was her trap, and she despised me for it. Me being Hateful ruined her life. That forgiveness you've just shown, she would never give me that. She would never... love me...'

Gabriel fell onto his knees, sobbing.

Lucifer watched, not going to him. 'What happened to her, Gabriel?'

Gabriel didn't respond until his sobs turned into something that made Lucifer's skin crawl.

Laughter, but not his laughter. His Fallen's.

'I killed her,' it said, speaking much like Korai. Gabriel looked up, his eyes already shifted into violet and crimson. 'That was the only way to free her. Gabriel could never do it, so he asked me to rid her of her suffering, and his.'

'But it was a lie, wasn't it?' Lucifer said, knowing where this was going, remembering his first experiences with Korai. 'You said that to further twist him. You took advantage of him, and now he's running into you again, because he can't take what he's seeing. He cannot accept forgiveness, because he believes it is impossible for himself and his mother.'

'Indeed,' his Fallen agreed. 'So now I'm going to destroy everything, Lucifer. Let's see how far your faith in that failure extends once I've taken everything from you.'

'You'll have to deal with Korai first,' Lucifer said.

Gabriel's Fallen chuckled, not considering him a threat. ' I've always wanted to take on the traitor. Do it, Gabriel.'

He rose to his feet, as Gabriel took back control, looking at Lucifer while shaking his head, dismayed.

'I'm so sorry, Lucifer. VORUS!'

The Transformation was almost instantaneous, as violet and crimson markings appeared across his bare torso, along with the hue that filled his eyes and gravity-defying hair. The aura that encased him was vicious, signalling hatred and destruction.

Lucifer remained unmoved, knowing what had to be done. 'Mother. Father. Please stay back. I'm going to stop this man,' he said, closing his eyes and lowering his head. Then, his own Fallen filled him with power, power he kept restrained until the last possible moment.

He opened his eyes, then called out the name of the entity within him.

'KORAI!'

36

Valki

Diana and Pauli both stood upon the great wall of the Institute. There they could see Valki had not only returned alive from his attempt to contact the forces of the Eternal Mother, but he also guided a small army of Ethero Fiends.

As he walked alongside one particular Fiend, Diana wondered if Valki had turned against them. She sensed the nervous tension from her guards on the wall, who seemed unsure of whether to stand or prepare for defence.

'You don't think he's…' Pauli began, before trailing off, as though not wishing to pursue the thought.

'I don't think so. It wouldn't align with his goals,' Diana said, reaching for Pauli's hand. Of course, the connotations were obvious, but Diana no longer cared.

'Diana,' one guard spoke out to her left, an older Hateful man whose expression was dark. 'What do we do?'

'Stand here,' Diana answered. 'Pauli and I will meet them. Everyone else stays here.'

'Shouldn't the entire Council go?' Pauli asked.

Diana tried to give him a confident smile. 'If we're attacked, neither of us will make it back. If that happens, we'll still need leadership. I've decided Reni will take my place until the end of this situation. Another vote can take place among you later.'

The other Council members had agreed with this plan. Diana had hugged Reni before leaving, knowing the Hateful were in capable hands if anything happened. She felt immense pride at how far he had come, but Diana knew she could say the same about all the Hateful. They had accomplished so much.

I will save them. Somehow...

Diana released Pauli's hand and stepped off the wall. She extended her arms, tapping into her Elemental Blessing to summon strong winds that caused her Hateful jacket to flutter. Landing upon the snow-covered ground with grace, Diana relinquished her Blessing, and Pauli landed close behind. She stepped forward, determined to save those who had placed their faith in her. This meeting would decide everything. She needed to succeed.

They reached within twenty feet of each other. The Ethero Fiend beside Valki strode ahead of the group. This Fiend, she guessed, was the noble known as Helenia Acratis. Just looking at her, Diana could understand why the others feared her. The weather didn't appear to faze her even though she wore a fine black dress with ruby sleeves, which matched the colour of her blazing hair. Compared to the other Ethero Fiends, she exuded vitality.

'Oh my, you weren't joking,' the noble said, as she strode all the way towards Diana, stopping right before her face. The Ethero Fiend was a couple of inches taller, six feet at least.

She leaned towards Diana, allowing her to smell the strange musky perfume she was wearing, with tones of apple and something Diana couldn't distinguish.

'A human leader,' Helenia continued, her lips close to Diana's neck. 'Well, times have changed, haven't they?'

She turned back towards Valki, whose demeanour appeared even more controlled than usual, unreadable.

'I thought you were joking. When did you decide on a human leader?'

There was a strange familiarity to the way she spoke to Valki, Diana noticed. Still, Valki remained unmoved, as though not wishing to commit. The two aspects together filled Diana with concern.

After a moment of consideration, Valki shrugged. 'A couple of months ago,' he answered. 'Diana has been exceptional for us.'

Helenia's smile never wavered as she looked back at Diana, appearing amused.

'The will of the Eternal Mother grows, it seems,' she said. 'So, human leader of the Hateful, you wanted to see me?'

Diana was prepared, and looked Helenia in the eye, showing no fear. 'I want to know what you want,' Diana said, keeping her voice level. 'I wish to avoid conflict, not just between us, but also between yourselves and the rest of my race within Exia.'

An amused glint appeared in the noble Ethero Fiend's eye. 'War is inevitable, human,' she said, her tone final. 'The Eternal Mother is making her move, and we want to punish the Divinity for what he did to us all those years ago. You do not know how far your human ignorance takes you. If you did, perhaps you'd think differently.'

Helenia leaned forward again, her eyes boring into Diana's. 'Understand that the only reason I'm even listening to you is because my lover asked me to.'

'Your lover?' Diana said, frowning.

Helenia didn't respond, appearing preoccupied as she folded her arms across her chest. 'I also see potential within them, the Hateful,' she said. 'They possess power despite their broken minds. If they were to join us, we would stand before the Divinity, and make him regret his foolish pursuit.'

Helenia stopped to look at Valki, a certain hunger in her smile.

Diana feared the worst, as the noble Ethero Fiend stepped towards him, opening her mouth greedily as though ready to consume him. She then reached for his face, stroking it.

'You will be mine,' she said, before turning back towards Diana.

'It is already too late for your kind, human,' Helenia said. 'We've infiltrated your city, killing anyone foolish enough to be on the streets. Your DFA is dead, and you and your Hateful are the last bastion between us and conquering this city. Once Exia is ours, we will march to the other cities, and we will end thousands of years of humiliation and shame. This time, that disgusting child will not stop us. So, human, what can you offer me? Can you give me a reason not to send in the rest of the scorned to tear your beloved Hateful apart?'

Silence filled the air. Diana had to stay strong, despite her almost crushing desire to crumple to the floor. She didn't know what to say in the face of apparent hopelessness.

Which she knew Helenia wanted.

'You cannot tell me you agreed to this just to gloat and flaunt your strength,' Diana said, allowing some of her anger to show. 'No one doubts your power, Helenia. However, I refuse to accept that there's nothing you want. Why did you bother to come here?'

The noble smiled cruelly, as though confirming this. 'Oh, I like you,' she said, biting her bottom lip with satisfaction, exposing her two fangs. 'You're just like him.' She gestured towards Valki. 'So bold. Many have died speaking to me like that.'

Helenia looked back to her small army of Ethero Fiends, and they hissed and stepped away, as though terrified of her.

'Yet, there's a sadistic part of me that loves it. So bold, yet so desperate. So tell me, what would you give me to leave the Hateful alone?'

'This is getting ridiculous!' Valki spat. He turned towards Helenia in agitation. He moved towards the noble without fear, while gesturing at the Institute. 'You're just playing with your food, so tell us what you want! We want to save our kind, and we don't care what happens to the humans outside our walls. All we want to do is live our lives.'

'Valki,' Diana stammered, stunned at this turn from him.

Valki eyed her for a moment, before turning a stern gaze towards Helenia.

'This is survival, Diana. So, Helenia, tell us what you want!'

Horrified, Diana looked at the noble Ethero Fiend; she appeared enthralled by Valki, delighting in his outburst.

'What do I want? Hmm... I think you might already know the answer to that.'

'No,' Diana said, sensing where this was going. 'I won't sacrifice him to save ourselves. That's not an option.'

'Even if it protects all of you?' Helenia asked, sounding almost devious as she kept her hungry gaze on Valki. 'It's just one Hateful, human. Besides, you were so kind to send him to me before, and I love the way he speaks to me. So much restrained passion. Yes, I think I'd enjoy him, so why don't you let me have him? I'll promise to leave you alone.'

'Hang on,' Pauli spoke next. 'You'd change your mind, just like that?'

'Yes,' Helenia replied, keeping her hungry gaze on Valki.

Diana had a hard time believing that. It seemed such a sudden turn. Still, it didn't change her answer. 'I'm still saying no,' she said, trying to sound firm. 'Besides, we have no guarantee that you'll not attack us.'

'She's an Ethero Fiend, Diana,' Valki said, sounding more like himself. 'Their word is tied to their integrity and honour. She won't break a vow if she swears it.'

'Exactly,' Helenia said, as though that would settle the matter.

Diana scowled, seeing the blatant hypocrisy of the noble's words. 'You mean like the vow her and her kind have just broken by revealing themselves to the world?' she countered.

Helenia laughed. 'She's got me there,' she admitted, amused. 'The only reason I agreed to meet was because I want this Hateful man for myself. You don't realise how wonderful it is to find someone who is not of your kin but can speak your language. A mind so open and curious.'

The noble Ethero Fiend licked her lips, as though excited. 'Oh yes, I feel his hatred. His anger. I want to taste it so much. Give him to me, and I'll spare you and your Hateful.'

'Again, my answer is no,' Diana repeated, despising how weak her words sounded. 'I won't let you eat him.'

'*Eat* him?' Helenia asked, confused. 'Who said anything about eating him?'

343

Valki stepped forward, holding out his hand towards both Diana and Helenia, as though sensing a direction he didn't want this conversation to go.

'Diana, wait,' he said. 'If giving me up will save my kind, then I'll do it. You've already done so much for us. You saved us from our own purgatory. Unlike Hela and any other leader before her, you gave us the power to choose how we live our lives. I offer myself freely, if that's what she wants.'

He smiled at Helenia. 'After all, that was the plan from the start,' Valki said.

Diana froze in horror, realising why Helenia had reacted in the way she had. Smiling now, Helenia allowed Valki to come to her, reaching for her head and pulling it towards his. They shared a passionate kiss.

He set us up from the beginning. Oh Divinity, what have I done?

Diana watched them part, and Valki turned back to face her. His expression resumed its usual confidence.

'I had every intention of allowing the forces of the Eternal Mother to slaughter my race. I spent years dreaming of this, of the world beyond those walls. Reading forbidden books, discovering all these fascinating beings and creatures, all with rich cultures and languages. They were supposedly fiction, but I knew the truth. The accounts were too detailed. That was the author's mistake.

'I delved deeper, and the more I uncovered about the world hidden from us, the more I understood our past was a lie. As I told you before, Diana, I journeyed outside the walls, and those journeys led to me to the underground world beneath our feet. Like most Hateful, curiosity gripped me, and without hesitation I went to explore, approaching all who would entertain me. I listened to their stories, their hopes and dreams. Soon, I wanted to learn everything about them.

'I made acquaintances who evolved into friends. I had none among my kind. I heard of one particular being who fascinated me, so I approached her. When I did, I'd never seen a woman so beautiful. This was especially intriguing, considering that I had no interest in anyone beforehand. Then I saw how the rest of her kind reacted to her, the fear she commanded… It was intoxicating. I had to meet her.'

Valki stopped, as Helenia smiled fondly. Diana couldn't deny that the noble Ethero Fiend loved him; it was obvious.

'Helenia,' Valki continued, speaking as though he adored every syllable of her name. 'We fell in love, and she taught me everything. I learnt of her past, and that of her race. Helenia showed me the truth and what was to transpire in Exia, promising me we could still be together, even after she destroyed humanity and my race. By that point, I didn't even care. I was ready to watch my kind perish, and yet… you emerged, Diana. You changed everything, giving me an outlet for my talents, and an avenue to pursue my dreams.'

He looked sincerely at Diana smiling. 'You have saved my race. Because of you, I returned to Helenia to ask for one favour as a token of our love. "Do what you want with humanity. Make them suffer. As for the rest of you, no harm shall befall you, so long as we remain together."'

That's a fragile line to ensure our survival, Diana thought. Still, while Valki's betrayal didn't surprise her, the manner of it did. He had been plotting humanity's demise from the beginning.

He has complete power over us, and there's nothing we can do,

Diana knew, feeling defeated. However, a large hand gripped on her shoulder, squeezing as though trying to reassure her.

'It's alright, Diana,' he said. 'We'll—'

Pauli never got the chance to finish his words, as an explosion of violet and crimson erupted in the distance, emerging from the Rai District. In its wake, the horde of Ethero Fiends within Exia shrieked and roared, before scrambling in its direction.

'It would seem the broken Demon has awakened,' Helenia said, as she released Valki's arm, drawing her crimson sword. 'I will return, my love.'

'I will stay here for you, my love,' Valki said.

Helenia flashed him a warm smile, then vanished, as her Fiends rushed towards Rai. Meanwhile, Diana noticed his self-satisfied smirk. There was more to this.

'There's something else you haven't told us,' she said to him then.

'Forgive me, Diana. While some of my supposed revelation was genuine, most of it fuelled Helenia's fantasy of us. She now rushes towards doom, and our only chance of survival.'

'What are you talking about, traitor,' Pauli spat.

Valki rolled his eyes. 'Are you really so dense, Pauli?' he said, his tone sincere. 'When I read those books back in the Institute and discovered the languages and creatures within them I knew we were being lied to. That part I told you was true. However, while curiosity and wonder did grip me, they paled in comparison to the pressing questions that entered my mind – such as, if creatures existed that were in hiding. Why? It was linked to the past, and my instincts forced me to question what would happen if such hiding was forced. Would they desire vengeance? If so, what conditions would they require to unveil themselves?

'I arrived at some conclusions, and I searched for what I believed would be a "hidden world" kept from our races. That search led me towards The Place That Doesn't Exist in Seraphu, and from there I came upon Helenia. It made sense that a pseudo leader of the races beneath Exia would possess the information I desired, and so from her I extracted everything I needed to know. Then, I had to wait for the trigger, the one who would encourage them to make their move.'

'Megidra,' Diana said.

Valki nodded. 'Indeed, and once he committed the unthinkable, I invited Helenia to play her hand. From there, my biggest gamble relied on Megidra himself. I was confident that he wouldn't perish, and knowing his disposition, I believed he would seek atonement. It only made sense then that he'd befriend humans, and that he'd wish to protect them. Once I encouraged Helenia to speed up her plans, I knew it would force him to decide, especially after I asked Helenia to take out the humans at the DFA. That would leave him with one option to protect his precious humans. Now, despite everything, it would seem that he's made his choice.'

'Megidra's coming here?' Diana asked, trying to keep track of all this information. 'That explosion was him?'

'It was,' Valki confirmed. 'And now he must fight. Megidra has to destroy Helenia and her Fiends, or else his beloved humans will die. This gives us time to kill a noble while dealing a vicious blow to the forces of the Eternal Mother. Helenia was right about one thing: war is inevitable, but if we can save more humans and gain Megidra's power, then it gives us a chance.'

Diana nodded, unable to argue with Valki's logic. She was sure that he was right. War was inevitable. There was no running from that. Valki had given them a chance. Of course, it came with significant risks, and the possibility of Megidra's return would cause a wave of discontent within the Hateful.

But what choice do we have? After this, they'll come for us. We'll need him. We'll need everyone... But still...

'What are you after, Valki?' Diana asked. 'What do you actually want?'

Valki smiled, glancing back to where Helenia had raced off with her Fiends.

'You want to know my goal?' he said. 'It's a lot simpler than you'd expect. Everything I've done has been to prepare me for my dream. Learning about your kind, about your behaviour and interactions. It has all served the same purpose, Diana.'

He looked at her calmly.

'I wish to become leader of the Council of Exia, of Ethero itself.'

'Why?' Pauli asked, confused. 'It no longer exists. It's gone.'

'Yes, but I wish to create a new one. I want to establish a Council similar to Diana's, one on which every race has a representative. I want to establish a new Ethero, and I want to lead the Council to herald change. To achieve that, we must win this war. We must forge a world beyond gods.'

37

Gift to Humanity

Megidra struck the doors to Johann's church, listening to nervous voices fall silent. He didn't doubt they understood it was him, their Devil, the one who had caused all of this to happen, changing their lives forever. Yet, now was not the time to think about that. Megidra knew he could reflect in solitude, but only once the humans were safe.

His only goal was to take them to the Institute.

To his surprise, he sensed no fear. Nor did he dread what would face him when he returned to his home. None of it seemed to matter anymore.

With almost Hateful focus, he kept his gaze fixed on the door, his body possessing the will to move, to act.

To save.

The door opened, revealing Marienne. Megidra refused to turn his gaze away from her, knowing she deserved more respect than that. Even in their brief time, he had felt something for her, feelings he wasn't sure he deserved. Marienne looked at him, sadness overcoming her.

'I understand if no one wants anything to do with me,' he began. 'But the DFA headquarters are no longer an option. The Fiends have already struck it, and I assume they've mobilised to take the rest of the city. There's only one choice left for you now. You need to come with me. I need to take you to the Institute.'

'The Institute?' Deion's voice said, as he and Johann appeared behind Marienne. The large black man seemed to be trying to restrain his anger. Deion was fighting an internal conflict, between knowing Megidra had saved him and his son, and knowing that Megidra was the cause for all of this. His teeth seemed to be clenched so hard that Megidra feared they might break.

'After everything you've done, how could you–'

Johann raised his hand to interrupt him, looking sympathetic. 'Please, come inside. Everyone needs to hears what you have to say.'

'We don't have time for that,' Megidra said. 'We need to leave.'

Both Marienne and Deion turned and walked away, as though signalling their disgust for him. A new fear rose within Megidra, one he hadn't considered.

What if they didn't come?

Johann watched them go before taking in a deep breath. 'They won't leave here unless you do,' Johann said, confirming that fear. Megidra realised how delicate the situation had become. He couldn't force them to follow him, that much he understood. Megidra nodded in acknowledgement before stepping inside the church.

Everyone turned to look at him, reflecting one of Megidra's oldest fears by doing so. He was surprised they weren't attacking him. He had hurt these people, except for Odeon and Ilara. He didn't know what to say. He took a breath, praying that they'd listen.

'You should despise me,' he began, surprised to sense calmness flood through him. Inside, Ryun emerged from him, filling him with the power of truth. Knowing that he was on the right path, Megidra continued.

'I ruined many lives, even before Anubi. None of you have any reason to trust me, to follow me. After all, I don't deserve your forgiveness, and neither do I want it, not anymore.'

Megidra bit his bottom lip, pausing. 'I wanted it to be different. All I wanted was to be human. When I was a child, my parents told me I was Cursed, along with my Hateful sister. They told us we were broken, lacking the capacity to understand, always fixating on strange things. Yet, to me, nothing about your kind ever made sense to me, either. I wanted to understand you, so I could understand what was wrong with me. If I figured that out, I believed that maybe then I could make you love me.

'However, as I grew older, the divide between us only seemed to grow. No matter what I did. No matter what I tried. I still couldn't solve this problem of understanding between us. By the time our parents cast us aside and we went to the Institute, I realised that all of my race shared the same problem. Love and kindness seemed far away for us.

'Then one day, everything changed.

'The only thing that came close to what I wanted was the bond I shared with my sister. I wanted love, to feel loved, so our bond as family was the closest thing. It gave me faith. Then, one of your kind scaled our wall, and the next thing I knew, my sister gained the love I craved. In that human, she found love and understanding. Jealousy and hate filled my heart, because it was like she didn't even have to try, and now I faced losing the one person who ever cared about me. I was so scared of losing that love that I feared no one would ever love me after her.'

Megidra smiled, knowing that tears were running down his cheeks now, doing nothing to stop them.

'The monster was born, the very monster my parents told me I was, and the Devil you all know me as today. I killed that human, my sister's lover, because I couldn't live with someone taking her away from me, especially someone whose race had scorned me my entire life. After that, my sister disowned me and banished me from my home. Now cast aside, I was truly alone. I had suffered the fate I feared most.

'To compensate for this, I delved into the furthest reaches of a poisoned dream, a deluded belief that I could unite us. After a chance meeting with the Captain of the DFA, I joined them. I believed in his words that the opportunity to work alongside your kind would help me prove we weren't that different. That one day we could stand together, by hunting down my kind, and punishing them for the crimes they'd committed.'

Megidra paused, realising how foolish such sentiments were. He wanted to rue his Hateful naivety then, along with his desperation. Still, he knew the story needed an ending.

Not a single human around him seemed to breathe, never mind utter a word. He found Marienne standing next to Destin, seeing her pain as she cried.

He realised she was upset over him, over what he was telling them.

'The humans in the DFA still hated me. No matter what

I did. No matter what I said. Even when I dyed my hair and changed my name, all I found was more hatred and rejection. The monster within blossomed, believing that one day I would learn how to become human, to remove the Hateful parts within me once and for all. Of course, it would take another one of my kind with a similar dream to expose everything that was wrong with me. You will all remember him.

'It was my responsibility to bring him in. However, he exposed my lies, and I had to face my sister again. I lost. Alone once more, pushing away my only friend, I unleashed the monsters that had once been the most vulnerable members of my kind. At that point, I no longer cared. I wanted to destroy this world for what it had forced me to become.

'Again, another lie, among so many. It wasn't until I'd committed those horrific actions that I realised what I had done, and what I'd allowed myself to become. Now, I don't deny what I've done. I acknowledge every life in here that I've ruined, along with those outside these walls. I no longer seek your forgiveness, because I don't deserve it.

'However, if you do not follow me, all of you will die. The Fiends will not spare you. I am your only chance. Even if afterword you choose to cast me aside and condemn me, I am willing to accept that. Please, accept this as my gift to you, to humanity. Let me guide you to safety. Let me give you the best possible chance of survival.'

Megidra breathed out then, knowing he had said everything. Seconds and minutes passed in silence, and Megidra feared the humans' response.

'Megi,' Deion said, causing the entire room to turn towards him as he stood with Johann. 'I'm not gonna lie to you. A

353

part of me doesn't want to forgive you for what you've done. Yet, we'd be dead without you. And, as much as I know many of us here would rather deny it, we cannot downplay our role in what led to Anubi happening. Yeah, it was you that committed those actions, but what choice did you have? Or, what choice did we present to you?'

Deion held himself then, frustration on his face.

'Beyond that, a part of me can't deny that I want to forgive you. A part of me that knows you as Megi, the Hateful guy who saved my kid, and who would do anything to keep us safe. Seraphu proved that, and so... I will follow you. I choose to trust you so you can get us to safety. If not, I will never see Destin grow older. I wanna see humanity survive.'

'And he will, Deion,' Megidra said, fighting back tears. 'I promise you that no human will die tonight. I will bring you all to safety.'

Megidra guided his group of over a hundred humans through the snowy streets of Rai, heading for the district of Orphani.

Towards the Institute.

There was no need to hide. No outside human group would dare attack them, not while the Fiends roamed the streets. As for them, Megidra already knew how he would deal with them. Inside, Ryun filled him with anticipation.

Are you planning on letting me out, Megidra? the Fallen asked. Megidra didn't bother answering. The Fallen knew the truth. They moved through the district of Rai without interruption.

But he knew they were watching, waiting for the perfect moment to strike.

They reached the centre of the city, a crossroads that led towards each district.

Megidra addressed the humans. 'Don't panic, but they'll meet us here. I won't let them harm you.'

Near the crossroads, black silhouettes were emerging from the snowy fog. Megidra remained calm, tapping into his Transformative Blessing and summoning his favoured curving blade on his right arm. The black shadows shifted into physical forms, revealing three Ethero Fiends.

'What are you doing, Hateful fool?' the one in front said, scorn in his voice.

Megidra stared into the black abysses that were his eyes. 'I'm taking these humans to my home,' Megidra said. 'You have two choices: let us pass or die. You have one minute to decide.'

The Fiend at the front glanced at the others before looking back at Megidra. 'And you believe we'll obey you?' it said, a simple challenge.

Megidra was unfazed. 'Yes,' he said. 'Because you know who I am, and who lives within me. So, stand aside, and I'll grant you the mercy of remaining alive.'

'You believe your word to transcend that of a noble?' the Fiend hissed, revealing his offence.

Megidra stepped towards the Fiend, allowing Ryun's power to emit from his body. 'No, of course not,' he said, watching as the Fiends shifted back. 'But he does...'

Megidra opened his arms, allowing Ryun's power to fill him.

More Ethero Fiends joined the others, surrounding the humans. Megidra knew they would watch him. He tapped into his Fallen power, creating five copies of himself. They all moved into position, circling the humans.

'Do not fear them, my friends,' Megidra said, allowing his

arms to fall, and his head to tilt slightly. 'After all, they should be the ones fearing me. RYUN!'

His Fallen aura exploded all around him, and Megidra felt his Hateful shirt and jacket burn away, leaving his torso bare and glowing with violet and crimson. Though his hair was short, it still rose towards the sky as though gravity no longer mattered. Megidra allowed himself to be swallowed by the power.

He gave way to the one who lived within him, the Truth-seeker.

'Well, I had not expected things to play out this way,' Ryun said, glancing at his bladed arm and free hand, before gazing up at the Fiends, who hissed and shrieked before reverting to their shadow forms, retreating.

Ryun grinned. 'You think you can run from me?' he said, allowing his copies to fade as he moved to step forward. However, Megidra stopped him.

'Really?' Ryun said, his feet planted on the ground. Feeling Megidra's desire for the task at hand, the Fallen glanced back at the humans, taking satisfaction in the terror with which they regarded him.

'That look will suffice,' he said, turning to see more silhouettes emerge. A lot more. Ryun shivered in anticipation. 'Ah. They come to us,' he said.

Beyond, a small force of Ethero Fiends emerged, headed by the female noble they had met in Seraphu. She had her sword drawn, and looked displeased.

'Truthseeker,' she said, addressing Ryun by his title. 'I didn't expect you to come to the aid of your broken vessel. I would've thought you regarded him as a disappointment.'

Ryun smirked, not believing this noble to be worth his

words. It didn't surprise him when the noble sneered in his direction, stopping a few paces ahead.

'So you obey his will now?'

Still, Ryun kept his smirk, folding his arms across his chest. 'I don't like the way you're speaking to me, Fiend,' Ryun said, his malice apparent despite his smile. 'You should be on your knees, praying to me.'

'I don't pray to traitors,' the noble remarked, which made Ryun chuckle.

'Now, now. Don't tar me with the same brush as Korai. You can only regard me as a traitor if I betray that which I represent. Last time I checked, I still stand for all truths – and myself, of course.'

'So you stand against us now?' the noble asked. Ryun noticed the slightest of twitching, showing that she was preparing herself for a fight. However, he responded by closing his eyes and shaking his head, portraying complete self-control.

'You ask the wrong question, little Fiend,' he said, before unlatching his right arm and shifting it into an enormous cannon. Tubes that pulsed a perfect violet connected it to his upper arm. Within its barrel a thrumming sound emerged. Ryun turned it on the Fiends.

'Do you all stand against me?' he asked, firing the weapon before anyone could answer him. The cannon discharged a single violet blast, causing those unfortunate enough to be in its range to disintegrate. Those lucky enough to remain scrambled away. Laughing with joy, Ryun turned the cannon towards some nearby tower blocks.

Megidra filled him with the urge to stop. Ryun tutted before shaking his head.

'Fine. I won't destroy this shithole,' he remarked, relinquishing the weapon. He was surprised to see a single body rise from the crater he had created in his initial attack. Squinting, Ryun realised it was the noble Ethero Fiend. She was bleeding from multiple cuts, and seemed close to death as she coughed up blood.

'I'm impressed. I wasn't expecting you to still be alive after that,' Ryun said.

The noble spat out more blood in indignation. 'I'm a noble,' she said disdainfully. 'It'll take more than–'

She didn't get the chance to finish, as Ryun held out a hand towards her, tapping into Megidra's Illusionary Blessing. He summoned a wave of control and sent it into the noble's mind, causing her to scream as she dropped to her knees, clutching her head in agony.

'You were saying?' he asked, before releasing her from his power.

Despite her obvious pain, the noble stayed on her hands and knees, gritting her teeth. 'I won't die like this,' she hissed. She motioned to reach for her sword just ahead of her.

Ryun tapped into Megidra's Elemental Blessing, summoning a bolt of light that he aimed directly at the noble.

She uttered her last scream as it burned her alive.

All around them, the agonised roars and calls of her Fiends sounded.

'We were always your superiors, fools,' Ryun said, lowering his hand. 'You would be wise to remember that.'

He turned to face the humans, seeing terror on their faces.

'Go. They won't touch you now, not while I'm here,' he said, before gesturing toward where he guessed the Institute lay. 'This is your best chance to–'

The ground beneath their feet rumbled, silencing Ryun. The Fallen's face dropped.

'No, it can't be,' Ryun said.

A colossal roar filled the sky, an almost mechanical bellow that silenced Ethero. It was a sound that confirmed his worst fears.

'Someone has awoken one of the great machines,' he said. 'The Titans.'

38

The Scorned

"*Your downfall*," Greene's mind repeated as he and the Tortured walked along the catacombs, travelling to the last location in their journey.

Dynames.

As expected, the walk was long while seeming short. The strange network of tunnels only scratched the surface of what Ethero was, to Greene anyway. The Tortured led him through the tunnels, and he followed silently. It gave him time to predict what was coming.

As he did this, he faced the "logical fear" his travelling companion had alluded to before they arrived at the land of Animus.

And the memory of what Forgiveness told him in the vision.

"*Faced with overwhelming anger and hatred, can you control it? Can you say no to your deepest desires and that of your entire race? Can you show them another way? That another path exists for them?*"

I... hope so, Greene answered in his own mind, though the longer they walked, the more his confidence diminished.

Something was going to happen to him. Releasing his ancestors would come at a significant cost. Greene wrestled with that as they wandered, trying to figure out the cost. Nothing came to him – nothing that made sense, anyway.

And so he followed, as the silent Tortured continued to walk with reserved dignity, his head shrouded.

'Our journey is almost over,' the Ethero Fiend said then, causing Greene to jump sightly at the sudden commencement of conversation. The Fiend moved as if he had never spoken. Greene quickened his steps to catch up with the Fiend, stepping alongside him.

'What do you mean?' he asked.

Silence met him, which meant either the Fiend was considering his answer, or he didn't believe the question worth answering. A sensation Greene had grown used to calling agitation rose, and he was almost sure the Tortured was smiling.

'We're almost at Dynames, Greene,' he said. 'You're about to reach the last piece of the Titan core. The power to free your kind will soon be yours.'

'Yes,' Greene replied, unsure. 'What's your point?'

'My point?' the Fiend asked. His smile faded, becoming a straight line. 'Have you considered what's about to happen?' he asked. 'Are you sure you're ready?'

Greene didn't answer that at first, frowning as he regarded the Tortured.

'Why are you asking me that?' he asked. 'After everything we've done, why ask that question now?'

'Because I know what started this quest,' the Tortured said. 'And I know what ends it. I was wondering if you've put together the pieces.'

Again, Greene said nothing. They had thrown many pieces at him. So many cryptic messages, as beings seemed to jostle with him as he sought to gain the power to free his kind. Barbatos. Forgiveness. Doomis. The Tortured. Throughout this journey, it appeared those around him knew things he didn't, while not feeling the need to share those things unless it suited their convenience. How did the pieces come together?

Especially when he wasn't sure which parts were the truth and which weren't.

'I don't know,' he admitted, shaking his head. 'All I can do is trust in myself. All my life, I've had to deal with beings who have always believed themselves above me and my race. I'm done with being a tool for them. All I seek is liberation for my kind.'

The Tortured seemed to consider this as they walked. Greene was certain he saw regret in him.

'Greene,' he began, his voice quiet. 'Understand that there is a cost that comes with all truth. What you're about to face is perhaps the greatest lie of all. You will face the greatest cost. I hope you're ready for the aftermath of discovering that truth, because once you discover it, you can never return to the point of ignorance. Truth changes everything, and this is something you cannot run away from.'

'What are you trying to tell me?' Greene asked, becoming more confused.

The Tortured didn't answer as they reached the end of the tunnel.

Greene heard the sounds of battle and human screams.

Greene froze at the sound, his mind recalling the sensations he had felt during Newman's descent towards darkness. The only thing missing was the gargled shrieks of his eyeless monsters. Hisses and powerful roars replaced these. It was the latter he recognised at first. Greene spun his head towards the Tortured.

'Doomis!?' he said, and the Tortured raised a hand towards the closed circular door behind them, tapping into his strange mysterious power that caused it to shake. It rotated to the right as the forever black sky met them, followed by the forest. The sounds of battle grew louder. As Greene stepped forward, he saw that they'd entered some kind of forest again, this one different from the others.

Rather than being surrounded by rain forest, a mist floated between the tallest trees Greene had ever seen, with thick tree trunks that were hundreds if not thousands of years old. The ground was soft, and thick roots rose from underground, creating a network that seemed to link them all together.

'What's happening?' Greene asked.

No answer came.

The Tortured proceeded, heading towards the path ahead. Greene ran in its direction, almost tripping over the roots. Still, he kept moving urgently.

A clearing appeared, and Greene saw a giant metal bridge connected to the natural landscape. Beyond, the screams of human beings combined with the vicious cries and roars of the Ethero Fiends in their group. He broke into a sprint, wanting to prevent what had happened in Exia.

I must stop them!

Greene reached the opening. There was a single figure on the bridge. He realised who it was. They had arrived at the last destination of their journey.

Dynames.

It was much smaller than Exia, sitting on a long metal spire that rose from a bowl in the ground. It formed into a shape like a spinning top, to which three metal bridges led. There were explosions and gunfire all around. Greene wondered how a single spire held that gargantuan weight.

Humans were fleeing down the bridges, scrambling in panic. Greene felt haunted, recalling his previous failure in Exia.

The figure on the bridge turned.

Barbatos.

'Ah, my dear Titanius,' the blue-skinned sorcerer said, opening his arms as though wishing to embrace Greene. 'You could not have timed your arrival better! The fun has already–'

Greene stepped forward and punched him square in the face. The sorcerer reeled back, somehow remaining on his feet, looking surprised. The look only lasted a few seconds, as black blood leaked from his nose.

'What are they doing?!' Greene exclaimed, gesturing towards Dynames, enraged. 'Why are you doing this?!'

After a few more seconds to collect himself, Barbatos smiled. 'Yuvi and Escara couldn't help themselves,' he said, grinning. 'And Doomis and Shallai intervened. What you're seeing are the results of that intervention. I guess you've had more of an impact on them than I expected. Alas, chaos displays its true beauty.'

'Yet you're the one standing here,' Greene said, disgusted.

The sorcerer chuckled. 'Of course!' he exclaimed. 'I've picked the best seats in the house! The main event begins with this.'

'What are you talking about?' Greene asked, noticing the

Tortured emerge from the forest. Barbatos regarded him without a word before returning his attention to Greene. He held out his arms and gestured to Greene.

'You, Greene. The main event is you! It always has been, ever since I first laid eyes on you, *Descendant*.'

He used the last word strangely. Even if Greene didn't understand what that term meant, he knew it meant something significant.

And something terrible.

He shook his head, looking over to the city where he now understood what was happening. Doomis and Shallai were fighting Yuvi and Escara in the middle of Dynames. Greene knew he had to stop them before it was too late. Still…

'Barbatos, what is all of this about? What are you?' he asked.

'So you want me to tell you the truth,' Barbatos said, understanding at once. 'Despite knowing I could lie. Well, we're beyond the place of no return. You have no choice but to proceed. I'll tell you what all this is about.'

Barbatos stepped towards Greene, leaning close to Greene's ear, as though he didn't want anyone else to hear what he was about to say.

'Vengeance, Greene, just like you,' he began, before stepping back, his grin returning. 'At the very beginning, once the Eternal Mother created Ethero and the Divinity, she handed him the means to create. So, he did.'

'The first beings he created were the Angels, the most perfect of all his creations - according to him, anyway. Nothing was ever good enough for him. Nothing.'

Barbatos' expression changed to one of disdain and hatred. Greene remained silent, knowing that Barbatos was telling him the truth for the first time.

'He began his quest to create beings in his image, the "perfect" being. The animals and creatures possessed no intelligence, but they were cute enough that the Divinity let them live. As for beings that would represent his "perfection", he first created humanity. You can predict how he felt about them. So intelligent, yet limited by their animal instincts. They waged war and slaughtered each other for fun, pursuing dominance that was the very opposite of the perfection the Divinity sought. Annoyed, he tried altering their minds, only to create a subset of humans that were more broken.'

'The Hateful.'

'Despite their power, having access to all the Blessings, the Divinity realised that they too were incapable of matching the image he wished to create for Ethero. He took more drastic measures, desperate to create his "perfect" beings. This time, he believed the issues all stemmed from their minds, so next he created a race with far fewer mental capabilities. Less capable of individual thought.'

'Us,' Greene said, knowing it was true.

Barbatos made no move to deny it. 'He viewed your kind as too subservient, lacking in free will. I don't doubt you can see the contradictory nature of his character now, but alas, he continued in his relentless pursuit. Injecting emotion back in, he created the Cybernetics, yet even they were not enough. In his rage, the Divinity blew the sun out of the sky, creating another new race with it.'

'Ethero Fiends,' Greene guessed.

Again, Barbatos made no move to deny it. 'Beings capable of incredible violence. Still, not good enough. The Divinity went back to the beginning, wondering what would happen if he gave his mindless animals intelligence. Hence, Animus were born. Yet, it was still not good enough. The divine father remained dismayed at his latest failure. Even if they were the closest to his ideal, nothing satisfied him. He was simply repeating the same mistake, never realising where it would lead.'

'Still, he made one last attempt. While mixing various aspects of all his creations prior, he created a single being, one that embodied every quality he sought in his "perfect being".'

'But the result was the same,' Greene guessed. 'Nothing was ever good enough for him.'

'Indeed,' Barbatos replied, his eyes blazing with hatred. 'How ironic, a being flawed and arrogant enough to believe that they could create perfection, never realising that he made beings in his image. Think about it, Greene. If all your creations are imperfect, when you see yourself as divine, "perfect", what does that say? What truth do you think the Divinity sought to extinguish?'

Greene said nothing then, sure that the questions were rhetorical. It all made sense now. It had all converged towards this point, to reveal...

'You were that final being. The last child of the Divinity,' Greene said.

'Yes,' Barbatos said. 'I was that last attempt. And just like all the others, he discarded me, scorned for my imperfections. I was never good enough, and neither were the others. So, I approached the one who made him, the Eternal Mother. We made a deal after I discovered her displeasure with what the Divinity had done. I would harness her power, and I would destroy him and what he treasured. With that power, I created the Demons that could match his Angels. From the rage of your kind, I helped create the Titans.'

He leaned towards Greene once more.

'I was the one responsible for the war, Greene. I took the title of Child of the Ether as defiance to my father. Yet, humanity and the Hateful stood against us, along with his Angels. Of course, my enemy, Forgiveness, has told you the rest. Now, I seek to finish what I started. So, my dear Titanius, unleash my Titans. Expose the ultimate lie. And kill everyone.'

Before Greene had the chance to speak, Barbatos clicked his fingers towards the Tortured.

'Take him to the tree,' he ordered. 'Do not let Doomis and Shallai intervene.'

The Tortured nodded dutifully and raised his hand towards Greene. He felt the Ethero Fiend's power take him, rendering him unable to move. Greene felt himself lifted then, as the Tortured motioned him towards the bridge.

Towards Dynames.

Greene couldn't fight it. The Tortured's strange power was so strong that he felt like a human infant in the arms of its parents, without the capability to move or speak. He could only watch as the Tortured carried him across the bridge, hovering in the air just above the metal bridge.

'I'm sorry, Greene,' the Tortured then said, sounding regretful. 'But this world cannot continue as it is. This is our only chance to change it, to end everything.'

But why? Greene wanted to ask, but he was unable to speak. Then he heard a gargantuan roar in the distance. Doomis. It sounded like a victory roar, as though he had just won a mighty battle.

'It would seem that Yuvi and Escara have perished,' the

Tortured commented, matter-of-factly. 'It wouldn't surprise me. The Executioner is a force of nature. A being born of pain and suffering like me, turning that into his greatest strength.'

Again, Greene said nothing; it would be pointless to try. This was inevitable. He couldn't stop this.

He would awaken his ancestors.

I understand what Forgiveness was trying to stop, Greene thought, picturing everything from the visions. Since the beginning, they had warned Greene of what was coming. Though Greene had always known something was wrong with the sorcerer, he had never imagined how intertwined he was with the history of Ethero. He had been waiting for this, working towards the perfect moment.

When he could ruin his father's world.

'*GRASHIVA!*' Doomis boomed, and Greene watched the Fiend emerge from the city, taking his first few steps onto the bridge they were walking across. He was bleeding from fresh cuts, wielding his giant black great sword in one hand. The Tortured had been correct in his estimation, but neither did he baulk at Doomis' emergence. He just continued to advance, as though Doomis weren't even there.

'GREENE!' Doomis called out. 'I'LL SAVE YOU!'

'No, you won't,' the Tortured whispered.

Doomis leapt into the air towards them, bringing up his sword with both hands, ready to inflict what would be a deadly blow. However, the Tortured raised his free hand in the same direction Doomis was falling, ensnaring him in the same power in which he held Greene. The Tortured released Greene and he crashed into the ground. Greene pushed himself to his hands and knees.

'Why did you release me?'

'Because it will take all my strength to hold Doomis,' the Tortured said. 'And, because you know I can crush him if you decide to wander from your destiny. Now go, get the relic.'

Greene fell silent, glancing between Doomis and the Tortured. Doomis was struggling in his fellow Ethero Fiend's power, fighting to break free.

'Don't listen to him,' Doomis gritted out. 'Run.'

'Where's Shallai?' Greene asked. 'Is she in the city?'

'You don't have time to find out, Greene,' the Tortured said, drawing his fingers closer, causing Doomis to cry out in pain.

'No!' Greene called, 'Please! I'll do it! Just don't hurt him!'

'Then move, Titanius,' the Tortured ordered, menacingly.

Greene turned and headed towards the city of Dynames.

It was much smaller than Exia, probably no larger than a single district of that city. Like all the other cities, it was made of metal and had many connected buildings. A few single towers rose beyond them all. Dynames had an almost circular shape, as the city seemed to have been built out from a point in its very centre.

That's where the last tree was.

Death and carnage surrounded it. Clearly, Yuvi and Escara had caused much damage and chaos before Doomis had intervened. Vehicles were upturned, and even dragons lay dead alongside many human corpses.

Four strange arches surrounded the site of the tree, all connected with strange objects standing atop them, reminiscent of metal gargoyles. They reminded Greene of something; something that made little sense to him.

They look like us, he noted, *only more machine-like.*

Greene moved towards the arch that led straight to the tree. He saw a figure lying against it with a glowing carapace; a female.

'Shallai!' Greene knew at once, kneeling down, praying that she was alright. Though she appeared damaged and hurt, Greene could make out the soft rising and falling of breath.

'I will take her too,' the Tortured said, before Greene could touch her. 'Keep moving, Greene. It is time.'

Greene glared at the Ethero Fiend with gritted teeth, but obeyed, rising to his feet before looking at Shallai, as she floated in the air.

'I will get us out of this,' he said then, despite doubting she could hear him.

With resolution filling him, Greene turned towards the tree. He crossed the distance between the four arches and the shimmering white barrier that encased the tree, knowing that only he could enter.

He did, and all went silent, except for a soft hum surrounding him.

To his surprise, nothing changed in the world around him. No vision came. Nor did the roots move to ensnare his ankles. Except for the falling golden leaves, his emergence appeared to have no effect.

Greene reached within his jacket pocket, pulling out the incomplete Titan core, which vibrated as though in anticipation.

This is it, Greene thought, as the last relic pulsed and vibrated, responding to the core in his hands. Greene was about to climb up to retrieve the last piece, but it flew towards him, connecting with the Titan core, and causing Greene to black out.

At first, there was nothing. He was in some kind of void,

which eerily reminded him of the third vision. This time, a deep rumble ran through his entire being. Something dormant had awoken. Greene tried to move then, but couldn't. The sounds of moving mechanical pieces and gears emerged as soft whispers surfaced, sounding as though they surrounded him.

'Descendant.'

'He has come! At last!'

'We have waited for this moment. It is time to awaken.'

'Now, humanity and the Divinity will pay for what he did to us. We will crush his world! Kill them all!'

'Lay this world in ruin!'

'Trample over them! Lay them to waste!'

More and more voices came, each echoing similar sentiments. Despite his initial desire to argue, to plead, they wouldn't stop. They just kept coming, voices that Greene recognised as his Titanius brothers and sisters spoke, as though every repressed feeling they ever had now flooded into him.

At first, it filled him with power, power beyond his wildest dreams, and he had the strange sensation of things emerging and latching onto his body as he steamed again. Then he felt rage and unstoppable, insatiable hatred. It didn't seem to matter if he could fight it or not. He didn't have a choice. This was the anger of an entire race.

And he would unleash it upon Ethero. He reared his head and screamed into the black void, only to hear it come back to him as a mechanical roar.

Then, a presence filled him, as the power of the core latched itself onto him, making him its heart.

The heart of Dynames, the World Breaker. One of four

great machines that, until now, had been hidden from the world.

Hear me, all Titaniuses, it said. *My name, is Greene. I am speaking to all of you, using the power of our ancestors, of the Titan core that has granted me control of the Titan known as Dynames. We have risen. I have exposed the lie, and I present to you the truth behind our kind, the truth that has led to every single one of us being imprisoned and forced to serve as slaves. My only goal is to liberate my kind, and make humanity pay for what it has done to us. The beings of the Divinity and the Ether have lived under sworn oaths to protect the truth from our kind. Now that I am speaking to you, they will stop at nothing to exterminate us, knowing the power we possess.*

I won't let them have their way.

I will begin my march, to trample and destroy all the settlements that the other races occupy. Then, I shall awaken my brothers, who humanity has made a mockery of us for so long, never realising what lies beneath their feet. Together, we will crush and obliterate all life, until Titaniuses are all that remain on Ethero.

Barbatos watched as the city of Dynames shook and a great mechanical roar filled the sky. He smiled with smug satisfaction as the Tortured landed alongside him. The Ethero Fiend still held Doomis and Shallai in his power as they witnessed the great unveiling that they had kept humanity from since the beginning.

The cities where they had built their homes had been on the dormant bodies of the Titans.

This is it, Barbatos revelled, watching as the metal bridges folded in towards the Dynames, while the single spire that held the city split in two and formed two legs that were as tall as the Institute's towers. The rest of the city began to fold and expand in different places as human screams filled the air. It was too late for them, Barbatos knew, as some fell from a great height, while others were crushed within the transformation. Soon, Dynames formed two arms and a central body.

'The ultimate humiliation of his ancestors,' the Tortured said, addressing no one. 'One of the great Titan's Dynames.'

'Magnificent,' Barbatos said as he sat on the ground. He watched as one arm shifted into an enormous claw, the other a hammer. A single red eye formed in the head with no neck, and the mechanical monstrosity known as Dynames bellowed another mighty roar. It then turned towards what Barbatos knew would be its closest relative, beginning its march as the world shook beneath its feet.

Towards Kyrios.

This time, Forgiveness cannot stop me.

39

Forgiveness

Korai stood before his fellow Fallen, Vorus, with a calm gaze, their auras almost intertwining as they regarded each other. Of course, neither Lucifer's parents, nor the humans and Hateful in Kyrios, would understand what was happening as they entered the streets. Still, everyone who witnessed this moment would never forget it. Such a sight had not been witnessed since Ethero's beginning. The world would never be the same after today.

The Destroyer stood before the Traitor.

Vorus was smiling with eager anticipation.

'Brother. It's been far too long,' he said, before kicking into the air, where his power kept him afloat. 'Who would've thought it? Thousands of years have passed, and we will end what we started.'

Korai repeated the same motion as Vorus and floated in the sky, reaching the same level as his brother.

'Why do I sense you don't care about that, brother?' he said. 'You only care about destruction.'

'Now, now, no need for hurtful words, Traitor,' Vorus

replied, though his smile showed Korai wasn't far from the mark. 'Why can't I have both?'

'Because mindless destruction is just that: mindless.'

'I don't recall you having an issue before,' Vorus said. He turned his right palm towards the sky and generated an energy ball of violet and crimson that pulsed with power. He held it casually towards Korai.

'It was only when you met your sweet little Angel that you changed, brother. Tell me, was she worth it, now knowing that it led only to postponement of the inevitable?'

Had his brother spoken those words before, back when he didn't possess the knowledge that both Orphani and his son lived within Lucifer, Korai knew he would have reacted differently. Yet now he kept calm, knowing the truth.

That Forgiveness had planned for this, and now everything pointed towards his emergence.

Korai had expected what had transpired between Lucifer and his parents to draw out Forgiveness, but it hadn't. That meant there was still something missing, a last piece Lucifer needed to uncover. Until then, Korai knew he would do everything in his power to aid Lucifer, the Child of Healing. He knew to trust Orphani's judgement. Her assurance, kindness and love had been what Korai needed. They made him fall in love with her. He intended to honour that love.

He would see this through.

'Nothing to say, Traitor?' Vorus prodded.

Korai returned his focus to him. 'I once had a different name, brother. Now I know why. From the beginning, everything has led to this. Whether you believe it, it doesn't matter. I will represent my original designation, Traitor or not. I am the Guardian.'

Korai extended his right hand, calling upon the Sword of Greyr. It sparked into life with a golden radiance like a shining star. It formed into the black and silver sword with glowing golden text etched upon its flat blade.

Korai felt a strange sensation within the blade.

It's as though Greyr's presence is still alive, trapped within it. Is that possible? Is he reacting to me?

Then, realising that taking his eyes off Vorus was foolish, Korai returned his gaze towards his brother.

'I thought you intended to destroy everything?' he said. 'Why are you waiting?'

Vorus shrugged. 'I just wanted to catch up,' he said, raising the pulsing ball of electrical energy in his hand. 'That's why I created this, Korai.'

Oh, shit, Korai thought.

Vorus grinned before turning the ball of energy towards the floor. 'Protect this, brother,' he said, as the ball erupted into a single beam of concentrated power. It raced towards Lucifer's parents in their home. Knowing he had seconds to save them, Korai dived, tapping into the Transformative Blessing as he landed, cocooning both himself and them in metal. He prayed it was enough.

Vorus' attack made contact.

First came a boom, then a tempest roared. Korai sensed his cocoon being launched into the air. A storm of tearing metal and a host of human screams followed. Seconds passed, and Korai knew what he would find once he released Lucifer's amplified power, knowing that it was his enhancement along with the Blessing that had saved his parents. Inside, Lucifer thanked Korai, now playing spectator to what would come next.

The battle between brothers.

Korai relinquished the Blessing, rising from Lucifer's shocked parents to find a scene of devastation. Some of Kyrios had been obliterated, with only faint metal skeletons that were once buildings of the housing section remaining. Korai rued how many had probably died in the attack. Panic erupted in the streets, as humans and Hateful lucky enough not to be caught within the blast scrambled to run away. Korai looked up to see his brother still in the air, waiting for him.

Korai launched himself into the air and headed straight for Vorus. He drew the Sword of Greyr in both hands before swinging upward with all his might as the sword glowed.

'Too predictable,' Vorus commented, turning to the left, missing the blade's arc. As Korai surged past him, Vorus used his momentum against him, swinging a hard right kick into his back, sending him tumbling through the air. Korai recollected himself before he crashed onto the floor, shaking his head to restore his senses.

His brother sent a single energy blast heading towards him.

Korai had milliseconds to respond, just bringing the Sword of Greyr before him to intercept the attack. It had taken the lethal sting out of the attack, but not the overwhelming force carrying it. It hurled Korai into a building with almost backbreaking force. He crashed into a wall with a loud groan, feeling it bend from his impact. Korai coughed out blood, sensing weariness he hadn't felt in years engulf him. This wasn't the same battle he had shared with Ryun. Vorus was the strongest fighter among the Fallen.

I need to move, Korai told himself. He peeled himself off the metal wall, and forced himself to look up, sensing his vulnerability.

Vorus was right there, his arms folded as though amused.

'You've got rusty, brother,' he said. 'I was expecting more.'

Korai smiled at that before spitting out blood. 'You believe I'm done?' he asked.

'If I wanted it so, you would be dead by now,' Vorus responded.

Korai then saw many forms appearing across the rooftops, running towards them.

'Then you should've done it before they came,' he said.

Vorus frowned in confusion, as though sensing what Korai had meant.

He was met by the Physically enhanced fist of Mika.

She caught him hard across the jaw, sending the Fallen reeling before Korai took advantage of the opportunity. He switched his right arm into the giant cannon, charging and unleashing a single blast that caught his brother square in the chest. The blast sent Vorus hurling into the air and then crashing into a building, metal groaning in his wake.

Korai relinquished the Blessing, feeling fatigue and pain all over his body.

'You alright?' Mika asked, turning towards him.

Korai nodded. 'Yes. Thanks for the help,' he said, straightening himself. 'Are you all here?'

'Certainly are, Prince,' Setsu emerged, landing alongside Korai. The confident Hateful man shot Korai a strange look, causing Korai to frown.

'What is it?' he asked.

'Hmm…just trying to come up with a name for you. Prince belongs to Lucifer, so I'm not sure what to call you.'

'I don't believe that's essential right now, Setsu,' came

Lionas' commanding voice. He landed before Korai, moving in his strange half-animal form that Lucifer had seen when he'd first met Silver Wing. Kyrn and Liesa landed on either side of Lionas and Setsu, as they all faced the direction where Vorus had crashed.

'Keep your distance,' Korai instructed. 'Do not engage with Vorus directly. Do not take any chances. I'm the only one who can fight him.'

'Got it. We'll stick to ranged attacks,' Lionas replied.

Korai was glad Lucifer had told them what had happened in Exia, including his experiences with Korai and his battle with Ryun. It made coordination much easier. Korai reached down for the Sword of Greyr, drawing it in both hands.

'Stay behind me!' Korai said, before launching himself at Vorus, ascending before switching his grip on the sword. Korai threw all of his strength behind a downward stabbing motion, crashing through the smoke and dust his brother had generated by crashing.

He was met by the clang of metal, the sword sinking someway through.

'Wait!' Korai bellowed, his eyes widening in realisation. A hand shot for his throat, forcing him to release the Sword of Greyr as he struggled under a suffocating grip. Many heavy punches followed, in his face, gut and face again. Korai then found himself thrown into the air like a rag doll, deciding to use this reprieve to recover and surge high into the sky. He knew Vorus would follow him. As beams of energy chased after him, Korai performed spins and somersaults to evade the attacks, ending with a giant backward loop.

He tapped into Lucifer's Transformative Blessing, changing his hands and forearms into giant enhanced revolvers, launching blasts he hoped would hit Vorus.

He heard a loud grunt and looked up to see Vorus fall.

Korai pursued his brother. He switched from the Transformative Blessing to the Elemental, summoning boulders that he engulfed in flames, casting a rain of molten rock towards his brother. This, too, made contact.

But they froze instantly, and Vorus turned them into dust.

Vorus hovered in the air, waiting. Korai met his brother in a head-on attack, tapping into multiple Blessings at once. First, he chose the Illusionary, conjuring hundreds of copies of himself, all attacking at the same time. He also tapped into the Transformative Blessing, summoning Lucifer's favoured bladed claws but much bigger, with ridges across the blades that stretched towards his arms.

His brother responded by raising a single hand towards him, summoning multiple balls of energy at once. As Korai braced himself for what would come next, Silver Wing moved to intervene. Lionas dived in first, clawing and slashing, while Mika closed in on the opposite side with her Physical Blessing. With that, Vorus abandoned his attack, before extending his hands towards both Hateful.

'No, you don't!' Setsu yelled, dropping right on top of Vorus with a Transformative war hammer, aiming for his head. Vorus launched himself forward with a roll, trying to get away.

He fell right into Korai's path.

Korai stabbed both enhanced Transformative claws towards his brother, as the blades across his arms ripped free and extended forth. Korai winced, but proceeded with the attack, sure it would be lethal.

He was wrong. Vorus decided against rolling onto his

feet, as Korai would've impaled him as he rose. Instead, the Fallen rolled again, this time going underneath Korai's arms. Before Korai understood what was happening, Vorus rose, his muscles bulging with the enhanced power of the Physical Blessing, swinging a powerful uppercut into Korai's jaw. The blow almost knocked Korai out cold, and he felt himself being lifted into the air. Vorus rose with him, using the momentum of his punch to carry him towards the same point that Korai reached the apex of his rise. Then he spun in the air and struck him with a powerful kick.

Korai gasped, before finding himself launched in the air again. This time the trajectory was short, and he crashed hard against a city wall again. Still, Vorus wasn't done. He surged towards Korai, aiming another powerful fist at his brother's face. Korai was defenceless to stop him, as he was the blows that came afterward. Vorus unleashed a relentless assault, punching, kicking and striking every vulnerable spot.

I can't... stop him... Korai realised, as Lucifer screamed inside to take back control. However, Korai could barely articulate himself, becoming limp like a rag doll as Vorus continued his assault. It seemed his brother intended to beat the life out of him.

'Lucifer!'

'Prince!'

The voices of Silver Wing emerged, their panic obvious. Korai could hardly see now, barely conscious. Kyrn and Liesa rushed at Vorus, bladed weapons raised.

But Vorus was ready.

Korai recognised the trap then, as his brother grinned before turning. With almost blinding speed, he struck down both members of Silver Wing before switching his right arm into a colossal Gatling gun, raising it as it spun.

'Now die, Silver Wing,' he growled. However, before the weapon could unleash what everyone knew would be a torrent of death, Mika dropped from above, launching a hard kick at his head. It delayed the attack, but it didn't affect Vorus. He reached his free hand towards her, catching her ankle before slamming her hard into the metal ground.

'Mika!' Lionas bellowed, as Vorus tutted his disapproval, watching as Lionas dived towards him, his right hand shifting into a bladed claw, ready to strike his foe. This time, Vorus stepped forward, somehow catching Lionas with his free hand by his neck, before choking the life out of him. Korai knew he only had seconds to do something, groaning as he tried to peel himself off the cold metal wall.

Vorus turned his Gatling gun towards him.

'Oh, you don't get to live to see this,' he said, shifting his gun into a giant blade, which he then stabbed toward Korai.

He was stopped by Setsu, who dropped between the two Fallen brothers, taking the full brunt of Vorus' blade in the stomach.

'NOOOO!' Korai cried, his voice meshing with Lucifer's before the Fallen lost his power, falling unconscious as Lucifer stumbled forward in his wake. As Setsu fell, Lucifer dropped to his knees next to him. He gazed at the gaping wound across Setsu's stomach.

'Setsu! Setsu!' Lucifer cried, scrambling to stop the bleeding. He knew he had seconds to do something. As Lionas croaked within Vorus' grip, the Fallen regarded him with a disgusted sneer, before tossing him away onto the ground.

'Pathetic... all of you. Do you not see it, how much

Gabriel protected you, knowing what would happen when he unleashed me? I am the Destroyer, and I will lay waste to this city. So, Lucifer, where is your forgiveness now?'

Lucifer didn't have an answer for him. What could he say? Korai had failed. He couldn't stop the being before him. Just like before. Just like with Ven. He was going to lose them, all of Silver Wing, his parents, his home. So soon after discovering his revelations. What good were they now? Lucifer gazed at Setsu, knowing that the Hateful man was going to die. He had failed him like he had failed Ven.

'I've not changed,' he muttered as tears streamed from his eyes. 'Despite everything I promised. Despite everything I've done and discovered. It was all for nothing. I've-'

The sudden grasp of Setsu's hand interrupted him. 'Don't listen to him, Prince,' he said, his voice still somehow audible, as blood ran from his lips. 'He's wrong. You have changed so much. If it weren't for Mika, I was almost afraid you'd take the human girls from me.'

Lucifer almost laughed at that. Even at a moment like this, Setsu was still himself.

'Setsu,' Lucifer whimpered, no longer caring how pathetic he sounded. 'I'm so sorry.'

'Don't worry about it,' Setsu said, still smiling. 'But he's wrong, Lucifer. He only says that because he's hurt, just like you were. But you changed; you became one of us. You realised your mistake, and you became someone better because of that. Gabriel needs to see that more than ever now, that even after all he's done he won't break you, that you represent the thing you've been seeking all along: Forgiveness.'

His light was fading, Lucifer knew that. Lucifer brought

his ear towards Setsu's mouth.

'I keep telling you. Tie your hair up. I promise you, Mika will love it.'

Setsu exhaled for the last time. His eyes went hollow, and his grip on Lucifer's hand eased.

As Lucifer watched him die, he was engulfed by emptiness.

'Setsu!' Lionas cried, dismayed.

Lucifer didn't move, just reflected on the words that he had needed to hear.

'Represent the thing you've been seeking all along: Forgiveness,' he said. 'That's it. That's the last piece I've been missing. To forgive, you must embody forgiveness. Despite the pain. Despite the hatred of this world and its beings. Forgiveness rises beyond it all, and I am so tired of watching my race hurt each other. We perpetuate the same cycle again and again. It has to end. I must choose the other path.'

He looked at Vorus then, as his eyes glowed a perfect white.

'Forgiveness,' he repeated, rising to his feet as a calm silver aura projected from his body, similar to Korai but representing the exact opposite. The power that emerged through Lucifer now was one of tranquillity. Just like Korai, his hair changed into the same colour as his aura, rising in the air in gentle waves. However, the markings across his body were gone. Everything about him radiated peace. Vorus staggered back, stunned.

'Impossible,' he murmured. 'All this time, he was referring to you.'

'No, he wasn't,' the being that had once been Lucifer said. 'He was referring to that which I embody, that which your Hateful needs beyond all else. This battle is over, Vorus.'

The Fallen gritted his teeth, before stabbing his giant blade at the being before him, but he evaded the blade as though in slow motion. Vorus attacked again and again, but the silver being moved with effortless grace, closing the distance between them, before raising his hand towards Vorus, smiling with complete tranquillity.

'This is over, Vorus,' he said, gently placing his hand on the Fallen's chest. Vorus disappeared from that single touch, reverting to Gabriel, who gasped in surprise.

'Now, you're forgiven,' the being said. Gabriel fell back on the floor, unconscious. Allowing his hand to fall, the being turned and regarded Lionas, the only one conscious around them, who regarded him with wonder and reverence.

'Who are you?' he asked.

The being smiled. 'I am Forgiveness,' he said, before he floated into the sky, 'There is one more who requires forgiveness. I will go to him now. Please, see to the others, including Setsu.'

Lionas nodded.

Forgiveness continued to rise into the sky, focusing on where he knew death was heading to them, bringing a lost soul that needed guidance.

His guidance.

'I'm coming, Greene,' Forgiveness said, launching himself in the direction of the Titan approaching from the Darklands. Dynames.

40

Awakened

The great Titan known as Dynames had already begun its march. The World Breaker caused tremors like earthquakes with each step. Its joints, grinding from the lack of movement for thousands of years, groaned and seethed. It was coming for its brothers, for all of Ethero.

And it would kill all of its enemies.

Within, Greene found himself lost in a haze of long-repressed rage, his own and that of Dynames and all his kind. Everyone had been walking across his ancestors' body. Every step had added to the mockery that had become his kind's existence. The more Greene thought about it, the less he wished to pursue the path of Forgiveness. Ethero and its creatures did not deserve forgiveness.

They all deserve to die.

Tell me, do you really believe that, Greene? After everything I showed you? a voice called out to him: Forgiveness. Greene struggled to hear it beyond the outcries of his brothers and sisters, and the terrible hate perpetrated by the ancestor he now served. Greene shook his head.

Stay away! I want nothing to do with you!

Oh, I know, Forgiveness said, sounding sad. *I told you this would happen, that you had to fall before you could rise again. However, unlike my vessel, you can stop this. You don't have to repeat the mistakes of those before you. You remember what happened to Newman, don't you?*

He did. One could not forget such a horrifying tragedy. Greene shook his head, opening his eyes to find darkness enveloping him.

It's too late, he said, knowing it to be the truth, allowing Dynames to continue on its course. *I've already ruined the lives of all the humans who lived in Dynames. I have failed, Forgiveness, and a part of me isn't ashamed of that. Now, I can free my kind after years of servitude.*

Is that what you really believe? Forgiveness asked, the simplicity of the question catching Greene off guard. *Then tell me, how has awakening Dynames freed your kind? They remain trapped in Exia, slumbering with their eyes always open?*

'What do you mean?' Greene asked aloud. He sensed Forgiveness' presence around him. It was growing, somehow.

Do you want to know the difference between you and the others, Greene? Forgiveness asked. *Do you wish to know that which distinguishes you as the Descendant?*

Greene sensed a trap.

Forgiveness considered his next words, as his presence continued to grow, far beyond any of the visions.

You are a Descendant because you are awakened, Greene, he said. *Your race's senses and emotions had to be dulled, because peace required it to be so. That's why your race became subservient. What separates you is that you were born with your senses and emotions intact, which was amplified by Barbatos' potion. It is this aspect that has always separated you from your kind. Just like how I embodied the power of myself, my mother and my father within one of the first scorned, I gave the power of the Descendant to you.*

'But why?' Greene asked.

Because I needed to see if one of you could look past the hatred, Forgiveness answered. *For after I defeated your ancestors, it was me who caused your race to change. Without it, your kind would call upon the Titans again, and they would lay the whole of Ethero to waste. However, I decided I would place the power of a Descendant within one of you, so that you could experience everything that was wrong for your kind. I knew Barbatos would sense the opportunity and would compel you towards awakening your ancestors.*

That is why I created the trees, Greene, to test your resolve. With each relic you gathered, I gained a moment to speak with you, to show you another way. Unfortunately, to gain the power to free your kind, I needed you to awaken the Titan so that you could face the anger and rage of your entire race.

But now you can guide them towards another path.

Now, only you can decide. Continue with the hatred that brought your kind to this point, or accept my gift and free your kind once and for all. You cannot have both, Greene. You must choose.

'But how can you free my kind?' Greene asked. 'What is your "gift"?'

The power to awaken all Titaniuses, to open their eyes from their slumber, and to give them the choice you will present to them.

The path of Forgiveness, and...something else that will become important in the coming weeks and days.

'What do you mean?' Greene asked, his suspicion rising.

'What are you hiding from me?'

Your true form, Greene, Forgiveness said. *The Titans may be your ancestors, but the actual form of your kind is quite different. Should you choose my path, I can lead you towards discovering this form, and you can grant this to your kind. Only then will Titaniuses become what they should have always been: Liberated. Free.*

And powerful.

As Greene pondered this, Forgiveness raced across the sky like a shooting star, heading towards the great Titan of Dynames. The World Breaker was still, which told Forgiveness his conversation with Greene was working. He landed on the Titan's chest and stood looking into its single glowing red eye.

'Forgiveness is the freedom to choose, Greene,' he whispered. 'As long as you choose the path of hate and retribution, you will never be free. Please, release Dynames from his pain. Set your kind free, and speak to them through the true power of the Descendant.'

'The Speaker.'

41

Preparations for War

Diana walked alongside Pauli and Valki, examining the great wall that was their last defence against the coming war. Even if Megidra brought down Helenia, that fate was certain. She didn't know how they might survive what was to come.

We have so much to organise. Will it be enough?

Diana's mouth tightened into a line, fearing what was coming. As she tapped into her Elemental Blessing and summoned wind to scale the wall of the Institute, she put on a brave face. The Hateful and humans among them would need that. If they were to survive, they would need every advantage they had.

Diana landed on the wall and the guards mobilised to meet her, their expressions expectant.

'Prepare for war,' she commanded, noticing how tired her voice sounded. 'They'll be coming back.'

Disappointment washed across the Hateful then.

Diana didn't know what else to say, disgusted with herself as she looked away.

'Look, Eren's returned!' one guard said, filling Diana with hope she knew felt out of place. She saw Eren leading a large group of humans across the no-man's-land between the Institute and Exia. Diana looked over to Valki, who smiled back.

I wish I could trust you.

'Help them get across the wall. I'll coordinate with Reni to make sure everyone inside is safe,' she said, before leaping off the wall.

Diana had not expected to be called back by Pauli so soon. Fearing their enemy had mobilised, she had rushed back, only to find a stand-off had occurred between the new group of humans and her guards in the Institute's grounds.

What's going on now? Diana wondered, as she regarded the small band of humans who had entered a stand-off with the surrounding Hateful, who were angry about something. It took her a few seconds to realise they had surrounded one individual who was on his knees, hands raised in the air. He looked Hateful.

Diana approached, noting that he was only partly dressed, wearing scruffy and torn clothes from the waist down, while his torso was bare and covered in what looked like violet and crimson tattoos. Realisation struck her.

Megidra.

Diana stepped into the ring that surrounded the infamous traitor, causing the Hateful to bristle in fear.

'Diana, no!' one guard yelled, 'He'll-'

'I will not hurt her,' Megidra said, remaining on his knees with his hands raised in the air. He turned his gaze to Diana. 'Besides, we've met before. Though, I must admit it surprised me to hear you had reached such a station. A human leader of my kind. You've done a lot since we first met, Diana.'

'I could say the same to you,' Diana said, holding back her anger about what had happened to Hela. 'Why did you come back?'

'I wanted to give them the best chance of survival,' Megidra said, nodding towards the group of humans surrounded by those armed. 'I don't care what happens to me, but please don't turn these humans away.'

'That's bullshit, Megi!' one of the armed humans spat, a large black man who held a machine gun. He fixed his fearful glare towards Diana. 'He's saved our lives! He's changed!'

That appears to be the case, Diana thought, recalling the last time she'd seen Megidra; he had almost killed her to get to Lucifer.

'Diana,' Pauli said, his nervousness obvious. 'What should we do with him?'

'Megidra deserves to die for what he did!' one of the Hateful guards said, drawing many nods from the rest of his race. Diana's mind turned to Valki, and how he'd essentially set this up. He had seen something in Megidra worth bringing him in for. Diana sensed there was something unavoidable about this. She returned her gaze towards Megidra.

'You killed Helenia Acratis, didn't you?' Diana asked. At first, the question seemed to catch Megidra unaware, but he nodded. Diana understood then: they needed him if they were going to survive. Despite her personal feelings, she was sure Valki was right in doing this.

'He's not to be harmed,' Diana said. A stunned silence swept all around her. She could tell how unpopular her decision was among the Hateful. They needed justification, and she would give them one.

'You all know what's coming. If we're going to survive this, we'll need him. He'll be our strongest fighter.'

'But that doesn't excuse what he's done!' one guard spat, a young female.

'Absolutely,' Diana agreed. 'We'll return to this once the war is over. At least with him on our side, we have a chance.'

Diana looked around at them, making sure everyone was listening. 'In addition, unless ordered by me to do otherwise, he'll remain by my side at all times. I will see to him myself. Should he move to betray us, everyone has my permission to act, but only when I say so.'

'Diana!' Pauli gasped his eyes full of fear. 'This is madness! You cannot seriously–'

'They're coming!' a voice called from the wall.

Diana tapped into her Blessing to scale the wall once more, landing within seconds to see what the guard had meant.

The forces of the Eternal Mother had entered the no-man's-land. Alongside her, Megidra and Pauli appeared, looking out at the same sight.

'This is it,' she said. 'Get ready everyone!'

The Hateful scrambled, leaving Diana to wonder how they were going to stand. However, as they watched the forces approaching them, a rumbling sounded beneath them.

'What is that?' Pauli asked.

Then someone called out. 'There's something behind us!' they said. 'From Exia Mountain!'

'Exia Mountain?' Megidra said, frowning. He looked at Diana, confused. 'That's where the Titaniuses come from.'

'The Titaniuses?' Pauli said.

Then an army of Titaniuses poured out of the mountain, shaking the ground, moving with greater speed than the forces of the Eternal Mother. They split and circled the wall, filling Diana's heart with dread. She'd never seen them act like this. Since Anubi, she had intended to send scouts to find them, yet here they were, some climbing the wall, heading towards the Hateful.

'Don't attack!' Diana shouted. 'Not unless they attack first!'

They didn't. Instead, the Titaniuses moved past the Hateful as though they didn't exist, their entire force moving towards the front of the wall. They positioned themselves between the Institute and the Ether's forces.

'What's going on?' she asked, as a single Titanius approached her, taller than usual for his race, emitting a strange steam from his body.

It stopped before her. 'Hello there, human,' it said. 'It would seem we got here in time.'

'What are you talking about?' Diana asked. 'Why are you here?'

'I would've thought that was obvious,' the Titanius said, speaking in a pleasant monotone voice. 'We're here to stand alongside you.'

'Stand alongside us? Why?'

'Because we are free, thanks to the Descendant, the Speaker,' the Titanius said. 'So we've chosen to forgive. We will stand alongside humanity so that it survives. We wish to create a future together, now that we're free.'

Diana nodded, not understanding, but happy to accept the help.

From out of nowhere, hope had arrived.

The war to decide the fate of Ethero was about to begin.

The end.

Also by Kieran McLoughlin

The Hateful: Acceptance
https://dl.bookfunnel.com/2my7sgl3pc
The war for Ethero has begun.

In the aftermath of finding Forgiveness, for himself and his past, Lucifer must now face his greatest challenge yet.

To uncover the power that could change the fate of Ethero forever: The Healing.

However, to do so, Lucifer must face his ultimate test, a militia of Hateful who is set on eradicating humanity and creating a utopia for all Hateful alike.

The charismatic Raphael, who possesses the desire to make this dream a reality, leads them. He will push Lucifer to his very limits. The ultimate battle is coming.

And the chaos sorcerer, Barbatos, after years upon years of planning and manipulations, is finally ready to unleash a power more harrowing than has ever been known.

Meanwhile, both Megidra and Diana must work together to make their last stand against the forces of the Ether. They have assembled to annihilate the remnants of humanity, Hateful and Titanius defenders, who seek to hold on to the last bastion of Exia, the place once scorned by humanity.

The Institute.

Lines have been drawn. The stakes have never been higher. The fate of Ethero now rests among the few who must do battle one last time.

For if Ethero is to survive, it must heal…